# IN THE BLUE LIGHT OF AFRICAN DREAMS

Paul Watkins is twenty-seven and the son of Welsh parents. He was educated at the Dragon School, Eton and Yale. His first novel, *Night Over Day Over Night*, was nominated for the Booker Prize. His second novel, *Calm at Sunset, Calm at Dawn*, won the 1990 Encore Prize for best second novel. This is his third novel.

'*In the Blue Light of African Dreams* places its characters in a Godless hell: subjected to extremes of physical discomfort and emotional distress they become existential heroes and dismal outsiders. The novel is set in the war between the French Foreign Legion and the Saharan Arabs in the 1920s. Charlie Halifax, an American pilot who deserted from the French air force during the First World War after a terrible accident, has been sentenced to 20 years in the Legion. Scarred, haunted by his tragic childhood, blackmailed and bribed by his corrupt commander, Halifax sinks into apathetic despair – all the while listlessly playing with the fantasy of escape... The stuff of gripping adventure is pinned down into something more sinister and desperate by Watkins's continuing emphasis on motive, treachery, illusion. Watkins writes in cool, tight, unsentimental prose; his descriptions can be stark and powerful, and his grip on the nerve-ends of his characters relentless.'

*Observer*

'*In the Blue Light of African Dreams* is the third novel by a remarkable young writer. It is an unusual book because Paul Watkins excels in a sort of writing which is rare in English, and even American, fiction... It is written with an unusual precision, with a care for the shades of meaning in language, and with an honesty in its portrayal of men under stress... it is quite clear that Paul Watkins, who is only 26, is the outstanding novelist of his generation yet to have appeared. He has now really established himself... At the moment, comparisons with Malraux and St-Exupéry don't seem absurd.'

*Scotsman*

'This is a splendid adventure story... at 26, Paul Watkins has become the writer of his generation whose future course will be watched with most interest... Watkins has been compared with Hemingway. A less common peril for the younger writer than it used to be, the comparison continues to be largely injurious... Mostly, though, all the comparison means is that those of us who confine our reading to good writers do not often come across a celebration of courage and the masculine skills. Bad writers, hosts of them, are busy about it all the time. Watkins deserves better than this. The second half of the book, in which Halifax and Ivan escape to Paris and set out to beat Lindbergh to the first Atlantic crossing, moves towards an ending which casts a redeeming glow of the imagination across eveything which has gone before... Watkins is a writer who cannot fail to make a success of his career.'

*Sunday Telegraph*

'Watkins is a fine, exact writer... The aerial scenes are remarkable and unfussy and the narrative moves with a sureness that suggests a card-sharp facility for plotting. The book shows once again how war, and in particular the Great War, has settled into the common imagination; what is remarkable about what Watkins has done is his ability to invest even hackneyed settings and occasions with a fresh impact and vision.'

*Times Educational Supplement*

Paul Watkins

# IN THE BLUE LIGHT OF
# AFRICAN DREAMS

VINTAGE

FOR CRW

VINTAGE

20 Vauxhall Bridge Road, London SW1V 2SA

London Melbourne Sydney Auckland Johannesburg
and agencies throughout the world

First published in Great Britain by Hutchinson, 1990
Vintage edition 1991

Printed and bound in Great Britain by
Cox & Wyman Ltd, Reading

ISBN 0 09 965890 9

# Part One

# Morocco

# 1926

# 1

HALIFAX FLEW IN from the desert, a thousand feet above the sand. When he reached the coast, he turned north and followed a line of waves breaking jade and white against the beaches.

His strut wires hummed with the speed. He pulled down his goggles and undid the strap of his leather flying cap, the sun jabbing at his eyes. When the town came in sight, he eased his plane down to four hundred feet and throttled back the engine. A shepherd's hut slid by underneath. Goats scattered into thorn bushes. He saw fishing boats rising and falling on swells near the harbour. Fishermen pulled in their nets and emptied onto the decks a silver-flickering mass of fish.

Runway. He centred his fuselage on the cleared ground and throttled back again. A man waved to him from the mosque tower. The white stone houses of Mogador were blinding in the light.

He could feel sweat between his palm and the leather gauntlet that gripped the control stick. The ground slipped out of focus as he came in to land. He bounced once and then settled. The tail dragged. He throttled back until the engine stuttered.

When the speed was gone, he motored towards the hangar. As he neared the wide arc of corrugated iron, he cut his engine. The grey blur of his prop rattled into the smooth bars of two propeller blades. His plane rolled to a stop as quiet settled around him. Dust from his landing drifted past.

Heat rested on Halifax's shoulders. His lips were dried out and cracked. He unhooked the glasses from around his ears and set them in his pocket. Then he blinked for a while at the out-of-focus dials on his control panel. After kneading the blood back into his legs, he unbuckled his seat straps and jumped to the ground. He staggered and then stood, pain from cramped muscles prising at his knee joints.

3

'Ivan!' Halifax stood facing the hangar, the hum of his engine still throbbing in his muscles. 'Ivaaan!'

Heat dribbled up from the roof of the hangar.

After waiting for a minute and hearing no answer, he left his plane and walked home through the streets. It was still the hot part of the day. The shops had closed. Blue wood shutters lay flat against the walls.

Halifax had a room on the roof of the Hotel Smara. He always felt it in his calves when he walked up the stone staircase. It was dark in the room and the air smelled salty from the sea. He peeled off his leather jacket and put his goggles, flying helmet, gloves and revolver on the table. Then he sat down in a chair on the balcony, hands behind his head.

Sleep smoothed at his face. This was the time of day he looked forward to most. He felt his breath grow slower and deeper.

A minute later, footsteps echoed in the hall outside his room. The door opened and someone walked in. A man blocked the sun. 'Hello there, Halifax my friend!'

Halifax opened his eyes very slowly, light streaming in. 'What do you want, Serailler?'

'You always think I want something, Charlie.' Serailler sat down in the other chair. He reached across and patted Halifax on the knee. 'I just came to see how my old friend Charlie is doing.'

'You never come up here unless you want something.'

Serailler sat back and the chair creaked. He undid the top button of his uniform jacket. Old sweat had dried into white dust around the collar and the back. 'All right. Fine. I do want something. You're flying out to meet the Touaregs today. Now, in fact. You're delivering a case of rifles and ammunition. Everything must be done today.'

'My flying orders are for tomorrow.' Halifax rummaged in his pockets for the orders. He found the piece of paper, thin and yellow and almost dissolving in the moisture from his fingertips. Then he put on his glasses so he could read. 'It says I do reconnaissance tomorrow at ten. Here. It's all here. You signed the damn thing.' He held out the orders to Serailler. 'Besides, I just got back from patrol.'

Beyond the town walls, waves exploded on the rocks, echoing through the narrow streets of Mogador.

'These are new orders.' Serailler took the paper and crumpled

4

it up. 'Unwritten orders. You leave in half an hour.' He found himself a cigarette and lit a match, shielding its flame with the thin web of his palm. His eyes closed and his cheeks bowed in as smoke streamed down his throat. The smoke leaked in grey slivers from his mouth and nose.

'Look, Serailler. Why don't you send someone else for a change? I just got . . .' Back from patrol, he was going to say again, but fell silent. It wouldn't do any good. He sat back, folded his arms and stared past Serailler at the stone walls that ringed the town. They were the walls of a fortress, built by the Portuguese in the 1600s when they dealt in slaves and gold dragged out of the desert. Their bronze cannons still jutted from the ramparts, aiming out to sea. 'Why can't you send Rollet or Labouchere? They could do it just as well as me.'

'But I'm ordering *you*. I don't trust anyone else to do the job right. Don't kid yourself. You know you're the man for the job. You always have been.' Serailler rested his hand on Halifax's knee. 'Of course, you could always say no. Try something new. Surprise me after all these years! Say, No, Captain Serailler, I have decided not to follow your orders anymore and would prefer to be transferred to an outpost in the desert. Serailler, you would say, send me to a place like Sidi Arak. Send me out into the sand so I can rub elbows with those Arabs. I want the challenge of knowing that if they get hold of me, they'll use my skull for a paving stone in one of their mosques. Is that what you want to tell me, Halifax? Is it? Because if you're going to tell me' — he reached across and gently slapped Halifax's scarred face — 'tell me now.'

Halifax walked into his room and came out with his leather flying jacket and goggles and the belt with a revolver in its holster. The sweat had cooled in his clothes. His jacket was heavy with it.

Serailler was smiling. He stood leaning against the balcony wall, the stub of the burning cigarette still pinched between his thumb and index finger. 'I'm your ticket home, Charlie. Do things right and one day soon I'll sign your discharge papers.'

'How soon?' The words sounded worn out in his mouth. He asked without listening for Serailler's answer.

Serailler shrugged. The almond-smelling oil in his hair gleamed in the sun. 'You're better off here in Africa, anyway.' He waved his hand out to sea. 'What do you have back in

America? A job in a coal mine. You want to go home for that?'

Halifax shuffled halfway down the stone staircase to the street. Then he turned and walked back. His face reappeared in the doorway. 'I never told you I worked in the mines. How did you find out?'

'Ivan told me.' Serailler snorted and pinched the cigarette dead, saving the few brown shreds of unsmoked tobacco. 'He tells everybody everything.' Serailler smiled and Halifax couldn't help smiling with him.

For almost seven years they had been living in the same town. Now they saluted only out of sarcasm. They never used rank except to insult each other. None of their arguments lasted for long and none carried any weight. So few of them in Mogador who had ever seen anything of the world beyond Morocco, they had no choice but to huddle for company and forgive almost anything.

Serailler followed Halifax down the stairs. His voice bounced off the damp walls. 'Just be glad I'm looking after you. You'll stay alive here. You know how badly it's going for us in the desert now. Dozens of outposts have disappeared, even in the last few weeks. The desert just swallows them up. Be glad I keep you on the coast. If you go inland, you'll die like everybody else.' Serailler put on his sunglasses; the round lenses were dark, dark green against the blaze of sunlight off the waves.

Sand blew across the airfield, scrabbling against Halifax's boots as he walked out to his plane.

Ivan Konovalchik crawled from under the wing. He had gone out to refuel the machine and then fallen asleep underneath, using an empty fuel can as a pillow.

Ivan worked in the aircraft hangar and repaired the planes that flew out of Mogador. Before he joined the French Foreign Legion and came to Africa, he had served as an officer in the Imperial Russian Cavalry. His family had owned huge stretches of land south of Moscow but lost everything in the Revolution. He was the only who made it out. All of the others were killed.

Halifax strapped himself back into the cockpit. Warmth from the wicker seat reached through his clothes and pressed against his back. 'Where are Labouchere and Rollet?' He looked down at Ivan. 'Did they go out on patrol already?'

Ivan tucked his hands into the pockets of his baggy boiler suit. 'They went out two hours ago. I already packed the guns and filled your tank.'

Halifax kicked his heels against a metal case under the seat. It was meant for Cooper bombs, small hand-held explosives that pilots threw like grenades onto the Arab strongholds. The Coopers had been taken out and replaced with rifles. 'What do we have this time?'

'A dozen Austrian Mannlichers with Spanish armoury markings.'

'Bullets?'

'Some.'

Halifax pumped pressure into the fuel tank and set the throttle. He thought of the weight of the guns and the strain they would put on his engine. How much more did a dozen rifles weigh than the rack of Cooper bombs? He started to think it through and then stopped because he wouldn't be able to do it without a pencil and paper and because he knew that Ivan would already have figured it out.

Ivan stabbed the toe of his boot in the dirt. 'Labouchere and Rollet aren't too happy about Serailler changing your orders all the time, especially now with the way things are going for us in the desert. They think if you're going to be anywhere, you should be up there with them. Out on patrol.'

'I know I should. Don't you think I know that? One of these days I'll tell Serailler to fly the guns out himself.'

'That would be funny.' Ivan grinned but his eyes stayed serious. 'I'd like to see you say that to Serailler, and then I'd like you to send me a postcard when you arrive at Sidi Arak. We can add your name to the list on the Legion memorial.'

Halifax flew at seven thousand feet, about as high as he wanted to go. He was flying the same type of plane he had flown in the war in France. The garrison at Mogador had three planes, one for each pilot. The machines were all single-seat Spad V11s, patched together so many times by Ivan that whole sections of engine casing had disappeared under repair work.

The purple Atlas Mountains rose up in the distance. This was the Rif, a region of hills that stretched from the first brick-

coloured sand flats of the Sahara all the way to the Mediter-
ranean. Even after years of fighting against the French, Arabs
still held the Rif. To Halifax, it seemed impossible that anyone
else would ever own the land.

The war in Morocco had begun in 1911, when France sent in
Foreign Legion troops and began fighting Arab tribesmen for
control of the country. Then the Great War broke out in 1914,
and France turned its attention away from Morocco. At the end
of the World War, while other troops went back to civilian life,
the Legion was rearmed for service in Africa. Guns, planes and
men used in the trenches of the western front were sent out into
the sand against Arab tribesmen.

Along with Frenchmen, and Russians like Ivan Konovalchik,
there were Germans in the Foreign Legion. Most of these
Germans had fought against the Legion in France only a few
months before. Englishmen joined the Legion, and Turks, and
Americans like Charlie Halifax. They were people who had
nothing to go home for or who couldn't go home or who had no
home when the Armistice came in the winter of 1918.

Vibrations from his engine shuddered through the canvas
and wood of the fuselage, numbing Halifax's feet. He followed
scratches of road and passed over towns made from red mud,
hedged in by date palms and cactus. These towns weren't on
the map he had fixed on two rollers inside the cockpit. The idea
was that as he passed over the different regions, he could roll
the map forward to see where he was going. But the map ran
out after twenty minutes of flying time. A ragged-edged block
of black and orange strips covered the paper all the way to the
end of the map. Written in red between the strips was ZONE
D'INSÉCURITÉ, the place of no safety. The French didn't hold the
land and couldn't guarantee the safety of anyone who went
there. No one called it the zone of insecurity. Instead, it was
called the Bled.

During the years since he had arrived in Morocco, he had
flown to towns in the Bled that his orders claimed had been
taken by Legion troops and were secure. When he got there, he
found the places empty. No traces of fighting or struggle, no
message left behind. And he had flown over the towns as a
mass of dark-cloaked Arabs heaved across the flimsy barricades. The tiny khaki speckles of Legionnaires struggled
against the black tide before it swallowed them up.

8

The shadow of his aircraft followed him like a grey beetle across the ground. Now and then he leaned out into the slipstream of his prop and breathed clean air. The rest of the time he sat in a haze of castor oil fumes from the engine's lubricating system, feeling his stomach complain and go sour. In France, he and all the others in his squadron used to drink blackberry brandy to stop themselves getting the shits in midair from all the castor oil, then burped blackberry burps while they peered into the sun, searching for German planes.

Sun warmed the leather of his flying helmet. After a while, he took it off and let the wind cut through his hair. He flew towards the Sahara, south of the region where the Arab leader Abdel Krim held out against Legion troops.

After an hour, Halifax reached the wadi where the Touaregs lived. The Arabs called them Blue People because they wore indigo-dyed cloaks that stained their skin. They lived at the edge of the sand and out across the dunes. The Touaregs weren't Arabs. They were here before the Arabs.

The wadi looked like a tear in the earth, a sudden cluster of green and water and flat-roofed houses in the middle of the sand. Here the desert seemed to be only a thin veil that hid rivers, and trees and people, and in this place the veil had been ripped open, showing what grew beneath.

He brought his plane in on a clear stretch of ground, cutting the engine just before the Spad's wheels touched the ground. The machine rolled to a stop and suddenly there was nothing but quiet and air boiling in the heat. Sand lay in waves of coppery dust. Halifax climbed down from the cockpit and stood rubbing his knees, which were stiff like an old man's knees. Then he sat under the wing of his plane, waiting for the Touaregs to appear.

For years, ever since becoming commandant of Mogador, Serailler had been running a black market business and using the Touaregs as middlemen. He sold guns to the Arab tribesmen, the same Arabs who were fighting against the Foreign Legion. They had to get their guns from somewhere, so they bought them from the enemy, from Serailler.

First he sold rifles from the Mogador armoury, listing the missing guns as broken or stolen in his monthly reports to Casablanca. Then he began buying weapons and ammunition from Spain and smuggling them down into Morocco. The guns came via the Canary Islands, which lay just off the Moroccan coast. Canary Islands fishermen made the deliveries to Moroccan fishermen out at sea.

The Arab tribesmen paid for their rifles with gold, which came from some place beyond the Sahara, beyond a stretch of desert called the Erg Cherch. As far back as Roman times, gold and black slaves from Central Africa had come out of the Erg Cherch. The Spanish, who owned a region south of Mogador, called it the River of Gold.

For centuries, the Arabs had traded gold and slaves for salt — weight for weight, gold for salt — because there was not enough salt on the African plains beyond the desert, and the people there would have died without it. Whole tribes were carried away as slaves to pay for the salt.

The source of the gold stayed secret. Arab armies that had marched into the desert to find it never came back.

Now the war against the French had broken down the trade routes to central Africa. The Arabs needed guns to stay alive, and they paid for them, the way the people beyond the Erg Cherch had paid for the salt, with gold.

From where he sat, Halifax could see nothing of the wadi. The desert seemed to stretch out unbroken. Serailler had told him always to stay up on the edge, never to go down the paths that led to where the Touaregs lived. The paths were narrow and scattered with amethyst crystals. Fossils in the shapes of giant snails bubbled up from the rock.

The man who worked for Serailler before Halifax came had been murdered by the Touaregs. Serailler wouldn't tell Halifax how, so he had to find out from Ivan.

The dead man's name was Leclerc. He was sent down to Morocco as a reconnaissance pilot after several months on the western front in 1917. Ivan said he thought the man had bought his way down here, since he'd told Ivan he knew his luck wouldn't have lasted any longer in the air over Verdun.

Serailler had owned Leclerc the way he now owned Halifax. One word from Serailler, the Foreign Legion commandant of Mogador, and Leclerc could have been posted to one of the desert outposts, away from the safety of the coast. So Leclerc had done what he was told, like everyone else in Mogador.

Leclerc had never seen the Arabs who came for the guns; he

only saw the Touaregs. They were the bankers, keeping a few guns and a little gold for payment.

Serailler once tried to cheat the Arabs by sending a shipment of guns without magazines, with the idea that he could charge extra for them next time. The Arabs took the Touareg in charge of the guns, cut off his head and threw it off the cliff of the wadi, down onto the houses below. So when Leclerc arrived one month later with the magazines and another shipment of guns, the Touaregs nailed him to the runway with spikes and left him there. They took what they could from the plane and abandoned the rest. By the time Serailler sent out another plane to see what had happened, scorpions were nesting in Leclerc's chest cavity.

The first time Halifax flew out, only a week after arriving in Morocco, the Touaregs kept him waiting until after dark, then they crawled from the sand and surrounded his plane. They lit sticks wrapped in tar-soaked cloth and held out these torches so they could see Halifax but he couldn't see them. The Touaregs took the guns from the chest under Halifax's cockpit seat and checked the bolts while Halifax stood with his hands in the air, waiting to be shot. As they moved around him, Halifax could just make out that one man was wearing the safety harness from the seat of Leclerc's plane. Another had his flying goggles.

They looked at the scars on Halifax's face, touching the smoothness of healed skin, peering at him while heat from the torches drew sweat from Halifax's body. Then they handed him the gold they'd been given by the Arabs, badly refined and poured into moulds like coins with no markings on them.

The next time he flew in, the Touaregs didn't keep him waiting. They brought him water and tangerines and didn't point a rifle at his head.

A dozen Touaregs formed out of the heat haze, first legless and headless, then suddenly whole and in front of him.

Their skin was darker than the skin of the Arabs. They looked more like the slaves who came from beyond the Erg Cherch. Their purple-black cloaks had hoods, which they wore against the sun. With the hoods pulled up, their faces were completely hidden.

Halifax kept his flight goggles on. He could see the men a little more clearly through them and knew they kept their distance

11

from him as long as he wore the lemon-coloured lenses and smooth flying cap.

The group of Touaregs stopped a short distance from the plane. One man came closer, touched the tips of his fingers against his lips and his chest, then held out his hand for Halifax to shake. In the hollow of his throat the man wore a bead of red amber, held around his neck by an old leather thong.

Wind blew at the capes of the men who had come to watch. They stared and didn't speak, squinting from the pain of sun in their eyes. Beyond them lay the wreck of Leclerc's plane. Its canvas was gone and only the metal frame remained.

Halifax brought out the rifles. They looked even older than the Spads. The wood of the stocks had been oiled so many times that it was almost black. The bluing on the barrels was peppered with rust.

The insides of the barrels must be pitted like soft bread, Halifax thought, and he wondered how many of them blew up in the faces of the Arabs who tried to fire them.

The Touareg picked a gun from the stack and lifted it, as if he would know from its weight whether Serailler had cheated them again. He went through the whole pile, the worn-down skin of his hands curving against the stocks. The other Touaregs rose on their toes, mouths open from the concentration of staring.

The Touareg finished with the rifles and walked back to his friends. The cloaks closed around him, and Halifax stared at the men's ankles, which was all he could see of their bodies. The rest stayed hooded and shapeless, tangled in the mass of cloaks. To Halifax, they looked like a group of Capuchin monks.

When the Touareg untangled himself, and returned to Halifax's plane, he carried a black metal box. Whenever Halifax saw the box, he knew everything had gone all right and that he could go home soon. It was the same kind of box that his father had used for holding the deeds to his house and his will and stamps from foreign countries that he took out now and then and held up to the light so he could see the watermarks.

The Touareg sat opposite Halifax, cross-legged on the ground, and opened the box. It was filled with the unstamped gold coins that the Arabs used for buying Serailler's rifles. The Touareg counted out four coins for each rifle. He mumbled as he squeezed each coin through his fingers. Wind carried away the sounds as they fell. Suddenly the Touareg looked up, chewed at his lip and asked himself a question. He asked himself again, then smacked his fist down on the coins and started counting over again.

Halifax smiled, hiding it with the back of his hand.

The Touareg pretended not to notice, but he smiled too, under the hood of his cloak. When he had finished counting, he sat back, hands gripping his knees, bare feet pale on the soles. Then he pointed to the others, who still stood gaping. The Touareg reached across, running his hand over the scars on Halifax's cheek.

It was the scars they had come to see.

Halifax tucked the coins into a cigar box that Serailler had given him — Cuban cigars, Punch half-coronas, the box so old and the cigars smoked so long ago that the smell of tobacco had gone from the dry reddish wood. The box disappeared underneath Halifax's seat and the Touareg spun the prop to get the engine started. He was good at it now, after years of not being good.

Before Halifax set the plane rolling down the runway, the Touareg handed up something large and white that had stayed hidden in the purple cloaks of the group. It was the skull of an animal, with big empty eye sockets and its teeth missing, the skull of a camel. The Touareg weighed it in his hands, as if it were another rifle. 'Sellayeh,' he shouted over the hammer of the engine.

'What?' Halifax peered at the bleached slab of bone.

The Touareg made a fist and beat on the skull. 'Sellayeh.' He took a knife from his belt and gouged it in the eye sockets. 'Sellayeh.'

'Serailler?'

'Sellayeh.' He touched the pads of his fingertips one more time against the scars on Halifax's face, then he threw the skull into the cockpit.

Halifax circled the wadi at five hundred feet.

The cloaked men stood around the rifles, looking up at the plane, shielding their eyes from the painful sun. Shadows lay like knife blades at their feet.

He didn't know what the Touaregs saw in his scars, except that they were smooth like the balls of amber they wore at their

13

throats, and looked deliberately polished, as if he had done this to himself on purpose.

In August of 1918, his plane took a burst of anti-aircraft fire over the Menin road, between Ypres and Polygon Wood in south-western Belgium. Halifax saw the shell as it reached the crest of its rising. He watched it move slower and slower, catching the light on its smooth copper sides, until it seemed to be hovering over his plane.

The explosion blew his canvas fuselage to shreds and tore a hole in his radiator. The machine kept running, but Halifax lost altitude and couldn't get back to his airfield at Bergues, across the border into France. Cooling fluid leaked from the broken radiator and overheated his engine in a couple of minutes. The fuel began to burn when he was still about a hundred feet above the ground, searching for a place to land. He beat on the guns, trying to dislodge the bullets so he could throw them over the side and stop them from bursting in the heat. He swayed the plane from side to side, hoping the fire would burn out before it reached him in the cockpit. From his days in flight class, he recalled the Falling Leaf Technique, seeing again the instructor swing his arm back and forth, holding the wooden model of a Spad. He knew even then that the technique wouldn't work.

The engine blew up. A sheet of burning oil sprayed back across the side of his face and his hands and his chest.

He didn't remember undoing the harness, couldn't remember jumping out. Suddenly he was just falling through the air, clawing at his eyes and slapping at flames that fluttered from the charred leather of his jacket. Cartwheeling down, he saw a forest, hedges, grass, a lake. They raced out of focus as he fell. Woods pulled apart into the pompoms of each separate tree.

Then a jolt shoved him into black and cold and hissing all around. I'm dead, he thought. I'll be damned, I'm actually dead. He spread his arms in the dark. Water. He was in the lake. He rose slowly to the surface, broke through and breathed. Trees crowded down to the bank. Smoke from his plane sifted into the clouds.

He didn't remember reaching the shore. The next thing he could recall was the face of an old woman and lying in the back of a cart pulled by a horse. The woman's hands appeared

14

suddenly close to his eyes. She touched at his face and he screamed from the pain and she screamed as well, jumping back from where she knelt beside him.

Potbellied clouds rode past in the sky. Halifax's head jolted back and forth over the rough wood of the cart. His boots were filled with water and his clothes felt heavy and reeked of smoke. Then greyness appeared like a sieve across clouds and sky, the grey turning to black like at the bottom of the lake.

Now I'm really dead. The thought trailed through his head and the black crashed down on top of him.

He woke up in a field hospital near Dunkirk. For weeks after that, the only memory he had was of pain. Pain far beyond the place he thought pain would end. Friends from his squadron came to visit him, their faces like owls from sunburn on their cheeks and the pale moons where they wore their goggles in the air. They gave him a new uniform. Nurses damp-sponged his body and said please not to cry out. His legs were in casts because they had broken when he hit the water, and so were his ribs. How many are broken? he asked, and the doctor said, How many have you got? Food moved like slivers of glass down his burned throat. His days became segments of boredom. The white walls seemed to shudder around him. Sometimes it looked to him as if everything were white — white clothes, white bandages, white puss from under his fingernails until they turned black and fell off.

The left side of his face had been scraped clean by the fire. The scars that remained looked like new wax. The skin, which was purple in the beginning but faded to white after a couple of years, stretched tight across his cheek-bone. He spent a long time looking in the mirror, teaching the muscles to work again. His face looked like a skull wrapped in wet rice paper.

In the weeks of convalescence, he taught the skull to speak. 'Cheese,' he said to the mirror. 'No, really, thank you.' He pretended not to take the glass of champagne a pretend woman offered him. 'And how do you do?' He held out his hand without the fingernails at his own reflection in the mirror.

The doctors in Dunkirk told him he could be back in his plane in two months. The first few times he heard this, he pictured himself in his Spad and flying patrols the way he'd been doing before, but gradually these pictures went away.

All he saw was himself on fire and falling. Again and again, falling and burning. It occurred to him that the only reason he had survived as long as he had was because of luck. After the fall, he felt his luck disappear. The mashed bodies of crash-burned pilots staggered in and out of his sleep. He forgot everything except the idea of running away. All his thoughts converged on it. It ran a groove through his head, channelling all the strength he had left into plans for getting home.

As soon as he could walk, Halifax put on his new uniform and left the hospital. He boarded a train heading for Cherbourg and got halfway up the gangplank of a ship en route to America before being stopped by the military police. They took him to the Leffrinckouke military prison, not far from his hospital in Dunkirk, and the war ended two weeks after he arrived there.

Halifax was appointed a lawyer, who told him he'd be subject to French military law. The lawyer said there wasn't much else to tell. They sat in Halifax's cell on mats made of hemp rope and clicked their tongues at the bad luck. Everyone thought the war would go on much longer, perhaps even for years. Halifax's French was almost fluent by then. He dreamed in French. When he was angry he yelled in French, and when the lawyer had gone, Halifax sang himself to sleep in French.

The court martial tribunal gave him a choice of being shot or signing up for twenty years with the Legion. They needed good pilots, they said. Within three weeks he was down in Mogador, speaking French and trying to learn Arabic, his burns still purple and healing, flying out to the Touaregs with guns for Serailler.

Halifax sat for a while in his Spad. The sun had gone below the sea and heat from the day was fading. He unstrapped himself, climbed down and walked to Serailler's office. On the captain's desk, he set the cigar box filled with coins. Next to it he put the camel skull.

'What am I supposed to do with this?' Serailler prodded the skull with the tip of an unlit cigarette. 'What do those little blue bastards think they're doing?'

'It's a token of their respect.'

'Respect?' Serailler moved the white mass from one end of his desk to the other. 'Do they really respect me?'

'Of course they do.' Halifax grinned at the skull.

Serailler was silent, then he nodded. 'I thought perhaps they did.'

## 2

MOGADOR GLOWED PURPLE in the sunset. Halifax sat on his balcony, watching Ivan in the other. Ivan tore strips of bread off a flat Moroccan loaf and stirred them in a pot of apricot jam before stuffing the mess into his mouth.

Ivan lived in the town, in a tiny room at the end of an alley that was always barricaded with laundry hanging out to dry. There weren't enough troops in Mogador to bother with building a garrison.

Ivan pointed at the cannons that stood in a row along the fortress ramparts. He aimed his finger at each one of them and called out the years when they were made. '1680. 1634. 1710. 1710. 1710. 1698.' The dates had been stamped into the bronze; thin, ornate numbers set above the royal crests of Portuguese kings.

The Portuguese used Mogador as a place to unload slaves from central Africa. They drove blacks up the same rampways used now by Arab fishermen. The slaves were chained to heavy iron rings fixed into the walls of the port. The rings still hung there, thinned by rust and age. From Mogador, the slaves were brought to the West Indies and America.

The Spanish wanted Mogador as their own slave port and tried to storm the town sometime in the early 1700s. But the Portuguese were waiting for them with their heavy bronze cannons and the Spanish ships sank in the harbour. The town walls still carried marks of Spanish grapeshot. The Spanish tried again a few years later, but this time they came by land. The Portuguese couldn't turn their guns around fast enough and the Spanish wiped out the garrison, locked the Portuguese into their own barrack rooms and burned them.

The Spanish held Mogador until the 1800s, when France took it over.

The French and the Arabs in Mogador had always stayed

apart. They didn't trust each other, most of them couldn't speak each other's language and very few Arabs wanted to be known as friends of the French Foreign Legion. Only a couple of local Arabs had signed up as militiamen. The French didn't like them and their own people didn't like them, but the money was good.

Halifax had stopped trying to be friends with the towns-people. He would never speak enough Arabic to understand what old women said when they stopped him in the street and waved their shopping baskets in his face and stamped on his boots with their henna-tattooed feet. He'd never wear Arab clothes and never find a woman here and never set foot in a mosque. But by now he was used to the man who stood in the mosque tower and called out across the town summoning Muslims to prayer. And he was used to mint tea and bitter oranges and goat's meat and ungutted sardines cooked over coals and eaten with fingers that always got burned. He was used to the heat and the glare and the clattering, twanging Arab music. He had a place in the town like all the other white men, but it was a place for white men and not for anybody else. That place would disappear as soon as they did. It was understood.

When Ivan had finished calling out the dates of the cannons, he pointed to where the sun had just ploughed under the sea. 'Georgia.' He aimed a little to the left. 'Florida.' To the right. 'New York. Maine.'

Halifax had taught him the names of all the states along the East Coast, and now when Ivan came up on the balcony, he recited them, pointing to where he thought they lay beyond the horizon.

Ivan pulled a page of newspaper from his pocket. 'Heard about the Orteig Prize, Charlie?'

Halifax shook his head and yawned. Sleep wandered through his body, shutting out the lights.

'Thousands and thousands of dollars for the first plane to fly nonstop from New York to Paris or the other way around. Says here that all the big names are going in for it.' Ivan squinted at the print. 'Fokker. Fonck. A man named Sikorsky, who says he's a Russian aristocrat.' He folded the paper and skimmed it across the balcony. 'If people believe him when he says he's a Russian aristocrat, then why the hell don't they believe me when I say the same thing.'

'Because you're an aircraft mechanic on a grubby airfield in the middle of nowhere. He's probably rich and cultured.'

'I'm cultured. I used to be rich.'

'He's in America.'

Ivan wiped the smile of orange jam off his face. 'That's the real reason isn't it? I should never have joined the Legion. I should have gone to America.'

'Why didn't you?'

'I couldn't afford the ticket. Still can't. When you go home, you let me know. I'll climb into your suitcase and come along.'

Halifax took the pot of jam away from Ivan. He scooped some up with his finger and let the sweetness rest on his tongue. 'Don't start that again, Ivan.'

'But when are you going to make your break?'

'I made my break a long time ago, and it didn't work. Look around, Ivan!' He waved his arm across the town and out at the scrubland that grew before the desert. 'There's no way to get out. Nowhere to run to.'

'It's not true.' Ivan rolled the bread into little pellets and dropped them on the ground. 'There's got to be ways out.'

'Then you take them. You find a way out and go back to your own country.'

'I don't have a country anymore. They stole it in the Revolution. If I went back, they'd kill me. I'm better off here.'

Halifax's throat felt full of dust. 'Well, maybe I am too. Did you ever think of that?'

'Oh, sure.' Ivan had made pellets out of the whole loaf. They looked like hailstones on the tiled floor. 'So we're both happy. We just couldn't be happier, could we?'

Halifax folded his arms. 'Maybe not.'

Halifax woke in the night and couldn't keep his eyes closed, so he walked down to a café called the Dimitri. It was late but the café was crowded. Most people slept for a few hours in the afternoon, when the sun made it too hot to be outside. Then they stayed up half the night, wandering from café to café.

The walls of the Dimitri hummed with talk, and slow-moving fans cut spirals in the smoke. Halifax drank mint tea and watched the crowds.

The Dimitri served only coffee and mint tea. The coffee machine gargled black juice and spat it into heavy white cups, which waiters topped off with goat's milk. They made the tea by stuffing a pot with mint leaves and adding boiling water.

Serailler's face appeared in the doorway. He squinted through the smoke until he caught sight of Halifax. Then he weaved past tables crowded with Arabs until he reached where Halifax was sitting. Serailler sat down, pulled out a handkerchief and smeared the sweat across his forehead.

'Bad news.' His skin looked green under the café lights. Twice a month, Serailler travelled up to Casablanca, where a doctor gave him small doses of arsenic as a treatment for syphilis. The sea-green crystals had bled the poison into his skin. It clashed with his blue uniform jacket and khaki trousers.

'What's the matter?' Halifax warmed his hands on the tea glass.

Serailler craned his neck around the café, as if following the path of a fly. Then he snapped his head back to face Halifax again. 'Sidi Arak fell today.'

'Arak?' A picture of the fortress popped into Halifax's head. He saw it again from the air, thick stone walls with three rows of ditches beyond them. Sidi Arak was built on a patch of brown water, fenced in by a few bowed palm trees. Sand stretched out for miles in all directions.

'Yes, Arak.' Serailler nodded. His whole body shook with the movement. 'Arak and a couple of other outposts. The Arabs here on the coast are talking about a great storm coming out of the desert. Are you listening to me? A human storm! Abdel Krim is heading for the coast. Everybody says so. He's heading right for Mogador. He'll probably be here by Christmas.'

Halifax thought of the dust trails of charging Arab horses. He saw Legion troops on the walls of Sidi Arak fire and reload and fire at waves of Arabs riding out of the sand. 'He won't reach the coast.'

Serailler slapped the flat of his hand on the table. 'You don't understand! In the last few weeks, Legion troops in the desert haven't just been driven back. They've been swallowed up. I'm telling you, he's heading for the coast. And there's another thing.'

Halifax drank the last of his tea and looked for the waiter, who sat on a stool in the corner. The man stared slowly back and forth across the room, waiting for his pupils to fuse with anyone who looked his way through the smoke-foggy air. As soon as he

21

caught Halifax's eye, he heaved himself off his stool and walked across. Serailler asked for coffee and Halifax ordered more tea. The waiter left through a screen made from strips of leather on which glass beads had been threaded.

'What's the other thing?'

'There's a man coming to investigate the sale of guns to the Arabs. Spanish guns.' From his pocket Serailler whipped out a sheet of yellow paper. 'They even sent a telegram!'

The coffee machine spluttered behind the bead curtain.

Serailler tried to calm himself. 'We're finished, of course.' He twisted his mouth into a grimace of accepting total defeat. 'They must have captured some of the rifles. Must have traced the guns back to Spain and then traced them to me. Straight to me.' He jabbed his thumb against his chest. 'I'll go to prison if this inspector finds what he's looking for. They'd lock me up. I couldn't stand to be locked up. I'd sit there and rot for the rest of my life.'

'They wouldn't bother keeping you in a jail. They'd shoot you. It would be the firing squad.'

He nodded, again, nostrils wide. 'If I was lucky.'

'And what about me?'

Serailler raised his eyebrows. 'I don't know. I hadn't thought about it. I guess they'd shoot you, too.'

Halifax thought about firing squads, thought about himself on his hemp mat in the Leffrinckouke prison cell, hearing the blast and echoes of a squad in a courtyard nearby. The executions had been out of his view, but often they had woken him at sunrise.

'Ever seen a firing squad?' Serailler scratched at his hands and elbows, as if he had begun to itch suddenly up and down his arms.

'No.' Halifax didn't look up to meet Serailler's gaze. He didn't look up because he was lying. A memory had come back to him, suddenly and clearly and freezing out his other thoughts. He remembered a man executed against the wall of a barn near the airfield where Halifax was stationed. This was in the fall of 1917.

A truckload of Military Police had brought the man, who wasn't tied up or blindfolded. His eyes were bulging and shut with bruises. The MPs seemed in such a hurry, as if they were afraid of getting caught. They set him against the stone foundation of the barn, which was as high as the man's chest.

Six men stood back and emptied their revolvers into him. They didn't stand back very far, only five or six paces. In the seconds before they fired, the man with the bruised face raised his head and peered at the MPs down the length of his nose, trying to see out from welts that covered his eyes. He wore baggy wool trousers, a shirt with no collar and a waistcoat. He was barefoot. When the first bullets struck him, he spun around and hit the wall with his face. The rest of the bullets hit him in the back. After the MPs finished firing, one soldier from the squad walked over and shot the man one time in the head, then they wrapped him in a rain cape, put him in their truck and drove away. Halifax had watched this from behind a fence that ran the length of the farmer's field. He never found out what the man had done.

'I've thought out what I'll do when the inspector arrives.' Serailler began counting off points on his fingertips. 'First we have to dump the guns. Dump everything. I'll just have to cut my losses. We'll do it tonight, give us plenty of time before this inspector comes. Then when he gets here, he can have his little investigation. If he gets anywhere near my business, he will suddenly vanish. There will be an inquiry. I will handle it personally. I will travel up to Casablanca and demand answers and will show considerable outrage at the clumsy paperwork of the people I have ordered to look into the matter. I will send out expeditions from Mogador into the surrounding countryside in search of clues. They will return empty-handed. I will send longwinded reports. In attempting to get to the bottom of the matter, I will spend the month's entire government budget for Mogador in one week. The inquiry will fizzle out. It will drown in its own paperwork.'

When the waiter arrived with the tea and coffee, Serailler stopped talking and looked down at the table top.

Halifax dropped three heavy brass coins into the waiter's palm and turned back to Serailler. He remembered the smell of chipped stone from bullets that struck the barn wall. For a moment now, his nostrils seemed peppered with it. 'This inspector doesn't stand a chance, does he?'

'Not really.'

Halifax stared at the yellow tea in his glass. Again he thought of the executed man, his body bent the wrong way up against the stone wall. He opened his mouth to speak but said nothing.

Suddenly it was himself peering from bruised eyes at the Military Policemen in their cigar-smoke-blue uniforms, revolvers held out and waiting to fire. He breathed in. 'I'm not flying any more trips out to the Touaregs.'

Serailler crushed a lump of sugar with his first three fingers. He crumbled the white grains into his coffee. 'Well, well.'

'Now that you're in the business of killing government inspectors, you can fly your own damn trips.'

'I could have you shipped out of here in ten minutes.'

'And where the hell would you send me? Sidi Arak? That'll be a bit hard now that it doesn't belong to us anymore.' As he raised his voice, an Arab at the next table turned and mouthed the work 'Arak.'

The people in the café began to whisper. Arak. Sidi Arak. It spread from table to table in the cramped space of the café. It echoed from the walls.

Halifax felt panic bubble up inside him. He fought against the urge to run away.

They walked down a narrow alley. Beyond the fortress walls, breakers gasped in foam and struck the rocks and blew apart. The sound of them hammered the town.

Halifax felt sea spray touch his face as they walked out onto the beach. If Serailler dumps them, Halifax thought, then maybe it will end. Maybe he'll just never get started again. 'Are you really going to throw all those rifles away?'

'If I don't, they'd be found. Any place I can think of, that inspector can think of, too.' Serailler tapped a finger against his temple. 'They get inside your head, these people. They get you to say things you don't mean to say. They're trained for it.'

They crossed the empty sand in darkness to where Serailler had hidden a rowboat in the dunes. Halifax dragged the boat down to the surf. Serailler pretended to help, resting his hands on an oarlock and walking with the boat as Halifax tugged it over the sand.

The bow reared up as it touched the waves. Serailler jumped in. He pulled an oil lamp from under his seat and hugged it to his chest. Halifax pushed the boat further out, until the water was up to his chest. He felt his trousers billow in the strong current. Then he climbed in and took hold of the oars. As the oar blades dug into the waves, spirals of green phosphorescence exploded in the black water.

They rowed out to an island called The Purpuraire. It lay in the surf beyond Mogador and used to be a penal colony. The Portuguese held Spanish prisoners there in the days when both countries fought for the land. Dungeons had been hacked into the rock. Some cells were ankle deep in water even at the lowest tides and chest deep at high tide. On moon high tides, water came up to the roofs and drowned the people inside.

Fifty years before Charlie Halifax was sent to Africa, the entire population of The Purpuraire died from an outbreak of scarlet fever. Even now, Arabs wouldn't go near the place. Fishermen ran their boats through shallow water to reach the port of Mogador rather than pass through a deep channel that ran beside the island. They said the place was unclean. They called all the white men in Mogador unclean, too.

Serailler and Halifax jumped from the boat as the bow ground against the beach. Serailler set the lamp down on dry sand, then grabbed the tow rope and pulled at it without strength, jumping back when a wave hissed over his feet.

They both dragged the boat above the waterline and walked up a small flight of steps to the prison. The huge hall was empty now, where prisoners once ate at long tables. Torch holders still jutted from the walls. Dirt lay inches thick on the floor. Serailler lit the lamp and started walking down one of the corridors. He kept the rifles in a prison cell. It was dry in the cell, except when spray broke against the tiny window opening.

The rifles had been bought up by people who were used to dealing in guns. Whenever the Spanish state armouries cleared out guns they thought were worn and too old to use anymore, these dealers acquired them. Most of the weapons came from the Great War. Some were even older.

Halifax and Serailler carried the rifles to a ledge where part of the prison had collapsed and slid into the water. One after the other, they tossed the guns into the sea, throwing up white spray and more green flickers of phosphorescence.

Serailler rubbed at the dirt on his hands. The flame of his oil lamp shuddered in the wind. 'I can't stand it on this island. Can't stand it in the prison cells. And those oubliettes are even worse. I can't tell you how many times I wake up at night and think I'm in one of those cages.' The muscles quivered in his jaw.

Halifax was enjoying the job of throwing Serailler's rifles away. It left him lightheaded, and grinning when he knew Serailler couldn't see.

Oubliettes were holes dug in the rock. They were big enough for only one person to stand in, with no room to sit or lie down. A metal cage closed over the hole. The Portuguese shut the Spanish officers in the holes and left them there to rot. In Serailler's nightmares, someone put him in an oubliette. He had a fear of locked doors. The door to his office was often shut, but he never locked it. Even to talk about the oubliettes made him twitch like someone in a seizure.

'After all, what can they do if they catch me?' Serailler laughed, the noise like the cawing of a cow. The laughter rolled off the stone and back in his face. 'What can they do? Send me to Africa?'

Black waves smacked against the island.

'This is a real pisser.' Serailler chewed at his lips. He was calculating the loss. Seventeen rifles at four gold coins each. Gold coins at roughly one ounce apiece. Price of gold on the Paris market. Whispering noises sputtered from his mouth as he multiplied and added in his head.

'You can afford to lose one shipment to the Touaregs, Serailler. You can afford to lose several. You must be one of the richest men in Africa thanks to all this.' Halifax picked up the lamp and walked back into the prison.

'I am rich, aren't I?' Serailler followed him in. 'I believe I'm filthy rich. When I'm done in the Legion, I'll move to Normandy and buy an apple orchard. And I'll never come back here again. I won't even allow myself to dream of the place.'

'Where do you keep all your money?' Halifax felt his ears pop with changed pressure as a wave struck the window of the cell. Water sprayed onto the floor.

'No place you can get at it. It's in a numbered bank account in Casablanca. I don't make the deposits myself.' Serailler squinted at Halifax, spinning his mind to think of something that would change the subject. 'You're a good friend to me, Charlie. A good worker. I won't forget it. If you help me get rid of this investigator, I'll write out the discharge papers for you.'

Halifax kept hold of the lamp. Its light rocked back and forth on the walls. He stood in Serailler's way, blocking the path back to the rowboat. He could tell from the way Serailler switched from one foot to the other that he felt trapped. Halifax stayed where he was. 'For years you've been saying you'd sign my discharge papers. And for years I've been doing exactly what you tell me to do. Sign my papers now, Serailler. Let me go.'

'When the time is right, maybe.' Serailler moved to take the lamp. He reached out, his fingers stretched to grasp the wire handle. When Halifax made no move to hand it over, Serailler slowly pulled back his arm, the fingers curling closed. His bony shape slipped past and he began groping his way down the corridor.

'But when is that? When's the right time?' Halifax called out, the darkness cupped around him. He knew he couldn't trust Serailler's kindness and his promises. Serailler was always kind when he got nervous. He knew that by tomorrow they'd be back at each other's throats.

Halifax didn't know if he was asleep.

Maybe I dreamed all my time in Africa, he thought. Maybe I'm still up in the air, still in the summer of 1918, searching for a place to land after the anti-aircraft shell blew my Spad to junk.

He remembered the strain in his eyes as he searched across the fields and towns with brick-coloured tiles on their roofs. He was looking for a place to land. His engine was dying away, coughing and starting and dying again. Fuel spattered and streaked across the windscreen and all over the guns, and he smelled the taste of castor oil. His spit tasted of gasoline. Get the ammunition out, he thought. Pull back the slide and get the belt out before this whole thing catches fire and the bullets blow you to shreds. He beat his hands bloody on the smoking metal of the Vickers gun. Then his engine died and the Spad glided down at the fields. He knew his engine would burn. Side to side, Falling Leaf Technique, sway from side to side and maybe the fire would go out. The windscreen started to melt. He smelled the canvas going up in flames. Side to side, falling leaf. The smell of his hair burning. The canvas of the gun belt burning. Smoke from under the cockpit. The wicker seat burning, too. It won't do any good to scream. Side to side until the fire goes away.

He lay face down on the bed, still wearing his clothes. For a while he listened for footsteps, in case someone had heard him cry out and now was coming to check on him.

No footsteps came. Waves beat at the walls of the town. It was

27

the middle of the night. He sat on the end of his bed and let his eyes grow used to the dark. Then he undressed slowly, hanging his shirt on a wire hangar, top button fastened. His buttons were made from mother of pearl. The original wooden ones that came with his shirt had rotted away. On a wooden peg at the back of his door, Halifax hung his leather belt and the revolver in its holster. Other than his clothes, all he owned was a rucksack, his glasses, three handkerchiefs, a watch and the flying goggles. The gun was an old French Lebel that belonged to Ivan. Halifax had borrowed it from him years ago and never gave it back.

In the last rustling of his thoughts before he fell asleep, he tried to shove aside the dream of his burning plane. He tried to remember what he looked like before his engine caught fire, but the picture stayed old and far away.

Serailler grabbed one of his khaki-suited Arab militiamen and threw him across the courtyard of the commissariat. The Arab tripped and fell. Quickly he stood, wide-eyed and trying to speak.

Serailler got hold of the man again and shook him back and forth. 'The inspector *must* be coming up that road! It's the only way he can get here!'

The Arab raised his hands. 'He wasn't there! Nobody was there!'

'The telegram said he was due here yesterday.'

'Captain, the road was empty! We have waited two days already.' The Arab tried to untangle himself from the knots of Serailler's fists.

'Listen to me. If that inspector gets past you and arrives in this town without me being informed about it, I will drag you out to the prison island and stuff you in one of those cages and I will leave you there.' Serailler let go and tried to knead the blood back into his hands. 'Go back and wait until he comes.'

The Arab saluted. The toes of his boots were chafed into suede. When he was outside the commissariat, he spat on the ground, looked back at Serailler and walked quickly away.

Serailler noticed Halifax standing at the entrance to the courtyard. 'That fucker doesn't think I'm serious.'

'What are you worried about if we already dumped every-thing?'

Serailler wasn't listening. 'I want someone with that inspector every minute that he's here. I want you to escort him around. I want you to get him drunk as often as you can. I want you to keep him amused. I want you to make him think this town is run by priests.' He began to pace. 'They must know about me, Charlie. It's the only answer. Otherwise he'd have come along the coast road by now. I tell you, they get inside your head, these people. They always think one step ahead.' Suddenly he stopped pacing. 'Do you thing they would send me to prison in Morocco or in France?' Without waiting for an answer, he went back to pacing. 'How long do you think I'd last in prison? I've been giving it some thought.' His head snapped up. 'Well, answer me!'

'I don't think you'd last very long.'

Serailler shook his head, pacing and pacing. 'I don't think so either.'

Ivan and Halifax sat on the balcony at the Hotel Smara, reading week-old issues of *La Presse* and *Le Relais Midi*, which had arrived that morning by truck.

'Look,' Ivan pointed to an article. 'This is about the Orteig Prize again. Says here that a couple of weeks ago, this man Sikorsky tried to make the crossing from a place called Roosevelt Field on Long Island. Says here the plane had hundred-and-twenty-horsepower engines, four of them, and fifteen thousand pounds of fuel. They didn't even make a test flight, they were in such a hurry to take off.' He read some more, mumbling, the tone of his voice rising and falling as he skimmed through the story. 'They didn't even make it into the air. Plane crashed. Two of the four-man crew died.'

They stared at the grainy-grey web of a newsprint photograph. It showed the plane and all the barrels of fuel it would hold lined up in front. Ivan traced his finger over the print. 'There's another man named Admiral Byrd who is building a machine. Fokker, the same man who built all the German planes in the war, he's building one as well. A pilot named Lindbergh is getting a company called Ryan to build a smaller plane than the other competitors. And then two more men, Davis and Wooster, are using a converted American bomber.'

'Anybody else?'

'Somebody called Chamberlin is working with Wright-Bellanca to put a machine together.'

'Who's the favourite?' Halifax tried to read over Ivan's shoulder.

'Doesn't say.'

'Where do they all get the money to build those planes?'

Ivan sucked at his teeth. 'Maybe they sell rifles to the Arabs.'

Halifax hooked his hands behind his head. He wiggled his nose to get rid of an itch and his glasses bobbed up and down. 'I went out with him to the island last night and we dumped all the guns. It was the most fun I've had this year.'

'Listen, Charlie.' Ivan folded the paper. 'This could be your chance.'

'Chance for what?'

'To bring Serailler down. You could tell the inspector everything. Say Serailler forced you to fly those guns out to the Touaregs. Say you had no choice. It would be the truth, after all. Maybe,' — he held out his hand as if a raindrop might fall into it any second — 'maybe they would let you go.'

'They wouldn't believe me.'

Ivan sighed and sat back. 'Of course they would! You know every damn thing about what he's doing. They'll listen to you. They'll have to. This inspector really has Serailler scared.'

'It's the inspector who ought to be afraid.' Halifax picked at his nails. 'Serailler says he'll sign my discharge papers if I keep working for him.'

'What? Are you trying to tell me that you trust him? How many years has he been feeding you that line?' Ivan took hold of Halifax's chin and brought their faces close together. 'He'll never do it.'

'It's the only chance I've got.'

Ivan banged his fist on the chair. 'He'll never let you go! He needs you. Anyone else might be able to wriggle out, but not you, Charlie. They court-martialled you, remember? They made you sign on for twenty years. You'll be here another fifteen! And you know how much will be left of you by then?' He pinched the air in front of him. 'This much! Nothing!'

Halifax slumped back in his chair, feet on the balcony wall. His boots were silhouettes against the violet sky.

## 3

A WHITE PLANE circled Mogador. It was a seaplane, its fuselage broad like the breast of an albatross. On its wings it carried the red, white and blue bull's-eye design of the French Air Service. It landed smoothly in the harbour and then motored to the pier.

Ivan and Halifax stood where they always stood when they had nothing else to do, on the balcony at the Hotel Smara. They strained their eyes to make out what was going on. A sheet of newspaper blew from Ivan's hand and wafted out over the town.

Two men climbed from the cockpit. One wore a leather coat that came down to his knees. The other was dressed in khaki. The man in the leather coat walked across the wing of the plane and tied it to some dock pilings with a coil of rope. The other stood by, yawning and stretching. His fists rose in the air and uncurled above his head. Arab fishermen watched from the decks of their moored boats.

Serailler arrived on the dock. He strode quickly across to the men and his arm reached out to shake their hands. Even from the balcony of the hotel, Halifax could see the miserable grin on his face. Serailler made wide sweeping gestures, taking in the whole town, and the two men followed with their eyes. Then Serailler nodded violently to something one of the men said. He led the one in khaki towards the commissariat. The other stayed behind. He took off his leather jacket, spread it on the ground and sat down. A minute later, a white feather of cigarette smoke wound around his head.

Halifax felt in his own neck and back the tiredness the pilot on the dock would be feeling. For a while after Ivan had gone downstairs, he stayed looking at the pilot's huddled shape.

As Halifax went out into the street and started walking towards the commissariat, he thought of the militiaman sitting in the roadside mosque, peering out into the blinding mesh of sun and desert while he waited for the inspector to arrive.

Halifax knocked on the door of the captain's office.

Serailler cackled behind the heavy slab of wood. 'You're so right. You're absolutely right!'

Halifax waited a moment and then knocked again.

'Come!' Serailler yelled at the door.

Halifax walked in, wondering if he should have polished his shoes or shaved. He scratched at his chin, then rubbed the toe of his right boot against his left calf.

Serailler stood. 'Private!'

'Private?' Halifax echoed the word. Then he remembered to salute.

Serailler pointed at the man in khaki, singling him out as if the room were full of khaki-suited men. 'This is Lieutenant Garros of the government's special investigation unit in Marseille. He is on temporary assignment with the Legion.'

Lieutenant Garros had the roasted pink face of a white man just arrived in Africa. He looked very young. The collar of his uniform shirt was too big for his neck. He stood and saluted Halifax.

Serailler brought out his bottle of Meukow cognac. The Meukow had been drunk months before and the bottle refilled with rotgut. He poured some into a white and blue enamelled mug for Lieutenant Garros. 'Don't have any glasses.'

Garros took the mug and looked at it for a while, then tipped the drink back and forth as if to see whether it would leave a stain on the enamel.

'Lieutenant Garros has told me that he expects our full cooperation.' Serailler drank some cognac out of the bottle and wiped the top before passing it over Garros's head to Halifax.

Garros cleared his throat. 'I want cooperation and I expect to get it.'

Serailler rolled his eyes, sure that Garros couldn't see. 'Private Halifax will be at your disposal. He will take you any place you want to go. He will coordinate any operation you might care to plan. He will remain at your side at all times.'

'I don't know if that's necessary.' Garros raised his eyebrows.

Serailler leaned forward until his chin was almost resting on the desk. 'This isn't Marseille, Lieutenant. This isn't Monte fucking Carlo. A man like you needs protection down here. Halifax has orders not to leave your side. He will obey them.'

'If you think it's —'

'I do.' Serailler leaned back and frowned. He stared at Garros. Judging and balancing and weighing. Always thinking. His mind like an anthill on fire.

'Where did you fly in from?' Halifax leaned against the wall. He held the cognac bottle by its neck and balanced it against his thigh. The alcohol burned in his mouth. You don't look more than eighteen years old, he thought.

'I came in from Casablanca. I spent three days there being briefed.'

'What type of plane is that down by the harbour?'

'It's called a Levasseur. The design is new. The navy's using them at the moment. I don't know much more than that.'

'I haven't seen it before. We're still using —'

'Have some more cognac.' Serailler snapped his fingers at Halifax and snatched back the bottle. The label was ragged and peeling. He took a drink, wiped the top with his sleeve and said again, almost shouting, 'Have some *more!*'

Garros didn't want any. 'I'd like to get a look at the beaches around here. Can we do that?'

Halifax shrugged. 'We'd have to go on foot.'

Serailler looked as if he were trying to swallow his teeth.

'Fine. We'll start now.' Garros set the enamel mug on Serailler's desk. 'If that's all right.' He nodded at Serailler and walked out of the room.

They listened to his footsteps fading down the hall. For the first time since the plane landed, Serailler stopped grinning. He took another slug from the bottle and slammed it down on the desk. The camel skull jumped. 'He knows. He can see right into my head.'

The Levasseur buzzed over Mogador and then headed north along the coast. In four days it was due back to pick up Garros.

Garros and Halifax watched the plane from the ruin of a Portuguese mansion in the dunes beyond the town. Squares of mosaic tiling the size of a thumbnail spread out across the floor of what had once been a large room. Sand covered it in patches. The remains of engraved pillars supported broken sections of arches, strangled in creepers and thorns.

'I saw this mansion from the air when I flew in.' Garros dug at the tiles with his heel. 'I thought it might be a good place to talk.'

'The café is a good place to talk. They have chairs.' Halifax was thinking of the pilot, up by himself over the sea. Blue above the blue below. Flying home with the strumming and thundering of the engine all through his body.

'I mean, talk privately.' Garros climbed one of the arches and looked around with a pair of small binoculars. Then he climbed down and brushed the dirt off his trousers. 'Do you know why I'm here, Private?'

'Serailler said —'

'I'm here to investigate the sale of guns to the Arabs. Rifles. Bullets. Does the name Mannlicher mean anything to you? It's the name of a gun. The guns that are being sold.'

Halifax blinked at him.

Garros smoothed back his cropped blond hair, then winced when his fingers trailed over the sun-burned skin on his neck. 'We believe these guns are being channelled through the Canary Islands.'

'You seem to know a lot about it.'

'Knowing about it isn't going to stop it. The Spanish aren't cooperating.' He sat down against one of the ruined pillars and covered his face with his hands. 'Jesus, my head hurts in this sun.'

Halifax took the handkerchief from his pocket, tied knots in each of the four corners and gave it to Garros. His father used to wear his handkerchief as a hat when he cut the hedge and worked in the rose garden in the summers back home. The first time Halifax tried it, when he was five years old, the hat covered his eyes like a splat of kneaded dough.

Garros put it on. The knots stuck out in little pigtails. 'I'm not used to the sun, not used to Africa.' He brushed away sand from the tiles near where he sat, uncovering a line of red squares, the colours still bright after hundreds of years. The line bordered a mosaic of two dolphins, the head of one touching the tail of the second, as if they were chasing each other in the water. Garros stood and began to speak, as if he hadn't meant to talk anything but business and now had to make up for lost time.

'My job here is to collect information. I expect that information to come from you. I expect you to provide me with names and places. I only have four days down here and I don't have time to go crawling around every side street in this dirty little town looking for clues. Is that clear, Private Halifax?'

'So why did you bring us all the way out here?'

'I needed some place where we could talk without being overheard. I need to know if I can trust you. Besides, it's often the commanding officer of a garrison who knows least about what's going on. You live in the town, don't you?'

'For several years. I have a room that overlooks —'

He waved his hand, cutting off Halifax. 'This job is my promotion. This job gets me a job in Paris. If my report stops the trade of those rifles, even if only for a little while, then I get where I want to go. If there's anything here, Halifax, I think you know about it.'

'Do you?'

'If this report succeeds, I can promise that the authorities will be told of your cooperation.'

'Maybe they'll make me a general.'

Garros walked closer to Halifax. He puffed up his cooked cheeks and sighed. 'There's no room for sarcasm in this, Private. There's room for people who want some recognition. There's room for a man who wants the next job up the ladder. It could be you in Serailler's office. Think about that. All you have to tell me is something I'm sure you already know. Who's involved? What's a couple of Arabs to you? Just give me their names and soon enough you'll be wearing your rank badges on your shoulders instead of on your sleeve.'

'Somebody back in Marseille must want you dead, Garros.'

'Why?' He left his mouth hanging open.

'To send you down here alone and not knowing who you can trust.'

'I can trust you, can't I?'

'How old are you?'

'Twenty-one.' Garros scratched at his handkerchief hat. 'How old are you?'

'Twenty-eight. How long have you been in this business, Garros?'

'Six months about. This is my first big assignment. I'm in line for promotion.'

'So you said.' Halifax turned away and put his hands in his

35

pockets. Mogador glimmered in the distance. A moment later, he heard the sound of Garros pissing in the sand.

Garros talked while he pissed. 'You're English or American?'

'American.'

'Were you a pilot in the war?'

Halifax nodded at the while walls of Mogador.

Garros buttoned up his fly. 'I read an article about you once in the paper.'

'I don't think so.'

'I did,' Garros agreed with himself. 'I'm sure I read an article about an American who flew for the French.'

'A lot of Americans did that.'

'But this one was an officer. A Captain, I think. He was one of those Americans who came over to fight before America entered the war. Some of them formed their own squadron. It was famous. They had a name for it.'

'Lafayette.'

'Yes! It was the Lafayette Escadrille. And when America finally did come into the war, the Lafayette Escadrille disbanded and all of its members transferred over to the American Air Service. All except this guy. He stayed on with the French because the Americans wouldn't accept him.'

'Why not?' Halifax blinked out to sea. 'Do you remember?'

'Yes. I do remember. It was his eyesight. You're him, aren't you? You've got glasses.'

'Someone else, I think.'

'He shot down dozens of planes. He was an ace. When I read the article, he'd just been awarded the Croix de Guerre. His picture was in the paper. I thought his name sounded like yours.'

'You're mixing me up with someone else. That was a long time ago.'

'I used to collect newspaper clippings of stories about pilots. I wanted to be one, but the war ended before I was old enough to join. I swear I read about you.'

Halifax shrugged. Heat leaned into him. He was remembering the surprising heaviness of the medal when he lifted it from its red case, remembering the soft blue silk of the ribbon.

Garros sniffed and shook his head. 'It's true, it was a long time ago.'

\*

36

Instead of returning along the same road, where dust had blown up in their eyes and caked in the spit at the corners of their mouths when they walked out, now they took a short cut along the beach.

Halfway back, they came to a patch of reeds. Halifax rested his hand on Garros's shoulder, stopping him from going forward. 'We have to go around and up through the dunes.'

'What's the matter? You afraid of getting a little muddy? Your clothes look like they need washing anyway.'

Halifax bent down, picked up a rock the size of Garros's head and threw it into the reeds. The stone landed in the mud and for a moment it rested on the surface, then it slipped under. 'The month before I arrived here, a Legionnaire took a walk along this beach and disappeared into this mud. The Arabs say it goes down for miles.'

Garros folded his arms, gripping at his biceps and frowning at the mud. 'You see, I can trust you. I always know who I can trust.'

Just before the town, children played on a long stretch of sand that lay uncovered at low tide. They ran down with the surf as it sucked back in the patch of a new wave. Each child carried a stick or one of the long bayonets issued to the Legion troops: cross-shaped spikes, two feet long with a brass clip for fixing onto the rifle. The local militiamen sold them and then reported to the supply depot that the bayonets had been lost or stolen. The children ran as far as they could down the beach without being caught by the waves, and jammed the bayonets deep into the sand. The child whose mark lay farthest out won the game. Older children stood by watching, too old to play but wishing they could join in.

Garros had taken off his shoes and rolled up his trousers. He lit himself a cigarette. For the first time in ages, Halifax caught the perfumed smell of decent French tobacco.

'Halifax, I've been having the strangest dreams since I came to Africa.' The cigarette wobbled between his lips as he spoke.

Halifax was thinking of Serailler and the way he had mapped out what would happen if Garros came close to finding anything out. He recalled the slow chopping movements of Serailler's hand in the smoky air of the café as he moved through each stage of his plan.

'Did you hear me, Halifax? I said I've been having the strangest dreams.'

'How strange? What about?'

'It's not so much what they're about. You know how it is when you leave a dark room and go out into a very bright day?'

'Yes.'

'You know how the light seems until you get used to the brightness? Everything looks blue.'

'Your dreams are that way.'

'That's it.' Garros tiptoed on the hot cobblestones now that they had reached the street.

Halifax smiled, the skin stretching on his face.

'It's true!' Garros laughed. 'Ever since I came here. Every night.'

Within a few months of reaching Mogador, the same thing had happened to Halifax so many times that he was used to it. He lay down in bed each night with the feeling of sapphires pressed against his eyes, through which dreams could be seen and remembered. And when the memory returned of going down in flames over Belgium, as screams broke from his throat and he began to feel the fire from his engine, these flames came back to him in cobalt blue.

Halifax took off his glasses and set them on the table of his room. Then he pushed them around with the tips of his fingers, as if they would move by themselves if he jostled them enough. Instead of wire temples, he had loops of cloth for wrapping around his ears. It was the only way he could find to keep his glasses from falling off while he flew in the Spad. The lenses were scratched by dust and too much polishing with a rough handkerchief or a shirt tail.

I should have bribed the doctor, Halifax was thinking. He had been thinking about bribing the doctor ever since the man turned him down for the American Air Service. Halifax had gone over and over the same few minutes, but changing them so that the doctor let him through. Money handed over and stuffed into a pocket. Handshake. Papers signed.

The doctor rode out to the Bergues airfield at six in the morning in a staff car. It was in the spring of 1918. He had come straight from Paris and looked beaten up from a hangover.

Halifax stood with two other Americans in a wooden hut at

the Bergues garrison. Tuttle and Metzger, he remembered their names. By the time the doctor arrived, they had already been waiting an hour.

The hut was normally used as a briefing room. Silhouette cards of German, French and British aircraft hung on the walls. The hut had no heating. Frost crusted the windows.

The doctor ordered Tuttle and Metzger out of the room and told Halifax to strip. He stood in front of Halifax and stared, as if he knew him from somewhere but couldn't quite be sure. 'How well can you see without glasses?'

'I'm always wearing them, sir, so why does it matter?' Halifax had expected a few questions. He thought he was ready for all of them.

'It matters because American pilots aren't allowed to wear glasses. Their eyes must be perfect.'

He knew then that he should have hidden them. But in the months leading up to the exam he had convinced himself that there would be no problems. 'If you look at my flight record, sir . . .'

'Oh, I will,' the doctor shouted and then winced as the hangover clamped down on his head. 'All's I've been doing since I got to France is look at records.' He took the glasses away and then made Halifax read a chart he had pinned on the wall.

Halifax read the first two lines and said he was having trouble with the third.

The doctor held the frames, looking with disgust at the old loops of cloth. 'They really let you fly with these?'

'Of course, sir. I have been flying one or two missions a day for the past six months. I have nine confirmed kills and two unconfirmed. I have been recommended for the Croix de Guerre.'

The doctor handed back the glasses. 'That's all fine and good, but the American Air Service will not accept you as a pilot. If I sign you over for active duty, I'll lose my commission' — he snapped his fingers — 'this fast. Look, I checked out men who could barely walk because of shrapnel wounds, men who practically have to be carried to their planes every day. I've checked out people who look fine on the outside but who can't stop twitching because their nerves are all fouled up. I approve these men because I can edge them past the regulations, but you I cannot approve. I'm sure you're good at what you do, but what you're asking me is out of the question.'

'But the French took me. For Christ's sake, I'm a good pilot!'

'I know that. And I know why the French let you enlist. Because you're an American. Those French pilots see you and they know who's side America is on in this war. They know you're the first of millions who'll come over. As soon as American troops get into this, it's over. There's so many of us, we'll trample the fuckers to death if we have to. That's why they let you enlist. It's an actual fact.'

'You won't sign my papers, then?' Halifax put on his glasses. The room moved in close and clear again.

'I will not. Nobody will. That's the story. Send the next man in on your way out.'

I should have bribed him, Halifax thought, still sitting at the table in his room. I should have threatened him. He wiped the lenses of his glasses with the edge of his thumb. I should have done whatever it took to change his mind.

Then he went downstairs and wandered through the streets.

'Halifax!' A whisper popped out of the dark.

He stood still. The alley was pitch black.

'Halifax!'

He turned his head slowly from side to side, watching for movement. Then a shape broke from the shadows. 'What's the matter with you, Halifax?'

He saw the white of Serailler's teeth.

Serailler peered at him for a moment without talking, and he gurgled in his throat. 'He knows, doesn't he? You don't even have to say it. I can tell from the look on your face.' He took Halifax by the elbow and led him toward the commissariat. 'I have arranged for the man's disappearance.' Then he stopped. 'Why aren't you with him?'

Halifax opened his mouth to speak.

Serailler hissed. 'At *all* times, I said!'

'He's asleep. I have to explain something to you.'

Serailler gurgled again. 'He's probably tip-toeing around town in an Arab cape with the hood pulled up. He's listening to conversations in the bars. He's asking questions.' He jabbed a finger in Halifax's face. 'I know you want to hurt me!'

'You're not seeing things clearly, Serailler.'

'I see everything!' For the first time, his voice rose out of a whisper. They walked to the commissariat. Halifax sat at a desk while Serailler paced the room. The steel lugs of his heels tapped against the floor like the ticking of a clock. A militiaman lay asleep on the bed of a cell across the hall. He hugged a thin and dirty blanket, looking uncomfortable even in his sleep from the starched uniform.

'Garros explained to me what he's doing.'

Serailler said nothing and kept pacing.

Halifax leaned forward in the chair. 'Garros doesn't expect to find out anything by himself. All he wants to do is sit there and let us write his report for him. The only investigating he's doing right now is trying to see how he can get himself back to Paris as quickly as possible. Any information he gets is going to come from me.'

Serailler stopped pacing and spread his hands on the cold stone of the office wall, like someone being searched for a hidden weapon. 'He's just trying to win our confidence. He's too clever. The man is torturing me.'

'He's only twenty-one years old. It's his first assignment in Morocco. Don't touch him, Serailler. You'll do yourself a favour just by leaving him be.'

Serailler went back to pacing. 'It could be a diversion. There could be another inspector who arrived without us knowing.'

'You're not listening to me, are you?'

Serailler pushed open the shutters of his window and yelled out into the dark. 'The whole place is crawling with spies!'

Halifax waited until ten in the morning, then went to see if Garros was still alive.

Garros had a room at the Hotel Smara. A breakfast tray lay on the floor outside his room. Skin had formed on the jug of warm milk used for mixing with the tar-black coffee.

Halifax knocked on the door.

The bedclothes rustled. 'Who is it?'

'Halifax. You all right?'

The door opened. Garros stood with a bedsheet wrapped around him. 'Did I oversleep?'

Halifax shrugged. 'We didn't set a schedule. Your breakfast is cold.' They both looked down at the damp bread roll, cold coffee and shiny puddle of apricot jam.

When Halifax opened the shutters, Garros shrank back from the glare.

A boot knife was stuck in the wooden bed frame. Halifax stared at it. Garros followed his gaze, then pulled out the blade and set it on the window sill. 'Someone tried to break into my room last night.'

'When?' Halifax thought about Serailler in the alley.

'Around two. The door handle turned.' Garros twisted his fingers in the air. 'It just turned very quietly, but the door was locked so they went away.'

'What did you do?'

Garros pointed to a hole in the door where his boot knife had stuck in. 'I'd have missed him anyway. So what do you have for me? Do you have a list of names? Any locations I should see for my report?'

'Nothing yet.'

'I'm counting on you, Halifax. I need those names.'

'If you want, we could take a look at the market settlement in Oujdim. It's about twenty miles down the coast toward Agadir. There are trucks that run there every week. People come in from the surrounding area and sell what they have. You might see something.'

Garros nodded. 'It would look good in the report, wouldn't it?'

'It would look very special, Lieutenant Garros.'

Garros and Halifax sat in an old army truck, wedged between Arabs holding straw baskets of eggs, slabs of meat wrapped in bloody burlap sacking and chickens in cages made from scraps of wood. On the roof of the truck were bundles of clothes and two sheep with their legs tied together. A heavy rope net held everything down.

The truck pulled out onto the desert road. Immediately the air filled with dust and exhaust fumes that blew up through holes in the rotted floorboards.

Halifax watched Garros closely. At first Garros tried not to notice the woman and child sitting next to him. The woman had moved back the heavy black veils of her dress and held out her breast to the baby. Now and then the child stopped suckling and turned its head away. The woman's nipple was a swollen bolt of flesh. Garros tried not to stare, but then gave up and watched.

The bus stopped at several settlements along the way to pick up passengers. There was no room, so people hung on to the sides. Over the sound of engines, Halifax could hear the sheep bleating on the roof.

As soon as the truck stopped, beggars crowded around. One man, with his face sheared off by leprosy, held up the fingerless stump of his hand. It looked like a slab of brown cauliflower. On the skin of his palm he had drawn a smiling face with charcoal, as if to show what he had looked like before the disease ripped him apart. Garros watched all of this, hands clamped on knees and nostrils twitching, and muttered to himself.

A beggar with no eyes climbed into the truck, led by a child. The beggar chanted, 'Allah. Allah. *Alllllah*.'

Garros held his hands out, ready to push the man away if he came any closer.

Garros sweated in the heat. When the truck reached Oujdim, he blinked at the cluster of flat-roofed houses that served as cafés for the merchants. Market stalls bordered the streets. The stalls were made of plaster and stone, all painted pink-red. Meat sellers occupied one row. Hollow-eyed severed goat heads rested on the counter tops. Carcasses hung on steel hooks. In another line of stalls, whole families sat cramped among baskets of spices that clouded the air. An old man crouched behind a wall of deep green leaves tied in bundles. He held some up as Halifax and Garros walked past. Halifax picked a leaf, crushed it with his fingers and breathed in the smell of the mint. Berber women in black clothes embroidered with red, green and yellow thread squatted over piles of eggs that lay on strips of palm leaves. The women looked up smiling, as if they'd laid the eggs themselves and had been congratulated on it.

Garros took hold of Halifax's arm. 'Why did you bring me here?'

Halifax waited until Garros had let go before he spoke. 'People sell guns in this market. They might not have the guns on display but guns can be bought. If you want them, find them.'

'But where?'

Halifax stepped into the shade of a pink-red market stall. 'You said Mannlichers, right?'

'Right.' Garros still stood in the sun, baring his teeth in the glare.

'Do you know what a Mannlicher looks like?'

Garros shrugged. 'It's a gun.' The air was heavy with spices and sweat.

'No.' Halifax held up his hands and shook his head. 'I mean, do you know what it looks like? If you held one in your hands, could you tell me what it was?'

Garros took out a handkerchief and started to tie knots in the corners, moving very slowly in the heat. 'Maybe I could. That's your part of the job, Halifax.' He looked around, his jaw moving back and forth as he worked up enough moisture in his mouth to speak. 'Let's go back.'

'You only just got here.'

'What good does it do to stay around.'

'It might help if you saw how these people live.'

Garros jammed the handkerchief on his head and started walking towards the truck. 'I don't want to stay in this place.' Then the handkerchief fell off, so he picked it up and held it in place. The face of his wristwatch flashed in the sun.

As they boarded the truck, Garros caught sight of a donkey harnessed to a cart, that was so loaded down the donkey couldn't pull it. An old man sat on the cart, whipping the donkey. The animal scraped its hoof in the dirt but couldn't move the cart. The harness straps had worn through the fur on its shoulders and left the flesh raw. Flies clustered around its eyes.

Garros watched for a moment, breathing hard through his teeth. Then he jumped down from the truck and ran across to the man. He grabbed the whip and snapped it, yelling that the donkey would live a lot longer if someone could at least take care of the thing. He shook his fist in the old man's face. 'I hope you end up as a donkey in your next life!'

Through all this, the old man looked around for someone to translate what Garros was saying. After a minute, he took a stone from his pocket, bounced it off the donkey's head and the animal finally began dragging the cart down the road.

Garros climbed back into the truck. He mumbled to himself again on the way home. Once he leaned over to Halifax and said, 'Makes you as mad as hell, doesn't it?' Dirt and sweat had formed a paste on his cheeks and forehead.

Halifax nodded vaguely at what Garros was saying, then turned away. He had learned to close down in the heat, like drawing blinds on a window. He had learned to live far away inside himself, finding reservoirs where it was cool and where he didn't have to breathe the red Moroccan dust.

Rollet himself held up his hand to the sun. A bullet had torn the flesh below his little finger. Blood ran down his wrist and into the sleeve of his flight jacket.

'Hold it up. That'll stop the blood.' Ivan ran into the hangar to fetch iodine.

Rollet propped up his bad arm with his good arm. His eyes were shut and his lips were dried out and bloody from deep cracks.

Halifax and Labouchere helped wheel his plane into the hangar. The machine had taken about a dozen rounds in the forward fuselage. The green paint was chipped away at the point of each bullet's puncture in the steel engine casing. One round shot the control stick out of Rollet's hands and he flew back holding the twisted length of metal that remained. The same round passed through his hand.

Labouchere seemed half asleep. He always looked that way. His eyelids stayed nearly closed and his long face drooped into the folds of his flying scarf. His Spad had also taken hits. They showed as black speckles on the plane's green-painted canvas. 'This has to stop, Halifax.'

'It certainly does.' He pushed hard to lift the Spad's wheels onto the concrete hangar floor.

Labouchere let go of his side and walked around to Halifax. 'No. You don't understand. What has to stop is you lounging around here on the ground or running errands for Serailler while Rollet and I go up and get our tits shot off.'

'You know I'd be flying with you if Serailler didn't give me separate orders. You know that.'

Labouchere ignored him. 'This time it was ground fire, Charlie. We were out strafing forward positions and the Arabs waited until we made a couple of really low passes before opening up on us with a machine gun.' Labouchere spoke quickly, faster than Halifax thought a man could ever talk who still looked half asleep. 'That's the first time I've seen automatic weapons in the hands of these people.'

'They probably captured them at Sidi Arak.'

'Doesn't matter where they came from, Charlie. It's not what I'm talking about. What I'm talking about is you not doing your job.'

45

'I'm doing what Serailler orders me to do.' So I can go home, he was thinking. So I can leave you and Rollet and these worn-out, shot-up Spads and go home.

'Not good enough.' The muscles twitched along Labou-chere's jawbone. 'Up until now we've all been doing exactly what Serailler tells us to do, and all of us for the same reason, which is that he has the power to transfer us to the desert. And you know as well as I do how many pilots come back after they've been transferred out there. Abdel Krim was just biding his time until the Legion overextended itself across half the fucking Sahara before rolling us up like a carpet. There's almost no place left where Serailler can send us. Rollet and I need you up there with us now, or in a couple of days we'll stand a better chance of survival if we run away and join the Arabs. Don't think Rollet and I haven't talked about it. He and I have seen enough ugly business here to know that it might be our only way out.' Labouchere's chest rose and fell evenly under the leather of his coat.

On the runway, Rollet sat in a chair that Ivan had brought him.

Ivan dabbed a cloth against the mouth of the iodine bottle, then touched it against Rollet's wound.

Rollet cried out and his body shook. His hand stayed raised in the air, as if waving goodbye to someone only he could see.

'Fuck Rollet!' Serailler was drunk. His office stank of cognac. 'Fuck Labouchere!'

'But they're right.' Halifax shifted from one foot to the other, already losing his temper.

'Why did you take Garros out to Oujdim today?' Serailler aimed a finger at Halifax. 'I'm having you watched!'

'I took him there so he would be out of the way.' He moved to open the shutters. The air was stale in the room.

'Close the window!' Serailler jabbed Halifax with the toe of his boot. 'I don't like daylight anymore.'

'I have to start flying patrols with Rollet and Labouche. They need a third man. If I don't go, then one of them could be killed.'

Serailler threw the cognac bottle across the room. It exploded into dark green fragments and a smell of alcohol billowed across the room. 'So let them die!'

Halifax stepped forward and clamped his hand over Serailler's face. He shoved him across the room on the tiny wheels attached to his chair legs Serailler bumped against the far wall. For a moment he only sat there blinking. Then suddenly he lunged for the desk. He opened the drawer and reached for a gun.

Halifax shoved him back again. 'Try to think straight!'

Serailler hit the floor, bouncing on his bottom. 'I'm going to have you shot. You'll be out at Sidi Arak by tomorrow. I'll have all three of you shot!'

Halifax took the gun from Serailler's desk, checked that it was loaded and grabbed Serailler by his collar. He rested the gun against Serailler's forehead. 'You know what I'm going to do?'

Serailler went cross-eyed staring down the barrel.

'I'm going to kill you right here. Then I'm going to that inspector and I'm going to tell him everything I know about you and your deals with the Touaregs. I'll tell the inspector you were going to kill him. I tried to stop you. There was a struggle. So I blew your stupid fucking head off. How's that for a plan, Serailler? I'll tell you how it is. It's better than anything else you've come up with lately.'

Serailler watched the rounded points of lead, waiting for the cylinder to roll counterclockwise when Halifax pulled the trigger. After a while Serailler opened his mouth and his face turned red. He started to shake. 'What am I supposed to do? They're closing in on me. Where am I supposed to go?' He rubbed at his eyes. Tears ran over his fingernails.

Halifax took hold of Serailler's cheeks and squashed them together. 'Listen to me. They are not closing in on you. If you can shut your mouth and do nothing until this boy leaves, you'll be all right.'

Serailler tried to stand up but fell back. 'I won't say anything. I won't do anything.'

Halifax opened the revolver and dropped the bullets into his pocket. He set the gun down on Serailler's desk and walked out.

Halifax was asleep when a man came into his room in the middle of the night. He stood at the end of the bed and beat Halifax on the feet with a rolled-up newspaper.

The first thought that popped into Halifax's head when he opened his eyes was that Serailler had come to murder him. And in his half-sleep it was Serailler's livestock face he saw and punched.

The man fell backwards, arms flailing, onto the cold tiles of the balcony.

With the door open, Halifax could smell and hear the sea. Waves trampled the rocks and fell back thundering into the dark. He walked out and peered at the man. 'Jesus, Ivan. I thought you were Serailler.'

Ivan rolled his eyes around in their sockets. He couldn't tell where the voice was coming from. Then he ran his tongue over his teeth to see if any were broken. 'I got a letter.'

'I had a big fight with Serailler and he tried to pull a gun on me. Jesus, Ivan.' He tucked his hand under Ivan's head and lifted it off the tiles, which were damp with spray from the ocean.

'I got a letter.'

'Who from?'

'From a woman who wants to be my wife.' Ivan smiled. His front tooth was chipped.

Halifax helped him inside. Ivan sat down in a chair and held on to the table, as if the room were sliding out from under him. 'You know in the papers sometimes there are notices from men who want to meet women and women who want to meet men?'

'Sure. Lonely hearts.'

'Well, I am a lonely heart. I sent in an advertisement about five months ago.'

'Why didn't you tell me?'

'You'd have laughed.'

Halifax scratched at the back of his neck. 'Now of course I wouldn't —'

'You'd have laughed yourself sick and you know it.' Ivan dug his nails into the pale wood of the table, anchoring himself in the swaying room.

'What did you write?'

Ivan took out his polished leather wallet, fished through bits of paper until he found the piece he wanted and gave it to Halifax.

It said, 'Displaced Russian aristocrat. Handsome. Educated. Independently wealthy landowner presently residing in Africa. Wishes to meet lady suitable for lasting relationship. Must be well mannered and prepared to travel to exotic locations.' Then it gave his name and the poste restante address for the Mogador post office.

Halifax handed back the paper. 'Is this supposed to be you?'

'Of course!'

'Do you expect anyone to believe it?' He put on his flying jacket against the chill. His thoughts were still garbled with sleep.

Ivan held up a sheet of lavender-coloured writing paper. His boiler suit bunched around his middle, making him look fat. 'This is the second letter she's sent me. Her name is Justine Dubois. She's a chambermaid at the Hôtel Président on the Champs-Élysées. In the first letter she said she was prepared to come down and meet me, but she needed some money for the voyage.'

'So what did you do?'

'I sent her everything I had.'

Halifax raked his fingers through his hair. 'Oh, Ivan.' Then he looked up and reached out to take the letter.

Ivan held it away. 'It's personal.'

'She'll never come.'

Ivan waggled the letter. 'She will. That's what she says here.'

'But you aren't wealthy, Ivan. You don't have any land. As far as I can see, you aren't very educated, and I don't mean any harm but you aren't all that handsome, either.'

'You just haven't seen me at my best. She wouldn't have written to me if I didn't give her a good picture of things.'

'You can't bring her down here now. Did you even tell her you're in the Legion?'

'Legion men can get married. I looked it up in the regulations in Serailler's office and it says so.'

'But not with the latest offensive and the rumours that Abdel Krim will be at the coast by Christmas.'

'It's too late, actually. She's already on her way.' He sucked in his cheeks and nodded. 'On her way. Do you think she'll like me?'

'You're an idiot.'

'I need you to lend me some money.'

'You're a fucking idiot.'

'I'm a lonely heart.'

'How much do you need?'

'Enough to buy some good clothes and material for new curtains.'

It looked as if a bear lived in Ivan's house. Piles of clothes

49

showed the marks where he had sat or slept on them. His drawers were filled with bread crusts and pots of unopened jam. He saved his cigarette butts until he had enough tobacco to make a new cigarette. The butts were stored in a metal can used for holding the Spads' ammunition belts.

Halifax took out his wallet and gave Ivan all the money he had. Then he fished under his mattress until he found his savings and gave him some of that as well.

Ivan counted the notes, smoothing them flat with his hand. He took out a pencil and a piece of paper and wrote Halifax an IOU. 'Could you help me make the curtains? Could you help me with the details when she gets here?' He looked obese in his boiler suit.

'I could try.'

'I know it's true that I don't have any land and I know I'm not handsome.' He doodled with the pencil on the table. Thick, heavy lines, over and over into the wood. 'But I used to have land. In Russia I had lots of land. I went to good schools. I never did any work when I was there but they were good schools all the same. And I used to be handsome. What do you know about handsome, anyway?'

'Not much anymore.'

'I didn't mean it like that.'

'I can't believe you wrote to a newspaper.'

'What?' Ivan rocked on the chair's back legs. 'You can't believe that after years alone in this place I'm doing the only thing I can think of to find myself a companion. Does that seem so strange? If you think it's strange, you should see how many other people put their names in the paper.'

'I just think it's strange that she answered the ad. This isn't a safe country.'

'It's safe on the coast.'

'For the time being. It just gives me a strange feeling, Ivan.'

Ivan grinned and spat. The white gob flew across the room and disappeared out of the window. 'There's a name for your little feeling. It's called jealousy.'

'No. Not jealousy.'

'What then?' Ivan scribbled on the table, losing his temper.

'I just know the truth about this place and about you.'

Ivan set down his pencil and stared for a second at the lines he had drawn. 'I told her some lies to bring her here. When she arrives, I'll tell her the truth. Then she can do what she wants.'

# 4

GARROS CROUCHED on the window sill of his room at the Hotel Smara. His eyes looked red.

Halifax brought in the breakfast tray. Garros climbed down stiffly and held out his hand like a crab claw for the tray. A small set of dominoes was spread out on the window sill. He'd been setting them up in a row and then knocking them over. Tiny rhinestones marked the numbers.

'Did you sleep?'

'Do I look like I slept? There are beetles in the bed. Most nights at home there could be a brass band in my room and I wouldn't wake up. But here there are beetles in the bed and I didn't sleep.'

Halifax tore a piece from the flat slab of bread, spread jam on top and handed it over. It was still warm from the oven. 'I have to fly a patrol this morning, so I won't be able to lead you around town.' He scratched the back of his neck, waiting to hear what Garros would say.

'I don't need you to lead me around. I want you to get me a list of names. Don't forget. Names and places and dates.'

'What if I don't have any names?'

'Find some.'

Halifax nodded, then turned to leave.

'I was hoping you could take me out to Cap Sim.'

Halifax looked back. 'Why there?' Cap Sim was a sandy point south of Mogador where carcasses of ships jutted from the surf and the wind made people blind.

'Why?' Garros stared, not sure whether to trust him anymore.

'Someone came to my room again last night. The person knew my name.'

'Who was it?' Halifax raised his eyebrows.

'I didn't see. He stayed on the other side of the door. Told me to meet him at Cap Sim this afternoon and to come alone.

51

Whoever it was knew the reason I'm in Mogador.'

You'll die if you go out there, Halifax was thinking. He tried to imagine Garros's sunburned face turned grey and dead. Serailler will kill you, he thought, and looked at Garros closely. Don't you know that? He'll kill you and he'll take his time doing it. 'I might be back by this afternoon. If the patrol goes well, I still might be able to take you out there. All we have to do is photograph a forward area and come home again. I should go with you to Cap Sim. They wouldn't have to see me there, whoever they are.'

'No. That might blow it.'

'Cap Sim is a dangerous place, Lieutenant Garros.' For Christ's sake, don't you see what's going to happen? 'No one could blame you for not showing up.'

Garros didn't want to talk. He picked up the coffee mug and held it against his chest, breathing in the steam.

Halifax pulled on his flying jacket, smelling old sweat in the wool blanket lining. He strung his goggles and flying helmet on his belt and set out for the airfield. The stone walls of the commissariat were pale in the morning sun. Hunched next to the commissariat was the Dimitri, busy with people and talk.

Serailler waved to him from a table at the café. He wore his dark blue Legion tunic with the blood-red collar. Halifax stopped in front of the table. 'Morning Serailler.'

Serailler motioned for him to come close. 'I didn't mean what I said earlier. I was drunk and don't remember what happened.' He reached out and took hold of Halifax's arm. 'I don't remember what I said.'

Halifax looked at the hand that gripped his jacket. 'Garros doesn't know about you. All you have to do is leave him be.'

Serailler let go but kept staring. 'They wouldn't lock me up, would they, Charlie? Not in some cage underground.'

They flew in a chevron above the scrubland east of Mogador.

Halifax looked across at Labouchere on his right, then at Rollet on his left. Only their leather-capped heads showed above the cockpits. He wished he knew the daydreams that unravelled in their heads.

Clouds jammed the sky at seven thousand feet, leaving dampness on the Spads' wings and on the pilots' faces. The wings shuddered as they passed through. In places the bleached curtain broke open, leaving vertical alleyways that stretched all the way to the ground. Below them were scattered farms and settlements. In the midday heat they showed no signs of life. The farmers fenced in their cattle with rows of cactus plants. When they had nothing else to sell, they collected the pear-shaped cactus fruit and brought them into Mogador. The fruit were sour and red inside and good against thirst.

Tiny streams in riverbeds winked silver and then returned to brown. Chalky scratches of paths led from village to village.

They passed over a mosque built of mud and red clay. It sat on a hilltop miles from any town or village. No roads led there. Halifax used the mosque as a marker to chart his course across the desert. The place had always looked haunted to him. He imagined himself in the dark coolness of the building, watching through a tiny window hole as his own plane went by overhead.

To shake away the daydreams, he checked controls, tightened his seat straps and readied the photographic plates in a camera attached to the fuselage. His job was to get as low as possible to the valley floor ahead of an outpost named Telaleh, then photograph the place to see if any signs of an Arab stronghold could be found before Legion troops advanced up the valley. Labouchere and Rollet had racks of Cooper bombs in the metal cases under their seats. They were to go in first and shell any fortifications.

Rock and sand swallowed the last peppering of scrub brush. The Atlas Mountains rose up in heat haze. They merged with brown fog on the horizon, forced down by the hard blue sky.

For Halifax, time in the air stayed separate from time on the ground.

In the summer of 1918 he was attached to the seventy-third Escadrille of the French Air Service. Twice a day his squadron travelled northeast out of Bergues, crossing German lines near Zillebeke in Flanders, and returned over what was left of the Menin road.

After weeks of surveying the dogfights, he couldn't understand why he was still alive. A constant panic threaded in and out of his ribs. He began to look at his time in the air as a payment for the time on the ground. Danger, then safety. Debt, then payoff.

He used to lie in his hut after dark, hearing trampling thunder from artillery barrages at the front, and all he could remember were the hours spent in his Spad's cramped cockpit. Everything else seemed fluid and pointless. He walked the ground like a person still asleep until the time for flying came again.

A road ran up to Telaleh. It lay parallel to a ridge of hills jutting from the ground. Tyre tracks gridded the sand.

They banked south along the roads. Gusts of wind curled over their planes like the crests of breaking waves. The Spads' wings shook with the force.

Then they saw black smoke, smoke from burning gasoline. A Legion truck was stopped on the road. Streamers of blue flame reached up from its cab, which had collapsed under the heat of fire. Several bodies lay beside the truck. The dead men had been looted. Paper and clothing were scattered around their inside-out pockets and emptied packs.

The pilots flew through the dark pillar rising from the truck. The reek of burned rubber pressed on their lungs. Halifax wondered for a moment whether the Telaleh garrison would be there at all, or whether it would be empty like other outposts he had seen, the dead Legionnaires carried away and hidden.

Telaleh lay at the beginning of a valley that cut through the rocky hills.

The buildings of the settlement were ruins now. Khaki Legion tents stood pitched in the rubble tucked like spider nests against crumbled walls. Stone barricades had been set up in the streets. Men squatted behind them, looking up as the planes passed overhead.

Halifax flew past the town, giving Labouchere and Rollet time to move ahead into a single-line formation. The valley was too narrow for a chevron of planes.

Labouchere and Rollet wheeled into the valley and disappeared.

The rock of the valley was steep and grey-red. It seemed as if the only thing that held up these hills was the shadow they threw on the earth.

The clatter of a Spad's gun reached Halifax's ears, muffled by the noise of his engine. Suddenly the shock wave of a Cooper bomb echoed off the stone walls.

White puffs of rifle fire spat from the rocks. A few Arabs broke cover and ran, long-cloaked and dark on the sand.

He set the shutter and took one picture, catching sight of Labouchere's Spad gaining altitude as it came to the end of the valley.

Black circles of Arab tents lay close to the mountainside. Tethered animals reared up as Rollet and Labouchere dived onto the settlement and dropped a row of Cooper bombs, which exploded in geysers in the middle of the camp. Tents flew apart.

Another picture.

More white puffs from long-barrelled rifles before the men panicked and ran.

Labouchere dropped another row of Coopers. The bombs wobbled, straightened out, then struck the ground where a group of men had stopped to form a firing line. They disappeared in the smoke. Now only a few tents remained. The others lay burning and in rags.

Three horses ran into the valley. They were still tied together, dragging their uprooted hitching post.

Another picture.

Faraway drumming of machine guns as Rollet and Labouchere strafed the camp.

A few miles beyond the valley, Halifax flew over an area of fertile ground fed by streams that bubbled up out of the rock. The fields were green with early wheat. Here and there he made out the headscarves of women who had been working in the fields and now were trying to hide. He wondered why they continued to farm when it was obvious the Legion troops would overrun them any day. They probably have nothing else to do, he thought. They have been farming these fields for a thousand years and their instincts won't let them do anything else.

Back into the valley. Sun cut a ragged line across the rock. The stone glowed above and showed cold grey below.

White slivers of tracer fire. Rollet dived down on an Arab who ran with his arms outstretched, weapon gone. The snake line of bullets from Rollet's gun overtook the Arab and he fell. Tracer sparked into the earth on either side of him.

Already the Legionnaires had begun an advance.

Halifax circled the town, taking a last picture. Then he landed on Telaleh's short airstrip.

A figure appeared from a dugout and ran towards him,

hunched over, arms down at his sides like an ape. When the man reached the plane, he was smiling. 'Charlie!' He hooked his hands over the rim of the cockpit. 'Did you bring me a present?'

Halifax pulled down his flying goggles. He felt pressure where the dirty velvet pads had dug unto his cheeks. 'No, Winslow. I couldn't find anything that looked like a present.' They spoke in English. Winslow was the only American Halifax had ever met in Morocco.

Halifax unbuckled his safety straps and jumped down to the ground, holding a leather satchel against his chest. It contained developed photographs from the previous week's reconnaissance run over Telaleh.

The two of them ran for the dugout.

'Not even a newspaper from home?' Winslow crouched behind a row of sandbags. They were made from old shirts and trousers stitched together and filled with dirt.

Rifle fire snapped in the distance. Pilots always had to run from their planes at Telaleh, in case Arabs were sniping from the hills. Several times in the past, Halifax had seen dirt fly up near his plane but never heard a rifle shot.

He caught his breath. 'Where am I supposed to find these papers, Winslow? I haven't seen an American newspaper in years.'

Winslow grinned. 'It's enough for me just to speak English.'

'Where's Captain Chaudon?' He slapped the leather satchel. Its handle was black with old sweat. 'I have to give these pictures directly to him.'

Rollet and Labouchere landed on the airstrip. They climbed down from their planes and ran toward the dugout.

Winslow was still grinning. 'Chaudon's in the town. He's waiting for you.'

Rollet and Labouchere slid into the dugout.

'Back in fifteen minutes.' Halifax took off his glasses, folded them into their metal case and put the case in his pocket. He leaned on Labouchere's shoulder as he climbed out.

Rollet took off his flying cap and used it to wipe sweat from his forehead. 'Do you have any tobacco?'

Halifax took a bag of tobacco and cigarette papers from his pocket and threw it at them, then he ran after Winslow.

*

They walked through the streets, dust the shade of curry powder kicked up by their footsteps stepping over the rubble of buildings crushed by artillery fire. At first Winslow couldn't remember where Chaudon had his new headquarters, since the last one had been blown up. Chaudon commanded the garrison at Telaleh.

In a few minutes they came to a house with its roof still intact. Winslow said this had to be the place, but the shutters were closed and it seemed empty and dark inside.

'So where is he?' Halifax stepped inside and felt the sweat cool suddenly on his face. 'I'd like to get out of here as soon as I can.'

Chaudon always tried to make Halifax, Rollet and Labouchere stay for dinner. Whenever they did, the Arabs used their planes for target practice, and sometimes they barely made if off the ground because their Spads were shot so full of holes.

Winslow slapped his palms against his sides. 'He said he'd be here.'

Halifax stayed quiet, wondering if he could get away with just leaving the pictures and not delivering them himself. He was thinking of his room at the Hotel Smara — cool, dark and echoing the sea. The chairs on his balcony warm in the sun.

Winslow cleared his throat and spat out dust. 'How come you're in the Legion?'

Halifax looked up, surprised. He had learned years before never to ask anybody why they'd joined. Almost everybody had something to hide. Many used false names when they signed up. They invented complicated lies about their pasts and could rattle them off like bulletins.

Whenever Halifax flew into Telaleh, he listened to the few things Winslow said, trying to catch hints of what brought him here. But Winslow let very little slip. It seemed enough for him to speak English about nothing at all.

'What business do you have asking that?' Halifax tried to raise some anger in himself, some indignation. But the anger didn't come. He only felt a little tired from the effort.

'Oh, no business.' Winslow sat down against the far wall, hands lying useless and palm up on the ground. 'I heard you were a pilot in the fourteen–eighteen war.'

Jesus, Halifax thought, does Ivan run some kind of a

newspaper? He looked out the door as someone walked past, hoping it would be Chaudon so he could get out and go home.

Winslow shrugged. 'It's nothing to me, Charlie. It's just talk.'

Halifax had a little hollow space inside him that needed to be filled with cigarette smoke. He reached for his tobacco bag and then remembered he'd given it to Rollet. He couldn't ask Winslow for his smokes. They were too valuable to give away out here.

'Why did you join the Foreign Legion in the first place?'

'Why don't you offer me a cigarette, Winslow?' He was angry for a smoke.

'Oh.' Winslow rummaged in his pockets and pulled out an old cigarette case. Brass showed through the worn-out silver plate. He opened the case and held it out.

Halifax looked at the three thin cigarettes in the case. 'I'm sorry, Winslow. You keep the smokes.'

Winslow picked the biggest cigarette and held it out. His dirty fingerprints showed on the rolling paper. 'Have it.'

'No. I don't want one.'

'Of course you do. Your hands are twitching. That's not good for a pilot. Have the damn thing. I can get more.'

Halifax lit the cigarette. The tobacco tasted stale and peppery.

Winslow settled back. 'I guess we never talk about those things.'

'I flew with the Lafayette Escadrille.'

'That's what I heard.'

Now Halifax found a little anger in his tiredness. 'So if you know, then why ask me?'

'I was just asking why you were here now. Why out on the middle of the desert? Why didn't you go back to the States at the end of the war?'

'It just didn't work out that way, Winslow.' The smoke burned his throat. This must be cut with corn silk, he thought, and peered at the pale flecks of tobacco in the mouth end of his cigarette.

'Try a drink of this.' Winslow pulled a flask from his pocket and handed it over. 'It's just that sometimes out here we run out of things to talk about. I forget what I can ask and what I can't. I forget, and when I remember I don't care. Abdel Krim will overrun this place any day now. Then it won't make any difference what I asked.'

58

Halifax took a mouthful. Alcohol. He spat it out. It tasted as if it had been filtered through dead leaves.

'I made it myself.' Winslow took back the flask and poured some down his throat. Then he shifted his cramped legs on the floor.

'You really think Abdel Krim will get this far?' Halifax tried to focus, drilling his eyes through the gloom.

'He's already here. We just haven't seen him yet.'

'You think?'

'I know.' Winslow smiled weakly in the dark.

Captain Chaudon appeared in the doorway. He was very tall and wore boots that came up to his knees. He carried a rifle by the barrel, as if it were a walking stick. He looked at Halifax, then turned to Winslow. 'Run after A Company and tell them not to advance any farther until I get back.'

Without saying goodbye, Winslow sprinted out of the house.

Chaudon took the satchel from Halifax and flipped through the photos. 'I don't know why you bother.'

'I beg your pardon, sir?'

'I know all the information in these pictures already. Known it for weeks. Probably knew it before you took the photographs.'

'Yes, sir.'

'Next time when you come, bring me . . . bring me —' he stuck out his chin and looked up at the ceiling — 'some good books to read! Yes, books, and some paintings to hang on these walls and some chocolate with nuts in it.'

'Chocolate with nuts, sir?'

'Look, these pictures you have given me are useless. So if you have to fly out here with something, if that's absolutely what the Legion wants you to do, then fly out here with some books and some chocolate. And what else did I want? I've forgotten.'

'Paintings, sir.'

'Right. A painting.' He spread his hands as if blocking out a space on the opposite wall. 'I'll hang it right there. Drop all the bombs you want but don't bother taking any more photographs. It's really no good to us. All right?' Then he smiled. 'Stay for dinner. As soon as we've secured the valley, I'll have the cook throw something together.'

'Have to get back, Captain Chaudon. I saw a truck on fire about five miles down the road. I wondered if you knew about it.'

'Oh, shit. Really? That was a reconnaissance group.' He raised his eyebrows. 'What about the men? Did they signal to you? Were they all right?'

'No, sir. Not all right.'

Chaudon nodded and walked toward the door. Loose bullets rattled in his pockets. 'Next time, Halifax, bring me what I asked for.'

They left the runway one by one. Halifax eased his Spad into formation ahead of Labouchere and Rollet. I should have asked Winslow some questions, Halifax thought. The same ones he asked me. Next time he won't feel like talking.

Late afternoon sunset glowed orange on his wings. He looked down at the burned-out truck as they passed overhead.

Dead men still lay on the road. The black remains of the truck looked like the husk of a beetle dried up on a window sill.

Ivan's voice echoed from the metal arc of the hangar. He was singing opera. First a high voice, then a low voice, then hums that broke now and then into la-la-las. He walked from the hangar, bellowed out the last few notes and bowed. He clapped for his imaginary audience and then for himself and finally he pretended to pick up the roses people threw to him on stage.

Labouchere, Rollet and Halifax stood watching. Their faces were grey with cordite from the guns. They sweated in their heavy clothes.

Ivan grinned. 'Busy day? Shot off all those nasty bullets? Did they fly up for fun in the sun?'

As the sun slid into the sea, the four of them sat in deck chairs outside the hangar. Their Spad engines muttered as they cooled.

Ivan sent one of the boys who hung around the hangar into town to fetch some mint tea. After twenty minutes, the waiter from the Dimitri appeared with their drinks on a tray. He wore black trousers and a short white coat.

Labouchere rolled cigarettes and handed them out. He tapped Rollet's leg with the toe of his boot and smiled. They both laughed at a private joke. The two of them lived in the same house near the market place, on a street that smelled of olives and fish. They had lived in the same house back in France.

When the sun went away, the sky turned turquoise and the heat began to fade. They stayed seated in their canvas chairs. The tea had all been drunk. Only the mint leaves remained in their glasses.

Ivan leaned across to Halifax. 'I had a look at that Levasseur plane, the one Garros came in on. Beautiful. Modern. With a dozen of those and the equipment to modify them for bombing and strafing, I could kick Abdel Krim so far back that he'd be paddling in the Red Sea in a month.' He nodded, agreeing with himself.

For a while no one spoke. Then Ivan shook Halifax's arm. 'What colour shall I make the curtains?'

'Why do you want curtains?'

'For Justine.' He frowned. 'Justine Dubois.'

'You don't need curtains. Nobody here has curtains. All you need is the shutters.'

Ivan sat back in the chair and rubbed his hand over his face. 'She'll be expecting curtains.'

Halifax wandered toward the commissariat. Under his arm he carried the camera and the new photographic plates of Telaleh. Suddenly he remembered Garros and the trip to Cap Sim. He walked faster, through the town gates and along an alley that bordered the fortress walls.

The Café Dimitri was crowded. Halifax peered inside. Two militiamen sat by themselves at a table. Both held knives and were leaning over something spread across the table top.

Halifax stopped and looked: the dominoes belonging to Garros. The militiamen were gouging the rhinestones from the black wooden tablets. They made a pile of the fake diamonds in an ashtray.

He felt the blood rush in his face.

The Arabs looked up, grinning. One of them pointed to an empty chair and asked if he wanted to join them.

Halifax left the café, ran up the commissariat steps and kicked open the door to Serailler's office.

The captain sat up. He had been asleep with his head resting on folded arms. The imprint of cufflinks showed on his forehead.

'You did it, didn't you?'

Serailler rubbed at his cheeks. 'Did it? Did *what*?'

'You killed him.' Halifax took a step forward toward the desk.
'Who?'

'Garros, you pasty-faced son of a bitch!' He kicked a hole in the front of Serailler's desk. The wood smashed and pale splinters shot across the room.

'Garros is on his way over to the Café Dimitri.' Serailler spoke very quietly. His hands lay flat on the desk. 'When you come to my office, you knock. When you talk to me, you say "sir" and stand to attention until I tell you otherwise. You do not kick holes in my desk. You do not raise your voice to me. Do you understand? Or shall I have you thrown into one of the oubliettes.' He sounded so different from the night before, so completely calm, that Halifax wondered if Serailler really had forgotten what happened and what he'd said about everyone being after him and about how the place was crawling with spies.

Halifax set the photo plates down on the desk. 'Garros went out to Cap Sim today and now I just saw some militiamen playing with his set of dominoes. Is he alive or not, Serailler?'

'He's alive. The man he went to meet is not, but Garros should be having his dinner by now.' Serailler looked at his watch. 'I'm supposed to be at the Dimitri in ten minutes. Poor Garros is a little shaken up.'

'Who did he go to meet?'

'Hassan Gharsi. I threw him across the courtyard the other day because he refused to stay at his post.'

'You mean out at the roadside mosque, where he was waiting for Garros to arrive?'

'Him. Yes. Hassan Gharsi. He decided to turn me in, so I had him killed.'

'How did you know about it?'

'The owner of the Hotel Smara overheard him when he went to talk to Garros in the middle of the night. The owner is a friend of mine.'

'How much did he charge you for the information?'

'Five hundred francs.'

'Who did the job?'

'The owner of the hotel. For another hundred francs. Let me ask you something, Charlie.'

'What?'

'Why are you so concerned with the safety of this man

62

Garros? If he does his job right, it's not just me who'll take the fall. It's you, too.'

'There's no need to kill him. There's just no need.'

'You're going soft, Charlie. You with the Croix de Guerre. You used to be one of the best.'

With slow and careful movements, Garros lifted a bowl of soup to his mouth. By the side of his chair was a live chicken in a box made from slats of wood badly glued together. The chicken's feathers were clean and white. It stuck its beak out through a gap in the slats and pecked at Garros's chair.

Serailler set his hand on Garros's shoulder. 'You feeling better?'

Garros looked up from his soup. 'I lent my dominoes to a couple of your militiamen. They gouged out all the fucking stones.'

'I'll have some new ones made. Does that chicken belong to you?'

Garros glared at him. 'Every time I eat something around here I get sick. Then I sit around making rude noises all night. This chicken —' he nudged the box with his foot — 'is going to be my first square meal since I got to Morocco. I'm paying that waiter to cook it for me.' He slammed down his bowl of soup. 'They should have given me more time to look into this. More time to investigate! Four days wasn't enough.'

'Not at all.' Serailler twisted a ring on his finger. On the ring was his family's coat of arms.

'That man knew what was going on. That man had names to tell. He wouldn't have taken the risk otherwise.'

'He didn't tell you anything?' Serailler chewed at his lip.

'Nothing!' Garros bug-eyed the café, staring at everyone. 'He was dead. Do you know what the fuckers did to him? They dug a hole in the sand at the low tide mark and buried him in it up to his neck. Then they let him drown when the tide came in again. They even stuck a rifle in the ground next to his body so I could find him.'

Serailler wiped Garros's spit off his own cheeks. 'That happens sometimes around here.'

'My report will have your names in it, gentlemen!' Garros was red in the face. 'My report will inform our superiors about your lack of cooperation!'

'But I put Private Halifax at your disposal. He's one of my best men.'

'He . . . did . . . *NOT* . . . cooperate!' Garros bellowed across the café.

'Floppy.' Ivan wobbled the wing flaps on Halifax's Spad. 'Floppy, floppy, floppy. These need fixing, Halifax.' He lifted his metal toolbox and shoved it into Halifax's arms. 'Guess what you're doing today instead of going out on patrol.'

'If we had a spare plane, I wouldn't have to stay on the ground.'

Ivan crumpled his face and let his mouth hang open. 'That's very profound, Charles. Maybe in your profoundness you can tell the main garrison in Casablanca something that will send us another.' He stuck his thumb against his chest. 'I in my baseness and stupidity seem to have a lack of communication with the main garrison. My attempts at subtlety have been ignored. Even such directness as "Give me a new plane, you fuckers" has met with no success. Now, am I to understand from your concern that you have a better idea?'

Halifax tucked the toolbox under one arm and scratched the back of his neck. 'I was only saying.'

Ivan tightened the strut wires and Halifax sat in a canvas chair with the toolbox on his knees. Ivan called for wrenches and screwdrivers and Halifax handed them over. Labouchere and Rollet took off on patrol. Dust blew up from their wheels and drifted over the town.

When the wires had been tightened, Ivan and Halifax went down to the beach and swam. They ran into the waves until the water tripped them and sent them cartwheeling into the surf. For hours they stayed in the sea. Their fingertips shrivelled and salt crusted in their hair. Then the sound of Spad engines reached them over the hiss and rumble of waves. They left the water and walked back to the airfield wearing only their trousers. The rest of their clothes and their shoes they hung around their necks.

Rollet and Labouchere had landed and parked their planes outside the hangar. Labouchere stood by his Spad. He clicked his tongue and walked in circles around the machine. Bullets had torn through the tail canvas and a line of puncture marks ran the length of his fuselage. Part of the exhaust pipe had been ripped open.

Powder from the Spad's machine gun stuck to Labouchere's face. He pulled his goggles down around his neck and lowered himself stiffly to the ground. He traced lines in the dirt with his fingertips. Socks showed through holes in the soles of his boots.

Ivan walked over to Labouchere. 'You all right?'

Labouchere nodded.

Ivan nodded back, then muttered at the damage. He wandered into the hangar and rummaged in his supply closet. Pots and metal boxes clanked to the ground.

Rollet chewed at his thumbnail. 'Those were brand-new planes they were flying. Labouchere almost didn't come back.'

'Planes? Another aircraft did this to you?' Halifax put on his glasses, hooking the pieces of cloth over his ears. 'Who were they? Did they have markings?'

Rollet shook his head. 'No markings, but the wings were painted with little lozenges of brown and light brown.' He made a diamond with his hands. 'The last time I saw camouflage like that was on German planes in France in 1918. I bet they're Germans. Probably mercenaries working for Abdel Krim. It's always the Germans who have to go and mess things up. Look at poor old Labouchere.' Rollet aimed a fat pink finger. 'The poor bastard got jumped by two of them at once.'

Ivan appeared from the hangar and sat down next to Labouchere. He began cutting squares from a roll of green cloth that he had pulled from his closet. On the ground next to him, he set a pot of glue.

'Where did this happen?' Halifax squinted up at the sky, in case the other planes had followed.

'Half an hour out towards Wadi Harazem. In the Bled.'

'What kind of planes were they?' Halifax kept looking up at the blue-roofed oven of African sky.

In all their years flying in Morocco, none of them had seen any planes belonging to anyone except the French. Until then, they had felt safe in the air, making reconnaissance runs across the Bled, taking photographs and delivering messages to outposts that had no other lines of communication.

Rollet pulled at his lower lip. 'I don't know what kind they were. I didn't see enough of them. They both went for Labouchere. I was trying to get out of the way.' He picked at his fingernails. 'I was manoeuvring into position. Then they went away.'

Labouchere sighed, rubbed his hands together and said something quietly to Ivan.

'What do you mean, it was other planes?' Ivan stood up. The green squares of canvas flickered off his lap. He turned and yelled at Halifax. 'Labouchere says there were other planes!'

Halifax nodded.

'Other *planes*!' Ivan said again. '*Aircraft*!' He began to stick the green canvas patches over bullet holes in the fuselage. He spread glue around the holes, then smoothed out the patches with his thumb.

Rollet stayed quiet.

Halifax took the revolver from his belt and emptied the bullets into his pocket, which he did at the end of every day. The bullets looked polished from years of being carried and never used. Heat from the day still pressed against his face. Salt dried white in his eyebrows. He started drifting into daydreams. It was so long since he'd even seen another plane, besides the Spads of Rollet and Labouchere, that he had trouble imagining what it would be like to feel hunted in the air again.

Rollet tapped him on the arm.

Halifax looked up, daydreams clattering apart. 'What?'

'They came out of nowhere, Charlie.' Rollet hugged his own ribs. 'We never knew what hit us.'


'This is your last chance,' Ivan whispered in the dark. 'You could still do it. You could still bring Serailler down if you told that inspector what's going on.'

The two of them walked along the beach. The moon was out. It burned in a trail on the water.

'It's no good, Ivan. I think Garros is as crooked as Serailler. He could be bought. He could be threatened. He could disappear.'

A wave broke on the beach and rushed over their feet.

'Well, then.' Ivan slapped Halifax on the back as if congratulating him. 'You'll be here for the rest of your life.' The wave sucked back in white foam and a boil of running water. Halifax felt the sand swirl around his ankles. 'I'm here as long as Serailler keeps me here.'

'It's not Serailler!' A harder slap against Halifax's back.

'What do you mean?'

Ivan stepped in front of him. 'You're keeping yourself here. *You!* You say it's Serailler and you say there's no way out of Morocco but it's not true. Why the hell can't you go home, Charlie?'

Halifax sat down on the wet sand. The next wave rumbled up and soaked his legs. 'I've been away too long.'

'It doesn't matter how long you've been away. It matters how much you want to go back.' Ivan crouched next to him, balanced on the balls of his feet.

'Look, if there's a plan, if there's a way out, then why haven't we thought of it?'

Ivan was quiet for a while. 'I don't know. What do you want me to say — because we're stupid? Maybe there wasn't a way before, but things have changed now. Serailler's cracking up with this investigator here. Abdel Krim is hammering us back into the sea. They have aircraft now. Get that into your head! It's only a matter of time, Charlie. Either we get out of here or the whole desert blows up in our faces.'

The next morning, the broad belly of the Levasseur set down in Mogador harbour.

Garros had been waiting for several hours. He looked as angry as he had been in the market at Oujdim. Serailler and Halifax stood at the dockside listening to Garros yell at the pilot. Suddenly his voice was cut off as the engine coughed and started.

When the plane had taken off, shedding a stream of water from its wings as it cleared the harbour, Serailler and Halifax wandered back to the Dimitri. Serailler jangled the change in his pockets. 'Those planes yesterday, the ones that shot up Labouchere . . .'

'Rollet said he thought they were Germans.'

Serailler coughed into his fist. 'They are.'

'How do you know?'

'They're from a Foreign Legion outpost in the north. One of them's an old-timer. Been in it from the start. I heard he was even in one of the Flying Circus squadrons in the Lille sector during the war. Maybe he shot you full of holes a few times. The other one's younger. They joined the Legion together. Rumor is that they're related. Father and son maybe. Anyway, both of them deserted. Went out on patrol and never came back. Up until today, we thought they'd crashed.' Serailler stopped walking. He flattened his lips, which made him look as if he were in pain. 'They were new planes, Charlie. They hadn't been used more than a couple of times. The best equipment made. And here we are, flying these plywood crates with wings on them. This is bad for us.' He watched as the last speck of Garros's plane disappeared up the coast. 'This and everything else. I should have had Garros killed.' Serailler started walking again, dragging his heels along the ground. 'I'd have been doing you a favour.'

'Serailler.'

'What?'

'Now that this is over, will you sign my discharge papers? We had an agreement. Sign the papers now.'

Serailler stood back. 'Now?'

Halifax nodded, not taking his eyes off Serailler.

'So that you can go home to your coal mine town and piss your life away? You don't get it, do you? I need you here. More than ever.' Serailler slipped into the shadows of the Dimitri.

Halifax watched him go, slowly breathing the scorched air. His leg muscles started to shake. He tried to stay calm in the heat.

# 5

HE WALKED DOWN Main Street in his sleep.

After years of remembering Brackenridge, Pennsylvania, where he had lived before he went to France, he had muddled the roads and houses and the faces of friends he grew up with. They stayed jumbled and out of reach. So he built a new town in his head and claimed new friends, patching them together with the fragments he recalled from before. He gave himself a job, better than the one he left behind in the mines. In this new town he had respect and credit in the shops. He kept everything clean and sunny, and it was a good place for children to grow.

In the town where he lived in his sleep, he was a person who had never been far from home. He had not been to the Great War and there had never been a Great War. He kept its people safe from the ugliness of Ypres and Verdun. The shadows of aircraft didn't sweep across their gardens and rooftops and they didn't lie awake at night, hearing the hammer of distant artillery.

But outside his dreams, he remembered standing in the mine shaft elevator, the weight of the Davy lamp in one hand, lunch box in the other. The elevator was crowded with people. When they moved, their steel helmets scraped against each other. Halifax looked up and saw sky chiselled away and fading as the elevator went down. He opened his eyes wide, getting used to the dark. The pit lights slid by. He was thinking that today they'd blast out another corridor, dig deeper into a coal seam discovered the week before. He thought of the huge corkscrew they used to drill blasting holes and the rough feel of the paper that covered the dynamite sticks. Six-hour shift and then home. Day off tomorrow. Going hunting for quail with his brothers, Tom and Henry, in the stubble fields outside Brackenridge.

Suddenly he was leaning against the side of the elevator cage. He heard shouting and felt a shudder of wind moving up the shaft. Explosion. It was all around him and rattling his bones and the elevator cage crashed against the stone wall of the mine shaft. He dropped his Davy lamp. People on their hands and knees. Gunfire? No, not gunfire. Something smashed against the elevator, then something else and then he cried out as a rock hit the underside of the steel floor, hurting his foot. Rocks bouncing off the metal and people screaming, the whole floor bulging from the impact of stones thrown up by the blast. The elevator cage swung back against the other wall and Davy lamps leaking fuel rattled toward him. His ears popped. Dirt and fragments of coal that had flown up over the elevator now fell down onto the backs and heads of the miners. The air was bitter with smoke rising from below. The shaft lights flickered and went out. Is the elevator still moving? No. The lights blinked again and then it was dark. He gripped the bars of the elevator cage and told himself it would be over soon so not to panic, not to scream like the others. When smoke made the air too hard to breathe, he pulled his shirt up to his face and tried to filter out the dust. Crash against the far wall. Look at the floor, will you look at the floor, it looks like it's got blisters. 'I can't breathe' they were shouting. Do what I do, thought Halifax. Do what I do and stop screaming. A rumble of more explosions deep in the mine but no pelting rocks this time. Elevator cable creaking overhead in the darkness. The smell of Davy lamp fuel. Smoke scrabbling up the sides of the shaft. They'll know about the explosion. The whole town will know by now and they'll be running up into the hills half dressed and barefoot and chattering. He saw it happen when he was about ten and a shaft caved in. The whole town heard it go. He was in school and Mr Lloyd looked up from his books at the head of the class and said, 'Oh, my God.' Everybody ran up to the mine. The streets were jammed and people screamed all the damn time and the old men tried to take charge and got left behind because they couldn't run fast enough. They stayed at the bottom of the hill, shouting orders from their fouled-up lungs.

The rumbling died down and Halifax stopped remembering the way it was when he was ten. If the elevator cables are snapped at the bottom of the mine, then we'll have to climb out, he was thinking. If the cables aren't snapped, they can get us out of here. They can't be broken, he thought. If they were broken we would have dropped. He waited, breathing as softly as he could through his flannel shirt. A stone bounced off the elevator roof. They must be at the top of the shaft now, the barefoot people and the kids let out from school.

The elevator jolted and the miners screamed again. It rose up a few feet and stopped, swaying. Started again and kept climbing. Through the grey filter of smoke, Halifax could see sky. Nobody spoke in the elevator. They all looked up at the sky, which unravelled at the top of the shaft. When they came to the top, Halifax waited for the whir of the elevator motor to die down and the locks to clank shut before he let go of the bars very slowly and shuffled with the others over dropped lunch boxes and puddles of Davy lamp fuel into the crowd. He walked down a line that the crowd had made for the miners, watching men step into the mass of people when they had found the ones they belonged to. He reached the end of the line and kept going down the hill, seeing the last old men struggling up and still yelling orders. He walked to the house where he knew both his brothers would be if they weren't down the mine and he found the place empty. He sat at the kitchen table, trying to remember what shafts they were working that day. People ran past in the street. He looked down at his shirt and saw the part he had placed against his mouth and it was black with dust. 'Maybe some of my toes are broken,' he said out loud, surprised at his own voice in the kitchen. He tapped his right foot in its heavy boot against the floor and felt the sharp pain that he thought must be some fractured bones. He wondered if the company would charge him for the lamp he lost. I'm not thinking straight, he told himself. What shafts are Tom and Henry working today? Which shafts were in the explosion? Think. 'Can't think,' he said to the table. Then he put his face on the bare wood and fell asleep.

For weeks after the blast, Halifax woke up gasping for air in the middle of the night. He knew right away what he'd been dreaming of. He was down at the bottom of Brackenridge mine.

He dreamed of walking slowly along black corridors, feet crunching on coal dust, water leaking through his boots. His hands slipped along the walls, trailing from one angled surface to another. 'Tom?' he said to the darkness. Sometimes his dreams gave him a Davy lamp and the beam rocked back and forth across the coal seam, glistening. Other times, he only had his hands to paw the ground in front of him, looking for his brother.

Seventy-three men were in the mine when it exploded. Twenty made it out through emergency tunnels. The other fifty-three disappeared under the roof collapse that followed the explosion. Halifax's brother Tom didn't come out. Henry wasn't in the mine that day. He was in town at a bar, asleep with his face on the counter.

In the days before the search parties gave up, crowds churned the ground around the mine shaft into mud. Women and men knelt praying in the rain. Its pattering made strange musical notes on the corrugated iron roof of the elevator. More crowds gathered around the mine offices, waiting for the daily posting of information about anyone who might have been recovered.

Smoke and dust billowed now and then from the shaft, as if something were breathing down below. The old men retreated into the bars, their orders about how to run the rescue changing into complaints about how it should have been run.

There were no bodies. Children waited outside the emergency tunnels, shining lamps down the empty openings and listening for voices. They shouted into the tunnels, hearing their words come back in fragments off the walls. No bodies. Always in the past there had been bodies, something to bury, at least.

Rescue teams tapped at rocks that blocked the tunnels, then pressed their ears to the wet stone, straining for a signal from the other side that miners there were still alive. Charlie and Henry went down every day with the rescue teams. Holding their lamps out in front of them, they lit up the stooped bodies of the men walking in front, wandering ankle deep in run-off water until they came to the place where rubble blocked the tunnel. They cut through yards and yards of it, trying to find a clear space in which the trapped men could have survived. The rubble was solid. The roofs had come down completely. The search teams brought out lamps and lunch boxes and helmets left by the survivors as they ran. The teams appeared at the ends of emergency tunnels and walked home along coal slag roads with the children who'd been waiting for them.

The whole town was carpeted with coal slag. It sparkled in the alleyways and rustled under foot. It smelled bitter after the rain. Mountains of the stuff piled up around Brackenridge.

At the end of the first week after the explosion, Henry was still saying they could be alive. He sat at the kitchen table, still wearing his mining helmet, and rolled his fists back and forth on the wood. 'Sure, they all brought food with them. If they rationed it out, they could be all right. Couldn't they, Charlie?'

'What about air? And light? If they lit a match, they could cause another explosion.'

Henry unlaced his boots. 'We should be down there looking for Tom. That's where we should be.'

Charlie eased the braces off his shoulders and sat down at the other side of the table. 'We've been looking all day and all day yesterday.'

'I can't sleep.'

'We were looking the day before that, too.'

'We'd know it if Tom was dead. Wouldn't we just know?' Henry's fists rolling on the table, knuckle over knuckle.

'I'm glad Mother and Father aren't here to see this.' Charlie leaned across, took the helmet off Henry's head and set it down on Tom's chair.

'They had cave-ins and explosions when they were alive too, you know. They survived those.'

Charlie sat back and sighed. 'And if they'd been someplace else, they'd have survived a little longer maybe. Just living here turns your lungs black.' He looked at Henry, who had put his hands flat on the table in front of him. 'We'll go down again tomorrow, Henry.'

Henry nodded, staring at his hands.

No bodies. Too dangerous to drill any farther, the mine owner said. Drill farther and you might bring down another section. You can't tell what's balanced on what. You might set off another pocket of gas and the same thing will happen all over again. This will take time, a lot of time.

Other mine shafts reopened after two weeks. The owners said they couldn't afford to keep searching and holding up production. The shaft where the explosion took place was closed down.

In the dreams that sent Charlie Halifax back down in the

Brackenridge mine, he was always groping along the tunnels, looking for Tom and afraid of what he would find.

The death of his brother followed him around like a ghoul. He thought of the other bad things that had happened in his life: no money, no girl, parents gone. He'd been able to chase them away. But his dead brother never let up. Every time his mind grew quiet, Tom came scrabbling up the sheer walls of the mine shaft to the surface. Every time somebody said a thing that Tom might have said, Tom's dead face covered the features of the person who was talking. For a long time after the explosion, it seemed to Charlie Halifax that the memory of his brother would never leave him alone.

Waves pounded at the walls of Mogador. Halifax got up from his bed and walked out onto the balcony. For a long time, he only stood there. Breeze off the water ran goose bumps up and down his back.

He flew in low over the dunes. Labouchere and Rollet trailed behind. They followed the coast down to Cap Sim. Water spread out to the horizon, khaki where it rumbled up the beach. Beyond that, it was the colour of old bronze. The bow of a cargo ship jutted from the breakers. It had been there since the war, snapped in half during a storm. Waves punched through the open midsection and streamed from portholes at the sides. The stern lay farther out to sea, uncovered only when the tide was low. The metal had rusted to brown. Light caught on the windows of the bridge, stabbing at their eyes.

They headed inland, gaining altitude. Halifax followed the ground on his map until it disappeared into the Bled.

More news had reached Mogador that morning: another outpost had been overrun. A Legion patrol found a half-dead man in a truck by the side of the road not far from Telaleh. When he had recovered enough to speak, the man said that the entire garrison at Wadi Harazem had been bombarded with cannons and then charged by hundreds of Arabs on horseback. Orders arrived from Casablanca to fly out and take pictures of Wadi Haifa to see if the half-dead man was telling the truth.

Sometimes Halifax imagined he could reach down from the cockpit of his Spad, grab a handful of earth ten thousand feet below, and let it stream away through his fingers. The land below seemed so minutely fragile. It was same over Belgium in 1918. The ruins of Polygon Wood looked like the bristles of a vast hairbrush sticking up from the mud. Shell craters merged and became lakes; fingerprints pressed into the gray-white Flanders clay. The bombed-out towns below, with names like Zillebeke and Zonnebeke, had no more shape or solidness than the ash from a cigarette. Craters seethed with shadows. The whole country seemed to be boiling.

Sometime in 1923, he had read an article in the French paper *La Presse* about American pilots who came home from the war and found that all they wanted to do was keep flying. They couldn't live without strapping themselves into a cockpit every day and leaving the ground. And when the days were stormy, they stayed in the hangar, heads buried in the engines of their planes. They were happy only when talking to other pilots, and spoke a language outsiders couldn't understand. They frog-hopped across the countryside to stunt shows and fairs, giving rides to children and turning loops while the audience sat racked up on benches, squinting at the sky. To keep spectators from losing interest, an announcer bellowed through a bull-horn that the pilot was almost guaranteed to die. Men were hired to dress in women's clothes and walk out on the wing of a plane as it flew past the fairground. Pilots trailed banners advertising farm supplies and cattle feed. They flew through the open door of a barn and out the other side.

At the end of the piece, the reporter said these pilots weren't much different from anyone else – they were in it for the money. But Halifax was almost sure that this man had never spoken to the pilots. He had probably seen a couple of air shows and then tried to interview the flyers, but they must have ignored him.

Many of those pilots wished they were back in France. Even with nightmares crashing through their heads every night, they had begun to miss the crackle in their nerves when they dodged the bat-wing German planes. It was true in 1923 because it was true in the war.

Smoke from Wadi Harazem was a smudge on the horizon. Traces of the battle dappled the sand below.

They flew over Legionnaires who had run from the town when Arabs broke through the barricades. Footprints straggled through the dunes. The men lay butchered at the end, their paths crossed by the smooth trails of galloping horses.

The town was still burning. Dead Legionnaires clustered in doorways and on rooftops. Beyond Wadi Harazem, the Arab charge had ploughed up the stony ground. Horses and men were stretched out in front of the ruins. They had fallen in jagged rows when the Legionnaires fired on command. An officer had shrieked over the thunder of the charge to load and fire and reload. As each volley struck out, the Arabs fell. The legs of the horses were stiff in the sun. The dead Arabs in their capes looked like tiny pools of black water.

Wadi Harazem looked abandoned now. The Arabs had stolen the trucks, food and guns, and continued their advance. Their tracks trailed off to the north.

Halifax took pictures. Labouchere and Rollet circled the town.

Halifax had a canister to drop over the headquarters if it still existed. The canister contained three packets of morphine tablets wrapped in brown wax paper, a flare gun, a box of different-coloured flares and an instruction sheet showing what each colour meant to a pilot flying overhead. Leather straps held the canister to the cockpit floor.

Ivan had been stealing the morphine tablets. He spent his nights numb-nerved and stupid from the drug. He took only one at a time, but soon none would be left. Halifax had checked the slow and steady disappearance of pills from the canister. He signalled to Rollet and Labouchere, twisting his hand around and around over his head. They headed home.

Why the hell do the French want this country? Halifax thought. What do they think is out here? Do they still believe the rumours that the streets of Timbuktu are paved with gold?

He wondered if the men in the long, echoing government halls in Paris had forgotten how to run a country that was not at war. Maybe they needed to fall asleep at night knowing that some corner of the French empire was under attack, that in the morning there would be casualty reports to read. Fists smacking polished wood tables and ordering all lost ground to be retaken. Rows of artillery guns rocking back one after the other in the first barrage of a counterattack. The clatter of bayonets being fixed on rifles as Legionnaires move out in extended line.

Maybe the reports never reached them in Paris, of the first

Christians to dye their skin with henna, memorize the Koran and straggle across the Erg Cherch desert to Timbuktu. They were looking for the streets of gold, but the streets of Timbuktu were mud, like everything else in Timbuktu. Perhaps, back in Paris, they couldn't shake the picture of blinding yellow-metalled roads. Weight for weight, gold for salt. They couldn't get it out of their heads.

Halifax understood now why the Spanish allowed guns to slip out to the Canary Islands. They knew the guns would reach the Arabs. They knew the Arabs would use these guns against the French and both armies would wear each other down. Maybe they knew Serailler's name. The French were even building a railway across the Sahara, and the Arabs sabotaged it when they could spare the dynamite. The railway had become a symbol for the stubbornness of the two sides. Build it and blow it up. Build it and blow it up again. To Halifax, the whole business seemed suddenly clear: the Spanish were biding their time. When the French and Arab armies were exhausted, the Spanish would move in and take everything. Halifax pulled at his jaw with leather-gloved hands. 'It doesn't make any difference what you know,' he said to the control panel with its shuddering needles and chipped black paint. The wind howled in his open mouth.

Something flickered past in front of him. Then came the even rattle of guns. He caught sight of Labouchere dropping out of formation. A plane with lozenges of sand-coloured camouflage painted on its wings shot by underneath.

His stomach jumped. The shock of an explosion battered his face. He brought the Spad over in a slow arc. A hundred feet above, dirty smoke spread from an engine on fire. As he eased down from the air, he saw the burning plane. It was Labouchere. He corkscrewed, spewing black, and disappeared from view. Halifax craned his neck around, chafing it against the rough collar of his shirt, searching for Rollet.

Something cracked in his engine, then the windscreen exploded. All that remained of it was the copper fittings. One of the strut wires snapped. It whipped up and tore through the canvas.

In the sun's glare, he made out the shape of an aircraft. Its guns fired, clattering and smoking. Tracers fizzed over his head. He pulled back hard on the stick and kicked the rudder, flipping his plane through an Immelmann roll, which put him almost on top of the machine that had been chasing him. Now he could see where the marks of the French Air Service had been crudely painted over. The German turned and saw Halifax's shadow cut across his cockpit.

The German's plane swayed in and out of the fat ring sights of Halifax's gun. Halifax pulled the trigger, losing sight of his target for a moment in a wash of tracer smoke and the noise of the gunbelt feeding into the breech.

Rollet appeared on one side. He banked sharply away from another plane that had come down on him out of the sun. It was the other German, his wings a grid of camouflage.

The plane in front of Halifax rose up on its tail and passed over his head. An Immelmann roll, thought Halifax. This man knows what I know.

The Germans broke off and headed away to the east.

Labouchere had vanished. Rollet and Halifax searched the ground below for as long as they could without running out of fuel, but found no wreckage, no smoke, no signal flares dragging bright arcs through the sky.

All night they sat by the runway at Mogador. They set out oil drums filled with rags and gasoline and burned them, lighting a way for Labouchere in case he had landed and repaired his machine. He might be trying to come home in the dark.

Heat from the day quickly disappeared. They huddled in their coats by the oil drum fire. Several times, Rollet looked up suddenly and ran out onto the runway, thinking he heard the sound of an aircraft engine. Then he walked back to his deck chair.

Halifax smoked until his throat felt raw, wondering why the Germans had deserted the Legion. Maybe from far away they heard the rumour of gold and believed they could find it by working for Abdel Krim.

Serailler appeared with a bottle of his garbage cognac and they drank it. When the fire died down, Ivan threw in new strips of rag. Apricot-coloured ashes coughed into the air.

The Spads stayed on the runway. No one had bothered to put them in the hangar for the night. Rollet wanted to refuel and head straight out again, but both his and Halifax's machines were damaged and it was too dark.

Rollet rocked slowly back and forth in his chair. Now and then, he raised his eyebrows and moved his lips without speaking, like an old man gone senile and hearing voices in his head.

'Labouchere?' Halifax opened his eyes.

Serailler and Ivan lay sleeping in their chairs, chins on their chests. Only Rollet was awake. He peered at Halifax, elbows on his knees and fingertips pressed together. 'Dreaming?'

'I just saw Labouchere.'

Rollet leaned over and spat.

'He was right there in front of me.' Halifax pointed to the smoking oil drum. 'Right there.' He looked at Rollet. 'I could have sworn.'

Rollet moved his lips again without talking. Then he tapped his boot against Ivan's chair. 'Get up.' He nudged Ivan's leg. 'Get up!'

Ivan snapped awake.

'Go and fix the Spads. I want to take off at first light.' Rollet's eyes looked dried out from no sleep.

Ivan stood. 'Your radiator was hit in two places. I could work all night and still not have it ready. It may need replacing.'

'How about Charlie's plane?'

Ivan shrugged. 'A few struts gone. No windscreen. One hit in the engine grille, but that's no killer.'

'So fix it.' Rollet ground his thumbs into his temples and yawned.

Ivan shuffled cross to the Spads.

Serailler stayed asleep, calm-faced and pale in the dark.

Halifax took out his tobacco bag. It was empty. 'Shit. I want to go home.'

'Go.' Rollet waved him away. 'I'll call you when I need you.'

'I want to go home to America.'

'You still call it home?' Rollet's eyes were fixed on something in the air in front of him.

Halifax nodded.

'You can't go home, Halifax. You have to stay here and help me find Labouchere.' Halifax opened his mouth to speak, but Rollet cut him off. 'Do you think he's dead?'

Halifax stayed quiet for a moment. 'His engine was burning. He could be.'

'Then why didn't we find him? If he crashed nearby, we'd have seen the wreck.' Rollet slapped the palm of his hand hard against his forehead. 'I can't understand.' Again he struck his forehead. 'I'm thinking and thinking but I can't understand.'

'We'll find him, Rollet.' Halifax didn't know what else to say.

There was a creak as Ivan opened the engine casing on Rollet's Spad. The other two turned to watch. Ivan stood swallowed from the waist up in the Spad.

Rollet picked at his nails, then turned to Halifax. 'Maybe Ivan told you some rumours about me and Labouchere.'

'If he did, I don't remember.' Halifax shrugged. 'Ivan talks too much.'

'Well, the rumours are true.'

Halifax shrugged again. His mouth tasted bad and the skin felt tight on his bones. He wished he could lie down on the cool sheets of his bed and sleep. He knew Labouchere was dead.

Rollet's face was bleached with worry.

Halifax felt the balance of order built up over years in Mogador fall apart like rotted scaffolding inside him.

Serailler stood in his crumpled uniform. He hadn't shaved or washed. He looked down at Rollet and frowned. It was late in the afternoon.

Rollet continued to sit in his chair by the charred oil drum, head turned to the wind, listening for the hammer of an engine. His face was burned by the heat of the day. For a while he had covered his head with a piece of newspaper, but the paper was gone now, and Rollet still sat in the sun.

Serailler took a deep breath. 'I order you to get in the shade.'

Rollet looked up and blinked.

Serailler shook a finger in Rollet's face. 'At least get your stupid self into the hangar!'

Rollet dragged his chair into the half-moon dome of the hangar.

Engine parts lay on the ground. Some of them were punctured, showing the silver of clean metal where bullets had torn through. Halifax stood with Ivan next to his Spad. When Ivan asked for tools from his toolbox, Halifax handed them over. Every few minutes, Ivan would call from somewhere in the coils of pipe, asking for a different tool. Then his right hand would untangle itself from the engine casing and reach out. The swirls on his fingertips were outlined in oil.

Halifax stared at the copper marque of the plane's engine maker. It was attached to the front grille and done in lettering made to look like elaborate handwriting. A bullet had ripped it in half. The name Hispano-Suiza now only said Hispa.

Suddenly Ivan pulled himself out of the engine. His hair stood up in tufts. The forearm of his boiler suit was wet from sweat wiped off his face. 'I'll have to telegraph Agadir for new parts. It's all patches in there anyway. Patches on patches.' He dropped his wrench and it crashed into the toolbox. 'An engine won't work if it's made of patches.'

The Spad was old. In places, the grain of the canvas showed through the paint. The pine-green colour of its upper wings had faded to olive-blue. Cracks like black veins showed on the runner tyres. Halifax ran his hand down the side of the machine. 'The whole plane's worn out.'

'It's been worn out for months. They won't send me a replacement.' Ivan unbuttoned the wooden toggles on his boiler suit and scratched at the dark hair on his chest. 'Did I tell you I was making some curtains?'

'Yes.'

'Oh. Well, I still am.' He smoothed back his filthy hair. 'I've been feeling lightheaded lately. I believe I am almost in love.'

'Don't be in love yet. At least not until you've met her.'

'I can't help it. I'm lightheaded with love.' He grinned and crouched down to close the toolbox. When he stood up a moment later, he no longer looked in love. 'Labouchere is dead, isn't he?'

'Probably.'

They stared at Rollet. He sat by himself in the mouth of the hangar. Sun cut across his legs. The rest of him hid in the shadows. Rollet saw them watching and sat forward. His face appeared from the gloom. 'Do you hear something? Is he there?'

# 6

SERAILLER APPEARED IN the doorway of the Café Dimitri, peering through the smoke until he saw Halifax and Ivan. He was holding a thin yellow piece of telegram paper. He sat down at their table and slid the paper across to them. 'Labouchere went down near Telaleh.'

Halifax snatched up the telegram. 'What was he doing over there? That's almost half an hour's flying time from Wadi Harazem.'

Serailler shook his head. 'He obviously thought he'd stand a better chance ditching the plane at a Legion outpost rather than trying to make it back across the desert.'

'But how did he get that far when I saw his engine burning?'

'Maybe it wasn't him.'

'It *was* him. I saw.'

'Well, maybe the fire went out. How the hell do I know?'

Ivan took the telegram. 'It might not have caught the main fuel supply. It could have been a tracer round that set his exhaust burning. That kind of fire could have gone out.'

'Is he all right?'

'Seems to be. Like it says in the telegram, they have him at a forward post somewhere up the valley. This message was sent yesterday. They were probably under fire from the Arabs and wanted to wait until dark before bringing him in. Maybe he's bust his leg or something.'

'Does Rollet know?'

'He's waiting on the runway. You take your Spad and fly escort.'

Halifax turned to Ivan. 'Will it get off the ground?'

'It should.' Ivan shrugged. 'I fixed it as well as I could.'

Serailler snapped his fingers. 'Hurry up or he'll probably leave without you.'

\*

82

Telaleh wallowed in the shadow of the hills. Rollet brought his plane in first. A stream of dust scattered in the path of his landing. Halifax kept the nose of his Spad up until just before the wheels touched the runway. As soon as he cut the engine, he heard rifle fire in the distance. Rollet was already running for cover.

The face of an old man appeared over the side of Halifax's cockpit. 'They're shooting at us from the rocks, but they won't hit anything.' The man smiled. On his head he wore a white Legion cap with a black visor. The cap was squashed and looked as if the man had been using it for a handkerchief. The stubble on the man's face stuck out like slivers of ivory.

They ran across the open ground, heads down, shoulders hunched. When they reached the cover of the first building, Halifax leaned against the wall and caught his breath. 'Where's Winslow?'

'Winslow? The American?'

Halifax nodded, wincing as he heard a bullet strike metal in one of the planes.

'Oh.' The old man took off his hat and coughed into it. His lungs were ruined. 'The Arabs have him. He was on guard duty two nights ago and in the morning he was gone.'

'Why would they take him?' Halifax remembered Winslow sitting against the wall of Chaudon's headquarters with his hands behind his head. He saw his face very clearly. 'Surely they wouldn't just take him?'

The old man shrugged. 'Maybe they thought he had some information.'

'Do you think he deserted?'

'Where to? He's not much use to the Arabs, not Winslow. The guard post was in a real mess. Wherever he went, it's a sure thing he didn't want to go there.'

'You could try to get him back, couldn't you?'

'No.' The old man picked at something stuck between his teeth. 'We already know he's finished.'

'How?' Halifax thought of Winslow's pale face.

'We caught a woman out in their fields about two days ago. We caught her and we brought her back. When we got her into town we noticed that she was wearing Winslow's dog tag.' He pulled out his own dog tag, on a greasy leather cord around his neck. The tag was an oval disc made of zinc and perforated down the middle. It had the man's name on each side of the perforation. If a soldier got killed, one half of the disc was broken off for graves registration and the other half stayed with the body. 'She'd made it into a fucking earring, so we shot her.'

They walked down the narrow streets. 'Did you know Winslow?' Halifax pulled off his leather flight cap and felt the sweat cool in his hair. He wondered where Rollet had gone.

'I knew Winslow a little bit. All I really know is that he's an American.'

'Did you know any more about him than that?'

'I knew he made booze sometimes and sold it.'

'Why was he in the Legion? Did he ever tell you?'

The old man frowned. 'Why are you asking so many questions?'

They moved past a barricade made from two doors ripped off their hinges and reinforced with piles of earth. Men sat behind the barricades, eating stew with huge spoons from aluminium mess tins. The barricade men stared, and when Halifax had walked past, they laughed.

The old man stopped at a house, knocked on the door and walked in. As soon as Halifax was inside, he shut the door to keep out the heat.

'Halifax?' A tall man approached from the dark carrying an oil lamp.

The old man saluted. 'I brought you the pilot, sir. I brought him to you like you said.'

It was Chaudon. 'What do you think of my new head-quarters? The other one got blown up.' He set his lamp on a table. 'You've come for Labouchere, haven't you? I heard two planes come in. Where's the other man?'

'I don't know, sir. Someone else was bringing him.'

The old man saluted again. 'I brought him straight here, Captain Chaudon.'

For the first time, Chaudon looked at the old man. 'Bring me my dinner, will you?'

The old man beetled into the white light outside.

'Heard about Winslow?' Chaudon fiddled with the lamp, turning up the flame and turning it down again.

'Yes, sir.'

'They'll hurt him, Halifax. I feel sorry for that man. I can't even tell you what they're going to do to him.'

'Yes, sir.'

'I mean it, Halifax. Those pissers know how to make pain. If you ever get yourself captured, you know what to do, don't you?' He kept talking without waiting for Halifax to reply. 'You take that revolver of yours and you shoot yourself in the head. Before they can get to you. Either way, you'll end up with your skull as a paving stone for one of their mosques.'

'Where's Labouchere, sir?'

'Still out in the valley.'

'He went down in the valley?'

'He came from the other side. Probably he was trying to fly through the valley and land here at Telaleh. But he must have got caught in a downdraft. Either that or his engine gave out and he belly-flopped right into one of our forward posts. Anyway, that's where he is. We haven't brought him back yet.'

The old man reappeared with a mess tin. He set it on the table and saluted again. 'Stew, sir.'

'Stew?' Chaudon squinted at the old man. Then he bent down carefully over the tin and opened the lid. Steam puffed out. He jerked his head back from the heat and blew on his palm where it had touched the burning metal. 'You see, Halifax, we weren't expecting you to come out so soon. If you want to, you can go out and fetch him right now.'

'Why didn't you bring him back?' The air felt heavy with dried sweat and stale breath.

Chaudon reached behind his back Then there was the sound of a knife being drawn from a steel scabbard. Chaudon turned a trench knife in his hand until his fingers found the right grip. Then he stabbed the blade into the stew, pulling from it a knot of meat as big as a fist. 'See what they give us? At least if that grotesque bastard of a cook chopped up the things he threw into these stews, we'd think he put some effort into it.'

'Why haven't you brought back Labouchere, sir?'

'What's the hurry?' Chaudon bit into the meat. 'He's stone dead, after all.'

Halifax felt a numbness spread through his face. He met Rollet as he was leaving Chaudon's headquarters.

'I got lost.' Rollet jerked his thumb over his shoulder. 'They took me to the wrong house.'

The old man carried a stretcher. Halifax opened his mouth to speak with Rollet but nothing came out. He waited for Rollet to ask about the stretcher, but Rollet said nothing. He only followed them in silence. After a few minutes' walk, they reached the base of the rocks.

Gunfire clattered in the hills.

The old man took hold of Halifax's arm. 'Follow this path into the valley. It leads to the forward post. Watch for snipers. The last fifty yards of the path leads through an underground cave.' He walked away flatfooted, back towards town. 'Sorry about your friend.'

'What does he mean, sorry?' Rollet waited several minutes before asking.

The path moved in scribbles along the valley floor, protected by outcrops of rock and scrub brush. They stopped to rest and dump their jackets at a small slit trench. It was made for covering a section of the path. Cartridges lay scattered on the ground nearby.

'Labouchere is dead. They told me back in the town.'

Rollet took off his jacket and dropped it in the slit trench. He sat down heavily in the dirt and nodded, as if agreeing with a voice inside his head. 'I told you he was, didn't I? That's because I knew.' Then he bowed his head forward onto his knees.

'I'm sure he didn't suffer. I'm sure it was quick. At least we found him, Rollet. At least we know what happened.' Halifax said anything that came into his head.

'Save your breath.' Rollet stood and began walking up the path. Beyond him, desert merged with sky in ribbons of heat haze.

Their flying boots were no good for walking and already both of them had blisters on their feet.

Halifax kept waiting for Rollet to cry, for a breakdown and tears, but there was nothing.

They came to the mouth of the cave, which led through the side of a hill. Water trickled in the dark. They groped along the damp walls, treading in puddles of cold water. In places the puddles were knee deep. At the edge of the cave Halifax saw movement. One of the rocks seemed to shift. He stopped. The rock shifted again.

Rollet sloshed through the water behind him. 'What's the matter?'

Halifax held up his hand for Rollet to be quiet.

Something rattled in the dark. Metal ground against metal.

Halifax pulled out his revolver and crouched down, wincing as cold water rose up over his groin and his stomach. Then he pulled at Rollet's trouser leg and made him take cover as well.

His breath shuddered as he lowered himself into the deep puddle.

Halifax aimed the gun at the rock that had shifted. 'We've come for the pilot Labouchere.'

The rock didn't move. The cave was very quiet. The only sound was Rollet's shivering. Then the rock talked. 'What did you say?'

'I said we've come for the pilot.' Halifax felt his hand cramped around the butt of the gun. He saw the silhouette of a rifle being lowered.

'I thought you were saying a new password. They never tell us the new passwords out here. One of these days someone's going to get hurt.'

At the end of the cave was the basin of a dried-up well. The walls of earth, studded with rocks, rose up sheer to the surface thirty feet above. Footholds were hacked in the dirt. A large space had been dug into the wall. In the space were two ledges that served as beds. There were boxes of ammunition, several rifles propped together in a pyramid and cans of rations stacked neatly in a corner.

The man with the rifle watched them as they crawled from the cave. His eyes were big like an owl's, and like an owl he blinked very slowly.

Another man squatted in the dugout, forearms resting on his knees. Stuffed in his belt was a knife with a brass knuckle-duster at the handle. 'We thought you were the bloody Arabs.' In his hands he held a leather jacket. 'Two days ago, a pack of them broke into another forward post and killed everyone in it. So far they haven't found us. Claude was all set to fix you when he heard noises in the tunnel.'

Claude set down the rifle. 'I nearly did, too.'

'Make them some tea, Claude.' The squatting man ripped something from the coat and set it in a pile of white fluff beside him.

Halifax peered into the gloom and recognized Labouchere's jacket. The man was tearing out its sheepskin lining.

Rollet noticed too. He grabbed the jacket. 'What the fuck do you think you're doing?'

The man looked up slowly, then narrowed his eyes. 'Don't bother with the tea, Claude.'

'Why not, Albert?' Claude turned from where he crouched over a small stove. 'I already got the fire going.'

'I'm not sure these people are worth a cup of tea.'

'Where's Labouchere?' Rollet barked in the man's face. 'What have you done with him?'

Claude smiled at them from the corner. He didn't seem to notice the anger in Rollet's voice. 'He crashed almost right on top of us. He had his engine off so all we heard of it was a sound like rushing wind and then a bump and then whole clods of dirt start raining down on us. Didn't they, Albert?'

'Where is he? What have you done with him?' The ends of Rollet's fingers twitched.

'You will have to calm down, or Claude will get excited. Then I'll have to spend the next couple of days trying to calm him down again.' Albert winced as he spoke, as if he were not used to talking and found it painful.

'Have you buried him already?' Rollet's shirt stuck to his back.

'We were going to bury him tonight, as soon as it got dark.' Albert reached up to take the jacket from Rollet.

Rollet held it away. 'This doesn't belong to you.'

Albert jabbed his finger toward the light at the top of the well shaft. 'It's no good to him anymore.'

'You just left him up there, didn't you?'

Through all this Halifax stood by, hands in pockets, smelling the dampness of the cave. Now that Labouchere was dead, he only wanted to be gone. He didn't want to see him. He wanted all this to be suddenly far in the past.

'Listen!' Albert got up. He was taller than Rollet. 'He's dead. It's hard enough living down here in a filthy cave, hoping the damn Arabs don't drop in on us any time they feel like it. And I don't want a body stinking up the place. I had to walk all the damn way to Telaleh just to tell them we'd found a pilot. That's more of a favour than I've done anyone since I came to Africa.

Now if you want him, you can go and get him.' Albert spread his hands in front of his chest. 'All right?'

'How many times did we use this already?' Claude held up a tea bag by its string.

Halifax climbed to the top of the well. For a while, he was blind in the light, then he saw the wreck of Labouchere's Spad in front of him. Its wings had folded when it hit the ground. Both propeller blades were missing and only a stump of wood remained attached to the engine. The engine itself had torn away from the fuselage. The grille and casing sat gnarled and empty beside it. Labouchere lay face down beside the broken Spad, still wearing his flight cap and goggles. Beyond the wreck, grass and small trees grew in clusters as the sand gave way to fertile ground. In the distance were cultivated fields.

Rollet climbed up the sides of the well, digging his fingers into the soft earth as he moved.

After looking up at the rocks, then out at the fields, Halifax slithered across the ground towards Labouchere. He rolled the body over and put a hand behind Labouchere's head, raising it off the ground. White dust had painted Labouchere's skin. It was strange to see stubble on his face and his lips dried out and cracked. The pockets of his trousers had been pulled inside out. Claude and Albert must have searched the body before crawling back underground. Halifax removed Labouchere's flight cap and goggles.

Then Labouchere opened his eyes.

Halifax yelled and jumped back onto the smashed wing of the Spad. It collapsed under him and sent up a curtain of dust.

'What the matter?' Rollet had reached the top of the well. 'Are you hit?'

'He's alive! I saw his eyes move.' Halifax felt his heartbeat thudding in the arteries of his neck.

Rollet crawled across. 'Are you sure?'

'I swear, Rollet. He opened his eyes.' New sweat itched in his hair. He tried to stop breathing so hard.

Rollet knelt down and pressed his ear to Labouchere's chest. After a moment of listening, he whispered to Halifax, 'Are you positive?'

'Go get the stretcher.'

'They left him out here to die. They just stole his clothes and left him here to die. You saw what they did!' Rollet gaped at Halifax.

'Get the stretcher!'

Rollet climbed down the well. When he was gone, Halifax spat on his fingertips and rubbed them into Labouchere's eyelids. Labouchere blinked and the muscles twitched in his jaw as he tried to open his mouth.

'We'll have you back in Mogador in two hours, Labouchere. What do you think of that?' Halifax raised Labouchere's head farther off the ground and felt oil clotted in his hair. 'Thought you could hide from us out here in no man's land? You'll have to try harder than that. Can you hear me, Labouchere?'

Then Albert scrabbled out of the well. 'You better do something about your friend.'

'He's alive.' Halifax motioned for Albert to come and help.

'You tell your friend to calm the hell down.'

'He's alive. Get some water! Bring a stretcher!'

Claude appeared over the rim of the well. He crawled on his knees, trying to keep his hands in the air. 'Tell him to stop, Albert.'

Rollet appeared. He was carrying a rifle. 'Move. Take a look!'

'What are you doing, Rollet? Where's the stretcher?' Halifax squinted in the glare.

'Look!' Rollet herded them forward. 'He's alive!'

'I am looking.' Albert pushed away the rifle barrel, which Rollet held to his chest. 'I'm looking and all I see is a dead man. He was dead before and he's not any better now.'

'Tell him to stop, Albert.' Claude hunched his head down to his shoulders, hands raised to the level of his ears.

'You didn't even check, did you?' Rollet prodded Albert in the chest with the rifle barrel. 'You just took his coat and left him here.'

Again Albert pushed away the gun. 'Who the hell do you think you are to come flying in here from your soft jobs on the coast and tell us something different from what we know is true?' Albert raised a fist. 'What's the matter with you?'

Rollet looked at the fist.

Halifax reached out to take the gun from Rollet. He said very quietly, 'Rollet?'

In one fast movement, Rollet swung the rifle butt hard into

Albert's stomach. Albert bowed forward and dropped to his knees. Slowly he stretched his hands to the ground and tried to get up.

Claude lunged at Rollet, grabbed his arm and spun him around.

Rollet pulled the trigger. The rifle jumped in his hands and the gunshot slapped at the air.

Claude tripped back. For a moment he regained his balance but then fell. His back arched and he clawed at the wound in his chest. Suddenly he sat up and looked at Rollet and Halifax. He turned his head to the side and tried to spit.

The rifle blast still echoed in the rocks above.

After a few seconds, still facing to the side, Claude slid over until his forehead was resting on the sand. Blood spread across his chest. He closed his eyes and lay still.

Without speaking and without the expression changing on his face, Rollet chambered another bullet in the rifle. The spent case spun over his shoulder in a flicker of brass. He put his foot on Albert's chest and shoved him back to the ground. He set the gun against the man's throat and fired.

Rollet looked at the gun for a second and dropped it in the dirt. He walked toward the well, then turned back, as if he had only just remembered about Labouchere and Halifax. He wiped his hands on his chest and looked at his palms. Still looking at his palms, he said, 'I'll tell them what I did, Charlie. Just help me get him to the town and I'll turn myself in.'

Halifax looked around, up the side of the mountain and out across the valley to the wheat fields. 'No you won't.' He started dragging Labouchere toward the well shaft.

'Why not?' Now Rollet's arms hung at his sides. Claude and Albert lay dead by the ruined plane.

'We have to make it seem like the Arabs did this, that they showed up after we left.' He gripped Labouchere under his arms as he dragged him. Labouchere's heels left two grooves in the dirt.

'Why are you doing this for me?'

'I don't know, Rollet. If I thought about it, I'd probably do something different.'

They broke everything they could find in the dugout and hid the guns in a crevice of the cave, so no one would find them and it would look as if they had been stolen. They pulled the place apart.

91

Rollet and Halifax stumbled through the tunnel, carrying Labouchere on the stretcher. When they rested on the other side, soaked again in the cold water of the cave, Rollet watched Halifax closely, waiting to see what he'd do.

Rifle fire still coughed in the distance as they brought Labouchere into Telaleh.

They stopped at a house with a Red Cross flag on the door. A doctor lay asleep on a plank. It was propped up on two ammunition crates, which served as an operating table. Over his uniform the doctor wore a white apron, and around his middle he had strapped an officer's belt. He woke when Rollet and Halifax put down the stretcher.

While he examined Labouchere, Halifax stood in the doorway, looking down the street.

'He's dying. Not dead, but dying, I'm afraid. He's that pilot, isn't he?' The doctor spoke to Rollet.

Halifax kept his back to them and only listened. He lit a cigarette and pulled the smoke into his lungs.

'You can't move him. He wouldn't survive the trip back. I'll look after him and see if he recovers.'

Halifax heard a rattle and turned to see the doctor open a black metal box. From a bundle of wax paper, the doctor took a morphine tablet. He broke it in half and pressed one piece under Labouchere's tongue. Very carefully, he placed the other half back in the paper, then licked the white crumbs off his hand. He locked the black box with a key on a string around his neck. 'That's all I can do for now.' The doctor looked young, with curly dark hair and blue eyes.

'I'll stay.' Rollet looked from Halifax to the doctor. 'I'll stay until he gets better.'

'I'm trying to tell you that he won't be getting better.' The doctor held the metal box against his stomach.

'I'll stay.' Rollet blinked.

Halifax took hold of his arm. 'Let's go.'

'Stay,' Rollet said again.

The doctor set down the box. He was watching Rollet closely. 'There's no sense in it. You should go home. I'll let you know as soon as there's a change.'

'How? How will you do that?' Rollet stared at the doctor.

'I'll get the word out somehow. Don't worry.'

'No. I should stay.'

Halifax twisted Rollet around until he was looking him in the face. 'Get in your plane and come home.'

They walked out to the runway.

'I quit.' Rollet dragged his feet along the ground.

'Don't say that.' Halifax rested his hand on Rollet's shoulder and guided him toward the Spads.

'I just fucking quit.'

'Please, Rollet. You don't have to say it like that.'

Halifax flew behind him on the way to Mogador. Now and then, Rollet turned to look back at Halifax. Once he raised his hand and waved.

Halifax didn't wave back. He was thinking too hard. He swayed his Spad lazily from side to side, watching Rollet's leather-capped head sweep slowly in and out of the machine-gun sights.

Far off in the night, Halifax lay awake. 'I quit,' he said to the ceiling. He wasn't remembering Rollet. He was thinking of himself. Always the thunder of waves beyond the town wall, the sound of them rushing and pounding through his head. Now he thought of his brother Henry swaying in front of him, pug-faced and a little drunk. 'What do you mean, you're quitting?' Henry shouted.

Halifax stood at the bar. 'I'm going to be a pilot.'

'A pilot where?' Henry tapped his hand on the bar. His fingernails were scratched white. It came from the gloves he wore when he worked down in the shaft. The gloves had metal cones at the fingertips. After years of wearing the gloves, the tips of Henry's fingers were worn almost smooth.

'In Europe. I'll fly with the Lafayette Escadrille.' Halifax swished the beer through his teeth and swallowed. 'The ones we're always reading about in the papers.'

Henry lifted a mug to his lips and drank, then lowered it carefully down on the bar, as if afraid of making a noise. 'That war's got nothing to do with you. Not a damn thing.'

'I made up my mind, Henry.' He counted his change to see how many more beers he could buy without borrowing money. 'I'm quitting the mine.'

'You're quitting' – fat finger aimed at him in the honeyed light of the bar – 'because you're afraid of going back down there after the accident.'

Halifax stacked his coins on the polished wood, nickels and pennies and dimes. He knew he was drunk. Otherwise, he told himself, I wouldn't be stacking my pennies. 'Is that some great truth you think you've uncovered, Henry? That I'm afraid to go down there again? You're damn right I'm afraid. I realized a couple of days ago that if I didn't get out now, I'd be spending the rest of my life going up and down that elevator, waiting for the walls to cave in on me.'

'So you think you'll stand a better chance shooting Germans out of the sky? You'll die a lot quicker over there.'

'Look.' Halifax rested his forearms on the bar, feeling spilled beer soak his skin. 'We're all going to get called up sooner or later. You know as well as I do that America will declare war in a couple of months. Then we're all going over!' He waved his hand across the heads in the bar. 'If I leave now and learn to fly, I can get a commission when the American squadrons start forming. I'd be an officer, Henry! Then I won't have to come home to this. I can make a new start. They look twice at you if you're an officer. I could even stay on as a pilot if I wanted to.'

Henry sighed and pinched the bridge of his nose. 'But why do you want to go up in the planes?'

'It's the fastest way to get a commission,' Halifax said. But he was thinking of himself far above the fields and rivers, as far up in the sky as he could get. 'It wouldn't be like the mines. I'm tired of living underground.'

Henry raked his thumb across his forehead. 'What about Tom?'

'What do you mean? Staying here won't bring Tom back.' They were calling for more drinks at the end of the bar so Halifax left his brother and walked over. What the hell does he mean about Tom? Halifax thought.

Henry walked into the bathroom. While he was gone, Halifax decided that he didn't want to talk any more, so he bought a pint bottle of sour mash and put it in his pocket. Then he walked out into the street.

He sat on a doorstep and drank the sour mash. It was gone when Henry found him. Halifax had just thrown the bottle across the road and into the trees.

'Why did you walk off?' Henry looked as if he had been running. 'I couldn't find you.'

'What do you mean about Tom?'

'Oh, Jesus.' Henry raised his hands and let them slap down against his sides. 'I don't know what I mean. I mean the mine is what the three of us had. We belong to the mine, Charlie. You can't just pick up and leave.'

'I don't want to belong to the mine.' Dead leaves were blowing down the street. Falling off trees up in the Pocono hills and drifting down on Brackenridge. Bunching up under the hedges all fiery and crisp. Pumpkins meaty globes out in the stubble fields. 'Why don't you come too?'

'So I can drift around in one of those flying coffins and get shot into mashed potato by some German?' Now Henry was shouting. 'I'll stay on the ground. I'll stay *under* it with the people I know and the coal. You don't just quit on me! You don't just quit on me and Tom!' He folded his arms against the cold. 'I'll come back for you when the bar's closed. You think it over. In the meantime, you're not going anywhere.'

Halifax sat there for a while. He didn't know how long. The sour mash was a brass band in his head. It was a hard doorstep and his buttocks felt numb. He knew he was drunk out of his mind. 'I'll go home,' Halifax said to himself. 'I don't need Henry's permission.' He stood up, his butt feeling like two frozen loaves of bread. First he walked a little way down the road, then he turned around and walked back. He chewed at his lip and breathed in deep trying to clear his head, straining to remember the direction back home. His balance started to go, so he took a step backwards to regain his footing. But his footing didn't hold and he found himself going backwards again, as if shoved in the chest by someone he couldn't see.

He was lying face down at the edge of the road. It was soft and crackly in the dead leaves, and after a while he heard Henry coming to fetch him. 'Did they hurt me, Henry?' he shouted as his brother picked him up, thinking he must have been in a fight and had somehow forgotten the details. 'Did they hurt me pretty bad?'

'You're all right.' Henry gripped him by the shoulders. 'How you feeling now?'

'They'll make me an officer, Henry.' Halifax nodded at the dead leaves blowing down the road.

'Not this officer shit again.'

'If I can come back a captain, Henry . . . If I can fly one of those planes . . .'

'You can't even walk. You can't walk and you can't think straight. Wait for the morning, Charlie. Then see if you still want to go.'

# 7

HALIFAX OPENED THE shutters. A bolt of magnesium sunlight cut across his face. A voice called from the mosque tower. 'Allah! Allah! Come to prayer! There is no God but Allah. Come to prayer!'

'Hey!' someone yelled to him from down in the street. 'It's me! Here!' It was Ivan. 'I got something to show you.' Ivan bustled him downstairs and through the streets until they reached Ivan's house.

Halifax opened the front door and peered into Ivan's dingy front room. Sleep still crumbled from his eyes. His mouth was pasty.

Ivan gave him a shove. 'Go ahead. What do you think?'

The place looked tidy now. Clothes had been taken off the chairs and hung on wooden hangers in a closet.

'Very nice.' Halifax sniffed at the air.

'The curtains. What about the curtains!' Ivan moved past, mumbling in Russian. Light sifted through the fine blue cloth.

Slow spirals of dust twisted in the room. Ivan bunched the curtains in his fist and let them go again. 'What do you think?'

'Maybe you should . . .' Halifax cupped his hands and moved them towards each other. 'You could gather them in the middle. Pin them back. You know how people do.'

Ivan's mouth opened a little. 'No. No, I don't.'

'You know.' Halifax took hold of a curtain and held it against the window frame. 'It looks smart this way.'

'Well then, they might as well not be there at all.' Ivan slumped down in his chair.

Halifax played with the curtains for another minute, then sat on the bed. 'Ivan?'

'What?' Ivan stared through the open front door. A sound of scrubbing came from the alley. An old woman knelt in the street, washing her front doorstep. Her washcloth slapped against the stone.

'We have to get out of here, Ivan.'

Ivan stretched out his legs and tapped his toes together. 'I've been saying that for years.'

'I know. And you're right.'

'So why are you saying it now?'

'I don't want to rot here forever. I'm beginning to realize that Serailler's never going to set me loose. I just can't wait another fifteen years.'

Ivan looked up at the dirty ceiling, then squinted back at Halifax. 'What made you change your mind, Charlie?'

'I've been thinking about how I was before I came to Africa.'

'Justine will be here any day.' Ivan shaped his hand into a claw, and it looked for a minute as if he were going to tear down the curtains. 'Handsome and wealthy, I told her. Educated, I told her. I sent her all my fucking money. I love her and I've never set eyes on her.' He stopped himself from ripping the curtains down. The claw disappeared from his hand. 'Tell me you have a plan, Charlie. Tell me it's all figured out.'

'I can't do that yet.'

Ivan picked up a broom and started to sweep the floor. The brittle straw scraped across the tiles. 'So how were you before you came to Africa?'

'I was going to come back an officer. Then I'd leave the mines and find a better job for myself. I was going to prove I could do it.'

A message came from Telaleh: Labouchere had died without regaining consciousness.

His dog tag, the small disc made of zinc, arrived with the message; one half had been snapped off and used as a grave marker.

'We should bury him here in Mogador.' Rollet paced back and forth in Serailler's office. 'I'll go out and bring him back.'

'No you won't.' Serailler looked down at his desk.

'I have to.'

'He's already buried, Rollet. He's six foot deep by now.' Serailler spun Labouchere's dog tag on the desk. 'For Christ's sake, get that into your head.'

Rollet stopped pacing. He picked up the dog tag and stared at it. The imprint of Labouchere's name was lined with the salt of old sweat.

Rollet and Halifax continued to fly reconnaissance across the Bled. The front shifted daily. Short, vicious campaigns exploded in the desert. The dead were robbed and covered up with sand. No news of them spread beyond the battlefield.

Lines of supply were cut for weeks at a time. From the air, it became hard to distinguish Arabs from Legionnaires. The Legionnaires began to live like Arabs. In places, it looked as if the two sides had stopped fighting. They stayed together in the wreckage of towns, waiting for the orders that would send them back to war.

Halifax had no idea who saw the pictures he'd been taking, who deciphered them and delivered them in neat folders to the conference tables at Casablanca or Tangiers. Maybe some of them even reached Paris.

Over the next weeks, the two German deserters shot down three French planes from a garrison near El Jadida. Rumours spread through the town that Abdel Krim was buying aircraft fuel and parts from the Italians in Abyssinia.

French authorities posted a reward of ten thousand francs for the death or return of the two airmen.

It must be hard for them now, Halifax thought. If they were wounded and became useless to Abdel Krim, he'd probably hand them over. Or if one of the Arabs thought he could get away with killing them and then deserting to the French to collect his reward, he'd probably do it.

Rollet didn't talk. He stayed alone in his house.

When Ivan and Halifax stopped by to ask him out for a drink, he didn't answer the door. So they walked in anyway and found Rollet in a chair by the window, eyes closed but awake, his face gone grey from no sleep and no food.

Halifax rolled bits of bread in his fingers and threw them off the balcony. Bats cut fast arcs out of the sky and ate the little pellets. They were everywhere at twilight over Mogador.

Footsteps on the stairs. The door opened and someone walked into his room.

'Out here.' Halifax found his glasses and put them on.

It was Rollet. He walked onto the balcony and stood for a minute in silence, as if he had come to hear a message.

'I'm feeding the bats.' Halifax held up the lump of stale bread.

'Did you tell anybody about what happened at Telaleh?'

'No.'

'Not even Ivan?'

'Especially not Ivan.'

'Have you heard any reports from Serailler?' Rollet didn't look at Halifax when he spoke.

'No. I'd tell you if I did. Serailler would tell you himself.'

'I wouldn't blame you if you turned me in, Charlie.'

'I won't, though.'

'I can't forgive myself for what I did.'

'Oh, shut the fuck up.'

'I just came to say I would understand if you changed your mind.'

'If you want to get yourself killed, go ahead, but don't ask me to do it for you.' Halifax threw his lumps of bread off the balcony and watched it fall to the street.

Engines. Halifax put down his newspaper and looked at his watch. It was two in the afternoon. He opened the shutters of his room and listened, wondering if he had only dreamed the noise, since no one was due out on patrol until the next morning.

A woman stood on the roof opposite. From a wicker basket, she took white sheets and hung them on a cord to dry. The sheets were wet and moulded against her in the breeze. She paused, then looked towards the airfield. She had heard the engines, too.

The noise sounded closer now. It came and went in gusts that blew from the desert. Halifax picked up his flying jacket and goggles. He figured Serailler had changed the times on him again. He breathed in the mustiness of his jacket's blanket lining. It was a comfortable smell.

An explosion batted his ears. Then the roar of a plane overhead sent him down on his knees. Through the open door he saw a machine bank left and disappear back over the town. It was one of the Germans. The sandy lozenges of colour showed on its wings.

Another explosion rumbled through the town. Halifax grabbed his revolver and ran out onto the balcony just as a second plane cut low across the hotel roof and banked for another run over Mogador.

100

Screaming and raised dust came from the marketplace.

He ran down the steps and out into the street. Black smoke showed in the sky and he realized then what they had come for.

The streets were filled with panicked people. Arab women hid in doorways, staring up through heavy veils. Dropped shopping baskets and overturned vegetable carts lay scattered on the road. A dog picked up a loaf of bread and ran away with it.

From behind Halifax came the howl of a diving plane, then the hammer of guns. He jumped through the open door of a shop and landed on his face. The street outside thrashed with dust as machine-gun fire hacked into the dirt. He heard the smack-smack-smack of bullets striking a corrugated iron roof farther up the street.

A man with impossibly thin legs appeared out of the dark interior of the shop, whose walls were covered with bicycle wheels and parts. He prodded Halifax with his foot to see if he was still alive. Halifax stood and the man jumped back.

Dust was still settling as Halifax ran up the street. Black smoke dirtied the sky above the runway. From the other end of town came the snap of rifle fire.

A fast series of detonations drowned out the rifles. Then he heard screaming. He didn't stop. The Germans had dropped more bombs on the marketplace. His hips were aching, bone grinding against bone. He hadn't been able to run properly since the crash. The pain was making him sweat.

A Spad's engine coughed as it started. Halifax kept his hand clamped against his hip. 'Wait for me, Rollet!' His glasses had fogged up. Then he watched his own plane clear the runway, brushing through the smoke. Rollet turned sharply to fly over the town. The duck-egg blue of the Spad's belly rushed past, its black landing gear hanging down. Rollet must have jumped into the first plane he could find, Halifax thought.

The aircraft hangar spat flames and smoke into the air. A bomb had dropped through the roof and blown it open, ripping holes along the side with shrapnel.

Clods of earth rattled down around Halifax as he ran towards the other plane, which stood in take-off position on the runway. 'Ivan!' He looked from side to side as he ran, teeth jammed against each other from the hurt in his legs. 'Ivaaaan!'

Climbing into Rollet's Spad, he saw the two Germans from the corner of his eye. They were diving down on the runway. He watched the box frames of their engines and the webs of wings and struts. They began firing and Halifax ducked, knowing as he did that there was no point.

The drumming of their engines grew loud and then deafening. Strange claps shuddered in the air as bullets dug into the ground. The shadows of the planes darted past and Halifax raised his head to see them break off in separate directions. Then Rollet dropped out of the sun. He waited until he was almost on top of the Germans before opening fire. His dive was so steep and fast that he didn't stay in firing position for more than a second. His wheels almost touched the runway as he levelled out and began to gain altitude.

A gunshot came from near the hangar. Halifax ducked again, banging his face on his knee. When he looked up, hand over his bleeding nose and his glasses bent, he saw Ivan shooting at the Germans with a flare pistol. Ivan loaded the fat gun and shot off another flare, which hissed and burst nowhere near the Germans, sending down a flutter of green sparks.

'Ivan, help me start the Spad.' Halifax waved to him.

Another flare spat and popped over the runway.

'Help me start the damn Spad! Spin the prop!' Halifax pumped pressure into the fuel tank and tested the flaps.

The Germans circled Rollet over the town. Rollet twisted to stay clear of their guns.

'For Christ's sake, Ivan!' he grabbed the side on the Vickers gun and cocked it, hearing a bullet chamber and the belt rattle in its canister.

'Forget it!'

Halifax swung around in his seat. 'Spin the prop, you son of a bitch!'

Ivan stood barefoot in front of him, wearing his boiler suit. Smoke had powdered his face. Blood trickled down from a cut on his forehead.

'All right, I'll do it myself.' Halifax set the choke and jumped down, knowing that if he spun the prop and the engine started, the machine would move forward at once. He'd have to jump in and clear the ground before the runway gave out.

But now that he looked, there was no prop. There wasn't even an engine.

The German planes headed away from the town with Rollet following them. They disappeared over the dunes. Halifax watched, expecting Rollet to turn back, but he kept after them. Soon even the sound of them had gone.

'You shouldn't have let him go up.' He stamped past Ivan towards the rubble of the hangar. He reached the first long shards of metal from the roof, then saw the lid from a jar, a paintbrush Ivan used for spreading glue on the wings that had been hit by bullets, a barrel used for gasoline, puffed out like a balloon from the force of fuel igniting. He found one of the deck chairs and picked it up. The canvas was gone from the back. He pulled the chair onto its legs and sat down. Smoke from the hangar pinched his eyes.

Ivan stood on the runway and scratched his head with the barrel of the flare gun.

'Why did you let him go up alone?' Halifax's throat felt caked with dirt.

'He started the plane by himself. He did what you were going to do before you found out the engine wasn't there. I took both Spads out of the hangar so I could work on them. When I heard the planes I walked onto the runway and by the time they began their dive, I was running like a rabbit. The shock of the bombs knocked me over. I was out for a little bit. When I came to, Rollet was in the air. My damn boots are in there somewhere.' He pointed at the hangar. 'There wasn't much fuel in that plane. They may try to force him down someplace without damaging the Spad. I could see from here that their machines have taken a beating. They'll need new ones pretty soon.'

'Maybe.' Halifax pressed his hand against the pain in his hip. 'There's no point trying to find Rollet now.'

'None.'

'So we'll wait.' Ivan sat down on a bloated fuel barrel. 'We'll wait right here.'

Two people died in the bombing. Black flags flew from the mosque tower. Arabs crowded into the courtyard of the commissariat, wanting to know if they should evacuate the town. They stood on the ramparts of the town wall, watching for the dust cloud of Abdel Krim's army approaching. A line of men with knives formed outside the blacksmith's. They kept the man busy for hours sharpening blades.

Serailler stayed in his office and drank cognac. He had sent a wire to Casablanca, asking for a regiment of troops in case of another attack. He asked for machine guns and two new planes and a truckload of barbed wire.

When Ivan and Halifax came to his office to ask if news had come in about Rollet, they found Serailler in the dark. He babbled about a thundering tangle of horses and men and guns that would break from the dunes and swallow the town. 'With *my* guns! The guns *I* sold them!'

Casablanca answered his request. It said that Legion outposts continued to hold ground between Mogador and the army of Abdel Krim, so the town did not need reinforcements. The telegram ended with the word 'ridiculous.'

Several times a day, Halifax wandered over to the commissariat to see whether some word had come in about Rollet. Nothing. Search groups flew out of El Jadida to the north and Agadir to the south. There wasn't even a trace.

Ivan and Halifax sifted through the remains of the hangar, pulling out anything of use. They salvaged the engine of Rollet's Spad, which had been outside the hangar at the time of the blast and was not damaged. They fitted it to his plane.

After three days of quiet, the crowds went away from the commissariat courtyard. No new rumours spread. No dust clouds approached. No aircraft flew overhead.

The next morning, Serailler's face appeared in a window on the top floor of the commissariat, then a window lower down. Finally he stepped carefully into the courtyard. His chin was prickly with stubble and a blueness showed under his eyes. Slowly he buttoned his jacket, smoothed his hair into place and walked with exaggerated steadiness to the barbershop. The Arab barber covered Serailler's face with a steaming cloth and shaved him with a cut throat razor.

Serailler looked around and saw things were back to normal. He remembered that he was in charge. The coldness returned to his face. He walked across to the Café Dimitri and ordered bread rolls with jam for his breakfast.

Ivan grew a moustache. It was slow and painful to watch. He went cross-eyed trying to get a look at the thing when there was no mirror around.

On evenings when the supply truck arrived, he showed up at the marketplace, waiting for Justine Dubois.

The three of them tried to estimate when she would arrive. They calculated her travel to Casablanca and then the truck journey down the coast. As the time came closer to their guess, Ivan began polishing his shoes. They were old toe-cap shoes and the leather was dry and dusty when he took them from his suitcase. With a spoon, he scooped the black paste of polish from a tin and held it over a candle until the polish caught fire. It burned with a blue flame like salt. He poured the molten polish over his toe caps and left it on overnight. In the morning, he spat on the shoes and rubbed them with a cloth until he could see his face in the reflection.

Ivan stood next to the bus as the passengers climbed out onto the cobblestone square, picked their bags off the roof and shuffled away through the streets. Ivan wore new clothes that he had ironed himself. The crease on one trouser leg curved around until it reached his ankle. This was the fifth day of waiting.

Serailler and Halifax watched him from their table at the Dimitri. When Ivan saw that she wasn't on the bus, he walked back and sat at the table.

Serailler cleared his throat. 'I had a wife.'

Ivan nodded, looking down at the table top.

Serailler kept talking. 'I was transferred from Paris to a place near the Spanish border. A town called Hendaye. This was the beginning of my long slide down to Morocco. I got up to see my wife in Paris about once a month. The rest of the time, I did what everybody else at the garrison did. I went across the border on weekends and spent the time with Spanish whores. I remember I was coming out of a hotel room. It was morning and I was holding on to the Spanish girl's hand. We were going down to the restaurant across the road for some breakfast.' Serailler laughed, and the laugh turned into a cough. 'I walked out of the room and my wife was sitting in a chair at the end of the hall. She was wearing her best clothes and she looked beautiful. She never looked more beautiful as when I saw her that morning.'

Ivan faced the table, but he watched Serailler from under the dark blocks of his eyebrows.

Halifax turned his coffee cup very slowly in its saucer. He was thinking of the whores he'd seen in Paris during the war. They sat behind windows and smoked or knitted. When men who looked like customers walked past, the whores kicked at the glass with their slippered feet and shouted to come in, their voices muffled behind the windows and their mouths gory with lipstick.

Serailler sat back and pulled at his chin. 'I fell down right where I was. My legs just gave way. They thought I was having a heart attack. I *hoped* I was having one. One of the hotel porters carried me back to the room and lay me down on the bed. The two women stood outside the door and talked a little to each other. They were really quite pleasant. "It happens sometimes, sir," the porter was saying to me, "but it's no reason to drop down dead." From the bed I saw my wife and the Spanish girl out of the corner of my eye. I still couldn't move. The porter covered me with a blanket and asked me in a whisper if he'd like me to get rid of the women. I opened my mouth and said, "Muh."' Serailler laughed and slapped Ivan on the arm. 'What do you think of that? Muh! Worst day of my life and all I can say is "Muh."'

Ivan sat still for a moment, then raised his head. 'Is that the end of it?'

Serailler stopped grinning. 'No. It went on for a long time after that. But that's the end of the story.'

Ivan opened his mouth as if to say 'Oh.'

Serailler rolled his eyes at Halifax and slapped Ivan on the shoulder, a harder slap this time. 'What do you think you're doing, anyway? What if you get posted out into the desert? What's she going to do then?'

'She doesn't have to stay.' Ivan drummed on the table with his fingertips. 'I don't expect she will. She may not even arrive.'

'You look pretty suave in your new clothes.' Serailler picked at the cloth.

'You look so damn suave, you don't even know what to do with yourself.' Halifax tugged at Ivan's lapels.

Ivan grinned. 'When a man is as suave as I am, you don't ask what he does with himself.'

'There is one thing, Ivan.' Serailler folded his hands and set them on the table. 'One thing I am telling you as a direct order.'

'What?'

'Get rid of the moustache. It looks like a piece of old bellybutton fluff.'

Ivan pressed his fingers against the moustache, as if maybe it was a fake and he had stuck it on backwards that day.

Halifax pressed his lips together and nodded. 'Do it, Ivan.'

'But I had a moustache when I was in the Russian cavalry. No one said a word about it.'

'You were a major then. Nobody tells a major to saw off his moustache.'

'Bellybutton fluff,' Ivan said again quietly.

They all looked off to different corners of the jammed café. Voices boiled in the air. Now, in a moment of quiet when they had nothing else to say, they started thinking of Rollet again.

'He didn't just disappear. He has to show up somewhere,' Halifax muttered at the table top.

Ivan's voice was almost a whisper. 'He might not. People vanish all the time out there. They just vanish. He might stay missing forever.'

Halifax watched her climb down from the truck.

It was late afternoon. Heat from the day had begun to die down. She looked first to one side, then to the other, and finally straight into Halifax's face. She was short, with high cheekbones and dark eyes.

He wanted to shout across the space of ground between them that it was all right, he was not Ivan – Ivan's face was not buried behind old scars.

Against her chest she held a bag, which looked as if it had been made from a piece of Persian carpet. She walked toward Halifax with quick steps, holding out her hand. 'Justine.'

'Fine!' He shook her hand and nodded. 'I . . . I'm very fine, thanks.'

'I'm very fine as well.' She looked down at their hands, which Halifax continued to shake.

He let go. 'I'm not Ivan. Ivan's asleep.' He clapped his hands and rubbed them nervously together. 'It's just me here today.'

'Would you help me with my baggage?' She smiled a thin-lipped smile.

'Sure.' He grabbed the bag and held it to his chest.

107

She pointed to the roof of the truck. 'I have a few more things.' She smiled again. 'Who are you?'

'Charlie Halifax. I'm a pilot in the Foreign Legion.'

'English?'

'American.'

'I'd like to go to America.'

'So would I.'

'Well.' She looked around, taking in the pale stone of Mogador. 'Well, could you bring me to Mr. Konovalchik?' She wore a canvas jacket, like a duck-hunting coat. She had it buttoned up to the throat against the dust and the sleeves rolled back because they were too long for her. Someone must have lent it to her along the way and she had forgotten to return it.

'I'll take you straight there.' Halifax flipped a coin to the man on the roof of the bus, who handed down her bags and grinned with no teeth.

Halifax carried her bags across the square and down the alleys to Ivan's house. He kept opening his mouth to tell her about the different noises and smells. This is a wave about to break beyond the fortress walls. This is the smell of olive wood. There is no danger. Nothing to be afraid of. Soon your dreams will turn to blue. He said none of this. Instead, he turned to her every now and then and smiled.

She smiled back and made a quiet sound like a laugh before looking away.

Ivan lay spread-eagled on his bed, still wearing his boiler suit.

The first thing Halifax saw when he walked in were the soles of Ivan's bare feet. He set down her bags in the doorway.

The noise made Ivan open his eyes. He sat up. 'Oh, my God.'

'Hello, Ivan.' She held out her hand. 'I'm pleased to meet you.'

Ivan jumped off the bed. 'Please to meet you. Oh, Christ Almighty.' He turned away and tugged at the sheets, trying to tidy them. Then he gave up and lunged for his socks, hopping on the floor as he put on each one. After that, he jumped into his shiny shoes and tottered in front of her, regaining his balance. 'I am very pleased to meet you. Are you hungry? Are you thirsty?'

'Yes.' She nodded, looking around the room. 'Yes, it's been a long trip.'

Ivan looked at Halifax over her shoulder. 'Bring us some

food, will you, Halifax?' Then he faced her again and took her hand in both of his. 'I'm so glad you came.'

All the shops were shut. Halifax had to beg some bread and cheese off the owner of the Café Dimitri. When he returned to Ivan's room, the sun was going down. Ivan's place was empty.

He found them up on the ramparts that faced out to sea. They were walking slowly past the cannons. Ivan pointed at The Purpuraire, at the port and back at the town. Halifax stayed in the shadows, unable to hear what they said.

Ivan took her hand and bowed slightly forward.

For the first time since Halifax had known Ivan, he imagined clearly how Ivan must have looked as an officer in the Imperial Russian Cavalry. When Ivan turned to keep walking, light caught his polished shoes. Justine Dubois moved with even steps beside him, following the sweep of his arms with her eyes.

Halifax stared at them and nibbled at the bread and cheese. After a while, he looked down and realized the plate was empty.

Ivan and Justine held hands. Fragments of their laughter reached Halifax over the rumbling waves.

He went home to his room and lay on the cool sheets. Daydreams shuffled past behind his closed eyes. The dreams were blue and far away. Not enough energy to shut the door. Not enough energy to think of Rollet and Labouchere. After a minute, Halifax opened his eyes. The last blades of apricot sun grew pale across the floor.

# 8

'CHARLIE? CHARLIE?'

Halifax heard knocking at the door. He sat up and blinked. It was the middle of the night again.

Ivan's head appeared. 'Can I come in?'

'What do you want?'

'Can I sleep here tonight?'

'Did you have a fight already?' Halifax struck a match and lit the oil lamp. Light pooled on the walls.

'No, but I only have one bed. I didn't think to get her a room at the hotel. She has to have some privacy, you know. You don't mind, do you?'

Halifax rolled over and stuffed his face in the pillow. He felt the bed sag as Ivan lay down next to him.

Ivan was gone when Halifax woke in the morning. He found the two of them at the Dimitri drinking tea. From the way Ivan looked, Halifax could tell something had gone wrong. 'Shall I come back later?'

'No. Please.' Justine held her hand out toward the other chair.

Ivan sighed and folded his hands together. 'My land is in Russia.'

'I don't understand.' She pulled at a few strands of hair in front of her face and studied them. She wore a white blouse with tiny flowers sewn around the collar. 'I . . . I had . . . of course it's not very important, but you left me with the impression that your land was here.' She shook her head. 'Of course it's not important. I . . .'

'In Russia it would take half a day to walk from one end of my property to the other. My family had over a hundred people working for them.' Ivan's fists were closed and resting on the table top. A glass of mint tea steamed in front of him.

110

She laughed. 'But that land was taken from you. Those people who worked for you are running the country now. If they weren't, you probably wouldn't be in Africa.' She looked at Halifax and back at Ivan. 'Isn't it true?'

Panic showed on Ivan's face.

'You didn't say anything about being in the army.' Justine looked up at the pink brick walls of the town. 'I knew this wouldn't work. People said . . . people said I didn't have a chance. I wanted so much to believe I was doing the right thing.'

'Please,' Ivan whispered. 'Please, Justine.'

Her shoulders shuddered.

Is she crying? Halifax squinted, craned his neck out and stared. He couldn't remember the last time he saw someone cry. Then he looked across and saw fat tears moving down Ivan's cheeks. I'll be damned, Halifax thought. Two in one day.

'Why didn't you say you were in the army? I thought . . .' Justine burst out laughing, 'I thought . . .'

'I was an officer in the czar's Imperial Cavalry. I've always been in the army. It's all I've ever done. Please, I wrote what I thought I should write.'

'If you were an officer then, why aren't you an officer now?' Ivan sat back, eyes wide.

Halifax cleared his throat. 'Ivan's the most important man in this town. He keeps the planes flying. If he wanted to, he could be an officer. They tried to make him an officer but he refused.' Halifax breathed in, not knowing how far to stretch the lie.

'Why did you refuse?' She touched the sweat on her forehead with the tips of her fingers.

Halifax took a clean handkerchief from his pocket, knotted it at corners and gave it to her, same as he had done for Garros. He was about to tell her she should wear it against the sun, but Justine took the handkerchief and blew her nose in it. Then she nodded thank you and put it in her pocket.

Ivan ran his fingers through his hair and sighed, as if it bothered him to recall. 'I refused because I can be of more service where I am than in some office or ordering other people around. I've already been an officer once. I thought I'd give the other side a try.' Then he smiled a broad smile, so pleased with his story that he almost believed it himself. He knew Serailler would laugh in his face if he ever asked for a promotion.

'I see.' Justine tried to pick up the tea glass, but it was too hot

111

and she had to put it down. 'But how did you get to Africa in the first place?'

Ivan set his hand on hers. 'I'll tell you how I came to be here. I'll tell you everything you want to know. If you don't like what you're hearing, then you can get on the next boat back to France, and I will pay for your ticket.'

With my money, Halifax thought. He'll do the gentlemanly thing and pay for her ticket with my savings.

'You don't have to.' Justine sipped at her tea, leaving the glass in the saucer. She paused to smell the mint.

'I insist.' Ivan nodded.

'I don't expect that. All I asked was how you got to Africa.'

As Ivan began to speak, Halifax settled back into quiet. He could have told her the story himself, since he'd heard it, and versions of it, many times. Halifax listened only to see how Ivan would change what he told, what parts he'd build up and what he would allow to disappear.

'I was a junior officer in a cavalry group stationed in the Ukraine between 1913 and 1918. In the days shortly before the Revolution, landowners were being murdered and their houses burned by the people who worked for them, the *mujiks*. My job was to ride out to their villages and round up the people who were responsible. We had lists, you see. Lists of names from informers. We'd ride into a village first thing in the morning, before they were out in the fields. I'd read out the names on the list and tell them they had five minutes to be standing in front of us. Of course they hardly ever showed, and of course no one ever told us who or where they were. The informers weren't going to stick their necks out in public. So instead we counted the names on the list and burned as many houses as there were names. We carried heavy sticks soaked in tar at the ends. These we lit and threw in through the open doorways.'

Justine narrowed her eyes. 'What did you do then?'

'Then?' Ivan sucked at his cheeks. 'Then we watched the people who owned the houses trying to put out the fires with dirt and old blankets and buckets of water.'

'But that's horrible!'

'Some cavalry units burned people instead of houses. I'm only telling you what happened. I'm not saying it was a good thing.'

'What did you do if the people showed up when you called their names? Where did you take them?'

'To a town called Zitomir. I don't know what happened to them after that.' Ivan shook his head and looked at the table. The wood had been worn down so much that threads of grain stood out in ridges. 'Soon enough we couldn't go into the villages. Cavalry units were being attacked. Any officers with connections had themselves transferred out of there as fast as they could. I went back to Moscow and stayed with my family. My father was an architect. He built many of the roadways and drainage systems around Moscow. Because of that, he had the influence to have me sent home.

'One night after arriving home in Moscow, I was at a party. My sister was getting married to another cavalry officer named Godunov – I'd gone to school with him several years before. I stood on the balcony of the house where the party was going on and watched people down in the street. I think at the time' – he tapped his thumb knuckles against his temples – 'at the time I knew something was going on. The way people walked in large groups, the way they all talked in hushed voices and even the way they were dressed should have told me. But maybe I was drunk. For me, Moscow had always been safe. I didn't have the same instincts there as in the Ukraine.' Ivan spread his hands, 'Anyway, it wouldn't have made any difference. My sister came out on the balcony with the cavalryman who was to be her husband. Suddenly my sister took hold of my arm and pointed down to the street.

'Lying on the cobblestones was a man in army uniform. A dead man. Someone had beaten his head in, dragged him there and dumped him in front of the house. I heard the sound of footsteps running away. Then I realized that the whole area had gone quiet. I saw people in the shadows. Dozens of them, shifting around in the dark. Then I heard a rifle butt scrape on the stones.'

Ivan dragged his fingers down his chest, 'I remember thinking how ridiculous I must have looked to them, standing up on the balcony with all my brass buttons shining and my red tunic and riding trousers. I turned to Godunov and told him to take care of my sister. Then I ran. I left through the kitchen and all the cooks were gone. All the horses were gone from the stable. The music in the house was so loud that no one had heard them being led away. I ran home, stuffed a revolver in a rucksack, changed into some old clothes and kept running. By then I could hear shouting and windows breaking across the city. All the lights were out.

'I know what you're thinking.' Ivan stared at Justine. 'You're thinking that I shouldn't have run. Maybe you're thinking that it was the end of that world and I should have died with it.'

'I am not.'

'Yes, you are. Every time I tell this to people, they ask themselves why I didn't stay. Sometimes they don't say anything, but I know what they think.

'I kept running for weeks. I moved south. It took a long time for news to spread that the Winter Palace had fallen, that the czar had abdicated, all of that. For weeks, in some places, the *mujiks* carried on as they had always done, sometimes discovering that the landlords had fled only days after they were gone. I travelled mostly at night, and for food I dug up potatoes from fields. I made it all the way back to the Ukraine. It was the safest place to be then. A lot of people were on the move and many of them went to work on farms that had become collectives, organized by members of the Revolutionary Committee. I went to a farm and asked for a job, told them I'd been a labourer up in Moscow. The first thing they asked me was to hold out my hands.' Ivan held out his hands, palm up, with fingers slightly spread. 'If my hands hadn't been permanently calloused from riding horses, they'd have known I wasn't who I claimed to be. My hands were the only credentials I needed. They sent me to work in the fields. I cut wheat.' He stood and gripped an imaginary scythe. He began to swing it slowly back and forth.

The Arabs in the café were watching him, but Ivan didn't notice. 'People minded their own business at the collective. I lived in a hut with two other men. The only person who gave me a hard time was an overseer named Valudin. Valudin's house had been burned by cavalry troops the year before. Maybe I burned it myself. He was suspicious of everyone. One day I passed him on the road going home from work. He waited until I had gone by him and then shouted for me to come to attention. It was only one word but a word I had been conditioned to obey, and for one second my back went still and I stood still on the spot. He stamped over to me, looking up and down the road to see if anyone else had seen. He shook his finger in my face and said, "From now on, there's no peace for you."

'A week later, I was out in the fields cutting wheat. A man named Zivkovic should have been working alongside me but he had cut his hand on a scythe blade the day before and had to stay home. I signed his name in the work book so that he would still get paid. There were too many of us at the collective and too few overseers, so there didn't seem any risk in signing him in.' Ivan noticed that all the Arabs at the other tables had stopped talking and were gaping at him. He stopped swinging the imaginary scythe and sat down.

'At lunch break that day, Valudin walked into the field where I was working and dragged me to a building in our village called the Hotel. It was only a tavern but so many people passed out there every night and slept on the floor that it became known as the Hotel. Parked outside was a car that belonged to the regional commissar. Valudin walked me straight up to the Hotel's front door, opened it and pushed me in. He hadn't told me a thing. I just assumed he had found out who I was. Already I had given up hope of getting away. I just wanted them to get it over with quickly. I wanted them to be in a hurry and have other things to do and to spend no more time than was necessary putting a bullet in my head.'

Halifax took his eyes off Ivan and let them wander over to Justine, ready to look away fast if she noticed. He watched her carefully, following the curve of her cheeks, her nose and her chin. Her face showed worry. She was far away with Ivan, waiting for a bullet in the head a long time ago in the Ukraine.

'Valudin pulled a chair off a pile in the corner of the room and sat down. The commissar was in an office at the back, and a boy in a sloppy green uniform stood guarding the door. On the other side of the door I could hear the owner of the Hotel saying, "It's a vicious lie, comrade Commissar, a vicious, hurtful lie!"

'When the owner finally appeared from the office, he walked straight past us, out of the Hotel and across the street to a bench. He sat down, took off his hat and twisted it in his hands.

'Then the sloppy-suited boy read my name off a list – not my real name, you understand, just the name I'd given them at the collective. I walked into the office and stared straight ahead of me at the wall where the commissar sat at a desk. For the longest time, it seemed, I was just standing there. Then I heard him shuffle some papers.

'Suddenly he said, "*You!*" I looked down. It was Godunov, my sister's husband. He was sitting there in the uniform of a Soviet commissar, grinning at me like a monkey.

'We talked in whispers. He told me how he had fought his way out of the house that night I last saw him, and brought my sister out as well. For a while they lived in the attic of a shop belonging to a friend of his. Then one night my sister tried to go home and see if the rest of my family were still alive. The *mujiks* were waiting and they caught her and hung her from the front door. To save his own life, Godunov dressed in rags and joined the crowds in the street, helped to rip down buildings he should have been defending. The barracks where he had been quartered were burned to the ground. All the records were destroyed in the fire. When things had settled down and the Revolutionary Committee was set up in the Winter Palace, he walked in and applied for a job. He told them he was a student and they saw he could write, so they gave him a post and after a while they promoted him to officer.

'He showed me the report that Valudin had filled out, saying that I'd been writing down Zivkovic's name in the work book when Zivkovic was really still at home.'

'"How did Valudin know?" I asked Godunov.

'Zivkovic had gotten drunk the night before and fell head first down a well on the other side of the village. I hadn't heard the news. Anyway, Godunov kept stuffing cigarettes in my pockets. He said everyone thought I'd been killed. He smiled and asked me if I couldn't have done a little better for myself than work as a dirt-poor labourer in the Ukraine. He told me to wait outside while he had a talk with Valudin. Then he yelled and screamed at poor old Valudin for about half an hour, telling him not to waste the time of commissars and to get a shave and have a bath once in a while and mind his own business for a change.

'He put me in the trunk of his car when his driver wasn't looking and gave me a ride to the next town. Then he gave me some money and told me to head for Romania. It took me two months to cross from there, through Hungary to Austria. In Vienna I met up with other Russians who had fled the

Revolution. They gave me enough money to reach Paris. When I arrived, I joined the Foreign Legion.'

'Why?' Justine crinkled her eyebrows. 'Why join the Foreign Legion?'

Ivan smoothed his hand across his face. Razor stubble crackled against his palm. 'Because I was starving. And I got tired of asking for money from people who didn't have enough to lend me any.'

She twisted a finger in her hair. 'So this is what you meant when you wrote in the advertisement that I should be ready for travel to exotic locations.' Then she smiled. 'If my friends at the Hôtel Président could see me now, they'd die laughing.'

Ivan's face clouded over. He let go of her hand. 'I'll have the return fare for you in two days.'

Halifax watched and couldn't speak.

Ivan seemed to be shaking. He stared hard at the worn ridges of wood on the table, tired out from talk and nervousness.

If she leaves now, thought Halifax, this whole town will come toppling down on top of us.

'I didn't expect miracles from you, Ivan. I'm not sure I even expected the truth.' She reached for his hands where they rested on his knees. 'But you told me the truth just then, didn't you?'

Ivan nodded, still staring at the table top.

'Before you buy me a ticket home, why don't we spend a few days at least talking?' Her face was very calm. She watched him for an answer.

Halifax wanted to lean across and slap Ivan's face, wanted to grab hold of his collar and shake him and tell him to wake up and say something kind.

Ivan looked up. 'We could talk for a while, couldn't we?'

'We can talk all you want.' She smiled at him.

Halifax kept staring. He knew he was staring too much. When was the last time you saw a woman without a veil? he asked himself. When was the last time you saw one who wasn't wearing sackcloth, so the only way you could make out her age was by looking at her ankles? You should be ashamed, staring like this. You should at least try blinking your eyes.

'Tired of borrowing money from friends, are you?' Halifax shoved Ivan off his feet, into the path of an oncoming wave.

117

They stood in shallow water fifty yards from shore. Already they had spent an hour in the water. Their hands were like prunes.

Justine sat on the beach. With one hand she kept a book open on her lap and with the other she held an umbrella above her.

Ivan disappeared under the foam. Halifax closed his eyes as the sea rushed over him. Then Ivan's head popped up again. He spat out a jet of water. 'I got tired of borrowing from them, but I never get tired of borrowing from you!'

'We don't have anything to spend our wages on, anyway.'

Ivan wiggled his finger in his ear to clear out the salt water. 'You should get Serailler to pay you extra for making those flights out to the Touaregs, especially after all this time and because of what happened to Leclerc. Why don't you ask him for more money?'

'All I'm asking him for are my discharge papers.' A piece of seaweed scudded past. Halifax picked it up and draped it over his shoulders.

Ivan looked back at the beach to see if Justine had heard them talking, but she was busy reading her book. Then he turned back to Halifax and peered at him along the length of his nose. 'For God's sake, why didn't you turn him into that investigator? You could be going home.'

Halifax looked down at the foamy water and shook his head.

'You're no better than a slave.' Ivan started walking toward shore. 'Maybe you're right. Maybe you've been away too long ever to go back.'

An Arab rode into town on a donkey. He said he'd found a dead man in a plane. It had taken him more than a day to reach Mogador and he wanted a medal for the information.

Serailler, Ivan and Halifax drove into the scrubland.

The Arab sat in the front seat, pointing the way. Pinned on the grubby material of his cape he wore Halifax's Croix de Guerre. Serailler drove his old Rolls-Royce staff car left over from the Great War. It made him miserable to take it off the road and out across the rocky slab of the desert, wrecking the suspension system.

Ivan and Halifax sat in the back, wearing flying goggles against the dust. They knew the pilot was Rollet. The possibility that it might be someone else had not even crossed their minds.

Rollet's aircraft lay a two-hour drive east of Mogador, flipped over in a dry river bed. Rollet's body hung upside down, strapped into the cockpit seat. The ground was dark with spilled gasoline, and the smell of it clung in the air.

The Spad didn't seem heavily damaged. None of the struts had snapped, and the fuselage wasn't hit by more than a few bullets. It was Halifax's plane. Rollet had taken the only serviceable machine on the airstrip.

Halifax stared at his Spad. Strange to see his own aircraft crashed on the ground and another man dead in the cockpit. The green-painted canvas felt hot in the sun. Small arcs of sand, blown by the wind, sloped against the upper wing. Rollet's eyes were open behind the yellow windows of his goggles. A bullet had passed through his chest and splattered blood across the instrument panel. It was dried black on the glass covering the fuel gauge and speedometer. Flies gathered around Rollet's mouth and his ears and his nose.

Halifax released the seat straps and Rollet fell out onto the ground. The body didn't look like Rollet anymore. His face carried the fattened sameness of dead people not buried when they should have been. Breathing through his teeth, Halifax brushed flies away from Rollet's face, unbuttoned his jacket and searched the pockets for his paybook and wallet. Then he pulled at the cord of his dog tag until it broke.

Serailler stood nearby, red in the face from holding his breath. The Arab squatted above the riverbed. His little face peered from the hood of his cape.

Ivan and Halifax took shovels from the staff car and started to dig a grave. As they hacked at the pebbly earth, Serailler stood over the corpse and waved his hand to scare away the flies. The reek of the body swarmed around them. Ivan's shovel broke against a rock. After a quarter of an hour, the hole was only a few inches deep.

'Get away, you bastards!' Serailler punched at the black curtain of flies, which exploded and regrouped and he tried to drive them away.

The Arab shifted from his squatting position so he could watch. Halifax climbed out of the riverbed and tried to dig in the ground above the ridge. It was even harder, and his hands blistered into tiny white grapes on his palms.

They stopped digging. Ivan opened the fuel tank, spilling

gasoline over the corpse and fuselage. They took a spare gas can from the staff car and poured that on, too. Serailler drove the staff car away down the road and stopped. The Arab and Halifax were in the back. Dust billowed in their wake. It rose up and overtook them and continued along the trail. Only Ivan remained by the wreck. He waved his arm at the plane and jumped back. He began to run, clearing the ridge, and was still running when a sound reached them like a huge flag snapping in the wind. Then came the familiar black of flaming aircraft fuel.

By the time Ivan reached the car, the fire had already started to burn out. Smoke twisted up from the riverbed, frothed over the wreckage and disappeared.

# 9

'CAPTAIN SERAILLER HAS shut himself in a cell.'

'That's impossible.' Halifax looked up at the Arab militiaman who had just walked into his room at the Hotel Smara. Spread out in front of him were the parts of Ivan's revolver. He'd been cleaning them with gun oil and a cloth. 'Serailler would never do that. He's terrified of cells.'

'He's in there now, sir.' The man wobbled on his heels, as if he weren't used to being this high off the ground. 'You can see for yourself.'

The militiaman led Halifax to the holding cells. The commissariat stank of Serailler's cognac. Halfway up the stairs, he paused. 'This time, Mr. Halifax, he has gone mad.' The militiaman winced as he spoke, as if Serailler had heard him, as if Serailler would always hear what he said no matter where he was, and now he would be beaten for insubordination. 'The captain has gone mad and this time he's going to stay that way.'

Serailler was talking to himself. Halifax could hear him as he walked down the corridor. When he passed by Serailler's office, something caught his eye and made him stop. The old Arab who had led them to Rollet's plane was sitting in Serailler's chair. His bare feet stuck out from under the desk. The soles were worn smooth. The man wore Serailler's white Legion cap and looked very pleased with himself.

Halifax stood in front of the cell. 'What do you think you're playing at, Serailler?'

Serailler sat on the cot, legs crossed like an Indian. His eyes were half closed with the weight of alcohol in his head. 'Don't talk to me, talk to him.' He waved his hands at the old Arab. 'I just put him in charge of the whole garrison.'

'Have you cabled Casablanca to request new planes? They've sent us flying orders and we can't carry out the job.'

'The last time I cabled Casablanca they told me I was

ridiculous. I'm in prison, Halifax, can't you see that? Why bother me when I'm in prison?' He stood up and yelled. 'Why is everybody bothering me?'

The militiaman stood at the end of the hall, head turned slightly sideways to hear everything.

Halifax called to the man. 'Send an emergency cable to Casablanca. Tell them that Labouchere and Rollet are dead and that we require immediate replacements as well as three planes, or whatever they can send us.'

The militiaman nodded and left.

'I know,' Serailler talked in a very loud voice, 'I know how it feels to be a general whose army has been defeated and who has nothing left to do except dress in his best uniform, have a good meal and then blow his brains out. I know how those Romans felt when they lost their empire.'

'For God's sake, sober up, Serailler.'

'Why should I?' He sighed. 'Why should I?'

'If you don't get back in your office, I'll cable Casablanca and request that you be relieved of your command.'

'Oh, would you?' Serailler showed his teeth. 'Would you please?'

He smiled in a way that made him look as if he weren't really drunk.

Halifax pushed gently at the barred door of the cell. It squeaked open.

'You didn't lock it, did you?'

Serailler's face twitched. 'No.'

Halifax turned and walked into Serailler's office, past the old Arab, who was still wearing Serailler's white Legion kepi. The hat looked huge on his head. Halifax took a key off the wall, walked back to the cell with the old Arab following behind and locked it.

'What are you doing?' Serailler's eyes opened wide.

'What does it look like?'

Serailler spoke very softly. 'Open the door.' He walked to the front of the cell. 'Open it.'

They stood only inches apart.

'Should I ask the old man here?' Halifax pointed to the Arab. 'What do you think he'd say?'

Serailler's hands curled slowly round the bars. 'Please, Charlie.'

'If you don't do your job, then Abdel Krim may reach the coast. If he gets to Mogador, it's you he'll come looking for. You know what he'll do to you, don't you?'

'Yes,' he whispered.

'Do you know what Abdel Krim means in Arabic?'

Serailler wiped his forehead on one of the bars. 'It means . . . it means the slave of God.'

'And you know what they call you in the town? Do you know what name they've given you?'

'Is it any different from the name they gave me last week?'

'They call you the slave of the slave of God. I'm going to leave you here, Serailler.'

'I don't like to be locked in.' His whispering was barely audible. 'I can't stand it.'

'Just do your fucking job like everybody else.' Halifax unlocked the door.

Serailler walked into his office and the old Arab followed him with short, shuffling footsteps.

As Halifax left across the courtyard, someone called his name.

The militiaman appeared from the doorway. 'I sent a cable to Casablanca, Mr. Halifax.'

'Good. Let me know what Casa says.' He turned to leave.

'Mr. Halifax?'

'Yes?'

'There is a man in Captain Serailler's office who wants to know if he can have his donkey back. He has been waiting all afternoon and says he is very grateful for the gift of Captain Serailler's hat and he also says we can keep the animal if we really need to, but if at all possible he would like it back.' The militiaman stayed half hidden in the shade.

'Let him go home. Give him his donkey and as much food as he can carry and let him go home.' Then Halifax caught sight of the old Arab looking down from the window of Serailler's office. He must have no idea what's going on, Halifax thought.

The old man raised his thin hand and waved it at Halifax in one sweeping movement across the window space.

Ivan sat on the end of his bed. His hair was neatly combed. He smiled when he saw Halifax come in. 'Isn't she beautiful, Charlie?'

'We have to get out of here, Ivan.'

'She's the best, most caring person I have ever met. In the past, when I heard of people who met and got married only a few days later, I thought they were being idiots. But I see what happened to them now. I know how they felt.'

'We should leave here as soon as we can.'

'What?' He was still smiling.

'I mean it, Ivan. Serailler is out of his mind.'

Ivan snorted. 'He's just drunk.'

'Think about Justine. Is she still going to want to be your wife when you tell her this town was bombed a few days ago? Did you tell her we found Rollet dead out in the scrub yesterday? Did you tell her the ground was so hard we couldn't even dig a grave for him?'

'I didn't tell her any of that yet.' Ivan stood up. 'And I won't tell her if I don't have to.'

'What's she going to do when Abdel Krim gets here? What the hell are *we* going to do?'

'The same as we've always done. We wait for orders from Casablanca and then we do what they tell us to do. Look.' He stabbed his finger at Halifax. 'When I first wrote to her, none of this was going on. Rollet and Labouchere were still alive. The fucking Germans hadn't run off with Legion planes. They hadn't bombed the town. There weren't any damn government inspectors nosing around. When I wrote to her, I thought that we'd be here forever. Get this into your head, Charlie. I'm starting to see it myself. Maybe we can't leave. Maybe there is no way out.'

Ivan still had his finger resting against Halifax's chest when Justine appeared in the doorway. She held a wooden box. 'See what I bought?' She shook the box and something rattled inside. 'The key to the box is hidden in a secret place. I bought it from one of the carpenters who work inside those little cubbyholes in the town wall.' She wore a white headscarf and a long khaki dress. 'Oh, Ivan, this town is beautiful! Everyone takes their time. There's no traffic and no rain. Tell me.' She rocked back on one hip. 'Am I the only woman who answered your ad in the paper?'

Ivan smiled until it looked as if he might burst into tears again. He took the box from her and rattled the key inside. The boxes were all made on the same pattern. A panel at the back slid open to reveal the key, and then a panel on the other side to uncover the lock. Ivan sat down on the bed.

Justine sat beside him. 'You won't be able to get it, Ivan.'

Halifax found himself staring at Justine again.

Ivan turned the box slowly in his hand. The smell of olive wood spread through the room. 'I don't think I'm going to get this.' He smoothed his fingers over the polish. 'No. I don't think I can.'

Justine laughed and put her arm around his shoulder. She pressed her finger against one of the wooden grooves and opened a tiny chamber with the key inside.

'Amazing!' Ivan handed her the box, then looked up at Halifax. 'Isn't it amazing?'

Halifax no longer shuddered at night before he fell asleep, as shapeless blasts of colour rushed out of the dark. No memory of fire burned his face. Now it seemed to be a different person in the Spad over Ypres in 1918, or back at the airfield in Bergues and lying in a tar-roofed Besseneau hut, or half dead and soaked in a cart on the way to the hospital, with the face of a panicked old woman staring down.

He knew he could lay claim to these things but they still didn't seem to be him. He could tell what happened, remembering each detail, and feel less pain than whoever heard the story secondhand.

A cable arrived from Casablanca, ordering one pilot from Mogador to pick up a replacement aircraft from a garrison up the coast at El Jadida. The cable said that two new pilots would be arriving within a month.

'This must be for you, then.' Serailler handed the scrap of yellow paper to Halifax.

'What good is one plane going to do? I can't fly reconnaissance without a fighter escort.' Halifax buckled his belt and leather holster around his middle.

'Why don't you send them a cable? Complain to Casablanca.' Serailler raised his fist and shook it. 'Make your voice heard!'

Blinding light splintered off the white stone walls at El Jadida.

Halifax waited in the garrison mess hall while mechanics fuelled up the replacement plane, another worn-out Spad. It was cool and dark in the mess hall. He sat at a long wooden table drinking coffee from a tin mug.

A few Legionnaires sat by themselves, scraping food off metal plates with large French army spoons. Halifax stared at one man in a corner who was drinking a bottle of wine, keeping it hidden under his seat next to the wall. He peered around whenever he topped up his mug, not wanting to share it with anyone. The man was a corporal, unshaven and fat and old. He hummed to himself.

I know him, thought Halifax. I know him from someplace.

The man noticed that Halifax was watching him and shifted to hide the wine bottle. Then he took off his white kepi and smoothed a hand over his balding head.

In that movement, Halifax recognized the man. He stood slowly from his bench and walked over.

The corporal scowled and drank off the wine in his mug. 'It's not for sale. It's mine.'

'Major Degrelle?' Halifax sat down, resting his hands on the bare wood table.

The corporal screwed up his eyes. 'Who are you?'

'Charlie Halifax, sir.'

'Don't call me sir!' he tapped two fingers on his left sleeve. 'Can't you see? Corporal!'

'But you are Degrelle? Are you or not?' Degrelle had been the base commander at Bergues.

'I'm still Degrelle, yes.' He flicked his fingernail against the rim of the tin mug.

'I'm Charlie Halifax, sir. Seventy-third Escadrille. Don't you remember me, sir?' But you used to be so tidy, Halifax wanted to say. You were such an orderly and proud man. Not a man to stay unshaven and hide his bottle of wine.

Degrelle pulled out the bottle, poured a drop into his mug and slid it across to Halifax. 'That's all you're having.'

Halifax pushed the mug back. 'You don't remember me?'

'Charlie who?' His lips were dried and cracked.

'Halifax.'

'I think I recall.' Degrelle tapped a finger against his temple. 'Yes. Sure. Charlie Halifax.' He nodded and smiled.

'You don't have the vaguest idea who I am, do you? Why are you in Africa?'

126

Degrelle ran his swollen tongue over his lips. 'They broke me down to corporal, two months after the war.'

'But why, sir?'

He blinked at the mug in front of him. He didn't seem to hear. 'They said either I could sign up for Legion duty in Africa or they'd send me to prison for the rest of my life. They do that, you know.'

'What happened, sir? What did you do?'

Degrelle's eyes flicked up at Halifax. 'Various things. I swear I don't remember you, boy.'

Halifax climbed into the Spad.

A mechanic spun the prop, then stepped up to the cockpit. 'There's two replacement pilots coming down to Mogador from Casablanca. They're flying straight down. I don't know when they're coming. Could be today. Could be a week. Could be they've already arrived.'

The white stone of El Jadida turned yellow as Halifax slid his goggles down over his eyes and eased the plane up off the ground.

After half an hour, he saw the two new pilots heading south to Mogador, about half a mile in front. Their spider shapes stayed level, side by side. Halifax opened the throttle to catch up. The pressure of speed nudged him back into his seat, leaning into his forehead and cheeks. The revolver in its holster dug into his ribs. The coastline ran smooth towards Mogador. Clouds bobbed two thousand feet above the beaches. Sand veered away sharply under the waves, showing the darker blue of deep water. He flew in directly behind the new pilots. Just as he was about to join the formation, one of the men looked back. Sun winked off his goggles.

Suddenly one plane peeled away to the side. Halifax looked for the cockades of the French Air Service and saw only the crude brown diamonds that the Germans had painted on when they deserted to Abdel Krim. Now the other plane banked. The second German swung his plane into a firing line behind Halifax.

Panic scrabbled through Halifax's stomach. The shadows of wings flickered past his head. He stood the Spad on its tail and dropped down.

The Germans grouped above him, ready to move in. Halifax cocked the Vickers gun. A bullet clanked into the breech.

The two Germans split up. One came in from above and the other from below. Again Halifax pulled away, hunting for the space that might give him a firing line. He kept the engine on full and his strut wires bowed with the strain. With each twist in the air, engine on full, blood slammed into the top of his skull, then poured away with the coarseness of sand.

Tracer fire snapped through the canvas of his fuselage. Short, vicious shudders moved up through his feet.

He swept down once more to the side. Sweat greased the inside of his gloves. There's nothing more to do, he told himself, tasting the coffee he'd drunk at El Jadida, acid at the back of his throat. Wait for the shock. Wait for the pain.

He dropped into the ragged mountain of a cloud and was suddenly lost. The glare forced his eyes almost shut. He knew if he kept up the dive with his engine on, he'd tear the wings off the plane, and if he cut the engine, he might not get it started before they found him again. Halifax eased back the stick and rode up into the khaki sun.

The two Germans moved in smoothly on either side of him, boxing him in. Each movement of his they had blocked. He didn't have the speed to run. The lines of their new planes made his old Spad look clumsy.

He watched them for movement, ready to break away, to curve around and find a target. It was the only thing he knew how to do.

Clouds and empty sky waved past in the lines of his gun sight. He braced his legs against the pedals and moved his head from side to side, not understanding why they hadn't killed him yet. Air sucked in through clenched teeth. He felt almost impatient for fire to begin streaming from his engine, for the miserable looseness of his flaps when the cables had been torn away by bullets.

The German on the left waved his gloved hand.

Halifax opened his mouth and wind streamed into his throat. 'Bastard. Wave to me, will you, before you send me down? Well fuck you. I'll steer right into you and take us both down!' He yelled at the top of his lungs.

The German waved again and pointed to the ground.

Now Halifax understood. They wanted him to land so they

could have the plane undamaged. He slumped back, already exhausted, numb with surprise at being still alive. He mapped in his head the sharp jerk of the stick and easing of his left foot on the pedal that would bring him up into the belly of one of the Germans' planes.

The German on the right eased his plane down as his partner rose up on the left. Following their movements, Halifax began the slow turn in formation. It brought them out facing east, toward the desert. They moved through the last clouds bunched above the coast.

Halifax watched the Germans disappear in the white pastiness, then reappear. Their shape and colours returned to focus like a sudden gathering of particles. He rammed his head against the back of the cockpit. If you were younger, he told himself, you could have moved faster. You could have gotten away from this. He let his head fall forward and stared at his old boots.

Gunfire slapped at his ears. He cried out and hunched down, waiting for the shock. The coffee splashed into his throat. When nothing happened, he looked up over the padded leather rim of the cockpit. The German on the right shook his fist, warning Halifax to stay in position. Halifax looked at the man's leather-wrapped head and goggles, the face of a fly.

They herded him out past the scrubland and into the region of sand, moving closer and closer to the ground.

They'll kill you. He nodded, agreeing with the voices in his head. They may not kill you straightaway but they'll kill you. Remember what Captain Chaudon said. It makes no sense for them to do anything else. What would you do in their shoes, in their shiny black German boots? Would you let a pilot go back home so he could get in another plane and come hunting for you? Here you are thinking they'll shake hands and give you a canteen of water and point you to the nearest Legion outpost. And you know what they're thinking. They're thinking shallow grave and bullet in the head. He looked at one and then at the other, remembering the Immelmann roll he had seen one of them do over Telaleh. They have the same skills as me, he thought.

He recognized none of the ground below. There was nothing to recognize, only dunes and a few grubby palm trees living off the muddy water of an oasis.

The Germans slowed as they approached a flat patch of ground. Halifax figured they'd spotted it on their way out of the Bled. He couldn't see anyone waiting for them. They wanted his plane down on the nearest safe stretch of ground.

He circled once before coming in to land. The Germans hung over him in case he tried to run. He cut his engine and rolled to a stop. Then the Germans set down on the runway.

Halifax released his seat straps, took the revolver from its holster and set it against his front teeth. He rocked slowly back and forth. The muscles in his stomach knotted and bowed him over until his face was almost touching his knees. He thought about Winslow at Telaleh and what the Arabs must have done to him, heard again Captain Chaudon saying, 'They'll hurt him, Halifax. I can't even tell you what they'll do to him.' He moved the gun barrel from his teeth to his temple and closed his eyes. Pictures rattled through his head of French soldiers hanged by the Germans from barbed-wire nooses along the rows of poplar trees in Flanders, in the days when there were still poplar trees.

'They'll want information,' he said to his boots. He thought of the skulls of Christians used as paving stones in desert mosques. Sweat leaked into his eyes and stung.

Pull the trigger. For Christ's sake, get it over with.

He heard their voices as they walked toward the Spad. One of them was laughing. Their footsteps thumped on the baked earth.

Pull the trigger now. It's the right thing to do. Do the right thing for once in your life. Pull the trigger.

He closed his eyes so tight they hurt. The butt of the revolver dug into his palm. His stomach muscles ached. He rested his forehead on his knees and tried to breathe.

Think of Ivan. Think of Justine. You don't want to hurt them, do you? You'll hurt them if you sing like a canary to these Germans. Get it over with. It doesn't hurt. There won't be any pain.

One of the Germans called out to him. He heard their footsteps closer now.

Get it over with.

He scraped the forward sight on the barrel across his forehead. The metal tore into his skin. He smelled gun oil soaked into his palm and breathed the hot air rippling off the ground. It burned his lungs.

No plan is the only plan you have left. Suddenly he felt himself stand, almost falling from the rush of blood in his head. He turned to the right and looked at the nearest German, lining him up in the gun sight. The smile dropped off the German's face.

Halifax closed one eye. The German's body disappeared behind the black needle of the gunsight. He fired three times.

The first round struck the German square in his chest. His eyes opened wide and he jerked backwards, arms thrown out to the side. The second bullet punched through the top of his flight cap, closing his eyes and buckling his legs underneath him. When the third shot hit him in the stomach, he was already dead.

Something snapped over Halifax's shoulder. Then he felt a hard kick in his right leg.

He turned his eyes from the dead man to the other pilot, who held out a small automatic pistol at arm's length. Its barrel jumped as he fired again. A bullet cracked the air above Halifax's head.

This pilot was younger than the other. He seemed to be almost a boy, shapeless in the baggy overalls he used as a flight suit. The boy dropped down on one knee. His gun was empty. His breath stuttered as he rummaged in the holster for another magazine.

For the first time, Halifax realized he had been shot. He felt no sharp pain, only a dullness that spread through his body. His nerves were buzzing. All he could see of the wound was a hole in his trousers around the edge of his thigh. He steadied himself against the rim of the cockpit. Carefully he brought up the revolver until it was pointing at the boy. His other hand gripped the leather padding of the cockpit rim.

The German was still kneeling on the ground, trying to jam a new magazine into the butt of the pistol. His panic made him clumsy.

Halifax was careful when he aimed. He breathed in twice and on the third he kept the air in his lungs. He squeezed the trigger very gently and felt the revolver jump in his hand. The boy sat down suddenly and dropped his gun. For a couple of seconds he looked around, as if he could no longer remember where he was or what had knocked him down. Then he raised himself up very slowly until he was standing.

Halifax's leg seemed impossibly heavy. He propped himself

against the seat. The spark of ripped muscle and nerves spread down his leg and up the bones of his spine.

The young German slowly turned around and began walking back to his plane. He paced with his back straight, one hand held to the wound in his chest. He began to move faster, running and crying out as he got closer to his plane.

Halifax strained to hear the words.

The German boy yelled until there was no more air in his lungs and then tripped over onto the ground. He fell so hard and so quickly and lay so still that Halifax knew he must be dead.

Moving as fast as he could, Halifax pumped pressure into the fuel tank, set the throttle and he climbed down from the cockpit. The ache in his leg drummed through him. He grabbed the prop and pulled down hard, staggering back as the engine started. The Spad jolted forward.

He lunged at the cockpit and fell into the seat. Taking hold of the controls, he slowed the plane as it came near to a patch of sand. Then he strapped himself in and headed back, easing the plane off the ground.

He flew west, slouched in his seat. His stomach muscles clamped in bars below his ribs.

The bullet's small entry point showed through the tear in his trousers. Around the wound were other, smaller punctures in the flesh, which bled more than the wound itself. His whole leg was soaked. His socks felt spongy with blood, which pooled between his toes. He couldn't see an exit wound and couldn't move his leg enough to tell. The safety straps kept him pinned to his seat.

He tapped the fuel gauge with his finger. The tank was still half full. Every couple of minutes, he leaned out into the slipstream to breath clean air and feel the sweat cool on his face. Tiredness pressed on his shoulders and he wanted to sleep. His hands were sticky with blood.

His thoughts started to unravel. In his head he had already begun an argument with the Arab doctor back in Mogador. He knew the doctor would try to make him stay at the hospital, but he wanted to remain in his room at the hotel. 'Right,' he said, and the wind howled in his mouth. 'Mind's made up. Want to be in my bed. My room.' Then he was hungry and imagined trays of food in his room at the Smara. The trays were

132

everywhere, even on the floor. Bananas and oranges and plums crowding the window sills.

His leg felt bloated out of shape, but when he looked down, he saw it hadn't swelled at all. He blinked, trying to stay awake. His spit tasted of gasoline fumes.

He heard shooting in the distance and twisted around in his seat. White-burning tracer rounds fizzed past below. A plane roared out of the sun. As Halifax pulled up, the machine passed beneath him. It was the young German, not dead after all. He must have only passed out for a while, thought Halifax. Now he's come looking for me.

The German tried to bank around and Halifax followed him. The German's machine moved clumsily. The smooth movements from before were gone.

They began to circle each other, as if riding the edge of a huge ring in the sky. Halifax had seen rings like this made up of a dozen planes, in the air over Belgium. The first pilot to break and dive would be a target for the other.

The German wavered and then flew steady. Every few seconds, he turned to look at Halifax. He didn't have his flying cap or his goggles.

Halifax looked at the German and thought, How did you come this far with a wound like that in your chest? Don't you know you won't have enough fuel to get home?

They approached the coast. The ocean lay a few miles to the west. Clouds drifted past and the two planes carved through them. The German's plane straightened out, but suddenly he twisted and dived, almost stalling his engine as he misjudged the force of the turn.

As Halifax pulled in behind him, he saw pale sunlight catch the diamonds of paint on the German's wings. He couldn't feel himself breathing. His eyes hurt. Sweat dripped through the padding of his goggles.

The German dived fast.

Halifax's plane shuddered slightly as he moved it into the slipstream of the German's engine. He hunched down behind the machine gun. For a second he felt very calm, as the vortex rings of his gun sight locked on the German. It seemed to him he hadn't felt this calm in years.

Then he broke apart the German's plane with a belt of incendiary bullets. The machine fell away in black smoke and flames from the blazing fabric of its wings.

133

# 10

HEAT SHIMMERED UP from the airfield. Halifax brought the Spad down, rolling to within a hundred feet of the hangar. He stayed sitting in the cockpit, chin resting on his chest. The only thing holding him up was the seat straps.

Pain fogged his head. He couldn't tell if the engine was on, and kept pressing at the shutoff button. The noise of the prop continued buzzing in his ears.

'Ivan!' he called out and then left his mouth hanging open.

Mogador looked empty. The hangar sat in a clump on the runway. It looked like a cake that had collapsed in the oven. A speck of white flickered from the remains of the door. Halifax squinted at the speck and saw it was a piece of paper. 'Ivan!' The ache in his leg felt sharper now. It pulsed and bled through the shreds of his trousers. He unbuckled the straps and fell forward onto the control panel. It took several minutes to get out of the plane. He hobbled across to the piece of paper.

It was a note from Ivan. The words slid in and out of focus. Halifax touched the paper, trying to hold it steady against the breeze. His fingertips left red splats on the white. The note said, I AM AT HOME.

Justine opened the door. 'Oh, God.' She put her hands to her face and stood back. 'Ivan! Oh, God!'

'It's okay.' Halifax stumbled into the room, dragging his leg.

Ivan walked out of the bathroom. He was bare-chested and had shaving soap on his face. A towel was wrapped around his neck. He took hold of Halifax's arms. 'Sit down, Charlie. It'll be fine.'

Justine ran past him into the bathroom with a chamber pot. She filled it with water from a pitcher and came back into the room.

Ivan spoke in a quiet voice. 'Go to the hospital, Justine. Get

134

the doctor. Bring him here and tell him we'll need a stretcher and maybe some morphine.'

'But I don't know where the hospital is!' She shouted in his ear. 'How can I find it if I don't know where it is?'

Ivan wiped the soap off his face with the towel. 'Stay with him, then. Keep him talking. I'll be back in a minute.' He leaned down to Halifax. 'I'll be right back, Charlie.' Then he sprinted out the door.

Halifax turned to Justine. 'I'm not as old as I thought.'

'Who did this to you, Charlie? Are you sure you're all right?' She put her arms around him.

'I'm all right.' He smiled at the blur of Justine's eyes. 'They won't use *my* skull for a floorboard.' Then he slid out of her arms and fell on his face.

'Ivan!' He opened his eyes and sat up. He was in a bed, a hospital bed. The blank white wall of the room rose up in front of him. Through the open window, he heard children playing soccer. A glass with three yellow flowers in it stood on his bedside table. He looked at the water in the glass. Then he picked the flowers out and drank the water.

He remembered his leg and pulled back the bedsheets. A bandage covered the wound. He unpinned the bandage and looked at the stiches, done in green silk thread. Fifteen of them. The edge of the scar was yellowed from iodine.

The door opened and Justine walked in. 'I thought I heard you talking to yourself.'

He pulled the bedsheets back over his leg. 'I didn't know where I was. Am I all right?'

'The doctor says you're fine. He said the bullet tore some muscle on your thigh but there's no more damage than that. You should be up in a week. They say you're going to get a medal. Mr. Serailler says they'll give you another Croix de Guerre and send you up to Casablanca for a ceremony. The whole town's talking about it.'

'But how did they know what happened?'

She laughed. 'Oh, you don't remember? You were yelling it, as we brought you to the hospital. You were waving your arms and acting it out on the stretcher. We tried to calm you down but that didn't happen until the doctor gave you some morphine.' She nodded and laughed again. 'That shut you up, though.

And today a reconnaissance group from El Jadida found the wreckage of both planes.'

'One of them isn't wrecked.'

'Well, they'll probably give you another medal, then. Everyone's so pleased, Charlie. Even though I don't understand Arabic, I can tell that's what everyone's talking about. They keep looking up at the sky and pointing to the damage the two planes did when they bombed the town. Then they point to your room at the Hotel Smara and their voices get very solemn and full of respect. Mr. Serailler is so pleased that he's gotten himself drunk up in his office.'

'I don't remember telling anyone.'

'You should have heard yourself. You were a one man band.' She was wearing her shirt with flower designs stitched to the collar. 'Who's Henry?'

'Henry?'

'Yes. After you yelled at the Germans, you started yelling at someone named Henry. Then they gave you the morphine.'

'Henry was my brother. We worked in the coal mines together.' Justine folded her arms and leaned against the wall. 'When was the last time you saw him?'

Halifax wiped his palm across his forehead, trying to remember. 'On the deck of the ship I was taking to France. That was in the spring of 1917. I was trying . . .' He wiped his forehead again. 'I remember I was trying to get him to come with me. We were having an argument. He told me to come home a hero or not to come home at all.'

'Why didn't he go with you?'

'He said he had responsibilities to the mine. I told him he had the responsibility to get the hell out of there before he ended up like Tom.' When Justine opened her mouth to ask who Tom was, Halifax kept talking. 'Tom was my other brother. He died in a mine explosion. It was when he died that I decided to quit the mine.'

'But why go all the way to France?'

'We all knew we'd get called up sooner or later. America was gearing up for war. And I knew if I waited until then, I'd never be a pilot or an officer. So I decided to join a squadron of Americans who flew with the French before America entered the war. They were called the Lafayette Escadrille.' He looked up at her to see if she recognized the name, but she only stared at him and listened. 'The French took almost any American in the beginning. It was good propaganda. My plan was to be an experienced pilot by the time the Americans arrived. Then I'd transfer over to the American Air Service and they'd overlook my bad eyesight. They'd make me an officer, too, I figured. And I wouldn't have to go home to the mine at the end of the war. I could go back to something better. That was my plan.'

She nodded, lips pressed together. 'The Americans didn't take you.'

Halifax tapped at his glasses. 'Policy.'

'You were calling out things in English, so I don't know what you said. I only heard the name.' Justine walked to the window and looked out at the children playing soccer in the hospital courtyard. 'Shall I tell them to go somewhere else?'

'No.' He felt a little dizzy and lay back on the pillow. 'I don't mind.'

Justine turned away from the window. 'It doesn't bother you?'

'Let them play. I don't care.'

'I don't mean that. I was thinking about something else.' She folded her hands over her stomach. 'I mean about the Germans. You killed them.'

'It'll bother me later maybe.'

'Surely you could have let them go.' Justine narrowed her eyes. 'They were just trying to get away, after all.'

Halifax looked up, realizing that she didn't know about Rollet and Labouchere.

'You could have let them go.' Her voice had anger in it. 'That would have been a little more honourable.'

'When I started flight training at Avord, all people ever talked about was the honourable thing to do. I thought that's the way it would be. I thought that when the other pilot jammed his guns, you let him fly home. If it didn't look like a fair fight, you didn't pull the trigger. But by the time I'd gone through advanced training and made it to the front, all that had changed. What they taught me to do was go out *looking* for an unfair fight. When the man jammed his guns, you didn't let him get away. You kept firing until his plane caught fire and then followed him down to the ground to make sure he died. They said it was the only way that made sense anymore, the only way to earn respect.' Halifax pressed his sweaty face against the clean white sheets. 'They said it was the right thing to do.'

Justine stayed quiet for a while.

Halifax listened to her breathing. He wanted to drag her through the streets of Wadi Harazem, maybe show her the graves of Labouchere and Rollet. Make her understand.

'I have to tell you something, Charlie.'

'What's that?'

She put her hands behind her back. For a moment, she stared at the floor. Then, she looked up. 'Ivan asked me to marry him last night.'

'Congratulations!'

'I didn't expect him to ask me so soon.'

'You don't want to marry him?'

She raised her voice. 'It's just very soon.'

'So tell him to wait. He will. I know he will.' Halifax raised himself off the pillow, felt his head rock as if a wave had crashed inside it, then fell back down again.

'I think I'd like to marry him.'

'So go ahead.' He closed his eyes and tried to stop the swaying in his skull. 'It all seems simple enough.'

'But it's not simple at all!' She pushed off the wall and came to the side of his bed. 'I'm sick, Charlie.'

'So get better and marry him.' He didn't know how much longer he could stay awake.

'I don't think I will get better.' She reached in her pocket and pulled out the handkerchief Halifax had lent her. She held it out. The white cloth was speckled with blood. 'I won't get better, Charlie.'

For a while, he just looked at the handkerchief. Then he cleared his throat very quietly. 'That's blood.'

'Of course it's blood. I cough it up every night.'

Disease, he was thinking. Sickness that doesn't get better. What the hell is the name for the sickness that makes people cough up blood? Do other people catch it? He breathed out through his teeth. 'Does Ivan know?'

'No. He never kept quiet long enough for me to tell him.' She tried to smile.

Halifax shook his head. 'You could have told him if you'd wanted to.' What the hell is the name of that sickness, he kept asking himself.

138

She stopped smiling. 'But I didn't want to tell him. Can't you see that?'

'I wondered why a woman as beautiful as you might come to Africa and then stay when she found out she'd been fed a pack of lies.'

'Oh, but they're not lies.' She raised her hands and let them fall again. 'He *is* an educated and charming man. As far as he's concerned, he still owns that land in Russia. He's also a kind man. He's more kind than I ever would have expected. I had no place else to go, Charlie. I got so sick that I had to leave my job at the Hôtel Président. A doctor told me I should go somewhere hot and dry for my health. He suggested I go to the south of Italy, but when I read Ivan's advertisement in the paper, I decided to come down here instead. Look, don't tell Ivan what I've said to you. If anybody tells him, it'll have to be me. Understand me, Charlie. I would marry him and I would be very happy with him, but if I tell him the truth, I don't think he'll want to stay with me.'

'Give him more credit than that.' Sleep washed over him. Her voice sounded hollow and far away. He tried to see the sickness in her face but couldn't. Her cheeks looked red from the sun and her eyes were shiny and dark.

'Sleep, Charlie. You need some sleep.' She brushed her hand over his eyelids and closed them.

He heard the door close and the sound of her walking away down the hall. He listened to the children in the courtyard.

In the night, he began to sweat and heat flashed through the right side of his body. His leg stiffened until he couldn't bend the knee joint. The thigh muscle swelled so much he thought the stitches would pop. He climbed out of bed to open the windows and fell on the floor because his leg wouldn't support his weight. It was cool on the floor so he slept there, feeling his leg expand. Sweat pushed out of him in scratchy grains of salt.

When he woke later, he was freezing. He wrapped himself in the sheets and slept with the pillow over his face.

Fever dreams repeated and repeated in his head. He thought he was back at the hospital in Dunkirk, recovering from his burns. A man stood in front of him, wearing the rough olive cloth of an American soldier's uniform. Leather gaiters stretched from his ankles to his kneecaps, the colour of polished mahogany.

'Your brother Henry died last week,' the man said. Then, because the room was stuffy, he undid the top button of his tunic.

Henry was called up in July of 1917. He left the mine and went into training with the infantry. A lot of people left the mines that summer. He arrived in France in March of 1918.

Halifax wrote to Henry every other day for the first few weeks, and every morning at the flight training school in Avord, he showed up at the mail table and waited while the clerk rummaged in the piles of mail. 'It takes time,' the clerk told him. 'Sometimes it takes a great deal of time.'

After the first few weeks of receiving nothing, he began to write less often. Twice a week. Once a week. Telling Henry about the planes called Penguins, which had wings that were cut short so the plane couldn't get off the ground. They rolled up and down the training field with the instructors either jogging alongside or standing behind them in the cockpit and pounding on their heads with rolled-up newspapers. Telling about Paris, even though at that time he had only passed through there on his way to Avord. He described Paris in the way he knew his brother would imagine Paris.

Come home a hero or don't come at all. Every time he let his thoughts go slack, the words rose up like a chant. He caught himself repeating them.

He graduated from Avord and moved onto the advanced flight training school at Pau. One week into Pau, he received his first letter from his brother. Henry was selling the house. Too big for just one person, he wrote. People were talking about a union for the miners. The letter stopped at the end of the page, as if Henry had run out of paper. The other side was blank except for a stain of something that might have been split-pea soup. Best wishes from your brother Henry, it said at the end.

The next letter he received was when Henry joined the infantry. Again one page, and again nothing like the letters he had hoped Henry would write. When Halifax joined the French Air Service and was posted to the Seventy-third Escadrille at Bergues, he no longer had time to write and eventually lost Henry's mailing address.

Now and then, he looked down on the mashed earth around

the trenches, and he wondered if Henry was there. After a while, Henry and Brackenridge slid away behind thoughts of the war.

'Henry died at Belleau Wood.' The man with the mahogany gaiters stood at the end of Halifax's bed. 'He's getting the Congressional Medal of Honor.' The man leaned forward over the brittle white sheets. 'You *are* Charlie Halifax, aren't you?'

'Right.' Halifax stared with one eye past the piles of bandage on his face. The other was hidden under gauze. 'When?'

'Almost six weeks ago. I had some trouble tracking you down.' The American soldier looked around the room. Then he saw what he wanted and went to fetch the white wicker chair that stood in the corner. It creaked as he lowered himself into it. 'I've been on my feet since last night. The only place I could get on a train down here was in one of those red cattle wagons. You know, the ones with Forty Men – Eight Horses written on the side. It was so crowded that I had to stand.'

Halifax raised himself on his elbows. 'How do you know he's dead?'

'How?' The man tapped his fingertips together. 'Because I saw it happen.'

Then it must be true, Halifax thought, and lay back on the pillow.

'There was a bunker at a crossroads in the woods and we couldn't get past it. We ordered in some artillery but the first couple of rounds fell on our own people so we cancelled the barrage. It was a pillbox bunker. You know the type — gun slits on all sides and a steel door. Every time we got men close to it, they'd get shot. We threw grenades at them all day and some even went through the slits, but the Germans threw them back out again before they exploded.' The American sat back and crossed one mahogany leg over the other. 'It was holding up everything. The men ahead of us were getting cut off. You follow what I'm saying?'

Halifax thought of the bunkers he'd seen from the air. Some of them had been there since the beginning of the war. Bright yellow mould grew on the chipped concrete.

The wicker chair creaked in the corner of the room. 'So Henry said he could fix the bunker. Fix it, he said. He took a sack of explosives, just plain explosives that we used for bringing down bridges and some of the tunnels the Germans had dug. He crawled around the side of the bunker and got as far as the steel door before the Germans shot him. We thought he was dead and so did they. Then, when it got dark, Henry crawled the rest of the way and set the charges off right at the base of the door. Blew the whole thing off its hinges and killed half the men in the bunker. Thing is that Henry was lying on top of those charges when they went off. They're giving him the Congressional Medal of Honour — did I tell you that already?' He walked across to the bed. 'I swear I don't know why he did it. There was no chance he could have gotten away.'

'You said the bunker had to go.' The deep breaths he had to take for speaking raked at Halifax's throat.

'Sure, I said that.'

'So Henry got rid of it. What more do you want?' Halifax blinked his one eye.

The solider chewed at his lower lip. 'What do I want? Nothing, buddy. I just thought you might want to know.'

All night, on the floor of the hospital room in Mogador, Halifax remembered the soldier's visit in Dunkirk. The viciousness of the fever trembling through him didn't seem drawn from any strength he had left. It felt as if he were plunged into some electric current that switched on and off every few minutes. The anger of it never let up. He couldn't make it go away. He could only lie there and take it.

In the morning, when the freeze peeled back, he crawled across to the window sill and saw merchants opening the shutters of their shops. By nine o'clock, the children had returned to the courtyard. Their small faces peered around the stone wall to make sure the coast was clear, then they kicked in a ball and started another game of soccer.

Halifax's leg had swelled so much that it looked like a balloon held together by the green strands of the stiches. In the afternoon, the doctor removed a sliver of lead from Halifax's thigh that had broken off the bullet. By the following morning, the swelling was down and the fever had gone.

'Excellent, excellent.' Serailler pumped Halifax's arm, then stood back from the bed. 'You'll get a medal for this!'

'Oh, boy.'

'Don't be so ungrateful, Halifax. You're going up to Casablanca next week for the ceremony. They're very pleased with you up there.' Serailler reached in his pocket. 'I brought you an orange. Here, catch.'

The bright-coloured ball slapped into Halifax's palm. he closed his fingers around it.

When Ivan stopped by later, Halifax told him for the first time about Henry.

'I didn't know you had brothers.' When Halifax didn't answer, Ivan kept talking. 'So this man Henry told you to come home a hero or not to come home at all?'

'Pretty much.'

'Why didn't you ever tell me?'

'I don't like to think about it.'

Ivan breathed out sharply through his nose. 'All this time, and you're still keeping secrets from me.'

'I don't like to *think* about it!' Halifax shouted so loud, his voice left a ringing in his ears.

Five days later, he was standing in front of a major up in Casablanca, leaning on a cane. It was dark in the major's office. The shutters stayed closed. The major told Halifax he had just arrived in Africa. He sweated so much in the heat that his uniform looked a shade darker than Halifax's.

'Have a seat, Private.' He thumbed through the report that Serailler had telegraphed him from Mogador. 'Good stuff.' He nodded as he read. 'We're very proud of you. We did have a relatively full-blown ceremony set up. At least, we did until yesterday.'

'What happened yesterday, sir?' He didn't look at the officer. Instead, he examined the brass buttons on his dress tunic. Each button had LÉGION ÉTRANGÈRE stamped on the metal.

'Someone got a look at your service record.' He set down the papers. 'You know what I'm talking about. The desertion, the court martial, and so on and so on.'

'Yes, sir.' Halifax wanted to get on a truck and go back to Mogador.

'It's too bad. it's really too bad. You had a *perfect* service record. Exemplary! If you'd stayed on after the war instead of running away like that, I'd be the one saluting you and not the other way around. What made you do a thing like that?'

'I was trying to . . .'

'Look,' The major sat back and sighed. 'You were recommended for the Croix de Guerre with silver palms, but the Legion isn't going to give it to you. It doesn't hand out medals to deserters, no matter how well they perform their duty later on.' He laughed. 'Usually they aren't alive to perform it. Personally . . . Well, what good does it do you to hear what I think personally? Your recommendation still stands, of course, and the men are grateful and proud of what you accomplished. It's quite ironic, don't you think?'

'Sir?' Halifax wished the man would shut up and drown in his sweat.

'It's just a bit ironic. I mean, a deserter killing deserters. If anything, I thought you'd stick together.' He laughed again. 'That would make more sense to me.'

'Yes, sir.' Halifax stared at the floor.

'We did talk to your garrison commander, this Captain Serailler. We asked whether he thought we should perhaps reduce your sentence, so to speak. Allow you to leave the service.'

Halifax's head snapped up.

The major clicked his thumbnail against his front teeth. 'But your captain didn't seem to think it was a good idea. Since it's his decision, we had to go along with it. Presumably he had his reason.'

'Reason?' Halifax's throat dried out in the last couple of seconds. He croaked at the major. 'What reason?'

'Didn't think you were doing your job well enough the rest of the time, I suppose. But it doesn't matter, does it? What's done is done.'

Halifax travelled back that night. He and the driver were the only ones on the truck, so Halifax sat up front. They talked for a while and then fell quiet.

At two in the morning, they stopped at a village and bought skewers of meat cooked on an olive-wood fire. They ate while standing around the embers, their faces orange in the glow. The smoke smelled like church incense. The Milky Way ran in a smudge across the whole sky. Halifax had never seen it so clear. Before he climbed back into the truck, he heard an aircraft engine in the distance. At first he couldn't see the plane. Then a

144

star flickered as something passed in front of it. He made out the shape of the machine, black on dark blue sky.

'It's the mail plane.' The driver climbed into the truck. 'He's on his way to Tangiers from Dakar. He flies along the coast. I hear him sometimes when I stop here. I make this damn trip twice a week.'

'I thought he was coming in from the sea.'

The man laughed. 'Where from? America?'

'No.' Halifax climbed in and shut the door. 'No, I didn't think that.'

For a long time they sat saying nothing. Trees lined the road, filing past into the dark. Then Halifax started laughing.

The driver looked across. 'What's so funny?'

Halifax kept laughing. An idea had broken through his tiredness and the pain of his wound and left him wide awake.

After a while, the driver began to giggle. He slapped the steering wheel and grinned and handed over a flask of rotten brandy. They drank it all in a couple of minutes. Then they rolled down the windows and sang. Their voices slipped out across empty countryside.

'No medal?' Serailler sat with his boots up on his desk. 'Oh, that's too bad. I was sure they'd give you one. You should have told me that when you first got back. I haven't seen you in days. So how's your leg? Getting better?'

'They were going to let me go.' Halifax ground the brass cane tip into the floor.

'What do you mean, "let you go"?' Serailler folded his lips around the last three words.

'Let me get out of here.'

'Oh.' Serailler nodded.

'You told them not to.'

'I never did.'

'I saw the report. I *saw* –'

'Now, wait a minute.' Serailler took his feet off the desk.

'You told them I wasn't doing my job.'

'Those were confidential documents.' Serailler waved his finger. 'I'm going to have a word with those clowns in Casablanca.'

'You said I didn't deserve to be set loose.'

'Listen, Charlie –'

145

'You listen.' Halifax leaned across the desk and breathed in his face. 'I wrote down some things while I was gone.'

'What sort of things. Poetry?'

'I wrote down everything I know about you and your business and the Touaregs and the fishermen who come in here from the Canary Islands and where you put your guns and how much you sell them for. That's what I wrote down.'

Halifax hadn't slept for a couple of days. Something had locked in his head that wouldn't let him close his eyes. So instead he spent hours thinking out the way he would lie to Serailler. He measured each path it could take, digging his way into Serailler's mind.

'And what did you do with this little story of yours?' Serailler spoke very quietly, folding his hands like someone at prayer.

'I gave it to someone.'

'Who? Who the fuck did you give it to?'

'A friend.'

Now Serailler stood. His face was red. 'You don't *have* any friends! Get out of here. I don't have time to fuck around.'

'In one week, my friend will deliver that letter to the special investigating unit in Marseille.'

Serailler cackled. 'You idiot.' He ground his palms together. 'You small-time crook. No one will believe you. It would be my word against yours.' He kicked over his chair. 'I'll fucking ruin you for this!'

Halifax tried to stay calm. He watched Serailler closely, ready to grab the man's throat if he went for the gun in his desk. 'They'll believe me, Serailler. It answers all their questions. They'll see how it all fits together. How can they not believe me? It's the truth.'

Serailler's nostrils were twitching. 'You didn't do this. This is just a joke you're playing on your old pal Serailler. Tell me that's what it is.'

'This is no fooling around.'

'But you'd be signing your own execution warrant.'

'I've told them you forced me.'

'They won't care about that.'

'Don't think about me, Serailler. Think about yourself. How long do you think you'll get in prison? Twenty years? The rest of your life? Will they let you live at all?'

The captain mashed his heel into the tile floor.

Halifax nodded. He knew the pictures that were unravelling in Serailler's head. He had seen them in advance. 'Do they still have oubliettes?'

Serailler stared. 'Why are you doing this to me?'

'They were going to let me go.'

'But Charlie. I'll sign your papers, Charlie. There's just been a misunderstanding.' Serailler smiled and held his hand out.

Halifax swatted it away. 'You've been saying that for years.'

'Just keep working for me, Charlie. Just a little longer. I'm your ticket out of here.' Serailler talked softly now. 'Remember that.'

'If my friend doesn't hear from me within a week, the letter *will* be delivered. Do you understand, Serailler?'

Very slowly, Serailler lowered himself into his chair. 'So what do you want?'

'The first thing I want is my discharge papers. Now, not later. Not in just a little while. And I want fifteen thousand francs.'

Serailler swept his arm across his desk, shoving piles of paper and the camel skull onto the floor. For a second he glared at his empty desk top, as if he couldn't understand where everything had gone. 'Are you out of your mind, Halifax? Do you think I'd give you that kind of money even if I had it?'

'You have it. I'm the one who's been lugging your gold all these years. You have enough to give me what I'm asking for and still buy your farm in Normandy and never work another day in your life.'

'Look at you, Halifax.' Serailler's finger was jabbing at the air. 'You're an old crippled convict who comes busting into my office and ordering me around. Me!' He jabbed his thumb against his chest. 'Nobody gives me orders. I have friends, Halifax. They do what I tell them to do.'

'They bury people up to their necks in the sand out at Cap Sim.'

'Yes. That's exactly what they do. And what about *your* friends? Will they stand by you?' He rubbed the tips of his fingers together. 'Will they take a bribe? Will they do what you tell them to do?'

'One week, Serailler.'

Serailler's Adam's apple bobbed in his throat. 'I never did like you, Halifax. I never liked you and I never knew why and now I know.'

147

'One week.'

'I can't do it in a week.'

'That's unfortunate.' Halifax backed up toward the door.

'I can't do it, I said! I need more time!'

'There's one more thing, Serailler. I want you to sign discharge papers for Ivan as well.'

'Ivan?'

'He's coming, too.'

'Oh, you sons of bitches.' Serailler shook his head. 'Why is this happening to me?'

'You did what?'

'You heard.' Halifax locked the door to his room and slid a chair under the doorknob. Then he took the Lebel out of its holster and set it on the floor in front of him. He knew he'd be sleeping with his eyes open from now until the time he left Mogador.

Ivan worked up enough spit to talk. 'Did he actually give you the money? Did he actually sign the papers?'

'He will.' Halifax folded his arms across his chest. 'I know he will. And then we're going to win the Orteig Prize.'

Ivan pressed his hands to his face. Then he dragged his fingertips down his cheeks, leaving red lines in the skin. 'Why the hell do you want to win that?'

'What's the matter?' His eyes were growing used to the dark. 'Has someone already flown across the Atlantic? Did they already award the prize?'

Ivan shook his head. 'Not yet.' He looked at the chair jamming the door shut.

'Don't you think we can do it?'

'Of course!' Now Ivan was smiling. 'I'm sure as soon as we register for the Orteig Prize, all of those big names – Fokker, Fonck, Sikorsky – all of them will just roll over and *give* us the prize money! Why don't we just jump in the Spad and leave right now? There's only one seat, so I hope it's all right if I sit on your lap.' He sucked in a breath of air. 'Did you think about the plane, Charlie? Did you think about the machinery needed to make a journey like that?'

'Yes, I did. We'll make the crossing in one of those Levasseurs, the kind Garros arrived in. We'll buy one. You said yourself that Levasseur is a private company. The planes can be bought.'

Ivan pinched the bridge of his nose. 'It wouldn't have the fuel capacity.'

'So modify it. Take out everything we wouldn't need and fit extra fuel tanks. You said you could modify the Levasseur for carrying bombs, remember? Then you were going to shove Abdel Krim back to the Red Sea. Modify it for extra fuel instead. Surely you can do that.'

'Why do you need me? If you have it all planned out, why drag me into it?'

'I need a good mechanic. For Christ's sake, Ivan, who else am I going to ask? And I'll need a navigator for the flight. I can get us out of here, Ivan.'

'You can get us killed is what you can do. If you're sure it will work, why have you got us barricaded in here? Why is that gun lying on the floor?'

'For making sure.'

'Well, you're not the only one who's going to be making sure. Jesus, Charlie, did you really write a letter and leave it with someone up in Casa?' Before Halifax could answer, he held up his hands. 'Don't tell me. I don't want to know.'

'There are good doctors in America. Maybe they can cure Justine.'

Ivan raised his eyebrows. 'How did you know she was sick?'

'She told me before she told you.'

'She could have let me know first. At least she could have done that.'

'She was asking my advice. She didn't know if she should marry you.'

'Oh, she told you that as well, did she?'

'She won't get better here in Mogador. In America she has a chance. If we win the Orteig Prize, we can buy her the best care in the world.'

'And if we don't win it, we'll be dead.'

'I'm going, Ivan. No one's forcing you to come. I just can't stay here anymore.'

'You'd make the flight from Paris?'

'Right. Paris to New York or New York to Paris. That's what it's all about.'

'If Serailler finds a way out of this, I'll deny everything. I'll tell him I don't know a thing about your plan. I mean it, Charlie. It's self-preservation.'

'Does that mean you'll come?' Halifax felt his jaw muscles twitch.

'Don't smile!' Ivan made fists. 'There's nothing to smile about yet. Why can't we just get our discharges and take a damn ship across. Why can't we do that, Charlie?'

'Because it's the difference between going back with something and going back with nothing! I want to have something to show for all the time I've been away.'

'You're an idiot! *I'm* an idiot. And if Justine stays with me after all of this, then she's an idiot, too!' Ivan pulled the chair away from the door and walked out into the blinding sun.

For two days Halifax didn't sleep. He stayed in his room and didn't eat. Didn't wash. Didn't shave. He sat on his bed with the Lebel loaded and oiled and he thought about Serailler.

After two nights with no rest, it seemed to Halifax that he could even hear Serailler's thoughts. Angry whispers called to him from the hollow walls and whistled through the shuttered windows. Each puff of wind that rattled the door made him grab for the Lebel. He almost shot the chambermaid.

The owner of the hotel stayed out of sight. Halifax began to imagine tunnels and corridors inside the walls where the owner scuttled like a rat after dark. Peepholes appeared and disappeared.

On the night of the third day, Halifax walked out onto his balcony, still limping from the wound but no longer using the cane. He felt dizzy, so he lay down on the tiles and closed his eyes. I'm not tired, he told himself. I'm ready for anything. Just try and sneak up on me. Just go ahead and try.

After a few minutes of listening for footsteps above the rumble of the waves, he fell asleep. He had no more strength for wading through his calculations. Nothing could keep him awake, not even the thought of Serailler crawling through the shadows, bristling with knives and poison and guns.

Ivan brought him food. He took the revolver before Halifax could even wake up.

They sat on the tiles eating melon and bread.

'What did Justine say when you told her about the Orteig prize?' Halifax slit the melon in half with a boot knife and gouged out the mild-white seeds.

'She said she'd marry me.'

'Congratulations.'

'She said she would, but not straightaway. She said she'd wait until you and I have reached America. Then she'll take a ship across to meet us.'

'She'll definitely come?'

Ivan shrugged. 'She said she would.'

'And you?' Halifax packed a slab of warm bread into his mouth and followed it with water from a tin mug.

Ivan changed the subject. 'The militiamen at the commissariat say that Serailler hasn't come out of his office in two days. They say he sits in there and talks to himself. Sometimes he beats at the walls and they can hear him dragging his nails across his desk.'

'Do they know what's going on?'

Ivan shook his head. 'They think he went mad a long time ago. None of this surprises them.'

'So nothing's happened?' Halifax swallowed the bread. It slid in a knot down his throat.

'Something has happened, but I don't know if it's something good or something bad. It seems that this morning he opened the shutters of his office and stood there looking down at the courtyard. For a long time he just stood there. Then he ordered his staff car to be fuelled up. As soon as that was done, he drove off in it by himself.'

'He's gone to Casa to get the money.'

'Maybe.'

'At least now that he's gone, I can relax a bit.'

'No, Charlie. No, you can't. You can't relax until we set down that Levasseur in New York harbour. Do you understand?' Ivan picked up half the melon and sank his teeth into it.

'I need to know, Ivan. Are you with me in this or not?' His back hurt from sleeping on the tiles.

Ivan looked up from the melon rind. He said nothing. Melon juice dripped from his beard-stubbly chin.

Serailler returned the next day. He sent for Halifax as soon as he arrived.

Halifax walked into Serailler's office and shut the door. He pulled out the Lebel and aimed it at Serailler. On the desk was a leather satchel, the same one Halifax used for carrying photographs. Serailler looked at the gun. 'There's no need for that.'

Halifax could feel his elbows shaking. He lowered the Lebel. Serailler slid the satchel across the desk. When Halifax made no move to touch it, he unbuckled the straps and emptied out the money.

Serailler counted out the bundles, flipping through the notes so that Halifax could see it was all there; fifteen thousand francs in bundles of a thousand. 'This is just a loan, Halifax.' The green of arsenic treatments glimmered under his eyes. 'I have decided to treat this strictly as a loan.' Then he stood up and held out his hand. 'A gentleman's agreement.'

Halifax's muscles were cramped. He stuffed the Lebel in its holster and began to pile the money back into the satchel. His eyes hurt from the strain of looking all around the room.

Serailler kept his hand held out. He said again, 'A gentleman's agreement.'

'Where are the discharge papers?'

Serailled reached into his coat pocket.

Halifax pulled the gun out, pointed it in Serailler's face and cocked the hammer. Sweat burned on his chest and under his arms.

Serailler tried to stay calm. 'Do you want your papers or not?'

'Mine and Ivan's. Now.'

Serailler pulled them out and removed them from their envelopes. The cream-coloured paper was covered with Serailler's tidy, blue-inked handwriting. Halifax holstered the pistol.

He read something about combat stress and wounds on the piece with his name at the top and then something about long service and honourable discharge on Ivan's piece. At the bottom of each sheet was a red seal with the stamp of the Mogador garrison squashed into the wax.

Once more, Serailler held out his hand. 'This is just another piece of business for me.' He seemed to be struggling with the nerves in his face, as if at any moment he would no longer be able to control them. 'That's all it is for me, you understand. Now, this letter. It will . . . it will not . . . ah.' He scratched at the back of his neck.

'As long as nothing happens between now and the end of the week, Serailler.'

'I won't go to prison, you know. I won't let them lock me away.'

'You won't have to.'

Serailler gave a short nod. Then he went to his cabinet and brought out the cheap cognac.

Halifax kept his hand on the butt of the Lebel.

Serailler poured out two glassfuls. 'I was thinking about a standard rate of interest for the loan.' When Halifax's eyes met his, he tipped his head back and drank off the cognac.

By the time Halifax left the room, tears were running down Serailler's cheeks.


Ivan packed and repacked his one suitcase. First he tried to take everything he owned. He had boxes filled with old engine parts. There were mangled bullets that he'd pulled from the Spads. A frayed bow tie. An ashtray from the Café Napoléon in Paris. In the end, he threw it all away.

Justine spent her time sitting at the Dimitri. She drank glass after glass of mint tea. Sometimes she bowed her head forward and closed her eyes. The veins on her neck stood out and she reached up her sleeve for a handkerchief. She coughed as quietly as she could into the white cloth, speckling it with blood. Her eyes looked watery and she trembled with the force of convulsions moving through her.

Halifax still couldn't sleep. The gridded wooden butt of the Lebel had worn a permanent red crisscross in the palm of his hand. He dragged his bed in front of the door and spent his nights peering out through the keyhole to see if anyone was coming.

'I'm waaaiting,' he mumbled to himself in the dingy room, listening for the truck to pull into town. 'I'm waiting for the truck to Casablaaaanca, and if I wait any longer I'm going to go out of my miiiind.'


The day they left, Serailler stood on the road that led out of Mogador. He stood watching them and didn't wave goodbye.

Halifax thought about Serailler, alone now with the militiamen he'd been throwing across the commissariat courtyard for all these years. Halifax wondered if they'd rip the man apart.

Serailler was wondering too.

'He won't be alone for long.' Ivan squinted through dust

kicked up by the truck. 'Those replacement pilots are due in from El Jadida within a couple of days.'

They watched Serailler grow smaller and smaller as the truck drove away from the town. His face seemed to lose its features. Soon it was only a pink ball against the khaki all around. Then the dust swallowed him and he popped out of sight.

Two days later, they were standing on the deck of a ferryboat to Algeciras, in Spain. Tangiers wallowed in the distance, a pile of bleached bones riding the waves.

The land disappeared slowly into the sea. When it had gone, pyres of heat haze still rippled in the air, rising up through hard blue sky.

# Part Two

## Paris

### February 1927

# 11

HALIFAX SAT IN the cockpit. He kept very quiet and still. The plane's engine hadn't been installed yet. If he hunched down in his seat, he could see out through the front of the fuselage. A breeze blew in from the fields.

Footsteps and talking echoed around him. He listened to the creak of wooden lids prised off boxes, nails groaning as they came loose. He heard the rustle of hay used for packing material as the men pulled it out in bunches and threw it on the floor. Men grunted as they lifted aircraft parts from the boxes and set them down again.

Halifax looked up at the rafters of the barn. Dust shaken from the hay twisted around the beams.

He and Ivan had rented the place from a farmer two days earlier, as soon as they signed purchase papers for the Levasseur. The barn lay just outside the town of Le Bourget, a couple of miles from Paris.

The Levasseur was easy to buy. The company sold them one that had been returned by the navy for structural repairs. They corrected the faults and sold it to Halifax for less than he thought he'd have to pay. The whole business took two days. Halifax had walked into the company's office in a rented suit and told them what he wanted to do. Half an hour later, he was making a test flight over the city. The next day he paid for the plane in cash and it was delivered, wings removed, to the barn.

'Where did he go?' Ivan shuffled through the dropped straw, talking to the Levasseur delivery men. 'He has to sign these delivery papers. Did you see him?'

Halifax heard him click his tongue and slap his hand against his thigh.

'Jesus,' Ivan said.

Halifax stayed in the cockpit, not letting them know he was there. The walls of the fuselage curved up around him. Metal, cold against the pads of his fingertips. The co-pilot's seat was a mass of wickerwork beside him. In a minute I'll come out, he thought. In another minute.

A car pulled up outside the barn. It's engine rattled quiet. A man in a long coat got out and walked into the barn. Halifax watched him through the gap where the engine should have been. Wires hung down from electrical connections. The man stood with his gloved hands folded across his stomach, waiting to be greeted. He nodded and smiled and tried to catch someone's eye. Two people in overalls moved past him, carrying a crate. He stepped aside, smiling and nodding. He took off his coat and wiped his sleeve across his forehead.

'Why can't *I* sign them?' Ivan stood somewhere beyond the wall of the cockpit. 'What's wrong with *my* signature? Really? Well, fine. You find him.' Footsteps outside the barn.

Halifax breathed in the smell of the straw. It peppered his nose. I'll be there in a minute, he thought.

The man in the long coat breathed so loudly and deeply that Halifax could hear him. 'I am looking for Charles Halifax!'

One of the Levasseur delivery men walked up to him with a clipboard and muttered. The man took off his hat and wiped his forehead again. 'I'm not him. I'm looking for him.'

Halifax stood up in the cockpit. 'Here.'

Ivan was in the shadows, a cigarette stuck in his mouth, studying the man. Then he sucked the last smoke from his cigarette and stamped it dead on the floor.

'Philippe Merlot.' The man strode towards Halifax, who had climbed down from the plane and now stood with his hands in his pockets, watching the man come close.

'Charlie Halifax.' He pulled one hand from his pocket. His palm was dirty with engine grease.

'I know who you are.' Merlot smiled. 'I have an invitation for you from Mme. de Montclaire. She's the social director of the Paris Aero Club. There's a function tonight and she would like you and Mr. Konovalchik to be there. The press will be around. We all need good publicity.'

Halifax wiped the engine grease onto the chest of his overalls. 'Yes, I'm sure we do.'

'Seven o'clock. Formal. Shall I tell her you're coming?'

'You may as well, Mr. Merlot.' He looked around for Ivan, needing to see the familiar face.

Halifax peered into the crowded hall. The huge room blistered with punch bowls. 'I'll be damned,' he said.

'May I kiss your scar?' A woman stood in the doorway. She was packed into a black silk dress.

'Beg your pardon?' Halifax looked past her. The band's music was almost lost in the rattle of talk. The music worried him.

'Your scar. May I kiss it?'

'Do you have to?' The thunder of voices worried him, too.

'Yes! Yes!' She took one uneven step forward. 'It's a *must!*' After squashing her lips against his cheek, the woman stood back and clapped her hands together. 'Now, why have you come so late? It's past eleven, you know.'

'We had a hard time finding tuxedoes.' Halifax tried to smile. He and Ivan had fallen asleep on the floor of the barn and only woke up at ten o'clock. Justine stayed behind at the hotel room they had rented for her.

Halifax caught sight of Philippe Merlot, who stood under a banner that stretched across the hall. On the banner, in blue and gold letters, was AERO CLUB DE PARIS. Merlot grinned and waved, then dunked his glass into a bowl of red punch and walked across the polished floor. 'With me it was my wrist. When she first met me, I'd just broken my wrist playing tennis and all she wanted to do was kiss the bandage.' He sipped at his drink. 'That's Mme. de Montclaire. She can kiss anything she wants.'

Halifax's tuxedo didn't fit. Ivan's fitted worse. They had rented them an hour before the function and changed in the bathroom at the Gare du Nord.

'You're working on a Levasseur. Why'd you pick that?' Merlot rocked on his heels.

Ivan cleared his throat. 'Easiest to modify. Lots of fuselage space not being used in the present design. We're hoping to reconstruct the fuel system.' It was as if Ivan had never considered any doubts, as if there were no doubts to consider. He had made up a speech in the taxi on their way to the Aero Club. Now he twisted his hand in the air, shaping his words as they came out. 'We hope . . . we hope to make the crossing within a couple of months. It's a small plane, we realize this, but then we're not trying to send over a hotel.'

'Of course.' Merlot agreed in a very loud voice. 'I'm very interested in flying.'

'Are you a pilot?' Halifax watched Merlot shuffle his feet.

'No. I make clothes for people. Special clothes. You know, people who are too fat to buy their trousers at a regular shop, they come to me. Clothes for midgets. Whatever people want.'

Ivan nodded slowly. 'So are you training to be a pilot?'

'No. But I'm very interested.' Merlot made a sweep of his arm across the hall, keeping his drink in the glass. 'Most of the people here are only curious. Half of them would wet their pants if you took them up in a plane. Me included.'

'Have you always been interested in flying?'

'No, not really. But flying's the big thing this year. The pilot idea is big in clothes this year. You know, flying jackets, white silk scarves. The Aero Club's membership has doubled in the last six months. Last year the big thing was motor cars. They owned this hall last year. All everybody talked about was the Grand Prix. This year it's planes. Probably someone else will own the hall next year.'

When Merlot had gone, Halifax turned to Ivan. 'Don't tell them when we're planning to go. If you do that, they'll start a countdown.'

'We don't want to tell them we hardly have any money left, either.'

'No. I suppose there's quite a few things we don't want to tell them.'

They walked to a table and sat down. It was the only free spot in the hall. A man had passed out with his face on the white tablecloth.

Ivan picked up the man's hand and looked at his wristwatch. 'Past midnight. Was Paris much different in the war, Charlie?'

'I can't really say. After all, we've only been here a week, and most of that time I've spent in that little barn or in the Levasseur company office.'

'But from what you've seen so far.'

Halifax glanced around the hall. 'Well, it wasn't any less noisy. There always seemed to be parties going on. But we could never get enough drink or tobacco. You had to go without things like milk in your morning coffee. In fact, most of the time you had to go without your morning coffee. I only came here a couple of times on leave. I spent my time in a bar called the Chatham or sometimes in the lobby of the Hôtel de Crillon. You could always find some Americans there. It was the only place I knew where they'd still sell drinks in the air raids. There were air raids every night I stayed in Paris. After a while, it became just another background noise. I remember seeing a German Gotha bomber shot down and crashed on one of the bridges over the Seine. It was all in bits and pieces on the road. People were taking home odds and ends as souvenirs. I don't know, Ivan. I never calmed down enough to get a good look at the place. Whenever I came here, it was to blow off steam. I was always thinking about when I'd be flying again. The whole city was like that. It seemed as if everyone was just passing through. They were all thinking about going back to the front.'

A hand appeared on the shoulder of the passed-out man. 'Come on, Stu.' The owner of the hand spoke English with an American accent. On his chest was a white badge that said PRESSE in red letters. He shook the passed-out man, then smiled at Ivan and Halifax. 'This is my friend Stu. Get up, Stu. Time to go home.'

Stu fell off his chair.

Halifax helped the newsman lift Stu back into his seat. 'Looks like Stu's had a long day.'

The newsman stood back and smiled. 'You're Charlie Halifax. They said you'd be here tonight.'

'Right.'

'You don't remember me, do you?' The man was heavy and had jowls.

Halifax squinted at his face. 'No. Sorry.'

'Doesn't matter.' The man tried to keep smiling. He looked a little hurt. 'It's been a long time.'

'How long?' Halifax sat down.

'Nineteen eighteen.'

Stu muttered something, then slid forward onto the table again. His forehead cracked against the wood.

'Well.' Halifax offered the newsman a chair. 'Who are you?'

The man pulled an old photograph from his wallet. It showed a pilot standing next to a Spad. Painted on the plane was the flying stork insignia of the Seventy-third Escadrille.

Halifax held the picture close to his eyes. Then he took his glasses out of his pocket and put them on. He studied the face that grinned from the yellow-brown paper. He looked up. 'Tuttle?'

'Hello there, Charlie.'

'Will Tuttle!' Halifax started to laugh. 'You're so . . . I mean, you've really . . .'

'I'm fat.'

'Yes!'

'I was just too thin before.' Tuttle drummed his fingers on the table.

Halifax turned to Ivan. 'Ivan, this is William Tuttle. I flew with him during the war. He was in the Lafayette Air Corps.'

Tuttle was smiling again. 'Then I was transferred out and Charlie stayed behind. What did you say your name was?'

'Ivan Konovalchik.'

'Ivan's the co-pilot.' Halifax rummaged in his head for pictures of Tuttle. As hard as he tried, he couldn't take the thin shape of the Tuttle he remembered and expand him into the chubby man he saw now.

'Pleased to see you, Charlie.' Tuttle slapped him on the arm.

'What are you doing here? What are you doing in Paris?'

'I never went home.' Tuttle looked embarrassed. 'I work for the *Herald Tribune* now. The newspaper. I'm one of their chief editors.'

'I never went home, either. I stayed on with the Legion and went to Africa.'

'Ah-ha.' He nodded.

'I was in a crash. I got burned up.'

'Yeah.' Tuttle looked down at his drink.

In the first few seconds, Halifax had thought they'd be talking for hours, but already they had fallen almost silent.

'I'd like to do a story on you, Charlie. And you, too, Mr. Konovalchik, of course.'

Stu lifted his face from the table. 'Hello?'

'Stu's also with the *Tribune*, aren't you, Stu?' Tuttle held Stu's head in one hand and slapped him gently on the cheek with the other, trying to wake him up. 'How does that sound, Charlie? About the story, I mean.'

'Think it will do me some good?'

'Your backers will love it.'

'Backers?'

'Right. Whoever's putting up the money. Who is, by the way?'

'I am.' Ivan rubbed his hands together.

'I see.' Tuttle reached in Stu's pockets until he found a pencil.

162

He began to write on a small pad of paper. 'What nationality are you, Mr. Konovalchik?'

'Russian.'

'One of the new Soviets?'

'No. An old one.'

Halifax and Ivan had already agreed that Ivan would tell people he put up the money. They conjured up questions and answered them, weaving the story, cutting out the name of Serailler and his gold coins and the blue-cloaked Touaregs. They juggled lies into the truth until they were barely sure themselves where the two parts joined.

Stu yawned. 'Where's Mme. de Montclaire?'

'I don't know, Stu. Go find her.' Tuttle waved him away.

Stu got to his feet. 'She took my press badge. She said she simply had to have it. She said it was a must.' He wobbled off into the crowd.

Tuttle watched him go. 'I should look after him. He's not always like this. He's looked after me a couple of times. Say, how about I get some more information when I come out to see your plane?'

Halifax wrote down the directions to their barn on a piece of paper. 'We'll go up in the Levasseur. It'll be just like before.'

Tuttle smiled, the smile growing crooked and eventually falling away. 'I hope not.'

Halifax shook Tuttle's hand. It was a strong hand, with strong sausage fingers. He wondered how fingers like those could ever work a typewriter. 'Long time, Will.'

'Time enough for me to get like this!' Tuttle slapped his belly and laughed. Then he went looking for Stu.

The taxi drove through the empty streets. Silver balls of rain broke on the windshield.

'Was Tuttle a good friend of yours?'

Halifax lit himself a cigarette. 'I can't remember anymore.' He breathed in the smoke and felt it smooth out his thoughts.

Ivan took the cigarette, inhaled and gave it back. 'You know, I haven't done much flying. I wasn't trained as a pilot, just as a mechanic.'

'But you know how to take bearings and follow a chart. And you can fix what's fixable in the air.'

'Sure.'

163

'That's all I need you for.'

'I'm a little nervous about flying. That's what I'm trying to tell you.'

'You'll get over it.'

Ivan got out in the town of Le Bourget. They had rented a room there for Justine, in a hotel called the Châtelet.

Halifax's taxi dropped him off at the end of the muddy road. He walked down to the barn, trouser legs tucked into his socks so as not to dirty the tux. Inside, he bent a piece of copper wire into a coat hanger and hung his suit from the Levasseur's propeller piston.

Rain trampled on the roof. He lit the gas heater and lay down on a blanket in front of it. The taste of punch and cigarettes was sour in his mouth. After a while, he got up and climbed into the cockpit of the Levasseur. The glass covers of the instrument panel caught a vague grey light. Everything else stayed dark. He imagined vast plains of ocean stretching out beneath him.

He thought of Fokker and Fonck, Sikorsky and the others, saw himself scrabbling against everything they knew, against their money and against the time they had already put into the crossing. He thought of the outdated Spads he'd been flying across the Sahara, of technological advances he had never even seen but that others would be taking for granted. He saw his own plan balanced on threads of glass.

Exhaustion cradled him, and his body began to close down. Dreaming of flying, his dreams still peppered blue with the thoughts he brought from Africa. He slipped through tatters of cloud into sleep.

Most nights, Ivan stayed with Justine at the hotel and walked out to the barn first thing in the morning. The times he slept at the barn, he and Halifax would cover themselves with horse blankets and lie beside the gas heater.

Halifax stayed in the barn every night. He didn't like being away from the Levasseur. He couldn't sleep unless the broad white belly of the plane stood in front of him whenever he opened his eyes.

Halifax was still asleep when Tuttle arrived in his car. Tuttle wore a gabardine raincoat, and on a strap around his shoulder he carried a camera.

164

Still wrapped in the blanket, Halifax walked in circles around the plane, running his hands along the white fuselage. 'The structure is mostly sealed plywood, water-tight.'

Tuttle followed him, making notes on a grey pad of paper.

Halifax ducked under the engine casing and stood up on the other side. 'It's powered by a four-hundred-and-fifty-horse-power, water-cooled Lorraine-Dietrich engine. We plan to store almost nine hundred gallons of fuel in aluminum-alloy tanks centred between the wings. The wingspan will be forty-eight feet. As you can see, it has an open cockpit. The landing gear will jettison on take-off and the plane will set down in New York harbour.'

'All right.' Tuttle wrote it down. 'So much for the plane. How about you? Why are you trying to go from Paris to New York rather than start out at home?'

'Why are you a journalist in Paris instead of New York?'

Tuttle sighed and put away the note pad. 'I'm only doing my job, Charlie. People will want to know why you aren't starting from the other side.'

'Because I'm going home. I can't go home if I'm already there. Besides, I want to make the crossing in the Levasseur, and since that's a French plane, I thought I should try from the French side. How's that for an answer?'

'Fine. What about the Russian? What's he getting out of it?'

'Money. The Orteig Prize.' Halifax was stiff from sleeping in the cockpit. 'He gets to go to America.'

'Do you really think you have a chance?'

Halifax shrugged and eased himself down on the floor. 'I've been flying for a long time now. I just haven't had my name in the paper very much.' You have to look confident, he told himself. You have to look in control.

Tuttle took the camera from around his shoulder and gestured with it for Halifax to stand in front of the Levasseur. 'Let's do one of these.'

'How's Stu?'

'Stu is in his apartment with a pillow on his head. Stu is not very well today.'

Halifax heard the thump of the camera flash and went blind in the clap of magnesium. 'What happened to you when you left the Lafayette? I never saw you after that.' Tuttle closed up the camera.

'I flew out of Amiens for a month, then they promoted me to captain and made me an instructor. After the war, I quit the forces but stayed in France.' He scratched at his head. 'I probably couldn't tell you exactly why. I guess I just didn't have anything to go back for.'

'Do you miss the States?'

'Oh, sure. Baseball. Decent steaks. There must be a few other things. I have what I want here. Being away from home like this, I end up being more American than most Americans. It's a funny thing.'

After a moment of quiet, Tuttle pulled out his note pad again. 'I'd better write all this down before I forget. I'll see you at the Aero Club.' He jerked his eyebrows up and down. 'Where the élite meet to eat.'

Halifax stood in the shadows, hearing Tuttle start up his car. Perhaps he really doesn't know about my court-martial, Halifax thought. About my running away. Maybe the news never reached him. The tribunal must have kept things quiet. It would have been an embarrassment to broadcast the court-martial. They'd only just given me a medal, after all. Halifax stepped from the shadows and waved as Tuttle drove down the muddy road. White light from the camera flash stayed carved in full moons on his eyes.

Three days later, the *Herald Tribune* published an article about them. The headline read, 'A New Contender'. Under that was 'The Great Homecoming of Charlie Halifax.' In the picture, the Levasseur looked sad and naked without wings or a prop – the picked-over carcass of a huge bird. Halifax stood under the carcass. The grey and black of the picture made the barn rafters look like the rib cage of an animal that had swallowed him and the Levasseur.

The barn used to house a pair of tractors in the front section and horses in the rear. A partition wall had been knocked down to make room for the Levasseur. The farmer left equipment hanging from nails, pitchforks and a leather yoke for a plough horse, cans of oil, a workbench on which a vice had been bolted and left to rust. It all smelled of machine oil and manure. After living for a week in the barn, Halifax smelled of the same things.

Sometimes in the mornings, the farmer went walking in his cabbage field. His name was Deschamps. He wore knee-length rubber boots and trod through the mud down his alleyways of cabbages, head hidden under a floppy hat. He set out traps for rabbits, which invaded his field at night and chewed up his crop. They were old traps, with two semicircular clamps whose jagged edges closed together like jaws when a rabbit stepped on the trigger plate. He carried the dead rabbits and traps over his shoulder, a tangle of fur and chain and iron teeth crunched shut. At night, over the sound of rain that always seemed to fall after dark, Halifax often heard the crack of traps and the squeal of rabbits caught in the field.

Ivan took a thermos from his satchel. He poured some coffee into a small tin cup and handed it to Halifax, who stared at the black liquid, then looked across at Ivan. Ivan leaned over and looked down at the coffee. 'What's the matter? Is there a bug in it or something?'

'Try to get here a little earlier, can you? It's almost ten o'clock.'

'I got up at seven.'

'Maybe you should get up a little earlier.'

'I do, usually, but then Justine tells me to come back to bed.' Ivan grinned. 'What am I supposed to do?'

'Tell her no.'

Ivan stopped grinning. 'There's no need to rush things.'

'Yes, there is.' Halifax put down the coffee and kneaded his calves. They were sore from sleeping in the cockpit again. He preferred to be there rather than on the floor, where things scuttled in the dark beyond the soft arc of light sent out by the gas heater. 'If we don't hurry, if we don't work all the time, then someone else is going to beat us on the crossing.'

'Look, Charlie.' He pulled a loaf of bread from the satchel and tapped it on Halifax's knee, like a doctor testing reflexes. 'You'll make it to America either way. In fact, it would be a lot safer if you just took the boat. So someone flies there first. So what? Who are you doing this for, anyway? Are you still trying to prove something to your brother Henry?'

'I'm doing this for myself.'

Ivan dropped the bread onto his lap and clasped his hands together. 'Why don't you come out to Normandy with Justine and me this weekend? It's pretty in the spring.'

'No.' Halifax swallowed the coffee and felt it jolt his nerves. 'And you're not going, either. This is something I thought you

167

understood. There won't be any trips to Normandy. No days off. No going back to bed.'

Ivan folded his arms. 'It's going to take both of us to fly this plane. I don't want you giving me orders. All my damn life, all I've ever done is follow orders. First it was school, then it was the Russian army and then it was the Legion. That's the only reason I'm coming with you, so I can find a way out of clicking my heels and obeying every time someone raises their voice to me. You're not thinking about anybody but yourself. It makes you hard to be with, Charlie. And while we're on the subject, why don't you take a bath? You smell like an engine.'

'There's a barrel full of water outside. I wash in it every day.'

'Wash harder.'

Halifax took a bit of bread and let it dissolve in his mouth. He let the quiet grow.

'I need some money.' Ivan stood, knees cracking, and walked across to the Levasseur.

'Why?'

'I took Justine to a doctor, the same doctor she was seeing before she left for Morocco, in fact. I need the money for some medicine he prescribed.'

Halifax pulled out his wallet. 'How much do you need?'

'Two hundred francs.'

'Just for medicine?'

'Actually it's for some clothes as well. She says she would like some new clothes.' Ivan looked down at his boots. 'It wouldn't hurt her to have some, you know.'

Halifax gave him the fifty francs he had in his wallet. Ivan folded the money away in his fist like a magician.

'We don't have money to spare, Ivan. If we win the Orteig Prize, we'll have plenty. But not now.' Halifax stood and walked over to the engine, which hung in a large canvas cradle at one end of the barn. It had to be taken apart and cleaned before they mounted it back in the Levasseur.

The whole day's wasted already, Halifax thought as he stood with his arms folded, staring without seeing the tangle of engine parts. I bet Fokker doesn't waste his days. Or Fonck or Davis or Lindbergh. They're all out there building and testing, spinning their minds while I'm here eating bread and jam. Halifax promised himself no sleep until he'd made up the time. He promised himself no mistakes.

*

The next day, Ivan hadn't shown up by nine. Halifax did as much work as he could without Ivan's help, then started walking up the road to town. At the Hôtel Châtelet, he climbed the back stairs to Justine's room and knocked, trying to catch his breath.

Justine opened the door. She wore a dressing gown and had a towel wrapped around her head like a turban. 'Hello, Charlie. Haven't seen you in days.'

'Where's Ivan?'

'Still asleep.'

'Please wake him up and tell him to come out here.' He tried to smile but only leered at her.

Justine stepped outside and closed the door. 'Why are you in such a hurry all the time, Charlie?' She rested her small hands on his chest. 'Now, you come in and have a cup of cocoa and I'll get us some breakfast and then the three of us can take a bus into Paris and walk through the Tuileries. It's a beautiful day, too good to spend in an old barn.' She took her hands off his chest and held them together as if she were praying. 'Now, how does that sound?'

'Very good. Now could you please wake him and tell him to come out here?'

'Oh, for Christ's sake, Charlie! Go see him yourself!' She stood aside and clicked her tongue as he walked by.

Ivan slept in a cot in a tiny side room. Justine had the main bed.

Ivan was up from his cot, standing by the window in a nightshirt. 'Sorry. I overslept. Sorry.' There was blood on the pillow where Justine's head had been. Four different bottles of pills lay on the bedside table. Ivan worked his hands over his face, still half asleep. 'I'm sorry. We'll work late tonight.'

'No, you won't.' Justine shoved a cup of hot cocoa into Halifax's hand and held out a tangerine. 'You can both damn well take some time off.'

'Justine, we can't.' Ivan took off his nightshirt and began looking for his clothes. 'We have to do the work until it's done.'

'Please. Just this morning. Just for a walk in the sun.' She sat down on the edge of the bed. 'It's not fair that I hardly ever see you, Ivan.'

Ivan pulled on his trousers and wrapped the braces over his shoulders. 'Charlie, you need to go to the Meteorological

Office on the avenue Rapp. You may as well go today. You'll have to spend several hours talking to them anyway. How about if we all take the bus into Paris and we meet you later at the gardens on your way back? No time wasted. How about that, Charlie?'

'Yes.' Justine punched Halifax on the arm. 'How about it, Halifax?'

For several hours, he looked over the shoulder of the head clerk, in the Meteorological Office, following the smooth tracings of the man's finger across the Atlantic. Halifax studied the chart, drumming it into his head, until his eyes were dried out from staring.

He bought weather charts of the North Atlantic from the clerk, rolled them up and carried them down to the Tuileries, where he read them like newspapers. Ivan and Justine were late.

Children wandered around a little pond, where an old man rented small wooden sailboats and sticks for guiding the boats. Other children threw bread crumbs at the waddling pigeons. Then they threw bread crumbs at Halifax.

He couldn't keep his mind on the tiny figures and flowing lines of wind currents on the chart. Instead, he was thinking of his new start in America. But after several minutes, he still hadn't moved beyond the picture of setting his plane down in New York harbour. It seemed to him that as soon as he left the ground and headed west, a machine other than the Levasseur would be carrying him forward. It would thunder into motion and he'd have no way to control it.

He went back to the charts but had no concentration. So he paid the old man for a stick and a wooden boat and ushered it around the pond, sidestepping children and parents. A while later, he looked up and saw Ivan and Justine watching him. They held hands and smiled.

In the taxi on their way back, Halifax felt his cheeks warm from the sun. When they got to the Hôtel Châtelet, Ivan offered to come along to the barn and work, but Halifax said no. Even after all he'd said and the promises he made to himself, just then he couldn't bear dragging Ivan away from Justine and back to the barn. He waved them away and told the man to keep driving.

The taxi man's neck was red and pockmarked. 'What are you doing out at this barn?'

'Building a plane.' Halifax caught the driver's eye in the rearview mirror.

'What for?' He handed back a cigarette and then a lighter.

'I'm going to fly it across the Atlantic.'

The taxi man laughed, then looked in the mirror again. 'Oh.' He covered the laugh with a cough. 'I thought you were making a joke. Where did you learn to fly?'

'In the war.'

'I used to see planes fly over our trenches in the war. Maybe I saw you one time.'

Halifax remembered the uniforms of French soldiers in the trenches, remembered the shape of their helmets, like deerstalker hats, and seeing them wave as he flew overhead. He used to see the soldiers climb from their trenches and advance towards the stone-grey uniforms of the Germans, who loaded and fired their rifles, loaded and fired and loaded and fired. He saw puffs of smoke and figures falling and heard nothing above the even rumble of his Spad's engine. Everything going on below seemed calm and unhurried from a thousand feet up. The only times any noise reached him from the ground was when artillery fired or when he felt the shock of anti-aircraft shells bursting black nearby.

The taxi man dropped Halifax off at the start of the mud road and he walked the rest of the way in the twilight.

From halfway down the road, he saw that the door to the barn was open and knew he hadn't left it that way.

For a moment he stood in the entryway, sweating, hands on his hips. Then he felt something miserable wave up in his chest. Someone had broken into the barn and smashed the Levasseur's radiator grille, then they had cut through the canvas sling so that the engine dropped to the floor. They had broken the windscreen, too. Muddy footprints still showed on the ladder beside the cockpit. Only one person.. One set of footprints. A hammer from the tool chest lay on the floor.

Halifax searched the plane but found no more damage. He paced around the machine, calculating the losses, wondering if the Levasseur people would have replacement parts in stock, figuring how much he'd have to pay.

'Who would do this to me? Who would do this to me?' He sat

cross-legged at the entrance to the barn, knocking the hammer against the concrete floor. The rhythm of iron on stone echoed through the barn. Thoughts raced too fast in his head. He kept his eyes always open, watching for movement, hearing strange sounds in the night.

# 12

'WHAT DO YOU want with a shotgun?' Ivan stood at the entrance to the barn. He still looked half asleep and had done up the buttons on his boiler suit the wrong way.

'See for yourself.' Halifax pointed to the engine.

Ivan checked the damage, silently running his fingers across the dented grille. Halifax stayed sitting on the concrete, shotgun cradled in his arms, extra cartridges set out in front of him.

He'd bought the gun off Deschamps earlier that morning. When he heard Deschamps come around to check his traps, he asked if there was one to sell.

'What?' Deschamps held up a dead rabbit. The jaws of the trap were clamped shut around its neck. 'One of these?'

'No.' Halifax nodded towards the shotgun Deschamps carried under his arm for shooting crows. 'One of those.'

They walked to Deschamps's house at the far end of the cabbage field. It was small and made of stone with a thatched roof. Now and then, Deschamps stopped and scowled. He gave Halifax the same glance as when he rented his barn, not able to believe that someone would want the place.

A cat jumped out the front door as the men walked through.

Deschamps's wife stood at the kitchen table, chopping celery.

Copper pots and heavy iron frying pans hung on the walls. The farmer's wife took two bowls from a shelf, filled them with the celery, then gave one to Deschamps and one to Halifax. Halifax picked at the tiny green half-moons as he walked up the stairs, following the farmer's broad back and hearing the floorboards creak under his boots.

From under his bed Deschamps pulled a steel trunk. When he unlocked it and opened the lid, a smell of mustiness billowed up in their faces. In the trunk were three shotguns. One of them looked ancient.

Deschamps sat down on the bed and rubbed his hands together. 'Why do you want a gun? Those rabbits in my field belong to me. I don't want you shooting my rabbits.'

'This will be for dealing with trespassers.'

'Oh!' Deschamps beamed a grin at Halifax, bent over very slowly and picked up the ancient shotgun. 'This is the one for you, then. My father used this in the Franco-Prussian War. He dealt with several trespassers. Three German soldiers, I think. Maybe more than three. They're buried in the field somewhere. Every now and then, some of their bones get ploughed up.' He held out the gun. 'This is all you need.' Then he fished a pipe out of his coat and clamped his teeth down on it.

Halifax released the catch and broke open the barrel. He held the muzzle up to the window and looked down inside the barrel, using his thumbnail to catch the light and see any pits in the steel. There were many pits and the gun was no good, so he put it back in the trunk.

Deschamps sold him one of the others and they went downstairs for some lunch. Deschamps's wife scooped chicken with dumplings into heavy pottery bowls and set them on the table. There was red wine in the sauce.

Outside it rained, and the cat came back through the kitchen window. The wife and the farmer didn't speak as they ate. They seemed completely lost in their own thinking, spooning the food slowly and carefully into their mouths.

Before Halifax left, the farmer gave him a box of cartridges and asked him again to please not shoot the rabbits.

'Do you really think you need a shotgun? What about the Lebel?' Ivan opened a drawer under the workbench and took out the revolver. 'Won't this be enough?'

'Shotgun.'

'What's the matter? Can't you speak in whole sentences?'

'There might be more than one. Need to get them all.'

'Did you see who did it?'

'No.'

'The damage isn't too bad. It won't cost much to fix. The company will probably give us a deal on the parts.' Ivan walked across to where Halifax sat and rested his hand on Halifax's head, like a priest at a baptism. 'It's probably just some children.'

174

'I'll kill them.' Halifax scooped up the shotgun shells and put them in the pocket of his brown corduroy coat. He had found it hanging on a nail in the barn. The elbows were shiny with dirt and the collar had frayed through.

'Maybe it's someone trying to give us a hint, someone who doesn't want us to make the crossing. It could be one of the people we're competing against. Think about it, Charlie.'

'Could be Serailler. Did you think about that?'

'Serailler's still in Africa.' Ivan looked at him and shook his head. 'He's a thousand miles away.'

'But he had friends!'

'Maybe you'd better let me have the gun, Charlie. I'll make sure no one bothers us again.'

'I'll kill them all, Ivan.'

'No, you won't, Charlie. You won't be killing anyone.' Ivan took away the gun, gently unclamping Halifax's hands from the butt. 'Mme. de Montclaire has invited us to another party. Merlot stopped by the hotel room this morning and asked us. We should go, I think. Maybe we'll find out what the competition is up to. We need that kind of information. It wouldn't hurt us to make a few friends, either.'

'No.' Halifax raised himself up onto his feet. They were numb from sitting cross-legged on the concrete. 'There'd be no one to look after the Levasseur.' He walked outside to the rain barrel and pushed his head below the surface. The coldness pressed at his eyes. Water overflowed and spilled down the sides, splashing his shoes. He came up gasping for air, freezing trickles running the length of his back and soaking his buttocks.

'Did you hear what I said?'

Halifax shook his head. The cold clamped down on his muscles.

Ivan clicked his tongue. 'What I said was, we'll get Deschamps to look after the plane. Tell him if he'll watch the place for a night, we'll give him a ride. It's a good idea.' He was quiet for a moment. 'It's a great idea.'

'Don't fall asleep!' Halifax laughed and slapped Deschamps on the arm. Then he stopped laughing and peered in Deschamps's face. 'You won't fall asleep, will you?'

Deschamps looked up from his chair, which he had dragged

from his house all the way across the cabbage field. 'Who do you think you're talking to, boy?'

Halifax swallowed his spit. 'It was only a joke.'

Deschamps didn't smile. Threads of tobacco smoke rose from his pipe.

Halifax looked back through the taxi's rear window as they drove along the muddy road. 'He'll fall asleep, Ivan. Or he'll decide to go rabbit hunting and he'll forget all about the plane. Then whoever it is will come again and ruin things for good.' He pressed his fists into the leather seat. 'I know that's what will happen.'

'That farmer is a better guard than you'll ever be. At least he won't be shooting the first shadow he sees, or some little girl out picking mushrooms. Nothing's going to get past him. Don't you worry.'

Halifax imagined someone staring at the barn from the cover of the woods. This person crouched in the shadow of the trees, seeing Deschamps fall slowly asleep, his head bowing down onto his chest. Halifax then saw through the person's own eyes as he ran from the woods across the field, stopping now and then to listen and moving on. Halifax's breathing had become his breathing. He felt the other man's heart behind his own ribs. The man moved without sound into the barn.

Mme. de Montclaire wore a red velvet dress. She held out her hand as if it were a flipper. 'Did you both read the nice things Mr. Tuttle said about you in the *Herald*?'

'Yes ma'am.'

She crinkled her face and smiled. 'Good!' Then some other people came through the door. She turned and held her flipper out to them.

Justine walked over to a table and sat down. 'This is our table. This is our home base. If any of us gets lost, we'll come straight back here.'

Ivan went to fetch drinks. It was the same crowd, mostly. The noise was the same. The band rattled out fast tunes with trumpets and double basses faster than anything Halifax remembered from the war. The songs ended with a clatter of drums, as if the drummer had collapsed onto them.

Justine pulled at the sleeve of Halifax's tux and told him to sit down. 'I used to be a waitress here when the place was owned by the motor club. Do you see that girl behind the drinks counter there?' She aimed her finger at a woman in a black and white maid's uniform. 'I know her.'

'Go say hello.'

She sat back and chewed her fingernail. 'No. I can't remember her name. Anyway, she'd only think I was being superior.'

'You are superior. Your're the superiorest lady I know.'

She ignored this and reached across, resting her fingers on his forearm. 'Thank you for the medicine. I know things are a little tight for us now, and you didn't have to do it, but thank you anyway. I don't get a good night's sleep without those tablets. But last night I slept so well. See what a good mood it puts me in? See?'

Halifax started to speak and then stopped. Instead, he breathed out and looked around for Ivan.

'Were you going to say something?' With her fingernails, she tapped the band's drumming on the table.

'I was going to say that looking at you makes me wish I had put an ad in the paper, the same as Ivan did.'

She hid her smile with the back of her hand, showing the paleness of her fingers and the shallow creases in her palm. 'But look what you'd get. A dud! You'd end up with a dud just like he did. I'm a very superior dud, of course, but a dud all the same.' She stopped smiling and changed the subject. 'Will you get married and settled down after you reach the States?'

'Married and settled down,' he repeated.

'Yes.'

'Sure. I suppose.' Halifax nodded. 'Sure.'

Now the band took a break. A girl sat on the drum player's lap. He was trying to teach her how to play the drums with a thing like a small metal broom that made swish-swish noises when it sruck the surface of the drum. The girl swept at the drum and giggled, looking for a place to tap out her cigarette ash. The drummer held out his hand. The girl giggled again and shook her head, but the man nodded sternly and said something that made the girl shrug and tap the ash into his palm. Then he put the ash into the pocket of his white tux jacket.

'Well now.' Someone walked up behind Halifax and spoke very quietly in his ear.

Halifax turned. It was Garros. The sunburn had gone from his face.

'I heard you were in town.'

'Good to see you.' Halifax stood and held out his hand. 'How's it going?'

Garros ignored the hand and pulled a piece of paper from his pocket. It was an old newspaper clipping brittle and yellow with age. 'I was right about you, Halifax.'

The clipping showed a picture of Halifax standing next to his Spad at the Bergues airfield. The article beneath the picture said that he was the only American who still flew with the French now that the American Air Service had been set up. It didn't mention that the reason he stayed on was because of his bad eyesight. Instead, it said that he had just been awarded the Croix de Guerre.

In the picture, Halifax stood in front of the plane with his arms folded across his chest. He was smiling. The photo had been taken before the accident and no scars showed on his face.

Garros folded the clipping and put it back in his pocket. 'I had it in my scrapbook. Why did you deny it when I said I knew who you were?'

Halifax shrugged. 'I didn't want to talk about it.'

'I lost my job because of you. The investigating service read what I had to say about you and that hog of a captain down in Mogador and they didn't listen. They blamed me instead.'

'Sorry to hear it.' Halifax looked down at Justine. 'This is Justine. Justine, this is Mr. Garros.'

Garros didn't take his eyes off Halifax. 'If you'd helped me just a little bit.' He pinched a piece of air in front of him with his thumb and index finger. 'A little tiny bit . . .'

'Can I get you a drink?'

'No.'

Halifax sucked his teeth for a moment, not knowing what to say. 'So what are you doing now?'

'I work for a newspaper. The *Herald Tribune*.'

'I have a friend who works for them. What jobs do they have you doing?'

Garros was angry. It seemed as if every time Halifax opened his mouth, Garros took it as an insult. 'I run the obituary column. That's just for now. I have other projects.'

Halifax nodded and smiled and wished he'd go away.

Garros breathed in suddenly. 'I'm going to write a story on you.'

'Someone already has. Someone from your paper.'

'This will be a different story. This one will tell the truth.'

'Excuse me?' Halifax gave up smiling.

'You're a liar. You're a liar and a crook. How the hell does a man like you get enough money together to try for the Orteig Prize? Do you think people aren't asking about that? Do you think they believe that Russian friend of yours when he says he has all the money? If he has so much money, then why is he living in a cheap hotel with a woman who isn't even his wife?'

'Enough, Garros. You're in over your head again.'

'It's not enough!' Garros raised his voice too much and people turned to stare. 'You hurt me down in Africa. How do you expect me to feel about that?'

'How do I expect you to feel?' Halifax hooked his finger under Garros's chin. 'I expect you to be glad you don't know what it feels like to be buried up to here in the sand at low tide. If I hadn't helped you, that's where you'd be.'

Garros swatted Halifax's finger away. He could barely talk, his teeth were clenched so tight. He stalked away into the crowd.

Justine went back to drumming on the table top. 'Well, that was very pleasant.'

Halifax sat down. He crossed his legs and then uncrossed them. I have to stay calm, he was thinking. I have to stay in control. 'Garros is an angry little man.'

'Do you really think he wants to harm you?'

'I know he wants to, but I don't think he will.'

'Would he really have ended up buried in the sand if you hadn't helped him?'

'Probably.'

'And where does all the money come from if it doesn't come from Ivan?'

'He didn't tell you?' Halifax held his hands out, palm up, to see if they were shaking. It was something he did at the end of every day. He'd been doing it since the war. In the prison cell where they put him after he tried to run away, he spent whole days staring at his hands, watching his fingers shudder. 'Well, ask him to explain it some day.'

'He tells me bits and pieces. He said you spent some time in prison for desertion. Is it true?' She watched him closely.

He couldn't look her in the eye. 'Yes, in the Leffrinckouke military prison near Dunkirk. I deserted just before the end of the war.'

'How long were you in prison?'

'Six months, between the time I tried to board ship for America and the time I reached Africa. It was all very quick and efficient.'

'Did you almost make it home?'

'Not even close.'

'Why did you desert?'

'I was going to get killed if I went up again. At least, right then I was.'

'How did you know that?'

'I stopped feeling lucky. It used to be that if you ever heard a man say his luck had run out, you could be pretty sure he knew he was going to die. I knew if I went back up in the air I'd get killed. It seemed like everything I'd learned about flying was no use anymore. Seemed to me that the only reason I'd survived was because I got lucky.'

'But you know that's not true. They don't give the Croix de Guerre to people who just get lucky.'

He looked around again for Ivan, then sighed and turned back to Justine. 'They were right to put me in prison. Anybody who deserts probably thinks they have a good reason. The fact that they are probably going to get killed anyway if they don't desert is a plenty good enough excuse for most people. So you see, the army can't make exceptions. Anyone who runs away must be punished.'

'It's a good thing you weren't presiding over your own trial, I'd say, or you'd probably have condemned yourself to death.'

'Right.'

'But you're going home now.' Again her hand, with its tidy, polished fingernails, rested on his arm. 'I'll never understand why you waited so long. How could you spend five years in Africa when all the time you wanted to be home?'

'Because it was Africa!' He surprised himself with the loudness of his own voice. 'And . . .' He flicked the rim of his punch glass, ringing the crystal. 'And I didn't know if I wanted to go home. I didn't know if I could. I was going to come back a hero, you see. Come home an officer and a hero or don't come home at all.' He looked at her. 'Do you see?'

'I think so.'

Now he stared at her again. 'So I wouldn't have to go back down in the mines.'

There was shouting by the door. Ivan was standing in front of the doorman, bellowing at him in Russian. The man had backed against the wall. He kept his hands down by his sides and his neck sunk into his shoulders. People stood on their chairs to get a better look. Murmuring voices boomed through the hall.

'This is not what we need.' Halifax talked to himself, moving with Justine through the crowd toward where Ivan stood.

By the time they reached the door, Ivan and the doorman were laughing and slapping each other on the arm. People around them turned to one another and laughed too. Soon, all Halifax could hear was laughter.

'This!' Ivan swung the little doorman by the arm out to where Halifax stood with Justine. 'This is Corporal Baturin!'

'Hello.' Baturin nodded and smiled, not sure who Ivan was talking to.

'And this is my wife, Justine. She will be, anyway.'

'Hello!' Baturin spread his arms to embrace her, but Ivan spun him around to face Halifax.

'And this is Mr. Halifax. Baturin was my corporal in the cavalry in the Ukraine. I heard he made it out to Paris but I couldn't ever track him down. And here he is!' Ivan cracked him on the back with the flat of his hand.

Baturin jolted forward, still nodding and smiling.

'Mr. Baturin.' Garros appeared, punching his way through the cluster of people. 'I want to speak with you.'

Ivan said something in Russian when he saw Garros. He looked from Halifax to Garros and then back to Halifax.

Garros spoke so everyone around could hear. 'Mr. Baturin, I am Edouard Garros, from the *Herald Tribune* newspaper.'

Baturin winced. 'I don't read much in the papers.'

Garros laughed very loudly and then suddenly stopped. 'I'm writing an article about your friend Mr. Konovalchik. I was hoping you could answer some questions for me.'

'I hope so, too.' Baturin bent slightly forward, the brittle-backed bow of a servant.

'Is it true that Mr. Konovalchik was a man of great position back in Russia?'

'Major Konovalchik is Major Konovalchik. He led the charge at Zovi Rog. That's all I need to tell you.'

'And was Major Konovalchik a very wealthy man?'

'You could ask him yourself. You're staring right at him.' Baturin held his hand out to Ivan, guiding Garros's stare.

'But I'm asking you, Mr. Baturin.'

Halifax felt worry in his chest, a pressure, as if his arteries had clogged and now the blood was straining to pass through them.

Ivan stayed very still, eyes on Baturin.

'Well.' Baturin's chin edged back into his throat.

As Halifax caught sight of all the others watching, he realized that what Garros had said was right: people had been asking questions.

'Major Konovalchik's the richest man I've ever met. I've never seen all his land, but I've heard about it. I'm surprised you haven't heard about it. What was your name?' Baturin stepped forward.

'But that land is in Russia.' Garros shook his head. 'He doesn't have that land anymore.'

'I'm only telling you what I know. He's the richest man I've ever met. What kind of thing are you writing? What's it to you?'

The crowd began to mutter. They snickered at Garros and filtered back into the hall. A tall man in a tuxedo appeared behind Garros. 'I thought I told you not to come here anymore.'

Garros wheeled around. 'Oh, Anton. Not you again.' Then he lowered his voice. 'I paid my tab.'

Anton jangled some change in his pockets. 'Mme. de Montclaire doesn't care about your bills.'

Halifax remembered the man now. He was standing at the door when they walked in, glancing at everyone with short stabs of his eyes.

Garros pulled a roll of bills out of his pocket. It looked like a lot of money. 'Well, she should care about my bills. Here.' He peeled one off the roll and stuffed it in Anton's top pocket. 'Is that enough to shut you up?'

Now he's done it, Halifax thought. Now that son of a bitch looks dangerous.

'Just go,' Anton said.

'What's the matter? Isn't that enough?' Garros was talking too loud.

Anton took hold of Garros's arm and held it out straight with

182

a hand held under the elbow joint, pushing it the wrong way. Garros clamped his teeth shut with the pain and allowed himself to be walked out to the street. He flailed his arms at a waiting taxi. Then he stepped into the car and flailed his arms some more at the driver. The taxi pulled away from the curb.

The kitchen at the Aero Club was bright and noisy and crowded.

Baturin ushered Ivan, Justine and Halifax past cooks and waitresses to a small wooden table near the freezers. He opened the door of the walk-in ice locker and disappeared through a fog of condensation, which drifted out across the white-tiled floor. When he reappeared, he was carrying a small glass dish half filled with crushed ice. Sitting on the ice was another, smaller dish containing black beads of caviar.

'I was saving this.' Baturin set the dish on the table, then held up a bottle of clear liquid, which he'd been hiding behind his back. 'I was saving this, too.' He pulled the cork from the bottle. It had also been in the freezer. Frost was thick on the glass.

'Here somewhere. Here somewhere.' Baturin rummaged in a drawer under the table. 'We keep it here . . . Yes. Here.' He pulled out a small wooden spoon and handed it to Ivan.

A few of the waitresses watched. The cooks peered from between rows of hanging pots and pans.

'Where did all this come from, Baturin?' Ivan dug the spoon into the clotted black bubbles.

Baturin shook his head as if he couldn't remember. 'Don't worry about that, sir.'

Ivan tipped the full spoon onto his tongue and closed his eyes as he crushed the tiny beads against the roof of his mouth. Then his eyes popped open. 'Oh, Baturin. Sevruga malossol.' He sighed and his shoulders hung down. 'Oh, this is something, Baturin.'

Baturin handed over the bottle. 'Wash it down, sir.'

Ivan poured the vodka down his throat without letting it rest on his tongue. Then he fed Justine some of the caviar and slid the vodka bottle across to Halifax.

Half an hour later, Halifax was sitting in the ice locker on a frozen side of beef. A bucket kept the door propped open. The chairs had all been taken by waitresses, who sat around Baturin,

Ivan and Justine. The cooks stood with their hands on their hips, looking over the waitresses' shoulders.

Halifax swallowed another mouthful of vodka and watched Baturin, who waved his fist as if he held a sword and shouted in Russian. The cooks and waitresses who understood what he said were laughing, and the ones who didn't understand laughed too, but not as loud.

Baturin thought he was back at the charge of Zovi Rog. He hacked at the invisible enemy in front of him. He frowned and sweated and butchered, stopping now and then to explain something. When he was met with more laughter, he turned to Ivan and held his hands open, demanding confirmation that what was said was true.

When Ivan only grinned, Baturin went back to fending off the enemy.

'Mr. Halifax?' It was Mme. de Montclaire, who had stepped into the freezer. 'What on earth are you doing in here?'

For a moment Halifax said nothing, trying to straighten out his vodka-fuzzy head enough to speak and make sense. 'Conditioning!' he said suddenly.

'But what sort of conditioning?' She leaned down and looked in his face.

'Conditioning for the flight, ma'am. It's going to be very cold up there.'

'But of course. Oh, Mr. Halifax.' She sat down next to him on the side of beef. Her arms were painted with goose bumps. 'I know you'll be the one who makes the crossing.' She touched his cheek with the back of her hand. 'I have all the faith in the world in you.'

'Thank you, Mme. de Montclaire.'

'Oh now, who told you to call me that? Did I tell you to call me that? You must call me Agnes. If you don't, I'll be furious.'

'I wouldn't want to make you furious.'

Outside in the kitchen, Ivan stood with his back against the wall, arms spread and shouting with laughter.

Mme. de Montclaire put her arm around Halifax's shoulder. 'By the way, I'm so sorry about that disturbance with Mr. Garros. He's a man who is no longer welcome here.' She slid a little closer and lowered her voice. 'I should say he isn't welcome anywhere. He is a member of several clubs around town, or *was*. But he couldn't pay his debts so he moved down

184

to Marseille. Where the money has come from this time I have no idea. Probably it's from his uncle. He's the same one who found him that job in the south. He'd been fired from most of his other jobs.' She held open her hands. 'He simply didn't do any work. That's what I heard, anyway. He gambles, you know. That's why he left for Marseille.' She shook her finger in time to the words that rattled from her mouth. 'Too-many-debts-with-the-wrong-sort-of-people. Now, I'm just as much against these gamblers as I am against Mr. Garros, but a gentleman must pay his bills. If he doesn't' – she settled her hands in her lap – 'I'll have Anton break his face.'

'He just had a few questions.' Halifax didn't want to talk about it.

'Oh, but he was rude in asking them.' She ran her fingertips across Halifax's neck. 'You're so cold, Mr. Halifax. You'll be a block of ice if I don't get you out of here.'

'Conditioning.' The vodka scrambled his thoughts. He knew he couldn't keep making sense much longer. He didn't know if he was making any now.

A knife slammed into the wall next to where Ivan stood. Halifax jumped and Mme. de Montclaire fell backwards off the side of beef.

Ivan was roaring. Another knife hit the wall on the other side of him, sticking deep in the plaster.

Baturin walked up to Ivan and pulled out the knives. The cooks and waitresses shouted for him to do it again.

Mme. de Montclaire's legs were sticking up in the air. She waved her arms as if she were swimming. Halifax helped her to her feet.

'What is it exactly that you are doing, Mr. Baturin?' Mme. de Montclaire walked out of the freezer and frowned at Baturin, whose hands were filled with knives.

Ivan cleared his throat. 'This is how Corporal Baturin used to keep us amused back in Russia.'

Baturin was drunk. He sweated alcohol and grinned at Mme. de Montclaire. 'It's what I'm good at.'

'It's quite harmless.' Ivan moved toward Baturin, ready to take the knives away and still smiling at Mme. de Montclaire.

'It certainly is not harmless. Those are Sabatier kitchen knives. They are very expensive and I won't have them used to chop holes in the wall.'

Then Baturin got hold of her arms. 'Please ma'am.' He pushed her gently against the wall. 'Please.'

She glared at him. 'Mr. Baturin!'

Baturin stood back, and before she could say anything else he had thrown two knives. One stuck in the wall directly above her head. The other planted itself just to the left of her shoulder.

Baturin held open his arms. 'You see? It's what I'm best at!'

The kitchen staff applauded.

When Halifax looked back at the wall, Mme. de Montclaire had gone. The knives still jutted from the plaster.

'You'll be in trouble for that, Baturin.' Ivan watched her go. 'She didn't look too pleased.'

Baturin dug the knives out. 'She'll be all right.'

'Was it really what you did to keep everyone amused?' Justine held Ivan's hand.

Baturin laughed. 'Yes and no.'

'What does that mean?' Halifax's jaw felt so cold he could barely move it.

Ivan sat down at the table again. 'It means that sometimes when we needed some information from one of the *mujiks*, we stuck him up against the wall of his shack. Then Baturin would throw knives at the man until he talked.'

'I never hurt them.' Baturin picked a handful of ice from the caviar dish and spread it across his face. 'Not without orders.'

The hall was almost empty when Ivan, Justine and Halifax left the kitchen. Baturin hugged Ivan goodbye, then banged his heels together and saluted.

When Ivan had walked halfway across the hall, Baturin appeared from the kitchen to say goodbye again. Ivan told him to stop being an idiot and to remember that he was invited for lunch on Sunday. He patted Baturin on the back and pointed him towards the kitchen.

They had almost made it to the street when Baturin came out a third time. He wanted to know when he should arrive.

'At lunchtime, Baturin. I am leaving now. We have said goodbye three times already. I will see you on Sunday.'

The vodka boiled in Halifax's head. Things moved too fast and then too slow. Ivan helped him to the taxi, then sat in front and talked to the driver.

Halifax sat with Justine. 'You see,' he was saying, 'the way it

186

was in Africa . . . the way it was, was as if all of life started over again every morning.' He raised his hand to stop Justine from speaking when she opened her mouth. 'You see, everything that's living gets broiled to death in the heat. Only the rocks and sand are left. Do you see? Then in the night it gets cold because the desert can't hold any heat. The cold washes everything clean. Then life starts over in the morning.' He put his fists on his knees. It all seemed so terribly important. 'Do you *see?*' He sat back and breathed out and closed his eyes.

'Charlie?'

When he didn't answer, Ivan leaned across and patted him on the cheek. 'Charlie, do you want to stay at the hotel instead of at the barn?'

'No. I want to sleep in my barn.'

'All right, Charlie. I'll tell the man to take you home.'

When the taxi stopped at the Châtelet, Halifax felt Ivan pull the wallet from his pocket. Ivan took out all the money. He asked the driver how much the fare was to Le Bourget, then handed over the amount. The rest of the money he kept. Ivan returned the wallet to Halifax's pocket and slammed the door. Halifax watched this through the mesh of his half-closed eyelashes.

He was almost sober after that. He sat on the wide leather seat of the taxi and looked out at the fields, knee deep in mist. He didn't feel angry at Ivan for stealing the money. He didn't have the energy. You could have asked me for it, Halifax thought. All you had to do was ask. You know damn well I couldn't tell you no.


Halifax crept across the fields shuffling through mud in his new black shoes. Rows of cabbages stretched out into the dark. It was three in the morning. The vodka had convinced him that Deschamps was asleep. 'I'm going to surprise him,' he whispered to the cabbages. 'Surprise him,' the vodka echoed in his head.

Stopping at the rain barrel, he peered around the side of the barn. No sound. The air smelled of damp earth and rain. He took one step around the corner of the building and something bit him on the foot.

'Jesus!' He spun around and the thing that bit him held on, so he fell on this face in the mud. Halifax groped down the length of his leg, prodding the flesh to see if it was torn, and came to a band of metal that stretched around his foot and that he knew must be one of Deschamps's rabbit traps.

Deschamps appeared from the front of the barn. 'I have a gun!' He shouted into the dark. 'I know how to use it!'

'I stepped in one of your traps, Mr. Deschamps.'

'How do you know my name? What are you doing stepping in my rabbit traps?'

'It's me. Charlie Halifax. I was just coming in the back way.'

Deschamps prised open the trap. The teeth in the steel jaws left red welts on Halifax's foot. No one had been around, Deschamps said, and helped him across the floor to where the gas heater burned with an orange and blue flame.

Halifax sat up what he thought was a few moments later and saw the sky was light.

Deschamps was gone. He had set a lump of bread and a piece of cheese next to the gas heater.

Halifax looked at his watch: already eight in the morning.

Ivan was walking down the road towards the barn with his toolbox in one hand and his overalls in the other.

The sound of an aircraft engine came from the airfield at Le Bourget. A plane cleared the runway. Red bands had been painted on its fuselage to show that it was a training machine. It circled the airfield, then headed off towards the coast.

Ivan stopped to watch it. He craned his head back, mouth slightly open, squinting up into the sky. .

## 13

OFTEN HE LAY awake, listening to the tiny hiss of his gas heater. He thought about bringing his Levasseur down past the Statue of Liberty and Ellis Island and onto the smooth water of New York harbour. He couldn't find the pictures in his head.

You don't need to know what happens after that, he thought. It will all fall into place.

'We have to toughen up!' He paced back and forth in the barn. 'Starting tomorrow, we'll go to that gym on the rue du Coq d'Or. We'll lift weights and run the stairs. We'll get in training for the flight.'

Ivan stood up from the cockpit. He was bolting on a new windscreen, which had arrived that morning. 'Do you hear that, Justine? Charlie wants me to start lifting weights.'

Justine sat near the gas heater. She wore Halifax's corduroy coat, the sleeves hanging down below her hands. A purpleness showed below her eyes today. She kept saying she felt cold. 'Why are you going to do that? There aren't any weights to lift on the plane, are there? Why do you need to build up muscles if you're only going to sit there and steer the thing?'

'It's not just the muscles, it's conditioning. From now on, that's what we're going to do. I bet that's what Fokker does. I bet Chamberlin trains in a gym.'

'Are you starting up the Great Halifax Penal Battalion? Are you trying to outdo the Legion?' Ivan polished the windscreen with his sleeve.

'How else are we going to make it, Ivan? How can we just breeze past the others if we don't try to think like them and then think ahead of them? From now on, the crossing is all we're going to think about.'

'Do you mean that lately you've been doing anything else?' Ivan climbed down from the cockpit. 'I don't think so, Charlie.

You live in the damn barn with your plane. You sleep in your damn plane and you smell like your damn plane. Tell me something, Charlie.'

'What?'

'Do you talk to your plane?'

'Don't be ridiculous.'

'Do you take this plane,' – Ivan gripped the propeller bolt with one hand and held his other hand out to Halifax – 'to be your lawful wedded bride?'

'You do talk to the plane, don't you?' Justine walked up behind Halifax and put her hands over his eyes. 'Come on, admit it. Just a little bit?'

'Ridiculous.' He peeled away Justine's hands.

'You do. I know you do.' Ivan smoothed his thumb across the new blued metal of the grille and looked up, grinning.

Halifax searched for his cigarettes, hearing Justine's quiet laughter, then went outside for a smoke.

Justine went over and sat in the Levasseur. Her black locks of hair showed above the cockpit rim. 'I'm flying over Paris!' Her voice bounced off the roof of the barn.

'Are you, dear?' Ivan held the bolts to the grille in his teeth. He spat them out one at a time and attached them to the engine.

'What can I see?'

'What?' Ivan mumbled, the bolts still bitten between his teeth. Saliva dribbled down his chin.

'What can I see from the air?' The levers in the wing mounts shifted back and forth as she played with the controls.

Ivan let the last oily bolt fall from his mouth. 'You can see thousands of rooftops. Some of the rooftops have gardens on them. You can see all the bridges across the Seine. A couple of them are jammed with people but the rest are empty. You can see streetcars and the blue flashes their cables make on the electric lines.'

'Am I thousands of feet in the air?'

'Thousands and thousands.'

'I think I want to come down. How do I do that? Do I pull the handle this way or this way?' The levers shifted again in the wing mounts. Suddenly she took a deep breath and Ivan raised his head. She began to cough. She fought for air but the coughs came too fast, one after the other, ending in a choking sound.

Ivan fetched Justine's purse from the workbench and climbed

up to the cockpit. 'Which of these pills do you want, Justine? Which one should I give you?'

The coughing died down and she breathed again. If was as if someone had been holding her head under water.

'Which bottle of pills, Justine?'

'None of them!' She pushed him back. 'Can't you see none of them do any good?'

'That's not true, Justine. These ones in this bottle help you sleep, the ones with the red label give you back your appetite, these –'

'But they only make it worse for later. Can't you see that? Can't you see it doesn't do any good?'

Old photographs hung on the walls in the gym on rue du Coq d'Or. They showed teams that belonged to the gym: fencing teams, tennis teams, rowing teams.

As Halifax walked down the pale green corridor to the weight room, it seemed to him as if men in the photos on one wall were staring at men on the other wall. Their grey eyes fused in solid beams like the strands of a spider web.

The caretaker let them in before the gym was officially open. That way, they could exercise and still get a full day's work on the Levasseur.

While they lifted weights, the caretaker moved up and down the corridors. He had a bucket of sand that he emptied onto the floor. With a large broom he swept the sand from one end to the other, collecting dirt and dust. At the end of the hallway he gathered the sand back into his bucket. His whistling carried through the building.

Most mornings, they started by running the stairs barefoot. Their calves burned and their throats dried out and they breathed in the smell of old sweat that clung to the walls. Then they threw medicine balls at each other – fat, suede-wrapped balls with sand in them instead of air. The first time they tried it, Halifax picked up a ball and threw it at Ivan, who stood with his legs braced, ready to catch. The ball went straight past Ivan's hands and hit him in the chest. He fell down and the medicine ball rolled over his face and into the corner of the room. They also did pushups. Drops of sweat soaked into the worn wooden floor, so worn that they got splinters whenever they shuffled their feet. They lifted dumbbells, looking through the window at the city churning into motion outside. Afterwards, they showered in the long, tiled shower room, facing away from each other. A taxi brought them back out to the barn.

Ivan modified the Levasseur's fuselage to take an extra fuel tank. It was larger than the two standard tanks already in the machine. The new tank fitted behind the cockpit section and was made of a new type of aluminum called Duralumin. Halifax rewired the fuel lines so he could switch from one tank to the other without unbalancing the planes's load. At each turn in the copper pipe, he fastened a rubber seal to prevent cracking and leaking. They took out the radio because it was heavy and there'd be no chance to use it if they landed in the sea. The camera mountings also went, along with anything else that didn't look useful.

Halifax clambered in and out of the Levasseur, running his fingers over each weld joint and bolt, searching for weakness, fixing each fragment of the machine in his head. In his sleep he dreamed of flying. He felt in his muscles each strain against the metal. His veins and nerves twined into the wiring of the engine.

'I am gathering the details,' he said to himself after Ivan had gone home one night. He sat in the cockpit wrapped in a blanket, seeing the gas lamp's blue flame flicker on the ceiling. Gather the details, he thought. Put these in this pile. Arrange these in a row. Shuffle these others around until they fit together. Pay attention to the details. Make the small things work and the big things will work by themselves. Gather the details and see what you've got. Precision. I need precision so that when I've finished gathering the details I can mash them all together and stick them in the holes in my plan and see if they fit. Stuff them in and hope they'll cover the faults.

But they won't, said the voices in his sleep. You can't win this race only by wanting to win. Every time you ran for your life from German planes over Flanders, it was the bat-wing Fokkers chasing you. Every time you brought one down, there was always another ready to take its place. All of them belonged to Fokker, and Fokker is still in the game. René Fonck says he shot down more planes than Richthofen and maybe he did. He's spent more time flying than you ever will. This man Byrd says he has flown across the North Pole in a plane. There are others.

They know more. They have more. They think clearer thoughts, said the voices. They don't live in barns and they don't wash every morning in a rain barrel.

Halifax opened his eyes. He heard footsteps out in the foggy night. Slowly he climbed down from the plane, took hold of his shotgun and crept to the front of the barn. The mist breathed as it sifted past.

'Stop where you are!' he shouted at the screen of grey-white rolling and unfolding in front of him. 'Is that you, Garros? I'll kill you if you come around again. Can you hear me? Are you there?'

After a few minutes of hearing no footsteps, and nothing else either, he turned and walked back to his heater. He sat still in front of its blue and orange flame. He was afraid. His memories of war, the ones that had been unravelling slowly in his head ever since he went to Africa, seemed now to be replaced by something even worse, which wouldn't show itself, which would never leave him alone.

'Come to Sunday dinner. Justine and I have reservations at a restaurant in Le Bourget.' Ivan lay on his back under the Levasseur. He was refitting a new piece of exhaust pipe. 'Baturin will be there.'

'I can't. I have to check over the engine. The new grille isn't in properly.'

'Oh, you can't be serious.' Ivan let a wrench clank on the floor.

'It needs doing.'

'Look, you can't just leave us alone with Baturin. You know how he is. He'll never go away.'

'You're the one who invited him, Ivan.'

Ivan sighed. 'How about if I buy some food and bring it out here. Then could you have dinner with us?'

'I don't know, Ivan. The work . . .'

'The work will get done!'

They sat on wooden crates and drank Portuguese wine from heavy green bottles. The crates had held the replacement engine parts. Straw used for padding lay scattered on the floor.

Halifax gnawed on a piece of cold chicken, tracing his greasy fingers over a chart of the North Atlantic. 'This is the route. Do you see?'

Baturin was leaning over Halifax's shoulder. 'Oh, yes. It all seems clear enough to me.' He spoke too fast and sometimes in Russian. His breath smelled of sardines. Already he'd drunk a bottle of wine by himself.

Justine and Ivan sat together on a crate. Earlier, they'd been throwing straw at each other. The yellow threads stuck to their hair and clothes.

Baturin cleared his throat and they all looked up. He made a sweeping motion with his hands. 'I have something to tell you.' He licked his lips. 'I lost my job.'

Halifax swallowed a mouthful of apple. 'Why?'

Baturin sat down heavily on his crate, which looked for a moment as if it might collapse. 'That caviar I gave you – it didn't belong to me. It belonged to the Aero Club. The vodka, too. None of it belonged to me. Mme. de Montclaire found out and she fired me. She said I had it coming. She was not pleased about my throwing her kitchen knives and even more not pleased that I threw some of them at her.'

'Find another job.' Ivan shrugged. 'A new one.'

Baturin shook his head. 'Everybody knows I'm a thief. No one will hire me. I've done a terrible thing.'

'Well,' Ivan fumbled for words. 'Maybe it wasn't terrible, exactly. Maybe it was . . . it was . . .'

'Stupid.' Halifax took another bite of apple.

'Take me with you.' Baturin spread his arms. 'Take me to America, Mr. Hafilax!'

'*Halifax.*'

'Take me to America!'

Halifax glared at Ivan, then turned back to Baturin. 'You realize we can't take you in the plane. You realize that, of course, Baturin.'

'I could help!' He held out his hands. 'I could . . . I could read the map!'

'I can't even buy you the boat fare. We don't have enough money. If we win the Orteig Prize we'll have enough, but right now it's impossible.' Halifax looked at Ivan again, asking him with his eyes to get Baturin out of here.

Ivan set his hand on Baturin's shoulder. 'Maybe if we win.'

'But will you? What if you don't?' Baturin searched them for an answer. 'I have no place to go. I have to pay the rent for next month. Let me earn my way to America. Please, Mr. Halifax. I can do odd jobs. I can keep the place clean. I can cook. I work hard. Major Konovalchik can tell you that. Just take me to America. I won't ask for more.' He walked out to the front of the barn and muttered to himself in Russian.

Justine walked across and talked to him.

Ivan lowered his voice. 'Maybe you could give him the job of guarding the place when you're not around. He's not asking for much.'

'What do you think I am? A fucking missionary?'

'Look, if we win the prize, you can afford to send him. Tell him beforehand that if we don't win it, we can't buy him the ticket. By then, he'll probably have found himself another job anyway. Take it out of my share of the money if we win. I can't just let him starve on the street. He wouldn't have come to us if he didn't really need to.'

'This isn't part of the plan.' Halifax started checking the engine. He knew it was all right, but he didn't want to talk anymore. He wanted them all to go away and let him work on his machine. The only time he could relax now was in his barn, surrounded by wrenches and copper wire and engine grease and the smooth white panels of the fuselage.

When Baturin took Halifax's hands and shook them, Halifax just stared. He didn't hear the Russian's jabbered thank-yous. He didn't hear Ivan and Justine say goodbye. Instead, he went back and buried himself in the engine, studying the pipes of the cooling system. They wound together like sinews of muscle, familiar to him and alive.

Halifax and Ivan sat at the table of a closed café. For hours they had wandered through the streets of Le Bourget. Ivan said the voyage to America would take from fourteen to sixteen hours, and they would go plenty of time either side of that without sleep. They made up their minds to stay awake all night and every third night after that until they made the flight.

They found an open café and sat drinking coffee until the place closed down. They walked around the block until the owner and the waiters left. Then they went back to their table, unstacked two chairs and played chess on a miniature set that Ivan brought with him.

'What do you suppose Serailler's doing now?' Ivan picked at a flat cardboard chess piece.

'He's probably still in Mogador. Probably got one of the replacement pilots to make his trips for him.' Halifax watched a man walking his dog across the street. The man wore an overcoat but had his pyjamas on underneath.

Ivan buttoned his jacket against the cold. 'Justine hasn't been sleeping much lately.'

Halifax looked up from the chessboard. The grid of black and white squares flickered on his eyes when he blinked. Then it died away.

Ivan was staring down the street. 'She doesn't sleep and she doesn't eat. I have more in one meal than she has in a whole day. She weighs nothing.' He dragged his fingernails back and forth across his knee. 'I think sometimes if I didn't hold on to her hand, she'd blow away in the breeze.'

'She'll get better.'

Ivan breathed out hard through his nose. 'You sound like me when I'm talking to her.'

The streets were empty and dark. Cobblestones glimmered and mercury-coloured tram lines cut across them. An old man appeared from an alley, drunk and bad tempered. After stopping to shout at a mannequin in a shop window, he galloped across the street and fell over. For a while he just lay there talking to himself. Then he galloped off into the dark again.

Halifax's head felt bloated like a pumpkin from fatigue. The coffee kept his nerves chattering. 'Baturin had better be doing his job.'

'Don't you worry about Baturin. If I told him to hold his breath until he passed out, he'd do it. If I tell him to stay awake, that's what he'll do.'

Halifax thought about Baturin holding his breath until he turned purple. 'What are you going to do when you get to America?'

'The way my luck goes, I'll probably end up joining the army again. I'll see what comes along.'

Halifax nodded, too tired to have understood what Ivan said. A moment later, he looked up and Ivan had fallen asleep. He slapped his hand down on the table.

Ivan jumped out of his chair. He stood with his hands stretched out at his sides. 'Was I sleeping?'

'Right.'

'I didn't mean to.' Ivan sat down again. 'Once I horse-whipped a man for falling asleep at his post.' He ground his thumb knuckles into his eyes and yawned.

A bum with his trousers down by his ankles pushed a bicycle across the road. There was no rubber on his tyres and the wheel rims clattered on the stones. Now it was Halifax who nodded off. A minute later, his eyes snapped open. 'Was I dreaming?' He looked across at Ivan.

Ivan's head was resting forward, chin on his chest, eyes closed and face calm with sleep.

Halifax slammed the table top again. 'Stay awake!'

Ivan's head jerked up. 'Sorry!'

'We have to stay awake.'

'I *was* awake. I was thinking.'

Shivers rattled across Halifax's ribs. He held his jacket collar against his throat. 'The first time I ever stayed up all night, I was sitting in a tree waiting for the headless horseman to ride by. I was about six years old.'

Ivan yawned. 'Who's the headless horseman?'

'He was a ghost. An old lady said she saw him on one of the roads outside the town where I lived, so I went with my brother Henry to see if we could get a look at him.'

'Whose ghost was he? Why did he ride around without a head?'

'I heard he was the ghost of a British soldier who got his top blown off in the War of Independence. He was riding around looking for a new head.'

'Why were you hiding in a tree?'

'So he couldn't climb up after us. We thought he wouldn't be able to climb so well if he didn't have a head.'

Ivan shrugged. 'Well, if he could ride a horse, then I –'

'I was six years old, Ivan. I appreciate your explaining it all to me now, but right then I thought I was safe.'

'What were you going to do when you saw him?'

'Hit him with a stick.'

'Did you see him?'

'A man rode by on a horse, but he had a head.'

'Were you scared? What did you do?'

'We hit him with the stick. We thought he was the headless horseman who had already found a head.' Halifax remembered running through the woods, tearing his face on the brambles, trying to get away from the man they knocked down from his horse, yelling and stumbling after them. When he and Henry couldn't run anymore, they lay out of breath under a railroad bridge, hands pressed over their ears as the noise of an approaching train grew painfully loud. The lights of passenger cars flickered down through the track spacers. He thought of Henry's round face, cut and pale and suddenly closed back into the dark as the train rattled on down the tracks. When the train had gone, they stayed still and listened for the headless horseman. The air smelled of rusted iron and honeysuckle.

Halifax lit a match and held it out to the cigarette in Ivan's mouth. Ivan inhaled, nodded thank you and breathed smoke through his nose. Halifax blew out the match. 'I'm starting to think there's ghosts out at the barn. I woke up last night and was sure I heard someone. I ran outside but couldn't see a thing.'

'Do you think it's Garros?'

'It could be him.'

'He has it in for you, Charlie.'

'What am I supposed to do about it?' Halifax had been smoking all night and his mouth tasted like ashes. 'I can only sit around and wait for him to show his face again. I'll kill him if he does.'

'No you won't, Charlie. You spent too much time saving his life down in Africa to bother with killing him now. Listen, maybe he *will* do some damage. Maybe he'll do a lot of damage. Now that he's working for a paper, he could hurt us with bad publicity in ways we can't even think of. He may knock us out of the race. I just want you to be prepared for that if it happens. Either way, we'll still get to America. We may just end up taking the boat.' Ivan patted Halifax on the side of his face. 'Right?'

'I won't allow that to happen.'

'Stop talking like this. What the hell's wrong with taking the boat? We could get killed in that damn plane. It just wasn't built for crossing the Atlantic.'

'Once we've rebuilt the fuel system, it will make the crossing.' Ivan turned away and spat.

Just before dawn, the sky broke open into a yellow and white smudge on the horizon. A man in a tuxedo walked past. His bow tie was undone around his neck. He wandered down the middle of the road.

'Charlie?' Ivan's voice sounded gravelly.

Halifax looked over and raised his eyebrows, too tired to speak if he didn't have to.

Ivan sat slumped in the metal chair. 'Does Justine really look all right to you?'

'Sure she does. Her cheeks are red like apples. I'm sure she's getting better.'

'Yes.' Ivan nodded. 'I'm sure, too. Now that you say it, she does have a healthy colour in her face. Well, what do you know about that? Those damn pills work after all.'

It made Halifax feel ill to lie that way. The red in Justine's cheeks was fever red, veins carrying poisoned blood round and round in circles through her heart.

The first streetcars appeared, and men in blue overalls riding black bicycles squeaked past. The night shift was going home, leaving a smell of cigars in the air.

A boy carrying two boards tied together and a stack of newspapers set up his stand on the curb. The sign said LA PRESSE in Gothic lettering. He held up a newspaper and began a slow mumbling chant at people walking by.

Ivan bought a paper and took it back to the table. 'Says here there's going to be an air show at Le Bourget. They're going for the world air-speed record. That'll be fun to watch.'

'We're not going to stand around watching any damn air show.' Halifax took off his glasses and polished them with the untucked tail of his shirt. 'Today we reinforce the strut cables. If we have time, I want to attach the wings.

Ivan rolled the paper and slapped it down on the table. 'Well maybe Justine could watch. If it's all right with you.'

Planes howled low overhead. Wind carried the sounds of loudspeakers and applause from the airfield at Le Bourget, one kilometre down the road. Justine sat in a chair outside the barn and waved at each plane as it flew by. Baturin stood next to her, hands in pockets, looking straight up. Meanwhile, Ivan and Halifax were inside, refitting the struts and bolting new cable anchors onto each wing.

A sound of engines grew out of the distance. Suddenly the

roof beams rattled as a plane shot past. 'Come and see!' Justine called from outside. 'This one's doing a loop!' Baturin shielded his eyes from the sun and watched.

Halifax smiled, nodded and turned back to the cable wires, hearing the plane cut its engine as it reached the crest of a loop. Then came the sliding hum of wind through its wings when it dived at the ground. After a few seconds, the motor coughed and restarted.

The announcer's voice reached across the field, garbled by distance and the breeze. The buzz of a trapped fly. More applause.

'I'm learning English, you know.' Justine set a book in front of Halifax. It was titled *English is Fun and Easy!* 'I need you to help me with the exercises, Charlie.' She pulled a piece of paper from a pocket in her dress. 'You have to tell me if these are right.'

Halifax lined up the original bolt holes in each wing with the new cable anchors. He nodded at Ivan to refit the bolts.

Justine spoke as if her tongue were too big for her mouth, drawing out the words as she formed the sentence in English. 'How are you today?'

'Right.'

'Good. I thought it was.' She ticked it with the stub of a pencil, which she had pulled from behind Ivan's ear. 'The cat is in the wall.'

'On the wall. The cat is *on* the wall.'

'Oh. It couldn't be *in* the wall?'

'It could, but it would be dead.'

She scribbled it out, pressing the paper against her knee. 'The car arrested in the middle of the road.'

'Stopped. It stopped in the middle of the road.'

A plane cut in low across the cabbage field. It shrieked over the barn.

Baturin stood in the doorway. His head swung from one side to the other as he followed the machine. 'They're going for the world speed record now.'

Ivan and Halifax left their work and stood on the mud road that led to Le Bourget. In the distance, banners flew beside Le Bourget airfield. A small, single-wing plane appeared as a silver dot in the distance. It had already made several passes over the airfield, gaining speed with each run.

You're pushing the engine too hard, thought Halifax. 'I

wouldn't ever push an engine like that,' he said to Ivan.

'You're not going for the record, either.' Ivan kept his eyes on the plane.

The sound seemed to come from a different place than the expanding silver speck. The distant crowd cheered above the mechanical roar.

'I wouldn't ever do that to an engine.' Halifax shook his head, talking to himself.

Ivan turned, frowning. 'What?' He was shouting over the noise.

The plane shuddered. Now it was close to the barn.

'Wave to him.' Justine flapped her arm at the sky. 'Wave to him when he comes past!' She elbowed Ivan in the ribs and he raised his hand in a wave.

Too hard, thought Halifax, forming the words but giving them no sound. I couldn't ever do that. He thought of his own muscles twined around the bolts and pistons and copper wire, and the pain of the engine pushed too hard, ripping his nerves.

'Wave to him!' Justine was yelling.

Ivan raised his arm and moved it back and forth over his head.

Then a shriek came from the silver-winged plane and it spat out a stream of smoke.

See, thought Halifax. See!

The left wing dipped and dragged sideways through the air. The plane passed to the side of the barn, fifty feet above the roof.

Ivan still had his hand raised in a wave. 'Is this part of the show, Charlie?'

The plane slued around and rose as if it were trying to perform a sideways loop. At the crest of the loop it slued again, dropped and struck ground.

A noise almost like thunder. Its tail section broke off and bounced into some trees at the edge of the cabbage field. Both wings tore away. The fuselage rolled in a blur through the mud, carried forward by the speed of its flight. An orange-black boil of flame coughed out of the silvery body. From the smoke came shreds of metal and burning wreckage. The barrel of its engine continued to roll, free of the plane, scudding across the ground. Finally it stopped amongst the cabbages, wrapped up in fire and smoke.

Ivan and Baturin ran toward the crash. Halifax found himself chasing them, trying to get out of his mouth the words that it was too late. No point in running.

By the time he reached them, his bad leg knifing pain into him and holding him back, they were already standing on the path the plane had smashed through the even rows of pale green cabbages. Smoke rose up around them from clumps of plywood and metal.

'Let's go.' Halifax stopped, then put his hands on his knees and gagged for air. 'Nothing we can do. Let the others take care of it. Really.' He stood up again, throat raw. 'Nothing to be done.'

Ivan and Baturin stayed where they were, wide-eyed and searching for the pilot.

'He's dead. I can tell you he's dead.' Halifax took hold of Ivan's arm. 'Please.'

A few spectators appeared at the end of the mud road. They stampeded forward.

'Ivan.' Halifax pulled at his arm, catching sight of the running spectators, the pale ovals of their faces and their bright-coloured clothes. 'Let's not stand here and stare like the others.'

Baturin walked slowly away, his boots squelching in the mud.

Ivan brushed off Halifax's arm as if it were a bramble. 'It just dropped like a stone.'

'He lost power. He blacked out. A million things could have gone wrong. Ivan, please.'

Ivan looked at him. 'You didn't tell me it happens this way.'

'For Christ's sake, let's just go.'

The crowd trampled towards them across the field.

Baturin stood by the engine. It still sputtered blue flames and smoke. He bent down and then suddenly jumped back, flapping his burned hand. Ivan went to see.

'Come back to the barn!' Halifax yelled at them, hearing the thud of footsteps coming close. 'Back to work!' When they didn't listen, he hobbled after them.

Baturin had found the pilot. The man lay with his head, feet and knees touching the ground. The rest of him stayed moulded to the seat. His arms were gone, so completely torn away that it was as if they had never been there. Only a black froth remained of his jacket's sheepskin lining. Oil from the burst engine

202

covered his body. It had erased the features of his face leaving only the clear white of exposed teeth.

'Back to work.' Halifax gave Ivan a shove. Then he grabbed Baturin and pointed at the barn. 'You, too.'

The first spectators reached the crash. Two young boys stared down at the pilot. 'He must have been going a hundred miles an hour.' The other boy nodded. More people arrived, splattered with mud and chattering.

As they neared the barn, Ivan turned to Halifax. 'It's settled, right?'

'What's settled?'

'That we go by boat. If we quit now, sell the Levasseur for parts and stop renting the hotel room, we'll have enough to pay for the boat fare.' He waved his hand at Baturin, who was a couple of paces away. 'Enough for all of us. And we won't be broke when we get there.'

Halifax tried to stand straight. The pain in his thigh made him grimace. 'We're almost set. We can be making test flights by next week. Don't fold on me now, Ivan.'

'Fold on you? I've come too far with you already.' Ivan swung his fist back, then opened his hand and slapped it hard against his side. 'Haven't you seen enough? I've seen plenty. We can be on the boat by tomorrow.'

'Tomorrow we attach the wings to the fuselage. The day after that we install the engine. The day after that we check out the instruments.' Halifax was still talking about the instruments when Ivan turned his back and stamped off towards Justine, who had stayed by the barn. She looked up at him and said something. Ivan yelled in her face and kept walking.

Baturin shuffled through the mud until he came level with Halifax. He had his hands in his pockets, following Halifax's gaze. 'I think I need to go for a little walk. Is there anything you need from town?'

'I was right, Baturin. He pushed it too far and I was *right!*' Halifax waved his hand across the cabbage field, over the plane wreck and people who had gathered around to stare. They appeared and disappeared in shifting waves of smoke.

# 14

'HELLO?' A SHAPE appeared in the doorway. 'Hello?'

'Who is it?' Halifax untangled himself from his blanket.

A man stood silhouetted outside the barn. Behind him, yellows and pinks from sunrise spread out across the sky.

'Sorry to wake you, Charlie.' It was Will Tuttle. He took off his hat and walked in. 'I've come to get a picture of the crash.' He sidestepped past the Levasseur, eyes slipping over the whiteness of its fuselage.

'I think you got here a bit late. They removed the wreckage last night.'

'They did? Well, shit. The police told me it would still be here. That's why I didn't arrive any sooner.' Tuttle sat down on a packing crate. 'He was going for the world air-speed record, you know.'

'I know.'

Tuttle peered around the barn. 'That's what you get for not staying on the ground.'

They walked out to the crash site. Investigators had carried off all the mangled chunks of wood and metal they could find. The crowd took care of the rest.

Tuttle set up his camera on a tripod, squinted through the viewfinder and clicked his tongue. Then he set it up in another place and wasn't happy with that, either. 'Waste of a trip.' He looked up at Halifax. 'Goddamn waste of a trip.'

'Why?'

Tuttle sucked at his teeth. 'I need something that people are going to recognize. It's no good trying to photograph a field of beat-up cabbages.'

Before Tuttle left, Halifax boiled water for tea on the gas heater. He squashed the tea bag against the side of the mug and pulled it out with a spoon. 'I don't have any milk or sugar.'

Tuttle shook his head and reached out for the mug.

'Do you still want that free ride over Paris?'

Tuttle balanced the mug on his knee. 'I'm not sure I want to fly again. Maybe I'll send Stu instead.'

They were quiet for a while. Wind muttered through the rafters of the barn.

'Let me ask you something, Charlie. Do you have any idea what kind of money you'll be worth if you win the Orteig Prize?'

'Sure.' Halifax scratched at his temples, still trying to wake up. 'The prize money, twenty-five thousand dollars.'

'No.' Tuttle shook his head, then dipped his finger in the tea to see if it was cool enough to drink. 'Millions. Your name will be worth millions. Your autograph will get you free meals all across the country. Every nation in the world is going to be throwing medals at you. Your name on an aircraft engine is going to mean business for whoever gets to you first. I happen to know that you have been mentioned in several industry board meetings already. The thing is' – he rubbed his dry hands together – 'they want to know more about who you are. They want to know why you're lying low, so to speak. You got to a couple of parties at the Aero Club, you show your face, but they want to know why they haven't heard of you already.'

'I'll go to a few more parties.'

'They're looking for one of two things, Charlie. You've got to be either a hero who's already made a name for himself or an all-American boy with no bad image, no skeletons in your closet, a block of new clay which they can shape the way they want.'

'I haven't really thought about it.'

'Well, you should, Charlie. If you make that crossing, things are going to start moving very quickly for you. You'd better be ready to take the shock. A lot of people are going to come looking for you, and they're all going to be smiling, but very few of them are going to be your friends.'

'What are you trying to tell me?'

Tuttle rested his lips cautiously on the edge of the tin mug and took a sip. 'I'm telling you to keep your face clean.'

Halifax held up the pan with the boiling water in it. 'More tea?'

'No, thank you. When do you think you'll make the flight?'

'The Meteorological Office on the avenue Rapp told me the weather looks bad until May.'

'That's only a couple of weeks from now. Are you ready?'

'I will be.'

Tuttle nodded. He looked at the weather charts and maps, which almost covered one wall of the barn. Halifax's finger had worn a grey band across the flight path. 'Did you hear about Byrd and Bennett?'

'No.' Halifax turned off the heater. 'What happened? Where are they?'

'They crashed their Fokker Trimotor on a test flight. Byrd broke his arm and Bennett broke his leg. Extensive damage to the plane. Too bad, eh?'

'They'll fix it again soon. Broken bones heal fast.'

'People are talking about Chamberlin now. They're talking about Lindbergh and Davis. Makes you nervous, doesn't it?'

Pink streamers in the sky, and fog in blankets over the cabbage field. Halifax felt the sleep peeling away from his bones. 'Why shouldn't it make me nervous? Everybody thinks one of them is going to win. Nobody thinks I'm going to win. Why shouldn't it make me nervous?'

'What people think doesn't mean shit. Nobody's crossing the sea in a plane powered by opinion. You're pleased that Byrd is out, aren't you?'

'I feel sorry for him if he really is out.'

Tuttle grinned. 'No you don't.'

'Don't put words in my mouth, Will.'

'I wouldn't do a thing like that.' He grinned again as he walked out to his car, and grinned some more when he gunned his engine and turned it around to drive back up the road. Then he spun his tyres in the mud and slid into the ditch.

Halifax had to fetch a truck to pull him out.

Ivan showed up late again. He said Justine felt ill and had to go to the doctor. He asked to borrow some more money.

'How much do you need?'

'I'll take what you give me.'

Halifax gave him all the money in his wallet. As he handed it over, he thought about the night Ivan picked his pocket in the taxi. He wanted to grab Ivan by the collar and tell him he knew. Instead, he only stared. 'What's wrong with her?'

'Same thing. Do they have good doctors in America?'

'Of course they do.'

'Does it cost a lot of money?'

'If we win the Orteig, we'll have a lot of money.'

Ivan buttoned his boiler suit up to the throat the way he always did. 'Then we'd better win it, hadn't we?'

'So you're still with me?'

'It just shook me up to see that crash.' Ivan squatted down and opened his toolbox. He picked through the heavy iron tools. 'It just shook me up, that's all. I can't afford to be so reckless now' – he tried to find more words – 'what with Justine. It's not only for myself anymore. Do you see?'

Halifax looked down on Ivan's black hair. 'Sure, Ivan.'

'Oh, you will see.' Ivan still didn't raise his head. He was talking to the hammers and the wrenches. 'Soon as you get married, you'll see.'

With the wings attached, the Levasseur began to look like a plane. It filled up the barn.

A few people walked down from Le Bourget, they stood outside the barn and peered in. Over the space of a couple of days, the number of onlookers grew from three to twenty.

Halifax recognized the two boys who had arrived first at the wreck. They came most days, even though there was not much to see. When they got bored, they pulled out slingshots and hunted rabbits in the cabbage field, using bright-coloured marbles instead of stones.

On the twelfth of April, Halifax rented a flatbed truck and hauled the Levasseur out to the airfield at Le Bourget. It was a sunny day. Glare off the white fuselage stabbed at his eyes. As he filled the centre tank with gasoline, the air grew steamy around the fuel pump.

People stood by watching. The plane seemed even bigger in the open.

'Did you fix the landing gear?' He shouted to Ivan from the cockpit.

'Yes, I did. I fixed it so it won't release on take-off.' Ivan paced around the plane, checking the flaps.

'I hope so.' Halifax studied the instrument panel, tapping the small round dials to make sure no indicators were stuck.

Ivan's face appeared on the other side of the windscreen.

207

'What do you mean, you hope so? Don't you think I know what I'm doing?'

Halifax took off his goggles and stuck them on Ivan's head. Ivan blinked through the yellow lenses. Halifax slapped his hand down on the co-pilot's seat beside his. 'Are you ready to fly like a bird?'

The Levasseur was slow and heavy leaving the ground. Even over the sound of the engine, Halifax could hear Ivan muttering, 'Oh, shit. Oh, shit. Here we go. Oh, shit.'

The tail dipped just as they broke from the runway. Halifax climbed to seven thousand feet and banked left, feeling the engine hammer up through the floor. He leaned out and looked down at Le Bourget.

'Look, Ivan. Baturin's running around in circles. He's waving a handkerchief. Look!'

Ivan didn't move. 'I believe you.'

They reached ten thousand feet. The runway showed as a lime-green slash in a quilt of slate roofs and woodland. Halifax settled back into his seat, feeling the straps loosen against his stomach and chest. Ivan searched the dials for a sign of trouble. He moved his hand along the cockpit wall, as if to find a heartbeat in the steel.

The Levasseur was slower than the Spad, needing more space and time to pull out of dives, but it ran evenly and had power and showed no damage or malfunction when they brought it in an hour later, engine off and trundling across the grass.

Baturin ran beside them, still shouting and waving his handkerchief.

Before the plane even came to a stop, Ivan undid his straps and tried to stand up. Halifax put his hand on Ivan's shoulder and pulled him back down. 'You'll be out soon enough.'

'I just wanted to wave at everyone.' Ivan turned, smiling. 'I wanted to wave the way I'm going to wave at them in New York.' He thrashed at the air over his head.

'It runs beautifully.' Halifax rested his hand on the control panel. It felt warm from the engine's heat. 'Beautifully.'

'I just wish Justine could have seen us.'

'Why didn't she?'

Ivan shrugged. 'Didn't feel up to it.'

'You'd better go home and tell her all about it.'

'Come along. That way you can defend me when she says I'm making it up.'

People clapped when they climbed down from the cockpit. Someone took a picture. Baturin was singing in Russian.

Ivan knocked on the door of the hotel room. 'Justine?'

'Is that you, Ivan?'

Ivan spoke quietly, his lips almost touching the frame. 'I'm here with Charlie. Can we come in?'

'Of course.' The bedsheets rustled.

The air smelled stale in the room. Clothes were hung over the backs of chairs and piled on the dresser top.

Justine lay in bed. The skin looked tight on her cheeks. Spread out in front of her were test papers and the book she had been using to teach herself English.

'We went up in the plane today.' Ivan began tidying the clothes. 'You should have seen us.'

'I'm sorry I didn't come.' She smoothed her hands across the bedsheets. 'The doctor says I shouldn't go out unless I have to. Not for a while.'

Halifax nodded, looking past her at pill bottles lined up on the bedside table. There were more of them than he remembered seeing the last time he stopped by.

'Let's open these windows.' Ivan appeared from the closet, where he had been hanging up some shirts.

'No, Ivan. Please.' Justine winced and smiled.

'We were up around ten thousand feet.' Halifax took his hands out of his pockets and showed the angle of their climb with the flat of his hand. 'We could see all of Paris.'

'We need some fresh air in here.' Ivan brushed back the curtains and tried to lift the window. 'It's stuck.'

'Ivan, no.' She reached her hand out and wiggled the ends of her fingers.

Halifax stepped closer to the bed. 'Want me to look over your tests?'

Ivan forced out a laugh. 'The damn thing's locked. No wonder it won't open.' He turned the latch and pushed up the window.

'No!' Justine screamed. 'Can't you understand me?'

Ivan spun around. His eyes were open wide.

For a long time it was quiet in the room. Cold air touched their faces. The sun-bleached curtains wafted in the breeze.

'I saw that man Garros last night.' Baturin sat on an exercise bench at the gym, smoking a pipe.

Ivan said he'd hurt his back, so he couldn't exercise today. Baturin came instead, but only to keep Halifax company. The sound of his voice rose and faded over the grunt and squeak of the rowing machine, where Halifax sat and sweated.

Baturin had managed to find a room with a cook from the Aero Club. He arrived early in the morning and minded the barn while Halifax and Ivan went into town to the gym. Baturin spent most of his days at the barn. The nights Ivan and Halifax wandered through Le Bourget, staying awake with the bums and the dog walkers and the stray men in tuxedos, Baturin stood guard in the hangar, singing to himself and cradling the shotgun in his arms.

'Where did you see Garros?' Halifax felt his breath squeezed out of him by the pressure of the oars.

'I went back to pick up my stuff from the Aero Club and he was there. I don't know how he got in. Must have climbed through the bathroom window. Anton threw him out again. He made another fuss about saying he'd paid his bills and he should be allowed to stay. He was asking questions about you and Ivan.'

'Who did he ask?'

'Anybody who would talk to him. I guess he was hoping he'd find someone who knew you.'

'What kind of questions?'

'Nosy questions. He asked the waitresses if you talked to any of them, if you propositioned them. He asked if anyone knew how much money you had. If anybody knew what you did in the war.' Baturin puffed at his pipe. Leather-smelling smoke drifted through the room. 'He's out to make trouble. You know, I could stop him from bothering you.'

'How?'

'Well, it would be best if you didn't ask me that. You would just say, "Yes, he is bothering me." You would say it just as if you were saying it to yourself. And then I would perhaps go to visit this little man. In Russia, I visited people all the time. Often a landowner would be stirring up trouble, refusing to allow

Major Konovalchik's cavalry to cross his land. Or an informer would give us some bad information. I would visit these people and explain things to them in a roundabout way.' He twisted his hands in the air. 'A roundabout way, so I don't have to make any threats. They'd know what I meant. I can make things clear to this man Garros. All you have to do is nod your head.'

Halifax stopped rowing and wiped the sweat off his face. 'That won't be necessary. I don't think it's come to that yet.'

'Maybe not.' Baturin shrugged. 'But remember what I said, if the time ever comes. I know how to talk to the little people.'

Halifax lay on the floor, hands planted on the chafed wood, and did pushups. The muscles in his arms and stomach complained. When he had finished, he sat back and brushed the dust off his palms. 'Too bad about Ivan's back.'

Baturin looked up from his newspaper. 'He has a back like an ox, and you and I both know it. There is nothing wrong with his back.' He hid himself in smoke.

The next day, they flew the Levasseur as far as Caen, in Normandy, before turning around.

Every day for a week they flew the plane, making changes in fuel flow valves and lengthening exhaust pipes so that no fumes would reach them in the cockpit.

The crowd outside the barn grew sometimes to almost a hundred people. They peered into the gloom, chewing sandwiches and whispering to one another. Whenever they hauled the Levasseur onto their truck and brought it to the airfield, the crowd followed them down the road. The people reminded Halifax of refugees from a fallen country, traipsing after a cart loaded with their possessions, looking for safer ground.

At the end of the week, Ivan brought Justine over to the airfield.

She said she didn't want to fly, didn't want to go up in the air, but Ivan carried her to the cockpit and set her down in the navigator's seat. He held her in his arms the way a man holds his wife when he carries her across the threshold.

## 15

'How DO I look?' Halifax fiddled with his bow tie.

Ivan hunched his shoulders in front of the mirror. The cuffs of his dress shirt hung down like handkerchiefs. 'Like you were born in a tux.'

'Same tux as this, probably.'

The taxi puttered outside the barn. The driver had been waiting ten minutes already.

'It's only a little small.' Ivan pulled at his sleeves.

'Yours fits. Why can't I get one that fits?'

'It was all they had. If you'd come to the damn shop with me instead of babysitting your plane, you might be wearing the right size tux.'

'Is Justine coming tonight?'

Ivan shook his head. 'She's still feeling sick. She'll come another time. I might go home a little early.'

Baturin sat in a chair near the entrance. 'I should be at the Aero Club tonight, instead of guarding this plane.'

'We need you right here.'

'They'll mess everything up without me. You'll see. The service will be terrible.' Baturin picked up the shotgun and pointed the barrel down the road. 'One of these days, that Montclaire woman is going to come walking along that lane begging me to come back. As soon as she gets in shouting distance, I'll tell her to crawl the rest of the way.'

Anton stood at the door of the Aero Club. He stared at Ivan and Halifax with narrow eyes, as if he knew for sure they hadn't been invited.

Halifax looked at the band and his nerves rattled.

The players were dressed as mice. The stage had been covered with a yellow cloth, to look like a big piece of cheese.

Ivan chewed his lip. 'Merlot didn't say anything about a costume ball.'

They had arrived too early. The dance floor was empty and only a few people clustered around the punch bowls. One man dressed as a giant pink rabbit and another dressed as a pirate walked in past them. Ivan and Halifax left the hall and walked to a park across the road, thinking they could come back when more guests showed up.

Trees like black clouds lined the gravel path. Ivan stopped at the statue of a man on a horse, sword raised and mouth open in the last bronze-frozen scream of a charge. 'I swear Merlot didn't say a word about costumes.'

Halifax turned up the thin collar of his tux jacket and held it to his throat. 'I think I remember this place.'

'You do?'

'From the war. There used to be an all-night soup kitchen at the other end of the park. It's not too far from the station, and I used to go there early in the morning before I caught my train back go Bergues.'

'I could eat some soup now.' Ivan bent over to read the inscription on the statue, but the words were clogged with moss.

They passed a pond where ducks rested in clumps on the grass.

'Hey!'

They turned and looked into the dark, not knowing where the sound had come from.

'Hey!' A clump of rags rose off a bench near the duck pond. It was a tramp. He wore a heavy coat and had a belt made of string.

'You all right?' Halifax took a step forward, trying to make out the man's face.

'Been to a wedding?' He wobbled slowly around the rim of the pond.

'Just a party at the Aero Club.'

'You always have to dress up nice for their parties, don't you?' He was a barrel-chested old man with a squeaky voice.

'This time we'd have done better dressed like you are.' Ivan nudged Halifax. 'Let's go.'

They started walking again and the tramp shuffled after

213

them. He moved ahead and then stopped, blocking the path. He levelled his finger at Halifax. 'Your name's Charlie.'

Halifax stopped. 'How do you know that?'

'You're Charlie . . . Charlie.' The tramp lowered his head. 'Charlie somebody. Charlie Halifax!'

'How do you know?'

'I know . . .' The tramp stuffed his hand into his coat and pulled out a crumpled ball of paper. 'Because I can read.'

Halifax saw that the tramp had stuffed his coat with wads of newspaper. 'Why all that paper?'

'Keeps me warm. I know you because . . .' he unravelled the ball, squinted at it and shouted, 'There you are!'

Halifax saw his face under the web of creases. It was the *Herald Tribune* article.

'I knew it was you. I seen your picture in other papers, too.' The tramp held his hands behind his back and rocked from one foot to the other. 'Can you lend me some money?'

Halifax pointed to Ivan. 'He'll lend you some.'

Ivan rummaged in his pockets. 'I'm broke.'

Halifax handed the tramp a few coins.

The tramp kept talking, with his cupped hands held out, waiting for more. 'I read about you taking one of those new navy planes across the sea. I ought to tell people that's what I'm going to do. Then they'd invite me to some parties.' He let the coins clink into his pocket. 'Except it seems like one of you fly boys gets your picture in the paper, you don't live much longer after that.'

Halifax and Ivan walked on to the soup kitchen. They stood outside the door. Halifax hadn't spoken since they left the tramp.

He was remembering how many pilots in the war wouldn't allow their photograph to be taken. They thought it took away their luck. Now he wondered if his luck was gone, and if he'd had any luck to begin with.

'I can smell the soup.' Ivan pulled at Halifax's arm. 'Aren't you hungry?'

People raised their heads from the heavy pottery bowls as the two men in tuxes walked in. They were the same people who wandered through the streets all night, crisscrossing the silver tram lines and swearing at shop mannequins.

In the war, Halifax remembered the walls of this place were

plastered with recruiting posters and blackout warning signs. Now playbills and concert placards took their place.

Ivan didn't notice people staring. He grabbed a bowl off the stack and held it out to the woman behind the counter. 'No spoons?'

'People keep stealing them.' She ladelled out some onion soup. 'One franc.' Then she shoved him aside with her eyes.

Halifax found them a place at a table.

Ivan slumped down. 'No spoons!'

'It was always that way.'

Ivan slurped his soup from the bowl.

'This place used to be crowded all the time.' Halifax looked around at the scattering of people hovering over their food, remembering the French Infantry uniforms and the red breeches and blue jackets of the French Air Service. Always mixed in amongst them was the gloomy olive-brown of American and British uniforms. 'I used to –'

Ivan interrupted. 'Charlie, I need to borrow some more money.'

'We don't have any. You know that.'

'If you can afford to give money to that idiot in the park, you can damn well afford to give me some as well. It's for Justine.'

Halifax stuffed a few bills into Ivan's hand saving enough in his wallet for the taxi fare home.

Ivan thumbed through the money. 'Don't you have any more?'

'I'm giving you all I can spare. Honest.'

Ivan said nothing. He looked off to a corner of the room and nodded. Then he stuffed the notes in his pocket.

'I had a talk with Tuttle.' Halifax lifted the greasy soup bowl to his mouth. 'He says we'll be rich if we make the crossing.'

'The Orteig Prize is a lot of money.'

'He says we'll be even richer than that. Says companies will be after our names. The way he made it sound, we'll never get another moment's peace as long as we live.'

Ivan shrugged and looked down at the dregs of his soup. 'I think I can live without the peace.'

Taxis pulled up outside the Aero Club, unloading people in costume. The hall was crowded now. Ivan and Halifax filed in behind a man dressed as a pregnant nun and a woman with silver foil lightning bolts in her hair.

Merlot met them at the bar. He was in a Chinese pyjama suit, with a little pillbox hat and a stringy moustache glued to his upper lip. On his chest was a press-card sign on which he had written 'FU MAN MERLOT'. 'I must have forgotten to tell you two about the costumes.' He held up the stringy moustache and sipped at his drink. 'It was my idea to turn the band into mice. Pretty funny, don't you think?'

'Oh, yes.'

Merlot slapped Ivan on the arm. 'And pretty funny you two coming here in tuxes!'

'A ripsnorter.'

'This is our yearly fund raiser. Madame de Montclaire has us all in fancy dress so she can sneak up on people without them knowing who she is and then she surprises them and asks for money. A lot of people come to me for their costumes. I make clothes you know.'

'You told us. Yes.'

Merlot picked a cracker from a tray on the bar. He looked at the pink mush on top, sniffed at it and popped the cracker in his mouth. 'You two should be pleased today.'

'Why?'

'Chamberlin ruined his landing gear on a take-off. He was someplace in Canada. Anyway, he crashed his plane, and from the rumours I hear, you should be ready to go before he can rebuild his machine. Good news, isn't it?'

'From one angle, I suppose.'

'Oh, Chamberlin's all right. I wouldn't sound so jolly if he was dead, even though it would still be good news as far as you're concerned.' Merlot jammed in another cracker.

'We try not to see it that way.'

Merlot grinned. 'It comes to the same thing. By the way, I've been meaning to ask. Do you know a man named Edouard Garros?'

'I met him.' Halifax could feel heat from the crowded hall drawing sweat from his face. 'Why?'

Merlot shook his head as if he couldn't remember. His Chinese moustache swayed from side to side. 'He was here the other day. He asked if I knew you, and when I said I did, he started asking a lot of questions.'

'Mr. Garros is a journalist. I think he's writing an article on Ivan and me.'

216

'Well, you should watch journalists like that. From the questions he was asking, I can tell you he's only out to dig up your dirty laundry, or whatever the expression is. Not all journalists are that way, I know. Take William Tuttle, for example. He can't stand this sort of thing. Told me so himself.'

'Who did?' Mme. de Montclaire appeared from the crowd. 'Who said what? Are you three plotters plotting? I won't have you plotting at my parties.' She giggled and slapped Ivan on the arm. 'You *plotters!*'

They all grinned at her and said nothing.

'What are you dressed as, anyway? A pair of bookends?' She gave Ivan another slap.

Ivan laughed politely for a few seconds then stopped. 'And where's your costume?'

For a moment she looked surprise, as if she couldn't believe anyone could laugh for such a short time at one of her jokes. She held up a papier-mâché mask on a stick. It was painted to look like her.

'It's me!' She talked through the lipsticked paper mouth.

'Everyone thinks I'm only someone dressed as me, until I lower the mask. I've fooled dozens of people. Actually, some of them have been rather rude. In one case, I actually thought it best not to show who I really was.' She lowered the mask and set it on the table. 'I suppose you've heard about Mr. Baturin.'

'Yes ma'am.'

'He has been with me several years, and for several years he has been stuffing his imperial Russian face with my caviar, the club's caviar, which members of this club pay for and expect to get. This last episode with him throwing knives was just the last straw. I'm only sorry you had to be there to see it. I have suggested to Mr. Baturin that he look around for another line of work. Perhaps he should join the circus. I'm sure he could throw all the knives he wanted there.' She made Ivan and Halifax promise to give five per cent of the prize money to the Aero Club. 'If you win it, of course!' Then she drifted away into the crowd. Merlot shuffled after her in his long Chinese suit.

Ivan rounded up all the half-full drinks on the table, poured them into one glass and sipped at what he had made. 'What if Garros finds out about where the money came from?'

'Then we're fucked.'

'You don't sound too worried.'

Halifax leaned across the table and lowered his voice. 'What the hell can we do about it? The worst thing for us right now would be to look scared. Besides, what's Garros going to do? Go down and talk to Serailler? If he sets foot in that town, Serailler will murder him.'

'Look, I could send Baturin. He could have a little talk with Garros.'

Halifax sat back hard in his chair. 'I don't want to see any of that. Please.'

'You said you'd kill anyone who tried to stop you.'

'But he's just a kid. He won't do any harm.'

'All right, all right.' Ivan held up his hands. 'Maybe Serailler was right about you. Maybe you are going soft.'

'Serailler never said that.'

'He said it all the time.' Ivan sucked at his drink. 'All the fucking time, Halifax.'

They made so many trips to the punch bowl that in the end Ivan just carried it across to their table. By that time, Halifax couldn't focus on anything in the room. First the band had gone blurry, then the people dancing and now even Ivan, on the other side of the table, hovered in a sparkly patch of fog.

'I should check up on Justine, see that she's all right.' Ivan picked slices of lemon and orange from the punch bowl.

Halifax looked at his watch. It was two in the morning. 'So let's go.' He stood up and the room bobbed under his feet.

On their way out, they stopped at the bathroom. Halifax peed while Ivan washed his hands, then Ivan peed while Halifax washed his hands. On the counter above the sinks stood a jar filled with combs in the blue liquid disinfectant.

Across from the sinks, a man knelt in front of a toilet. His friend stood over him. 'Are you all right yet? You'll feel better now.'

They had hung their costumes on coat pegs – the big pink rabbit and the pirate suit. The man standing in the cubicle turned to Halifax. 'He feels better now. It's all right.'

The man on his knees spread his hands against the white tiles of the bathroom wall and retched.

Halifax picked a comb from the blue liquid and brushed his hair. Blood hummed in his ears like a generator. Which way does my parting go? he was thinking. Then something jolted his elbow.

It was Ivan. He held out the rabbit's head, which he'd taken from the coat hook. Halifax shrugged his shoulders, wanting to know what he should do with it.

Ivan walked quietly over to the pegs and lifted off the pink suit and the pirate costume. Then he bared his teeth and jerked his head toward the exit.

They left by a side door and were in the alleyway before Halifax had a chance to speak. 'What do we want these for now?'

'I'll return the costumes tomorrow, don't worry. We'll surprise Justine.' Ivan wedged the triangular pirate hat on his head.

'Why can't I be the pirate? I don't want to be a rabbit.'

Ivan handed him the rabbit suit. 'It's my idea.' He fitted the eye patch over his eye and strapped on the belt. Sticking from the pocket of the red coat was an old musket, which seemed to be real.

The rabbit costume looked like a pink boiler suit, with a blob of fluff stuck on the back for a tail. The head was large and hollow, made from papier-mâché, the same as Mme. de Montclaire's mask. Halifax put it on and looked out through the mesh of thin wire that ran across the rabbit's mouth. It smelled of cigarettes inside. His breathing came back to him in stuffy echoes.

They wandered across the park on their way to the Gare St. Lazarre. It was the only place where Halifax knew they could find a taxi at this time of the morning. Ivan rested his hand on Halifax's shoulder as they walked. He aimed the musket at the trees.

They went by the all-night soup kitchen, hoping there might be some coffee so they could sober up. Halifax's stomach felt empty, and the sour punch burned behind his ribs. The old woman who ran the place walked out of a back room carrying a mug of something dark and steaming. She stopped when she saw them, then looked at the door to see if anyone in normal clothes might be coming in as well.

Halifax looked around for signs of a coffee pot, but saw only the vat of onion soup and the table tops thick with bread crumbs. For a while the three just stood there not speaking.

Halifax only now remembered that his name was carved on one of the tables. He had put an X beside it every time he passed through. At the time when he first engraved his name, hacking it deep in the pale wood with a boot knife borrowed from an infantryman, he didn't expect to reach Paris again. One of the last things the instructor told them at the flight training school at Pau was that the average life expectancy of a new pilot on the western front was fifteen days. If they could make it beyond that, the instructor said, they might make it out altogether.

Halifax was daydreaming in the airless rabbit's head, thinking about the rail cars in which he rode back out to Bergues each time he returned from leave. They were red, without seats, only straw scattered on the bare boards. Soldiers lay side by side with the doors half open, watching black fields stutter past, knee deep in mist.

The woman put down her mug and reached for the soup ladle. Her hair stuck out in tight grey curls.

Halifax opened his mouth to ask if she had any coffee, but before he could speak, Ivan raised the musket to the woman's throat and told her to put all her money on the counter.

Halifax laughed, far away in the papier-mâché head. He raised his paw to touch Ivan's arm.

The old woman's face was very pale.

She reached into her apron, set a pile of crumpled notes on the counter and took a step back. Then she opened her mouth and breathed out.

Ivan stuffed the money into his pockets and ran out of the door.

The old woman and Halifax watched him go. Then they stared at each other. Her lips were trembling. Halifax looked back at the door, waiting for Ivan to reappear. For a while he kept turning his head from the door to the woman and back to the door.

Her eyes stayed fixed on the fat pink ball of the rabbit's head. After a moment of saying nothing, he heard her whisper, 'Please.'

Halifax ran outside and looked towards the shadows of the park, still expecting to see Ivan in his pirate suit. Suddenly he realized Ivan wasn't coming back.

Halifax couldn't run well in the rabbit costume. His legs swung out to the sides and his breathing sounded like thunder.

Ivan had stopped by the duck pond, hands on his knees and gagging for air. The tramp was nowhere in sight. Halifax ripped off his costume and tossed it into the bushes. His tux felt soggy with sweat.

Ivan took off his pirate suit and threw it away.

Halifax shoved him in the chest. 'You fucking idiot! We have to give that back before she calls the police.'

Ivan tripped back a few paces but stayed on his feet. 'I'm not giving it back.'

'What did you think you were doing?'

'I didn't think. I just did it.' Ivan turned and jogged towards the station.

For a few seconds Halifax stood by himself near the pond. The alcohol still churned inside him. Then he ran after Ivan.

They didn't speak in the taxi. Ivan looked straight ahead with his fingers knotted together.

The Hôtel Châtelet stood dark and locked like all the other houses on the street. Halifax paid the taxi man and waited for him to pull away from the curb. Then he spun around and grabbed Ivan by the coat collar. 'You may have ruined everything! You say you're worried about Garros and then you go and do a thing like that.' He shoved Ivan up against the hotel wall, banging his head on the stone. 'What the fuck is wrong with you?' He shook him and Ivan's head hit the wall again. 'I should never have brought you with me. I should have left you to rot out in the desert.'

Ivan didn't try to fight. 'Maybe you should have.'

'Are you so afraid to take the risk? You, who led the charge at Zovi Rog? If you're so terrified of dying, then why the hell did you join the Legion? Why the hell do you even get up in the morning?'

'I'm not afraid to die. I'm afraid to die stupidly.'

'You just didn't need to do it. There was no *need!*'

Ivan breathed in suddenly and showed his teeth. He clamped his hands on Halifax's wrists. 'Of course there was a need. I ask you for money and what do you give me? A couple of francs! I can't buy medicine with a couple of francs. I can't buy medicine or clothes or food. You don't know the first thing about need. You've stopped living like a human being, Halifax, out there in your run-down barn with your sorry-looking aeroplane.'

The last blurred echo of drink died in Halifax's head. 'I've been giving you money. I'm giving you all I can spare.'

Ivan gurgled spit at the back of his throat. 'You have more

221

money than you know what to do with. You're hoarding it like a miser. Justine is dying because of you.'

'You think so? Then tomorrow we'll go to the bank and look at my account and you can see for yourself. Are you that desperate for someone to blame?'

Halifax saw Ivan's arm twitch and then something exploded against the side of his head. His glasses flew off into the dark.

He was on the ground. His ear and his jaw felt numb. He tried to stand, but his legs had started to shake. Then Ivan kicked him in the stomach, lifting him off the pavement with the force of the kick. He lay on the road sucking in air but not feeling it get to his lungs.

Ivan reached down slowly and took hold of Halifax's throat. 'I should never have let us get that plane into the air. I should have ripped the damn thing apart when you weren't looking. If I'd done that, we could be halfway to America by now.'

Halifax held on to Ivan's fingers, trying to pry them loose from his neck. 'Why didn't you?'

'I *tried*, you idiot! It wasn't Garros who dropped the engine from its cradle and smashed the windscreen. It was me.'

Halifax let go of Ivan's fingers. He had no strength left in him. 'You? When?'

Ivan lifted his thumbs off Halifax's Adam's apple. 'The day you sat in the Tuileries reading your air charts from the avenue Rapp, I took Justine home because she didn't feel well. After that, I went out to the barn and smashed in the grille with a hammer and did all that other damage. I would have done more except I heard the farmer coming.' He raised Halifax's head until their faces were only a few inches apart. 'I didn't want to hurt you, Charlie. I just wanted you to see some sense.'

Halifax thought of the Levasseur's smooth white lines. His eyes fizzed. 'I thought you were working with me.'

'We don't have a chance, not against all those others. I kept thinking you'd realize what you were doing.'

'And what do you think now?' Halifax felt his consciousness slipping away piece by piece, like loose panes falling from a window.

'Now?' Ivan's hands closed again, tight on Halifax's neck. 'Now I'm just back to following orders. I'm building the damn plane the way you tell me to.' He pulled in air, a hiss through his teeth, and smacked Halifax's head down against the concrete. 'I don't give a shit what happens to us anymore.'

The door to the Hôtel Châtelet swung open and Justine ran out. 'Stop it!' She scratched and pulled at Ivan, grabbing his hair and yanking his head back, 'For God's sake, stop!'

Ivan let go. He stood up and brushed his hands together. He was breathing hard.

'You're acting like a couple of drunks.' Justine was shivering in her nightdress. Halifax caught sight of people looking down from windows in the house across the street.

Ivan folded his arms. 'We *are* a couple of drunks.'

She swung at him and the flat of her hand caught his cheek. 'I thought you told me you were friends. You told me he was the only friend you had, and now I see you trying to kill him. What the hell are you trying to do?'

'I wasn't trying to kill him. He's holding back the money. We need money to live and to pay the doctors and he has it and he won't give us any.'

Halifax raised himself on his hands and knees. 'It's not true.' He had trouble breathing. 'I'll take you to the bank tomorrow. Show you. Show both of you. I don't have any money. I don't have anything to give.' Then he fell back down on the pavement. 'My glasses.' He patted his nose, trying to feel them.

Ivan picked them out of the gutter. 'They're scratched.'

Justine pushed Ivan. 'Help him up. Get him to his feet and carry him upstairs.' She slapped him again. 'You frightened old man. Of course he's not holding back any money.'

Ivan didn't answer. He lifted Halifax and turned toward the door. Justine cried in quiet sighs as she followed them both up the stairs.

# 16

SUN WASHED INTO the room. Halifax woke up in Ivan's bed.
When he tried to stand, the pain in his stomach doubled him
over. His guts felt bloated, as if he had drunk salt water. Around
the place where he'd been kicked, the skin was purple-blue. He
left quietly and walked out into the street. Car tyres rumbled and
popped over the cobblestones. Pigeons marched up and down
the pavement with people on their way to work.

Halifax stood in a line at the Banque Agricole. The high ceiling
echoed with footsteps clicking on the marble floor. A bolt of
light shone through the tall window, bleaching the faces of
people in its way. He gave the clerk his account number and
asked for the balance. The clerk wrote down the numbers on a
piece of onionskin paper, then slid it under the brass grille that
separated them.

Ivan opened the door a little way. 'Where did you go?'

Halifax held out the bank statement.

'Oh.' Ivan disappeared into the room. The door swung open
by itself.

Justine was rocking slowly back and forth on the bed. She
held a handkerchief to her mouth and struggled for breath
before the next spasm dragged through her. Blood speckled the
sheets.

Ivan rested his hands on her shoulders. 'Should I call an
ambulance, Justine?'

She shook her head. Her eyes were shut tight from the pain
twisting inside. 'It's like this every morning. Don't you know
that by now?'

Halifax folded the paper and put it in his pocket.

Justine looked up and tried to smile. 'How do you feel today?'

Ivan made tea and fed Justine a series of pills. She stopped
coughing a few minutes later.

When she padded away into the bathroom, Halifax gave Ivan his figures from the bank.

Ivan crumpled the paper and threw it away. 'I don't want to see.'

They didn't talk about the night before. Halifax knew they would never talk about it.

Justine brought out her English book and made Halifax test her on the verbs. 'I have six more lessons to go and then, according to this, I will be able to converse with anyone who speaks English.'

'Not if your car arrests in the middle of the road you won't.'

She read out the title of the book in her warbling English. *'English is fun and easy!'* Then she set the book down. 'You two had better be off to work.'

'Ivan could stay here with you today.'

'No, he won't. He'll go to work.' Justine waved them away. 'A few of my friends are stopping by and I don't want Ivan stumbling over everything and getting in the way.' She smiled and hid her face behind the cup of tea.

She made Ivan close the shutters; the light was bothering her. 'Smile will you? And you smile, too. Both of you are about to make history and neither of you are smiling.'

Ivan took her hand. 'Are you absolutely sure you're all right today?'

She swatted him. 'Just get going to work. And make sure you don't start beating each other up as soon as I'm out of sight.'

'We've been beating each other up for five years. Why should we stop now?' Ivan let go of her hand.

'Just don't do anything permanent!' She stepped away into the darkness of the shuttered room.

Baturin sat reading a newspaper. He looked tired and cold. The Levasseur seemed to be leaning over his shoulder, its snout raised in the air. When he saw Ivan and Halifax, he lifted up the paper. 'Deschamps brought me the news and some breakfast. Did you read what happened?' He held open a double-page article, in the centre of which was the picture of a crashed plane. It lay crumpled in a small lake or a pond. The earth was gouged where the machine had touched ground and skidded.

They read over Baturin's shoulder. The plane belonged to Davis. It was a converted American Pathfinder bomber, and crashed a few seconds after leaving an airfield in Langley, Virginia. Davis was dead, along with his co-pilot, Wooster. Both had been trapped in the cockpit and drowned in a few feet of mud.

A photo, taken from the air, showed the specks that were people standing around the wreck of the plane. The machine lay broken and jagged like a corpse face down in the dirt with its arms spread out to the sides.

The article mentioned Halifax's name, and Ivan's. It said they were the only serious contenders remaining, along with Lindbergh and Chamberlin, who had repaired his landing gear.

Ivan finished reading, muttering the sentences to himself as he moved from paragraph to paragraph. Then he walked into the barn, took down his boiler suit from its peg and put it on. He went straight to work.

Halifax stared at the picture again. 'I want you to do something for me, Baturin.'

Baturin raised his eyebrows. 'What?'

'Go to the Meteorological Office on the avenue Rapp. Tell them I sent you. Ask them what day in the next two weeks will give us the best weather conditions for making a crossing.'

'Now?'

'Today.'

'What's wrong with Ivan? He seems in a bad mood.'

'Justine.'

Baturin nodded.

'I need that information today, Baturin. All right?'

He smiled. Then he clicked his heels together and bowed slightly. 'At your orders.'

'Just like that? You just decide we are going and that's that?'

'Right.' Halifax crouched under the Levasseur and helped take down the undercarriage, which Ivan had unbolted from the fuselage.

'But we have more tests to run. We ought to take it up in the air a few more times.'

'Why?' Halifax sat back on his haunches. 'Everything's set. You know it is. We should go as soon as we can. If we don't go soon, someone else will get there first.'

'It doesn't seem like the right time.'

'As soon as the avenue Rapp people say the weather is good, we're going.'

For a while Ivan said nothing, then he sat back hard on the floor and wiped his oily hands on his trousers. 'I'd better tell Justine.'

'Tell her tonight, but don't tell anybody else.'

When Baturin returned in the late afternoon, he was drunk. He waddled down the mud road, drinking swampy green calvados cider from a bottle. When the bottle was empty, he threw it against a tree.

The sound of breaking glass brought Ivan and Halifax from the barn.

Baturin's eyes were blotchy with tears. 'Major Konovalchik.' He took hold of Ivan by the shoulders and shook him. 'Major Konovalchik, sir.'

'Enough, Baturin. You're the only one in the world who remembers my old rank and the charge at Zovi Rog.' He untangled himself from Baturin's grip and walked back to his work.

'Major Konovalchik.' Baturin's voice was grisly from crying. 'Your wife.'

Ivan jumped. 'What about my wife?'

Baturin shrugged. 'Major Konovalchik, sir —'

'Enough with this ancient fucking name calling, Baturin. What about my wife?'

Halifax took a step backwards, away from the angry voice.

Baturin held his hands out, palms up. 'I went to see her at the hotel on my way back from the Meteorological Office. I didn't know she was so sick. I had no idea or I would have stopped by much more often. I am not the kind to neglect a friend.'

'Oh, for Christ's sake, stop snivelling. I didn't tell you because you didn't need to know. She'll get better, Baturin.' he looked at Halifax and laughed. 'Every time he gets drunk, he bursts into tears.'

'Oh, no, Major Konovalchik.' Baturin ground his knuckles into his puffy red face. 'I may be drunk, sir, but I know your wife will not be getting better. She won't get better because she's dead.'

The blood drained out of Ivan's face.

Baturin started to speak in Russian.

227

Halifax felt everything seal up around him.

He saw himself dragged years into the past. He was left sitting again in the flimsy tarpaper-roofed Besseneau hut that served as a debriefing room at Bergues. He saw his faded red Air Service trousers, flight jacket still buttoned and flying goggles pulled down around his neck. The flight officer stood at the front of the room, calling out the names of pilots who had died that day. Halifax patched faces to the names and stored them away. The flight officer's voice cocooned him in silence.

Even after dozens of times – always in the same room and always hearing names read out by the flight officer, until one day when Halifax had to stand up in front of the patrol group and read out the flight-officer's name – the same thing rattled through his head. Not something he had ever spoken of. It was a feeling of tiredness from knowing the length of time and the energy it would take for the dead man's family to recover.

Halifax drifted miles away, still thinking about the war as Ivan paced in slow circles, hands pressed to his face, his breathing so choked it sounded as if he were trying to suffocate himself. Baturin followed, resting his hand on Ivan's shoulder, his voice a constant purr.

Once again Halifax stood in the graveyard at Bergues, hands folded over his belt buckle as the service was read out and wreaths set carefully over the cross. If anything remained of the pilots and if their bodies could be found, they were buried in a cemetery behind the airfield. Widows drifted over the grass. Sons and daughters trailed behind.

Ivan broke from his pacing in circles and walked to the end of the barn. He reached the fuselage of the Levasseur, picked up the shotgun, which rested against one wing, set the butt on the floor and crouched down until the barrel was against his chest.

Halifax started towards him.

Gripping the end of the barrel with his left hand, Ivan reached down until his right thumb was hooked over the trigger. He closed his eyes. His teeth were clamped shut, lips peeled back.

Baturin raised his fingers to his lips.

'Noooo!' Halifax screamed and lunged.

Ivan pressed down on the trigger. Nothing happened. He opened his eyes and pressed down again.

Halifax caught him by the shoulders and they both collapsed on the floor. Halifax landed on his hands and knees, tearing his trousers and the skin of his palms. The gun slid under the plane. Ivan tried to get up. He reached out for the gun.

Halifax grabbed a handful of Ivan's hair and pulled him away. Then he took hold of Ivan's arm and twisted it.

Baturin walked over. In his cupped hands he held the blue cartridges of the shotgun shells. 'I didn't load the gun.'

'Give me one of those!'

Ivan struggled to get loose. He spluttered at Baturin. 'I order you to give me one of those!'

'What are you trying to do?' Halifax shouted in Ivan's ear. 'You think about the living!' He gripped Ivan's arm so hard that it would break if he tried to get away.

Red dots of burst blood vessels surfaced around Ivan's eyes.

Halifax barked in his face. 'Where do you leave us if you back out now? Did you stop to think you might not even get to the same place Justine's going? After all the houses you burned in the Ukraine? After years of priming Cooper bombs? You may not be going anywhere near where she is now. If you end up with anyone at all, you'll end up with me and I'm not looking forward to it! Are you listening?' The sound of his shouting bounced down from the roof.

Ivan had stopped struggling. His eyes were shut and he was crying.

Baturin set a hand on Halifax's shoulder. 'Shall I call a taxi to take him into the city?'

'How did she die?' Ivan's voice sounded nasal and slurred. 'Where is she?'

Baturin's breath touched the back of Halifax's neck. 'She walked out of her room at the Hôtel Châtelet and collapsed on the stairs. That's what they told me. They called an ambulance and it took her to the hospital and she died there only a couple of hours ago. They asked me to tell you she didn't suffer.'

Ivan struggled to get loose. 'It's not true! Of course she suffered. She said she felt better. I asked her if she felt all right and she said yes. You heard me, Charlie.'

Once more, Halifax felt Baturin's hand closed on his shoulder.

'A taxi? She's still at the hospital. She needs to be identified.'

Halifax nodded and turned back to Ivan.

'What am I supposed to do now?' Ivan rolled his head from side to side on the concrete.

'You come with me to America is what you do.' Halifax slowly let go of Ivan's arm and stood up. 'We'll stick together, the way we've always done.' He looked at his hands: dirt mixed with blood from his cuts.

Baturin had almost disappeared down the road to Le Bourget.

'What am I supposed to do?' Ivan stayed lying on the floor, still rocking his head back and forth.

# 17

IVAN KNELT BY Justine's grave.

Baturin and Halifax stood at the entrance to the cemetery, hands in pockets, watching Justine's friends climb into taxis and head back to Paris. It rained softly on the town. Crows argued in the trees across the road.

More than a dozen people had showed up for the service. They were all from the hotel where she used to work. Justine's parents and younger sister had gone to Canada two years before. Ivan couldn't reach them in time for the funeral.

The cemetery was called the Sacré Coeur. These two words appeared on the gateway, twined with flowers. All of it was made of bronze, all of it turquoise with age.

Baturin cleared his throat. 'The meteorologists say the weather will be good on the tenth of May.'

Halifax looked at Baturin from the corner of his eye. 'Maybe we shouldn't talk about this now.'

'I have to talk about it now. The whole business is eating me alive.'

'What business?' Halifax breathed in a smell of ploughed earth blowing off the fields.

Baturin kept his voice low. 'Will you make the crossing or not? I have to know. This is my life we are talking about too, you know. If you don't make the flight, then probably you'll take a ship. You'll still be going. But what about me? I'll be stuck here the rest of my life.'

'What exactly did the weathermen say?'

'They said that after the tenth, a ridge of high pressure will be moving across the North Atlantic. You wouldn't have much hope of flying through it.'

'Then we'll go on the tenth.'

Ivan stood up from the grave and started walking towards them.

Baturin rested his back against the mossy stone wall of the cemetery. 'That's the man who led the charge at Zovi Rog.'

'What about this?' Halifax held up Justine's white shirt with the flowers embroidered around the collar. Ivan shook his head, and Halifax set it on a pile beside his chair. The shutters were open. Maids had cleaned the hotel room. It smelled of beeswax and soap.

'And this?' Ivan held up Justine's English book. 'This I can keep, don't you think?'

'Of course.' Halifax felt something gritty in the pocket of Justine's coat. He pulled out the grit and saw it was tiny lavender buds.

Ivan turned the English book upside down and shook it, in case there was something hidden between the pages. 'What's that in your hand?'

Halifax emptied the lavender into Ivan's palm.

Ivan sniffed, almost breathing in the purple specks. 'I wondered why she always smelled of flowers.' He put the lavender in his own pocket. 'We'll send it all to America by boat. It'll be there when we arrive.'

'Of course.'

'Listen, Charlie.' Ivan pressed his fingertips together. 'We set aside enough money for Justine's boat fare to America. Why don't we just give it to Baturin? Let him go instead.'

'Sure.' Halifax brought out another of Justine's shirts. He folded it and put it on the pile. 'You're looking better today, Ivan.'

'I am?' He raised his head. 'You mean I was looking bad before?'

'You just seemed a little tired these past few days.'

'I am tired. I've never been so tired.' He started to lower his head.

'Ivan.'

'Yes?' He caught Halifax's eye, then quickly looked out the window.

'We have to go on the tenth. The weather's no good before then. No good after as well.'

'That's the end of next week.'

'The plane's ready, Ivan. It's ready to go.'

'Whatever you say.'

Halifax sighed and leaned forward. 'You're ready, aren't you, Ivan?'

'Whatever you say, Charlie.'

Halifax dreamed of the pressure ridge building in the west. Clouds piled on clouds, churning towards him in a grey wave. He tried again to turn his thoughts to home, beyond the flight, reasoning with himself that he would soon be there and would have something to show for all the time he'd been away. But he couldn't think past the storm. He would never get through. In the blue light that still followed him, as if he had only just walked in from the glare of sun off Mogador's stone walls, he imagined the Levasseur swamped and sinking in the ocean, far from land.

This colour and the things he saw in its light had become an enemy. He began to realize that if he couldn't leave it behind, it would keep his mind worrying and tire him and cause him to make mistakes. Thousands of feet in the air, where there was no room for mistakes and where his tiredness was dangerous, the instincts for flying that he had built up over the years might fail. Would fail. If they failed, this vision that walked across his face and kept him from rest would come true. The Levasseur would ditch in the sea, too far from land. It would take on water and sink. Even if he and Ivan survived the crash, they wouldn't last long in the cold water off Ireland or Nova Scotia or Maine. In moments of quiet, he imagined he could hear it – the constant rolling thunder of the storm.

The next day he went to the avenue Rapp. A clerk walked out from behind a smoky glass screen. His hair was parted down the middle and greased back.

'Got some bad news for you, Mr. Halifax.' Teletype machines clattered and buzzed.

'What is it?'

'Chamberlin left this morning. He's on his way across the Atlantic right now.'

Halifax let his breath trail out. He bent forward until his head rested on the counter.

'Sorry to be the one to tell you.' The clerk flipped through the Teletype reports.

'Where was he last seen?'

'Well, there's been no confirmation of anything so far, not even that the story is true.'

'Not true!' Halifax straightened up fast and felt the blood rush in his head. 'The only thing I want to hear from you is facts. What about those dates you gave me for clear weather? Are they true or did you just pull them out of a hat?'

The clerk scratched his sideburns. 'Sir, I –'

'I need some precision! Why can't I get any precision?' He wanted to punch the man. 'That's what I'm paying you for.'

'You're not paying us anything, Mr. Halifax.'

'Well if it *was* precision, I'd pay for it.'

Another clerk appeared behind the smoky glass, Halifax saw the blurred outline of his face and the rims of his glasses.

'I'm coming back here in one hour, and when I come back I want to know if what you told me is true. Understand?'

'Yes, Mr. Halifax.'

He walked to the Tuileries and sat on a bench. An old man sat next to him. The old man sucked at his gums and made slurping noises. When a plane flew overhead, both of them looked up, craning their necks and peering into egg-white sky. Then the old man went back to sucking his gums.

Halifax raked his fingers back and forth across his chest, imagining Chamberlin in a limousine in New York City, riding down Fifth Avenue. Ticker tape rained down from skyscrapers. Halifax saw himself reaching up from the crowd to shake Chamberlin's hand. 'That's it, then,' he said to himself. 'This is as far as we go.'

'How far who?' The old man leaned forward, lips rotating as they smoothed across his gums.

Halifax looked down at the pavement as he wandered towards the avenue Rapp. 'This is it, then,' he said over and over to himself.

When he swung through the door of the Meteorological Office, a clerk hurried out from behind the smoky glass. He had his sleeves rolled up and was holding a sandwich. 'Mr Halifax –'

'I'm sorry. I came to say I'm sorry. I didn't mean to doubt you.' Halifax chopped the air with the flat of his hand. 'I didn't mean to yell.'

The clerk smiled. 'That's all right, sir. It was a rumour

anyway. Chamberlin's still on the ground with a broken undercarriage.'

'He is?'

'That's right sir.' The clerk grinned and chewed his sandwich.

'Good,' he said quietly. 'That's very good.' He nodded and walked toward the door. He took hold of the brass doorknob and then stopped, wheeled around and went back to the counter.

The clerk quit chewing. 'Sir?'

Halifax smacked his fist down on the counter. 'Don't tell me lies another time. Things are very tense at the moment, do you understand? Very tense.'

'Yes, sir.' The clerk nodded slowly.

'It hurts me to hear lies like that. Right here.' Halifax pointed at his chest. 'It actually hurts!'

He sat in his Levasseur, memorizing the controls. Compass. Tachometer. Altimeter. Oil gauge. Fuel gauge. Left tank warning light. Right tank warning light. Clock. Horizon monitor. Throttle. Ignition. Undercarriage release. Engine thermometer. Water bottle. Flare gun. He stared at them until they stayed scribbled on his sight when he closed his eyes, until he would look automatically at the right spot when something needed to be checked.

Baturin swept the floor of the barn. He had packed his bags and was due to leave for America in two days. He hummed to himself as he swept.

Halifax heard a noise at the entrance and looked up.

A man in a trench coat stood outside. 'Come in from the rain!' Halifax climbed out of the cockpit.

The man walked into the barn. It was Garros.

Halifax dropped from the plane. His bare feet slapped on the concrete. 'What can I do for you?'

Baturin stopped sweeping.

Garros looked around the barn. 'I came here to make you a deal.'

'What kind of deal?'

'I know all about you, Halifax.' He tapped a finger against his temple. 'I've been asking questions.'

'That's what I heard.'

'I know you deserted from the Legion in the autumn of 1918. I know you were caught trying to board a boat to America. You were court martialled. The Legion gave you the choice of being shot or signing on for another twenty years. I know you were released only a short time ago. It wasn't easy finding out all this. People kept it quiet at the time. I had to pay some people to get at your records, but I got there. And now I know the truth about the great Charlie Halifax.'

'So?' Halifax felt sweaty-palmed. 'You came all the way here to tell me that?'

'No. I came to make you a deal.'

'I don't have the time for this, Garros.' Halifax shrugged. 'I'm busy.'

'You won't be busy for long. I wrote an article on you. I wrote down the truth. I'll even be handing it in to your old friend Will Tuttle. He's in charge of covering the Orteig Prize.'

'I thought you wrote the obituary column.'

'I do. But I wrote this piece on my own time. Do you know what's going to happen as soon as it hits the papers? Do you? I'll tell you. You won't get the Orteig Prize. They'll even pull your name off the list of competitors.'

'No they won't.' The tendons in Halifax's neck stiffened so much he thought they would snap.

'Of course they will!' Garros was losing his temper. 'They don't want some convict winning a prize like that. It's too special. They'll save it for somebody else. People like that beached whale Mme. de Montclaire, what do you think they'll say about you? What do you think they'll do? I'll tell you that as well. They'll make such a fuss that the Orteig Committee will be forced to kick you out.'

'What do you want from me, Garros?' He bit through his lip. Metal-tasting blood flooded into his mouth.

'It's not what you can give me. It's what your friend can give me, your rich Russian friend. Seems he really does have a lot of money, doesn't he?'

'What do you want, Garros?'

'Want? What do I want? Twenty thousand francs is what I want. You give me twenty thousand and I don't hand over that article.'

'There's no chance in hell I could get you that kind of money.'

'You're lying to me again, aren't you? You have twenty-four hours to give me that money. I'm being generous, Halifax.

You'll get it back with interest if you win that prize.' He shook his pale-knuckled fist in Halifax's face. 'You owe me, Halifax.'

'Why did you bother with all this, Garros?'

Garros shook his head, nostrils flared. 'You didn't have to stand there in that little room in Marseille while the commanding officer of the investigating unit hollered in my face and tore up my report and demoted me and finally decided that wasn't enough, so he discharged me. You didn't have to pack your bags and leave overnight. You didn't have to take the humiliation. That's why I bothered, because of the humiliation.'

'I saved your life down in Africa. I'm asking you to believe that.'

'Asking me? Why don't you beg me?'

Halifax watched him for a couple of seconds, saying nothing. Then he smiled. 'What if I could get you that money?'

'Then we'd be quits.'

'I'll see what I can do.'

Now Garros smiled as well. 'Good. I'm glad you see things my way. I'll see you in twenty-four hours.' He spun on his heels and started to walk away.

Halifax reached for the drawer under the workbench and pulled out Ivan's Lebel. He stepped toward Garros, holding the gun out at arm's length.

Garros turned. As soon as he saw what Halifax was carrying, he raised his hands in the air. 'Wait! Wait a minute!' His fingers groped towards the ceiling.

Halifax set the barrel against Garros's forehead.

'Wait,' Garros said again, but quietly, the energy gone from his voice. His hands dropped to his sides. Veins stood out on his neck.

Halifax pulled the trigger, seeing the blur of the hammer go back and then snap forward, his arm braced for the shock. The chamber was empty.

Garros cried out and shut his eyes tight.

Halifax cocked the gun again.

Garros went down on his knees. 'For Christ's sake!' He hooked his elbows over the top of his head.

Halifax bent down, aimed at Garros's temple and pulled the trigger again. Another empty chamber. He let his arm fall to his side, still holding the gun.

Garros crawled backwards. His knees caught on the material

237

of his trenchcoat. 'Jesus,' he kept whispering. Then suddenly he stood up and ran.

Halifax watched him disappear down the muddy road. He threw the gun into the field, hearing it land amongst the cabbages.

Baturin appeared beside him, still carrying the broom. 'I took out the bullets a few days ago, after Ivan tried to kill himself.'

'I know. I could see it wasn't loaded when I took it out of the drawer.' He sighed and looked at Baturin. 'But my pal Garros didn't know that, did he?' He breathed the rainy air blowing in from the field. 'We're fucked.'

'I could still pay him a visit.' Baturin scratched at his chin.

'What good would it do? You'll never get to him in time.'

Baturin sighed. 'No, probably not. I'll cash in my ticket and give you back your money.'

'No, Baturin. It's your ticket. I don't want it back.'

For a while they said nothing. The sun went down in ragged pink bars through the trees.

'I thought my plan would work, Baturin. The whole plan.'

'Yes, sir. But I don't think . . .'

'I didn't think it would come to this.'

'No, sir. But I really doubt he . . .'

'It's getting very hard to keep the fighting clean.'

Baturin sighed and rocked hard on his heels. 'So what?' His voice was clipped with anger.

Halifax had never heard that tone from him before. 'What do you mean?'

Baturin shrugged. 'So don't start sweating until you see the thing in print. Don't panic until you have to. Besides, Mr. Halifax, if you think this is unclean fighting, you wait until I start playing patty-cake with that little spot-faced fuck.'

Halifax blinked at him.

'Mmmm.' Baturin nodded, emptying the bullets from one hand to the other and back again. He was trying not to grin. 'You wait and watch the show.'

# 18

DIESEL FUMES COUGHED in Halifax's face as he walked behind the truck that carried his Levasseur. Its wings had been taken off and laid beside the fuselage. Fat coils of red-brown hemp rope lashed everything to the bed of the truck.

Ivan drove. Now and then he leaned out of the cab and grinned at Halifax.

Halifax looked back at the barn. Rain tapped on his head. Water ran off the slate tiles of the roof, channelled by a gutter into the rain barrel where he washed every morning.

Deschamps stood in his cabbage field. He wore his floppy hat and carried a shotgun. The chains of his rabbit traps were slung over his shoulders. When he saw Halifax turn, he raised the gun over his head and held it there. Then he wandered back towards his house.

A temporary hangar made of canvas had been set up on the airfield at Le Bourget. They rolled the Levasseur inside the hangar and reassembled the wings. Two army cots and the gas heater had been placed in a corner.

Ivan and Halifax tied down the entrance flap and stood for a while in the dark, saying nothing. Wind thumped at the walls. The smell of canvas filled up their lungs.

Ivan cleared his throat. 'It's been twenty-seven hours since Garros left.'

'Right.'

'Any news?'

'What? Since the last time you asked me a half hour ago? No, Ivan. There hasn't been any news.'

'How about the weather report? Did I ask you about that already?'

'The weathermen say there's still a high pressure ridge in the mid-Atlantic. They're hoping it'll die down by the tenth.' Halifax took a brass cigarette lighter from his pocket and spun the flint. The flame popped to life and the Levasseur jumped at them out of the dark. Suddenly its wings were over them. The engine grille hung open like a mouth.

Every time Halifax shut his eyes, a grey tide rolled in from the horizon of his dreaming. He saw the wall of the approaching storm. It churned in a slow avalanche over the waves, far out in the middle of the sea. Clouds spat lightning in his face. He heard the storm's slow pounding drag across the sea. It ploughed the waves. Nothing moved through it. Nothing got by.

Several times a night, he stood up from his cot and walked across to the gas heater. He squatted on the trampled grass, facing away from the plane, afraid to close his eyes and afraid to go back to sleep. The heater grumbled and hissed and lit his face with its pale blue flame.

'Ivan?' He stumbled into the hangar. It was completely dark. He breathed in the musty canvas air.

Halifax had spent his afternoon at the avenue Rapp. His pockets were stuffed with the latest weather reports. He took out his lighter and spun the flint. Sparks popped up around his thumb, but the wick didn't burn. He tried it again and nothing happened, so he got down on his hands and knees and crawled towards his cot, where he knew there was an oil lamp hanging from a nail in one of the support poles. He knew if he didn't crawl, he'd trip over something.

A match cracked into flames. Suddenly there was light in the tent.

Two young faces peered down at Halifax. A small hand held out the match pinched between finger and thumb. They were boys. They wore heavy black shoes and their bare knees were splattered with mud. Their socks hung down around their ankles.

Halifax started to get up. 'Don't I know you from somewhere?' He snapped his fingers. 'You're the boys who were at the crash that day. You're the ones who hunt Deschamp's rabbits with slingshots. I remember you.'

The match went out and the two boys started running. Halifax grabbed at the dark and latched on to a collar. Two hands clawed at his arm, then a kick struck his shin.

'He's got me! Come back and help! He's got me!' The boy threw another kick.

The other boy ran into the canvas wall of the tent, fell over, crawled out under it and kept running.

'Come back! He's got me!'

Halifax groaned with the pain in his shin. 'He's not coming back for you.'

The boy kicked him again.

'All right, stop! You kick me again and I'll kick you back.' He dragged the boy over to the support post, found the lamp and held it out. 'Now, light another one of your matches and set this lamp going.'

The boy fumbled in his pocket and Halifax heard the rattle of matches in a box, then a crack, and light spread again from the boy's hands. The boy held out the flame. His breath stuttered as he tried to hold back tears.

'How come you're crying?' Halifax still held on to him, fist knotted in the collar of the boy's wool jacket.

'Don't hurt me.'

'I'm not going to hurt you.'

'You're hurting me right now.'

'Well, if I let you go, you'll run away.'

'You'd run away too, if you were me.' The boy stood on the tips of his toes almost hanging in the air by his collar.

'How did you get in here? I'm supposed to have a man guarding the place.'

'He went into town to get some food.'

'How do you know?'

'I heard him. I was hiding right outside. He was singing opera music. Then he had a long talk with himself about soup and bread and cheese, and walked out of the tent. Me and Arnaud sneaked in. We only wanted to have a look at the plane. That's all we wanted.'

'Did you break anything?'

'No, sir.'

'Touch anything?'

'We sat in the plane for a while.'

'Damn it!' Halifax dragged the boy over to the cockpit and peered in. Their footprints dirtied the seat. 'You better not have broken anything.'

'We didn't. I promise. Please don't hurt me.'

'What makes you think I'm going to hurt you?'

'Once, when you were out at that farm place where all the

241

cabbages grow, Arnaud and I heard you yelling that you'd kill anyone who came around. You had a gun.'

'Oh.' Halifax nodded. He loosened his grip on the boy's collar.

'Are you going to let me go?'

'Sure.' Halifax lowered the lamp and the light slid away from his face. 'What's your name?'

'Albert.'

'You ever been up in a plane?' Halifax let go of his collar.

'No, sir.' The boy skipped a few paces out of reach.

'If you come by tomorrow at seven o'clock, I'll fly you over Paris.'

'No you won't.' He edged toward the entrance flan. 'You'll have the police waiting for me. You'll set out traps and catch me the same way that old farmer catches rabbits.'

Halifax shrugged. 'So don't come.'

'I didn't say I wouldn't come.' The boy darted out. His footsteps thumped away across the grass.

Halifax checked over the plane, wiping away the muddy footprints, running his hand over the control panels like a blind man reading Braille, checking for cracks, dents and missing parts.

Ivan's voice reached him through the thick canvas blanket of the hangar. 'I could take that plane apart and put it back together with my eyes closed. Charlie? Well, he flies the Levasseur, of course, but without me he'd be crawling around on his hands and knees.' The entrance flap swept back and Ivan walked in carrying a lamp. Shadows barged back and forth as the lamp swung in his hand.

Another man walked in behind him, one of the regular mechanics at the airfield. 'Where's Mr. Halifax?'

Ivan laughed. 'He's probably standing on a bridge over the Seine, flapping his arms and trying to make the flight, not only without me but without the Levasseur. The way I hear him talk, all he thinks he needs is a propeller bolted to his nose and a beer mug full of aircraft fuel and he'd be all set for the Orteig Prize.'

The mechanic walked up to the plane. 'You'd better not give him any ideas.'

Halifax hunched down the cockpit.

The mechanic tapped the metal engine grille. Tiny vibrations rippled through the plane.

Don't touch, Halifax thought. Get your fucking hands away.

'I don't give him any ideas he wouldn't eventually have by himself. It takes patience to deal with him, you see. And I am a pillar of patience.' Ivan cracked his knuckles. 'Now and then he just needs a shove in the right direction.'

You bandy-legged Russian cowboy, Halifax was thinking. You imperial chubby-faced pansy.

The mechanic cleared his throat. 'I should be getting back to the hut.'

'Thanks for the soup.'

'Not at all.' The entrance flap rustled and the mechanic slipped out.

Ivan hummed to himself. He walked to his cot and lay down.

Halifax listened to the sound of Ivan's boots dropping one by one to the ground. Then he took a deep breath and sighed very heavily.

'Who's there?' Ivan sat up.

Halifax slowly stood in the cockpit.

Ivan slid off his cot. 'How the hell did you get there?'

'I've been here a while.'

'Oh.' Ivan nodded and pursed his lips. Then he pointed toward the entrance flap. 'I was just out getting some food.' He looked hopeful. 'Asleep, were you?'

'No.'

Ivan scratched his head. 'I was just having a talk with one of the mechanics. Just a little talk, you know.'

'Two boys got in here while you were gone.'

'Did they?' Ivan winced. 'Is everything all right?'

'I told you not to leave the fucking plane.'

'Well, from now on, you won't have to worry about it. They're having guards stationed outside the hangar.'

'Who is?'

'The Aero Club is paying for them. Apparently, they think the crowds could get a little rowdy. Mme. de Montclaire sent her flunky Merlot to tell us this afternoon.' Ivan turned his head to one side and squinted at Halifax. 'See what happens when you listen to your old friend Ivan?'

'Sure I see. I end up standing on a bridge with a propeller bolted to my nose.'

'You shouldn't have just sat there and let me say rude things.

243

It's not fair. I didn't mean them.' Ivan jabbed his heel into the ground. 'I suppose you think I meant those things.'

Albert showed up at seven.

He brought his friend Arnaud. They stood side by side in their dirty shoes, with their socks down by their ankles.

'Ready for your ride?' Halifax threw a flight cap to Albert.

'What about me?' Arnaud stuck out his chin. 'Can I come too?'

'Only room for one more.' Halifax walked over to the Levasseur. He'd had it wheeled out earlier that morning.

Arnaud followed them to the plane. 'But we're smaller than you are. Two of us could fit in the seat.'

Albert put on Ivan's flight cap. 'You heard him. No room.'

'But it was my idea to sneak in!' Arnaud tugged at Halifax's sleeve. 'I thought of it.'

'You should have stuck around.' Halifax lifted Albert into the cockpit and strapped him in.

The mechanic from the night before left his hut and came walking over, looking for Ivan.

Halifax waved hello. 'I hear my co-pilot gave you quite a talk last night.'

The mechanic grinned. 'He had plenty to say.'

'Please can I come up?' Arnaud pulled at Halifax's hand. 'Could you go up maybe two times?'

'Maybe so. But it would only be a short trip.'

'Short's all right.' Arnaud stepped back as the mechanic ushered him away from the plane.

The Levasseur rose up above Le Bourget. Albert couldn't see over the rim of the cockpit, so Halifax tipped the plane almost over on its side to let him look out.

'My mother would kill me if she knew I was here.' Albert shouted over the drumming of the engine. The goggles nearly covered his whole face.

'Oh.' Halifax thought about it. 'Maybe we shouldn't tell her.'

'She says you're a bad man.'

'Why's that?' Halifax yelled back at him, eyes flipping back and forth across the controls, resting for a second on each needle in each dial, then moving on.

'She says people have seen you wandering around in the cabbage field in a tuxedo in the middle of the night.'

'That makes me a bad man? Do I look bad to you?'

'You look a little beat up.'

'But bad? Do I look like a bad man?'

'How should I know?' His voice was already strained from shouting.

'You ever heard of the headless horseman?'

'No.'

'*He* was a very bad man.'

He brought the Levasseur down after ten minutes because it looked as if Albert might throw up. Then he flew Arnaud, and Arnaud did throw up.

When Halifax landed a second time, Ivan was standing outside the hangar in his underpants. He had balanced a hand-size metal mirror on top of a fuel drum and was shaving himself with a cut-throat. His cheeks were clouds of shaving soap.

Halifax leaned against the side of the plane as he watched. He wished he had a son or daughter, wished he had a wife and a house and a job. Heat from the engine reached through to his back. 'Any news?'

'Not a thing.' Ivan scraped at his chin with the blade. 'Not one titty-fucking thing.'

Halifax let his flying gloves drop to the ground. The old leather was almost worn through. 'I'm not going to wait anymore.'

'What choice do you have?' Ivan pressed a towel to his face. His voice was muffled in flannel.

'I'm going to see Tuttle.'

'What good will that do?' Ivan's skin had goose bumps in the cool air.

'I can trust Tuttle.'

'Wait a minute.' Ivan wrapped the towel around his neck. 'You can't trust him. You don't know him anymore. Besides, he's a journalist. He makes a living off people like you. Why don't you go talk to Garros instead? Or let Baturin talk to him.' Now he stood only an arm's length from Halifax.

'I have to find out what's happening or I'll go out of my head.'

'Oh, you will?' Ivan tugged at the ends of the towel. 'The way you are right now, Charlie, you won't notice any difference.'

Tuttle was on his way home. He walked down the steps of the *Herald Tribune* building and fitted a hat on his head. He tried to

245

open his umbrella but it didn't work. He tried again, shook it, flailing raindrops. When it didn't work a third time, he smacked the umbrella against a brass handrail running down the length of the steps. The umbrella snapped in half. For a moment, he stared at the J-shaped stump of the handle. Then he threw it away.

Halifax raised his hand to say hello.

Tuttle stamped past, chin tucked into his collar.

Halifax skipped after him. 'Will. Hey, Will.'

Tuttle stopped. He didn't turn around. 'Charlie.'

Halifax watched Tuttle's broad back. The man's shoulders were wedged into a gray gabardine raincoat. 'I wanted to talk for a minute.'

'I thought maybe you'd be stopping by.' Tuttle walked across the street, still without turning around.

It was late afternoon. Cars and people jammed the road. Tuttle stopped at a newsstand and bought a copy of all the papers being sold except the *Tribune*. He rolled them into a thick bundle, which he shook at Halifax. 'The competition.'

Halifax shuffled to keep up. 'Can I buy you a cup of coffee?'

Tuttle glanced from under his hat. 'I guess.' Rain washed in streams along the gutter. He kept walking.

Halifax grabbed a handful of Tuttle's sleeve. The gray gabardine crumpled in his fist. 'What the hell are you so dog-faced about, Will? All I asked was if I could buy you a cup of coffee.'

'You're stupid to come to me, Charlie.' Tuttle raised his head. Water drained off the brim of his hat. 'How do you know if you can trust me?'

So you know, thought Halifax. He thought it and then he said it. 'So you know.'

'Maybe.'

His patience crumbled away. 'Don't get fucking mysterious with me, Tuttle. I don't have a damn thing to lose either way.'

'Why not?' He weighed the rolled newspapers in his hand, like a club.

'Because if I've lost anything, it's already gone.' Halifax spat the rain off his lips. 'Now do you want a lousy cup of coffee or don't you?'

Tuttle sat down at a table. He looked around for the waiter, then slapped his palms on the marble top. 'This is my table, Charlie. I've been coming here for six years and always at the same time and always the same table. If you were to sit here and it was this time of day and I wasn't here with you' – he jerked his thumb over his shoulder – 'they'd give you the boot.'

Halifax looked past Tuttle at the pepper-grey sky. People crowded under the red awning of the Café Fontenac, hiding from the downpour.

Tuttle tapped a coin on the table top, impatient for his coffee. He still wore his hat. 'I'm not supposed to talk about this. Just this afternoon I swore to my supervisor that I'd keep my mouth shut.' He took a deep breath and shouted across the room for two coffees. 'My supervisor is a frightening man. Every time I talk to him, I come away just glad that we're on the same side.' He waved the log of newspapers at Halifax. 'Now you, you're going to make me promise to break my other promise. I have bad dreams about things like this, Charlie. Little devil people stick me in my fat butt with pitchforks and dance around me in red suits because I broke a promise and any dumb shit knows about breaking promises and going to hell. Am I right?'

'You talk too much, Will. I like you but you talk too much.' Halifax's glasses had steamed up. He took them off and polished them.

Tuttle gritted his teeth and then sat back when the waiter arrived with the coffee.

The waiter removed Tuttle's hat and held it out to him. 'The hat, sir.'

'All right! I'm not stupid.'

Tuttle snatched it and set it on the table. 'The hat.' He pulled a handful of change from his pocket, sorted through it and dropped a coin on the marble. The coin spun, flickering.

For a moment, all three of them watched it, then the waiter snatched it up and disappeared.

'I know I talk too much.' Tuttle stirred his coffee with a little spoon. Brown-white foam gathered on the black surface. He lit himself a cigarette. 'I don't care. And I don't care if you like me, either. Why don't you just not ask me anything, Charlie. Because whatever you're thinking I know about, I know. I *do* know. But it's more complicated than that. I'm not supposed to tell you. Just get in your plane on the tenth of May and make the flight and that will be that.'

'I have to know what's going on. I have to know if there's any point in me risking my damn life in that plane.' He sipped at the coffee and felt his nerves jolt.

Tuttle put his face in his hands and sighed. 'Little pitchforks, Charlie. Little sharp pitchforks.'

'Oh, forget it then.' Halifax stood.

Tuttle pulled away his hands. 'Oh, stay and drink your coffee, Charlie. I didn't mean to snap at you. It's just that I've had a bad day. I don't mean to take it out on you.' He tapped his fingers on the table. 'Come on. Sit.'

Halifax settled back down in the chair.

Tuttle rested his elbows on the marble. 'About two days ago, a man named Edouard Garros came to my office. He ran the obituary column at the *Trib*. He wanted me to publish an article. It was an article about you.'

'Right.' Halifax lowered his head and watched Tuttle's hands. They were black with newsprint.

'I told him' – Tuttle stabbed his cigarette dead in the ashtray – 'I believe I told him he should use the reverse sides of the pages for writing out new job applications.'

Halifax looked up. 'You did?'

'I did. And do you know what the little fucker told me then? He told me he'd pay me five thousand francs if I made sure it was published. At a guess, I'd say he probably told you about this article he was writing.'

'Right.'

Tuttle grabbed a handful of sugar cubes. 'I'd guess he tried to blackmail you with it.'

'Right.'

Tuttle nodded, pleased with himself. 'How much?'

'Twenty thousand.'

The muscles along Tuttle's jaw quivered. He dropped the sugar cubes one by one into his coffee, five of them. 'Son of a bitch.'

'He was in debt.'

'Damn right he was. Gambling debts. And do you know how he was paying them off?'

'No. I know he's been flashing a lot of money around lately.'

'I'm not surprised. Writing obituaries is not the hardest job in the world, but it turns out he wasn't even doing half of them on

248

time. He kept telling the senior editor that he was working on a special project.' Tuttle sat back and growled in his throat. 'Project! His editor tells him the same thing I'd have told the man. Your job is to write obits. So write the fucking obits! Now, all this is nothing special. Some new man who doesn't do his job and gets fired isn't a big deal. But it turns out he was writing some of the obituaries, then finding out where the people lived who had just died. He'd check if they had any money, and if they lived by themselves, he'd go to their houses, which he made sure were empty at the time, and the bastard was robbing the houses of the dead people. Can you believe it? Special fucking project. The police pick him up. Now I have to write a story on *him*! I have to have it on the editor's desk by tomorrow. I'm going to be up all night.' He yelled at the waiter for a pastis. 'People have a low enough opinion of journalists without having to read about idiots like Garros, but since he was working for the *Trib*, it's in our best interest to have a story on the man, or the other newspapers will think we're trying to cover up.'

The waiter set the pastis on the table. It was a small amount of honey-coloured liquid. The waiter left a jug of water, and Tuttle added some to the drink. It turned banana yellow. Tuttle drained the glass and smacked it down on the table. 'Better.'

'Did you read the article, Will? The one Garros wrote?' Halifax picked at his fingernails.

'Yes.' He laughed. 'What's the matter? You think I don't know about that?'

'You do?'

'About why you ended up in Morocco? About the deserting?' Tuttle shrugged and rubbed his big hands together. 'Known about it for a long time.'

'How?'

'I learned about it just after the war.'

'You never mentioned it.'

Tuttle sniffed. 'Neither did you! Who the hell wants to talk about a think like that? Believe it or not, I don't care. I heard how badly you got burned up. I heard they were trying to get you right back into your plane. I'd have run the same as you did.'

'I thought if anybody found out, they'd take away my chance to compete for the Orteig Prize.'

'Most people just care about the flight. The people who only

249

care about the politics of the flight, or whether the flight fits into their social agenda, they don't matter. You know that, don't you?'

Halifax just stared.

Tuttle kept talking. 'The truth is, Charlie, if you win the Orteig Prize, someone's going to find out about it anyway, and by that time, any news on you will be news that someone will publish. By then, though, it won't matter much.' He snapped his fingers at the waiter and ordered another pastis. 'Have one, Charlie. Have a couple.'

Halifax drank and the alcohol brewed in his head. It made his spit taste of liquorice and rumbled up and down his spine until it found his brain. Then it quietly exploded.

Tuttle's mouth was becoming a blur. 'Now, I talk to you about winning this thing, Charlie, and I'm sure you will. But have I talked to you about losing? Have you thought about what will happen if you fail?'

'I'll be dead.' The pastis dissolved the tidy grey corridors of his thoughts. It felt as if someone had hit him in the face with a pillow.

'You may be. You may be.' Tuttle brushed it aside with a sweep of his palm. 'But what about if you come down just outside New York, say. Ten miles out, and some trawler picks you up. You're all right but the plane's gone and you don't get the prize. What then?'

Halifax shrugged. 'The impact, Will. I doubt –'

'*If*. I said if. Play the game with me, Charlie. If you lose the race, people are going to put as much energy into forgetting about you as they'll put into remembering you if you win. Do you see?'

'I guess.'

'Take Levasseur, for example. If you win, they'll stick your name on every piece of equipment they sell. They'll build a fucking altar for you, Charlie. And what about the Aero Club? They'll sail you back to Paris as soon as they can, and they will have a party in your honour, and that zeppelin-woman Mme. de Montclaire will slobber all over you. You can bet they'll charge a fortune for places at that party, and you can bet even more sure that people will pay any price to get in. But if you fail, they'll forget your name. Just like that.' He snapped his fingers but they were wet with sweat and didn't make a noise. 'Charlie

250

who? They'll say they knew all along that you'd never make it, and then when they find out about the desertion, they'll swear that if they'd known, they never would have talked to you. The Levasseur company will *bury* you, Charles, my old pal.'

Baturin leaned from the window of the Paris–Cherbourg train as it started to roll down the tracks. 'I'll make sure they have a parade for you in New York.'

'We'll be there before you, Baturin.' Ivan paced with the train.

'Oh, yes, so you will.' Baturin laughed, and his face became suddenly serious. 'Thank you, sir.' He looked at Halifax. 'Thank you.'

Ivan and Baturin spoke in Russian and burst out laughing and hugged each other.

Steam from the train fanned out across the platform. The train was moving too fast. Baturin waved once more and backed into the carriage. Ivan and Halifax watched until the last car was gone from sight. They caught a taxi to Le Bourget.

'What did you say to Baturin?'

Ivan grinned. 'I asked him for once to call me Ivan. I asked him and then I ordered him. Both times he refused. He said it would break his heart.'

'Well, who could blame him? After all, you led the charge at Zovi Rog.'

Ivan shook his head. 'My horse led the charge. I was drunk as a bum at the time and didn't know where we were going.'

Merlot stood outside the canvas hangar. He wore a brown pinstripe suit and carried a large briefcase. He looked at the hangar, frowning, as if he couldn't figure out how to get in.

Halifax spied on him from a hole in the canvas. He didn't want to talk.

Merlot waited quietly for another minute. Then he called 'Charlie!' at the grey-green wall of cloth.

'Oh, shit.' Halifax scratched the back of his neck. He was completely naked and had been asleep. It was the sound of Merlot's car that had woken him up.

'Chaaaarlie!'

'Wait!' Halifax wandered over to his cot, put on some trousers, and pulled the braces over his shoulders. 'Wait a minute!'

'Charlie.' Now Merlot's voice came from just the other side of the canvas. 'I was hoping you'd be in.'

Halifax swung back the entrance flap. 'Merlot.'

'Charlie!' Merlot's arm swung out and he walked into the tent. He shook Halifax's hand. The briefcase he carried had polished brass fittings.

'What can I do for you, Merlot? Do you want a free ride in the plane?'

Merlot laughed and shook his head. 'No, not me. No, I have come to talk with you about a proposition.' He set his briefcase down on workbench, which they had brought with them from the barn. Merlot opened the case. 'I've been working on this for a very long time.'

Halifax sat down on his cot and hunted for a cigarette, wondering when Ivan would come back from the avenue Rapp with the latest weather reports.

Merlot shut his briefcase and held up something that looked like one of Deschamps's dead rabbits. 'This is the product of many months of work.' He wedged the dead rabbit onto his head. It was a flying cap. He reached up and flipped down a pair of goggles that had been stitched onto the brim. All that showed of his face was a smile. 'It is a device which I believe will revolutionize clothing in the air. I am calling it the Merlot Air Hat.'

'Sounds good to me.' Halifax fitted a cigarette into his mouth. The dry paper stuck to his lips.

'You think so? Well, the proposition I have to make to you is this.' He walked out from behind the workbench. 'I will agree to supply you and Mr. Konovalchik with the Merlot Air Hat in exchange for a modest amount of publicity.'

Halifax shifted on the cot looking for his lighter.

Merlot held up his hand. 'Before you answer me, I should tell you that this garment will be very expensive in the retail marketplace. I am not a supplier to the masses. I am a supplier to a select few.'

'Midgets and fat people.'

'Would you like to try this on?' Merlot took off the hat.

'Not right now, thanks.' Wind beat against the canvas wall. Halifax looked up, hoping it might be Ivan.

Merlot held up one finger. 'I look upon my clients as my personal friends.'

'That's very good of you.'

Merlot put the hat back on.

'You're my friend, Charlie, and this is a superior piece of equipment.'

'I see.'

'Good!'

'*Can* you see?'

'I can see very well.' Merlot flipped up the goggles and blinked, then he walked over to the Levasseur. 'This is a beautiful machine.'

'Yes, it is.' It made Halifax nervous seeing Merlot so close to the plane.

Merlot groped his hands along the wing and the tail. 'What is it called?'

'Called?'

'What is its name?'

'I haven't given it a name.'

He nodded and sniffed. 'As I said earlier, I would agree to supplying you with my Merlot Air Hat in return for some publicity.' He fanned his hands across the Levasseur's blank white belly. 'Call it *Merlot*.' He moved his hands again, as if framing the words. 'Red letters. I'll pay for the art work, of course.'

'I don't think so, Philippe.'

'But why not?' Merlot whistled quietly through his teeth. 'After all, if you haven't given it a name, then surely you don't care what people call it. What's wrong with *Merlot*? Think of the free merchandise I'm offering you.'

Halifax scratched at his head, wondering how much longer he could stay polite. 'I think I'll do fine with the clothes I have on.'

'No, you won't. Look.' Merlot put on his rabbit hat. 'It's ahead of its time.'

'Have you tried any of the other competitors? Maybe they'd be interested.'

'Oh, I have had several inquiries already.' He swept his hands back and forth across the fuselage. '*Merlot*,' he muttered. 'It's so little to ask.'

'I think I'll leave the plane the way it is.' Halifax stood and moved toward the workbench, hoping he could find something to do that looked important.

'All right!' Merlot hid behind his suitcase as Halifax came closer.

Halifax saw he had a toothbrush in one of the slots made for a pen. 'All right what?'

'You wouldn't have to call it the *Merlot*. Instead, just put my name in smaller letters on the side. Smaller letters, you understand.' He blocked out a space between his palms.

'I'm really quite busy, Philippe.' Halifax picked up a pot of varnish. The liquid had dried and the paintbrush was welded to the bottom. He pretended to stir the varnish. 'I'm on a schedule.'

Merlot stuffed the flying cap back into his briefcase and snapped its brass locks shut. 'The offer may not last.'

'I understand.' He walked Merlot outside. They both squinted in the light.

'When will you be in touch with me again?' Merlot was hugging his briefcase. 'Tomorrow? Later today?'

'I'll give you a call. How about that?' Halifax took the unlit cigarette from his mouth and flicked it away in the grass.

'I don't have a telephone.'

Just then Halifax saw Ivan walking over to the hangar. 'Here comes my co-pilot. I'm sorry to leave you like this, Philippe, but we have a lot of work today. Stop by some other time.' He had smiled so much his jaw was aching.

'Perhaps Mr. Konovalchik would be interested in my product.' Without waiting to hear what Halifax would say, Merlot set off toward Ivan. With Merlot's back to him, Halifax waved his arms and shook his head at Ivan. Merlot stopped in front of Ivan, shook his hand, then squatted down on the ground to open the suitcase.

Ivan peered at Halifax.

Merlot put the Air Hat on his head.

Ivan burst out laughing.

Merlot stuffed the cap back in his suitcase and walked away with fast strides too long for his legs.

There was nothing to do.

The two guards sent by the Aero Club paced back and forth outside the canvas walls. Halifax listened to the slow tread of their boots on the grass. Their pacing reminded him of Leffrinckouke military prison and the heartbeat clack of steel-lugged heels on the floor outside his cell. He tried to think of some detail they might have forgotten, something to keep them up all night working. It seemed to him that the only time he could think straight was when he had no time to lose.

The Levasseur stooped over them, crowding the tent.

It was too quiet. He stood up and walked to the workbench. All the brushes had been set out in neat rows and the varnish pots cleaned and stacked. The tool boxes were closed and in their place.

Ivan took off his shoes and spit-polished them with a handkerchief.

'Why are you doing that?' Halifax drummed his fingers on the bench.

'Bad habit.'

'Do you think there's anything we've missed?'

Ivan snorted. 'Sit down and enjoy the silence.'

'I can't. I hate the quiet. Must be something we missed.'

'Nothing, Charlie.' He spat and rubbed the polish on his toe caps. 'Relax.'

Halifax went over to Ivan and crouched down. 'Do you miss Justine?'

Ivan looked up. 'Of course. Stupid question.'

'You've been so quiet about it. You haven't mentioned her since the funeral.'

'What's there to mention?' Ivan stopped polishing.

'It might help to talk a bit.'

'Talk about what? When I think about her, I can't believe she's dead. Do you see?' He tapped the shoe against his head. 'I can't get it into my head. It seems like every twenty seconds I catch myself making plans for what she and I will do when we get to America and then I remember she's dead. But I can't believe it. I saw the damn coffin go down and I refuse to believe it. Do you see what I'm saying?'

'Sure, Ivan.'

'Well, good. Because I don't. It should be the clearest thing in the world. She's dead. But it's not clear at all. The more I think about it, the less clear it seems. I wish to hell I could think about something else for a change.'

Halifax walked back to the Levasseur. He had more energy in him than he knew how to control. 'I can't think past the moment that we set down in New York harbour. I can't get past that point. Can't plan. Can't even picture it. I think there's something wrong with me.'

Ivan spat on his shoes. 'The both of us will be so surprised to be alive that even if we did have a plan, we'd be too shaken up to use it. Besides, there'll be ten thousand people waiting for us on the docks. We'll let them figure out what to do with us.'

'We should go now, Ivan. What's stopping us from leaving right now?'

'The weather's stopping us. You said the tenth, remember? Do you want to run head first into that storm?'

'No.' Halifax sat on his cot, arms clutched against his sides. 'I don't want to be in the storm.'

# 19

'WHAT'S THE MATTER?' Ivan stood at the edge of the dark, where the oil lamp's flame gave out.

Halifax lay on his cot. He shrugged under the weight of his blanket.

'Well, *something's* the matter with you.' Ivan folded his arms. 'You keep twitching your arms and your legs. It's keeping me awake.'

Halifax shook his head back and forth in the dent of his pillow. 'You're imagining it.'

Ivan went back to his cot and turned down the oil lamp. Sudden blackness poured down on top of them.

Halifax could see nothing at first. After a minute, he made out a sliver of twilight that showed through a crack in the hangar's entrance flap. His arm twitched again and he tried to stop it. He didn't want to tell Ivan what he was doing. For hours now, Halifax had been running through his head the sequence of dials on the Levasseur's control panel. His feet and hands flinched as he repeated the movements of take-off, landing and dodging wind pockets and waves of storm clouds that billowed up out of his thoughts.

He looked across and caught the shine from Ivan's open eyes. Now that his eyes were used to the dark, it seemed to Halifax that he could see Ivan's lips moving. He strained to hear words but caught only the squelch of the guards' boots outside as they paced around the hangar. They were infantry soldiers assigned to Le Bourget.

Halifax woke to the sound of arguing. He grabbed for his watch on the chair next to him, hoping he might have slept for a long time, perhaps even the whole night, and that now it was time to leave. But he saw he had only slept half an hour. Outside the hangar, the soldiers were turning newsmen away. The newsmen said it was important, and they knew Ivan, they knew Halifax. Said they'd been invited and a lot of shit was going to fly if they didn't get into that tent. There was some whispering as they tried to bribe the soldiers. Halifax heard the dead-leaf rustle of bills, then the soldiers barked at the newsmen, telling them to leave.

After a few minutes a noise came from the far end of the hangar. A head appeared where the canvas met the ground. A man struggled through and then stood.

Ivan lit the oil lamp, and he and Halifax sat on their cots, watching.

The man smiled. 'Evening.' He wore thick wool trousers. His knees were pasted with mud.

Ivan pointed to the entrance. 'There's a door, you know.'

'Yes. Yes.' The man kept smiling and shifted on his feet. 'I'm with *La Presse*.' He took out a pad of paper and a pencil. 'All right if I ask you a few questions about the flight?'

'Go ahead, now that you're here.' Halifax lay back on his cot. He stared at the ceiling.

The reporter crouched down and rested the pad on his knee. 'Is it true you're leaving tomorrow?'

'True.'

'And is it true that you signed a contract with the Wright-Bellanca Company for the use of your names if you make the crossing?'

'Where did that one come from?'

The man looked up from his scribbling. 'I guess it's just a rumour. How about the bets that people are putting on you? Did you know about them?'

'What kind of bets?'

'The Paris bookies have set the odds at five-to-two against. Do you have anything to say about those odds?'

One of the soldiers stuck his head into the hangar. 'You son of a bitch. Didn't you hear me the first time?'

The man with the muddy trousers winced. 'Only a couple more questions. Tell him to leave me alone for a minute, can you? I'm just doing my job. What about Africa? What did you think of the place?'

'It was very hot and we did not enjoy ourselves.'

The soldier walked across the trampled grass, his hand stretched out to grab the newsman.

'Did you think up this whole plan when you were down there?' The newsman spat out the words as fast as he could talk.

Halifax rested his head on his hands. 'That's right.'

The soldier hoisted the man to his feet and pulled him outside.

The whole day went by. In the evening, Halifax peered out through a tear in the canvas. Several cars lined the runway. People milled around them. Bunting hung from the gates at the entrance to the airfield. Halifax saw the Aero Club banner and the words 'Paris–New York'. The runway stretched off towards a patch of woods.

A soldier walked past. His grey-blue wool coat brushed against the canvas. Halifax was still peering through the tear when Tuttle's car arrived. Tuttle climbed out, smiled at the soldiers and started walking toward the hangar. The soldiers stood in his way.

'It's fine. I'm a friend of Charlie Halifax.' Tuttle smiled again and tried to push past.

The two men hooked their hands under his arms and started dragging him back to his car. Tuttle didn't struggle. He looked from one soldier to the other.

Halifax walked out. Fresh air cut into his lungs.

Tuttle pointed and said something to the soldiers.

'We thought. We have orders.' One soldier tipped his helmet back and chewed his lip.

'Doesn't matter.' Halifax shook his head.

Tuttle brushed at his arms, sweeping away the wrinkles in his coat. He opened his car door and they both got inside. 'Did you hire those guys?'

'Mme. de Montclaire gave them to us.' Halifax slumped onto the leather seat. The car smelled of old smoke.

'I came to say goodbye.' Tuttle sat wedged behind the steering wheel. The colours of sunset were pale on his face.

'There's a rumour that we signed a contract with the Wright-Bellanca Company.'

Tuttle nodded. 'I heard that one too.'

'Why haven't any of those companies come to us? You said they would.'

'They're waiting.' Tuttle opened the door and stretched out

259

his legs. 'Their waiting to see if you crash. They don't want their names associated with yours if you don't make it to the other side. Right now, the whole world's staring you in the face.' He tucked in his legs and shut the door again. 'I hear they've got a hell of a party lined up when you arrive in New York. Have you ever been in a ticker tape parade?'

'No.'

'You will be. I have a lot of money riding on you and your plane. You'd better win the prize, or I won't be getting much to eat for the next few months.'

Each time he woke, Halifax heard the muttering of voices. Rain tapped at the hangar roof, leaked through cracks and broke on to smooth wings of the Levasseur. He wandered paths of nonsense in his half-sleep. All through the night, cars continued to arrive. Sharp glare from headlights cut in through the hangar entrance. He listened to motors clattering to a stop as ignitions were switched off, then the bang of doors closing.

The clerk from avenue Rapp was due in at five in the morning with the latest weather report.

Halifax wanted to be gone. A fluttering kept up behind his ribs. It soured his guts and wouldn't go away. He wished something was broken so he could fix it. He wished someone would ask him some questions. He wanted to shave – shaving sometimes calmed him down. He swung out of bed, then thought of what Ivan would say, and lay down again. He imagined the slow scrape of the razor across his cheek, over his upper lip and down the length of his chin. It stopped the fluttering for a while, but the pictures fell apart and he was left staring at the green roof, where the storm itself seemed to be unravelling. He felt the stampede of thunder only just beyond the limits of his hearing.

The two soldiers paced back and forth, rifles on their backs. Ivan shifted on his cot. Halifax put his hands over his ears, trying to block out the footsteps, the whispers and the rustle of clothes. He looked at his watch. Then again, and again. After checking it more than a dozen times in half an hour, he put it in his boot, stuffed a sock in after it and threw the boot to the other end of the hangar.

There was a leak in one of the Levasseur's tyres – he could hear

260

it. He crawled across and checked the pressure and found there was no leak. Back to bed. Half an hour later, he was sitting in the cockpit, testing the lights on each instrument dial, on some hunch that the fuses had blown. The lights were fine. Halifax raked his fingers through his hair. There was too much noise in his head, like an orchestra tuning up. It seemed to him that the roots of his sanity were being tugged up one by one.

On his bed again, the stale smell of his own breath bouncing back off the pillow, exhaustion finally settled on him. The huge weight of his tired muscles pushed him down into sleep. He felt himself drowning and no longer cared.

His eyes popped open. Someone stood at the entrance. It was a man, shifting on his feet and peering into the gloom. Halifax watched him without moving. He recognized the face: it was the clerk from the avenue Rapp. He held a sheet of Teletype paper in his hands.

Halifax had imagined the man's arrival so many times that now he couldn't be sure he wasn't dreaming it. The man looked around, made nervous by the dark and the plane looming over him, and padded over the grass to the cots.

Halifax wanted more time. Suddenly unfinished business crowded into his head. I should have written letters, he thought, I should have written a will.

'Sir?' The clerk rustled the Teletype paper. 'Sir?' He stood over Halifax, looking down.

'Are you early?' Halifax's mouth tasted bad.

The clerk checked his watch. 'No, sir. Five o'clock. Right on time.'

'Is it good news about the weather? Read me the report, can you?'

Ivan snuffled in his sleep.

The clerk squatted down and whispered, not wanting to wake Ivan. 'Twenty-five-mile-an-hour head winds over Paris and as far as London. Then a small amount of storm activity over the Irish Sea.'

'A storm?' Halifax grabbed at the sheet. The print was too faint and he couldn't read what it said.

'Only a small one, sir. No threat. We estimate the flight will take you fifteen hours.'

'What about tomorrow?' He swung out from under the sheets. 'Would the weather be better tomorrow?'

'No, sir. There's a bad front moving up from the south. It'll be here soon.'

Halifax sat on the edge of his cot, fingers pressed against his closed eyes until flashes of colour burst in the dark. 'Were you the one I yelled at before?'

'Yes, sir.'

'I didn't mean to yell.'

The clerk's teeth showed as he smiled. 'That's all right, sir. Really. That's all right.'

Ivan held up the pocket mirror while Halifax shaved by the lantern's light. The mirror shook in Ivan's hand. Halifax wiped soap from the razor's flat blade onto a towel. Sleep peeled back from him now, and time seemed to be moving on its regular path again. The small thoughts that had been driving him mad went away. He felt each heartbeat shudder in his veins. He was hungry.

After he had finished, he held the mirror for Ivan, allowing his eyes to rest on the curves of Ivan's face, seeing each thread of bristle cut back by the sweep of the blade. A smell of almonds from the shaving soap filtered into his lungs.

Halifax dressed very slowly, feeling the smoothness of clean clothes and the hug of socks on his calves. He hopped into a corner of the hangar and retrieved his boots and watch.

A mechanic with scarred and dirty hands brought them breakfast. He sat with them, resting on his haunches, while Halifax and Ivan ate the orange smiles of cantaloupe, bread rolls stuffed with cheese and coffee gone a little cold from the time it took to reach them. Halifax was grateful that the man didn't want to talk. He knew he should say something, but the time seemed too choked with importance. He could find no words that fitted. He's wondering if this is the last meal we'll ever eat, Halifax thought to himself. In the end, he didn't even thank the mechanic for the food, and their eyes didn't meet. The mechanic smiled into space, forearms resting on his knees.

The first thing Halifax saw when he walked outside was a light in the window of the mechanics' hut. Condensation plastered the windows. He knew they must have been awake all night. The edge of the runway was jammed with cars. Lights flickered, cigarettes rising and falling from mouths. The sky was purple and grey. Soldiers stood on the airfield. All of them wore greatcoats that came down almost to their ankles and carried rifles with fixed bayonets.

Ivan and Halifax wheeled the Levasseur out onto the runway. Dew beaded on the wings and they brushed it off.

Halifax kept breathing deeper and deeper until he was dizzy. The scrabbling and fluttering had started in his guts again. Once more time bulged out of shape and went too slowly. He couldn't understand why Ivan seemed so calm. Then he realized that perhaps he looked calm, too. It was only inside that the small things were driving him mad.

Ivan checked the tanks as mechanics filled them. He listened to the rustle of fuel piping into the machine. Now and then, he turned towards the crowd and squinted, as if to find someone he knew.

A cluster of men with cameras stood behind the barricade of soldiers, snapped their fingers and called out. Bursts of magnesium flickered across the grass as they took pictures.

Halifax climbed into the cockpit and settled himself in his seat. The wicker creaked when he leaned back into it. He turned on the panel lights and the controls lit up with tiny balls of green. Closing his eyes, he ran over each of the dials in his head, then shifted the control stick and pedals as Ivan walked around the plane, checking the flaps and rudders. Flecks of rain patted the machine, leaving broken threads like Morse code on the windscreen. Yellow puddles of sunlight showed on the horizon.

'Hello? Charles? Hello?' A woman's voice. Mme. de Montclaire. Halifax wondered how she had got past the soldiers.
'I wanted to say goodbye.' She stood up on her toes. 'I wanted to tell you good luck. And I've brought you some food for the trip.'

She handed him a paper bag.

Halifax leaned out of the cockpit and took the bag. Mme. de Montclaire kissed him on the lenses of his goggles. Cameras flashed in the background. Mme. de Montclaire faced the newsmen and smiled. There were more bursts of blinding light.

'You look as if you're ready to take my place, Mme. de Montclaire.'

She was wearing one of Merlot's Air Hats, as well as riding boots and breeches. She looked down at her clothes, as if she had forgotten what she was wearing and had only thrown on the first thing she could find before leaving the house. 'Well, they say it's going to become the rage.'

'Mr. Merlot says, anyway.'

'Yes, Mr. Merlot.' She squinted. 'You aren't wearing the Merlot Air Hat.'

'No, ma'am.' Halifax pulled down the goggles, tired of looking through the spat of her lipstick marks on the glass.

Ivan snickered on the other side of the plane.

Mme. de Montclaire took off the hat and patted her hair into place. 'He assured me that you would be wearing his Air Hat on the flight. In fact, I expected to see his name on the plane here. He was telling everyone –'

One of the soldiers put his hand on her shoulder. 'You said one minute Mme. de Montclaire.' He looked over her shoulder and rolled his eyes at Halifax.

'Well, it hasn't been a minute yet. Besides, I made up that rule for other people, not for me.' She brushed his hand away.

The soldier pulled back the hand and looked at it, as if he had no control over where it went.

'I organized all this!' She blinked at the man with the gun, then turned back to Halifax. 'I just want to get something straight.' She rested her fingertips on her chest. 'I was led to believe . . . I paid a great deal of money . . .' Then she gave up talking.

The soldier led her away. Before she disappeared into the crowd, she turned and waved.

Ivan climbed in beside Halifax and strapped himself into the seat. 'Merlot had better leave the country before Mme. de Montclaire sends Anton to pay him a visit. I think Anton went to the same school of persuasion as Baturin.'

They both cackled so hard at the joke that when they stopped a moment later, they couldn't look each other in the eye.

Halifax pumped pressure into the fuel tank, opened the throttle and nodded to the mechanic, who stood ready with his hand on the prop. He felt the cold dabs of rain on his face.

As soon as the engine fired up, all other sounds moved away. Ivan checked the aluminium chart tubes welded to the floor under his seat.

Halifax still had a grin on his face. He pulled the seat straps down over his shoulders and buckled them. The cockpit was already warm from the engine's heat. He let his head fall back and looked up at the sky.

'All set?' The mechanic held on to the rim of the cockpit. His fingernails were black with oil.

'My call.' Halifax gunned the throttle and set his feet on the pedals.

Ivan had stopped smiling. Now he sat stone-faced, watching the green-glowing dials.

The mechanic stood beside the plane. In one hand he held a ring attached to a cable. The cable was bolted to the blocks. When he removed them the plane would go forward.

Halifax nodded to him and mouthed the word 'go'. The Levasseur jolted, then began rumbling over the grass. Car horns beeped and people waved from the runway's edge. The scrabbling behind Halifax's ribs mixed with the engine's hammering until he couldn't feel it anymore. For the first time in days, it seemed to him, he could take a full breath of air, his lungs not squeezed by muscles that were cramped from having nothing to do.

The cars and people merged into a blur as the plane gathered speed. Leaves on trees near the runway flickered pale and dark and pale in the breeze. Halifax opened the throttle and eased the stick back, feeling through his feet for any break in the even strumming of the engine.

The end of the runway appeared, hedges seeming to pull back around the Levasseur. The lines of spectators had gone, and on either side of the plane were empty woods. One wheel lifted off, then the other. The tail dipped as they rose into the air. Halifax pulled the release lever and their landing gear fell away. Trees filed underneath and the sky was lighter. Shreds of blue cut through the paste of clouds. Mist clogged the ditches and wallowed in the fields.

Paris spread out under them, winking lights and nudging the sky with its buildings. Silhouettes jabbed at the sunrise. Bead chains of car lights threaded up and down the avenues. Clouds glowed in the first break of sun, edged with brass and copper light. A train cut through the fields below, dragging a smudge of steam.

An hour later, they flew over Normandy. For the first time, Halifax allowed his back muscles to relax. He looked down at

Caen and then at Bayeux. Its red-roofed houses spread out around a grey cathedral. The cold air cleared his head. No useless clots of worry banged at his skull to get out. He saw a train pulling into the Bayeux station trailing a flag of steam. At an altitude of seven thousand feet, he could even see passengers on the platform. Black and white cows dragged their feet through the misty fields, following a farmer to a dairy. Halifax thought of the towns waking, baking bread and coffee brewing, the whole country pacing forward into motion. He turned to Ivan and saw him looking down, knowing the same things were going through his head. Even at this height, Halifax felt a part of the land. He knew that if he reached the other side, these people on the ground, all of them, would hear of it and speak of it. The train carriages would be filled with the gossip of his flight, of the new possibilities that would be opened up. Crossing the Atlantic, Halifax thought. I am crossing the Atlantic in an aeroplane.

Two press planes caught up with them as they neared the pink-sanded beaches of Arromanches. Newsmen's cameras flashed from the tiny round windows. The planes waggled their wings, then turned back for Paris.

The sun shoved back the night, gold-plating the side of the plane. Ivan and Halifax watched the coast fold into oncoming waves.

Halifax leaned forward to tap the dials, making sure the needles weren't stuck. The cold air numbed his wrists and face. Whenever he closed his eyes, he could trace in his mind the path of the engine's pipes, of the electric wiring and cables that controlled the flaps. It was as if he could feel the tension in them, nothing straining, everything in place.

As they crossed the English Channel at ten thousand feet, droplets of water on the windscreen froze into spider webs of ice. Threads of white foam ran like claw marks across the water below.

Ivan studied a map, tracing their course in the beam of a small flashlight. It was dark in the cockpit, since the sun hadn't risen high enough yet to pour in. Ivan huddled close to the light, as if it might give out some heat. He raised his head, saw Halifax watching, nodded, then went back to the map.

Halifax tapped him on the shoulder, a muffled nudge of

leather glove against leather jacket. Ivan looked up again, his mouth open slightly, O-shaped with worry. Halifax grinned and tapped him again, a little harder.

'What?' Ivan switched off the flashlight. 'What?' He had to shout over the engines.

Halifax eased the plane side to side. Sun filled the cockpit, and everything burned with a light the colour of marmalade. He couldn't stop grinning. It had been years since he felt this clear-headed, perhaps not since he was a child, and he thought of the hill roads outside Brackenridge, where he had walked in early summer, and the sharpness of the morning, an oncoming rush of green as the summer closed in. It was the light that made him remember. It was only his light, which broke open from his memory the sudden picture of himself at ten years old, and his brave face and uncombed hair. He thought of returning to the same hill roads and Brackenridge. He'd go there again just to see.

They climbed as they moved over the water, leaving the elephant-skin wrinkles of waves. The ocean seemed to smooth out as they gained altitude. The Levasseur flew along the southern coast of England at fifteen thousand feet. The English countryside was brown and red, the outline of its coast a sharp serrated line. Towns spread roads like tentacles through the fields. Crops showed different shades, hard-edged where stone walls or chalky roads blocked them in.

The engine strummed heavily. Ivan took out his note pad and wrote, HUNGRY.

'We only had breakfast half an hour ago!' Halifax yelled in Ivan's ear.

Ivan pressed his lips together. He scratched his chin with his leather-gloved fingers.

'We'll eat later.' Halifax had already begun daydreaming of porridge with cream and brown sugar, wondering what Mme. de Montclaire had packed for them.

Brown-red land gave way to tan and green as the sun rose higher in the sky.

They didn't try to talk much above the hammer of the engine. Every fifteen minutes, Ivan handed over a scrap of paper with the present bearing heading and the bearing correction. He wrote down the numbers and then spelled them out underneath so there would be no mistake.

With nothing to do except steer the plane, Halifax ranged along the corridors of his daydreams. He forced himself to remember his hometown, not the one he had imagined over the years but the real Brackenridge. He forced into his head the idea that the friends he had left behind would have buried him by now, assumed he had died in the war. He wondered if his name was carved next to his brother's on some war memorial outside the town hall. Again he breathed the smell of damp coal and diesel and rusting metal of rail cars piled with shining black rock.

A jolt moved through the Levasseur, fastening him again to the wicker seat and shuddering cockpit floor.

They dropped a hundred feet before Halifax could steady the controls.

'What's the matter?' Ivan clung to his seat.

'Wind pocket.' The shouting made their voices monotone.

'You did that on purpose, didn't you? You wanted to rattle my balls.'

'There'll be plenty more of those.' He looked across at Ivan. 'You having any thoughts?'

Ivan pulled down his goggles. His eyes watered in the cold and wind. 'After I came out of Russia, I used to think about America all the time. Everybody talked about going to America. Sometimes you'd think, from the way people talked that all of Europe was about to be abandoned. But I'm realizing now that . . .' His voice was already hoarse from shouting. He punched each word out of his lungs. Each word needed a breath. 'That a lot of people talked, and sure, a lot actually went, but for some people, I'm trying to say, it was better to have America as a place we could never reach. Each time I hit rock bottom, the way I did three times a week in Paris when I was begging off my friends, I always had it in my head that if things ever got too bad, I could go to America. I would be different in America.' Now his throat was raw. He squeaked and growled his sentences. 'But now I wonder how different I'm going to be. I wonder if this place can ever be as good as I imagined.' He made an irritated flip with his hand and looked down at his chart, ashamed of having spoken that way. He pulled up his goggles and his body seemed to contract as he studied the flight path again. A minute later, he switched the fuel flow from the central tank to the port tank and then sat back.

They both waited for the engine to change pitch, signalling some disruption in the fuel flow. Halifax kept his hand on the throttle, ready to change the air and fuel mixture if he needed to. Ivan gripped his knees and stared straight ahead.

No change came. The even thrum continued. Ivan and Halifax blinked at each other through their goggles.

There were long, complicated stretches of quiet. The cradling drone of the engine was so constant that Halifax no longer heard it or felt it. It became a new silence. Fatigue touched at his face, so he raised himself, bracing his neck muscles, and let the force of the wind slap him awake. He felt the goggles press back against his eyes. The chin strap of his flying cap dug into his throat.

They moved across the tip of Cornwall and over the Irish Sea. Cliffs snubbed at the ocean, purple and brown with heather and bracken. Sun caught on the steel fittings of the windscreen. It splashed into their eyes like white water.

Ivan took the charcoal pencil and wrote, TIME GOES VERY SLOWLY UP HERE.

Halifax nodded. His sense of time ballooned and shrank. Without looking at his watch, he had no idea how long they'd been in the air. It all depended on how smoothly his daydreams carried him, how close they brought him to sleep.

Heavy blocks of clouds shut out the Irish coast. The Levasseur skimmed over the white islands. Another landscape formed around the plane. Shreds of cloud arched over them like breaking crests of waves. As far as Halifax could see, a ruffled plateau stretched out towards the pale blue horizon, which compressed into a darker blue as it pulled near to the sun. He found himself looking at the puffed valleys and mountains, trying to decide where rivers would run if the landscape were solid, where towns could be built, where they might land if the engine gave out.

It was the first time since take off that he thought of any trouble with the plane. He let the worry slide away. He had nothing to do now but what he was already doing. I've already done the worrying, he thought, under my dirty blankets at the barn and at the tables of closed cafés in Le Bourget.

When he first began flying, he was always worried, but after months of working in his Spad, he trusted himself enough to know that if something went wrong, he would do everything that could be done. Beyond that, he figured, there was only luck. If his engine gave out, either he'd be close enough to the ground to land the plane before it dropped into a tail spin or he wouldn't. Either there would be a place to land or there wouldn't. He'd die or he wouldn't. He saw everything and thought everything in black and white.

All this changed after the crash. The black and white disappeared. As he lay in his hospital bed, it seemed to him that he could have spent his whole life preparing for the fire and the pain and the fall, and it would have done no good. Instead, he began to think the way the other pilots did, convincing himself that some talisman had taken root inside him, something unmentionable because of its preciousness. He gave himself the guarantee of growing old, unhurt and unpunished by nightmares and alive. Everybody did the same.

After the crash, this black-and-white idea of dying or not dying and nothing to be done about it splintered into so many degrees of wounding and maiming and death that it was all he could think about. Each avenue of his thinking, when the doctors told him he could be back in his plane in a month, ended with the same picture of himself encased in flames and falling. He had used up his talisman. The only guarantee he could give himself now was that he would die if he went back up. The only way out was to run, so he ran.

As they passed over Ireland and the Shannon River estuary, they saw on the map that there was no land between them and the coast of Labrador. The flight path Halifax had decided on at the avenue Rapp was to stay close to land for as much of the route as he could, crossing the Atlantic at its narrowest point, passing Newfoundland and the coast of Maine and from there heading straight to New York.

Ivan switched to the starboard fuel tank. He locked his fingers together and bent forward, yawning and stretching. Suddenly he looked up. 'Have you thought about turning back?' He raked his fingers up and down his thighs. 'This is the last point where we can turn back. I just wondered if you'd thought about it.' The wind howled in his mouth.

Halifax pulled Mme. de Montclaire's food package from

under his seat and dumped it on Ivan's lap. 'Think about that instead.'

They ate caviar and bread. The caviar came in a jar with a blue top that had Russian writing on it. The bread was hard and crusty. Ivan spread the black beads onto the bread and stuffed lumps of it in Halifax's mouth, then ate some himself. Afterwards they had sour green apples, the kind that come from Normandy and are used to make calvados. In the bag, Mme. de Montclaire had put two armbands with *Club Aero de Paris* done in gold and blue thread. She didn't leave a note. The last thing in the bag was a bar of dark chocolate. Halifax let the squares dissolve one after the other, pressured slowly between the roof of his mouth and his tongue.

There was the sea below. They had been in the air for five hours. At fifteen thousand feet, ridges of waves showed like the ripples of fingerprints. Storm clouds showed on the horizon. They were flexed muscles the colour of slate. Ten minutes later, the first shudders crept under their wings. Trembling rose through the cockpit floor and into their feet.

Ivan watched the clouds. With the charcoal pencil, he drew circles on his note paper. Circle after circle, one swallowing the other until the whole page was a whirlpool of black. He didn't look down. He kept his eyes on the storm.

Halifax was not surprised. He had told himself too many times in Le Bourget that the storm would have to come. He had imagined it and thought too many times of flying through it, his limbs flinching as he steered the plane in his sleep. He began to play a game in his head, telling himself that if he refused to think about the storm, it would go away. It seemed to him that the source of the grey clouds was inside his head. He felt that he was causing them.

The steely clouds were multiplying. They rose up in funnels, blocking out the sun, and stretched all the way to the sea. Raindrops broke against the windscreen sending clear veins of water streaking across. Drops veered into the cockpit. Halifax felt them strike at his shoulders and head.

Lightning flashed somewhere in the belly of the clouds, then thunder growled over the noise of the engine. Halifax strained to picture a clear sky, or being on the ground, landing in New York harbour, shoving back the ugliness of the storm.

271

Wind pockets tugged at the wings. Halifax's hands clenched as he steadied the Levasseur.

Ivan brought his face close to the control panel and lowered his goggles. He tapped at the glass covers and took another set of readings. He busied himself, allowing no time for the fear.

Halifax took Ivan's note, read the bearing and bearing change in spidery handwriting, then balled the paper. He held up his arm into the force of the wind and let the paper tear away from his fingers.

White pillars of lightning burst out of the clouds and shot down toward the sea. They looked brittle, like glass.

Halifax was blinded. Sometimes the thunder reached him, other times he felt only a brief pressure against his temples. Still unable to clear from his head that the storm was somehow his fault, he scribbled scenes for himself: waving to the crowd in New York harbour, seeing the Statue of Liberty. Each thunderclap shoved him back into his seat.

Lightning exploded in the clouds below. They lit up pink and purple and spat out thunderbolts. Head winds rose to forty-five miles an hour. Ahead, the wall of the storm had sucked all the light from the air. The Levasseur barrelled down clear alleyways. Grey mountains hedged it in.

'They said no storm!' Ivan yelled in Halifax's ear. 'They said clear skies!'

Halifax shrugged. His stomach muscles were pressed so tight against his lungs that he could barely speak. No talisman, he was thinking. No luck left for me. You are doing all you can do. Remember what you told yourself. You know your instincts are right. Anything that can be done, you will do, because you know the plane. You know each curve in its frame and each artery of its fuel system and you can feel through your bones how it's running.

'This isn't worth it!' Ivan shouted. He raised his hands and slapped them down on his knees. 'This is a piss of a way to die!'

The Levasseur rattled around them. Ivan lifted his goggles. 'I am not prepared to die.' Clouds around them coughed out streams of fire. The air gasped under them and they dropped a hundred feet. The altimeter needle bobbed in its case. Ivan cried out.

Pressure dragged at their guts. Halifax nosed the plane down under a cloud bank. The bank seemed to shift. It slid up towards

them and suddenly they were in it. Grey-black air clamped
down on the plane. He put the Levasseur into a climb, seeing
the altimeter needle shudder to the right. The clouds stayed
with them. He could barely see the wing tips. Cold raked up his
spine and the pain from his guts from clenched muscles was like
the leftover hurt after a punch in the belly. Rain drizzled into the
cockpit and smudged Ivan's notes. Water slipped off the wings
in white streamers.

They broke from the clouds and levelled off at twelve
thousand feet. Halifax veered off to the north, hoping to fly
around the storm.

Ivan switched back to the port tank. He scribbled on the
soggy note paper, NOT ENOUGH FUEL FOR DETOUR.

'No choice.' Halifax bellowed at him. His eyes ached from
searching back and forth across the dials.

Eight hours in the air.

The storm forced them down towards the sea. Halifax hunted
for a path, looking up over the ice-blurred windscreen to see a
way through. Raindrops pinched at his cheeks. Visibility
dropped to less than three hundred feet. Air speed was down to
a hundred miles an hour.

Ivan switched to the central fuel supply. Now all tanks
registered half empty.

Water sloshed in the cockpit, soaking through their boots.
Halifax couldn't feel his toes. Worry became a hard barrel
inside, barely held back by his ribs.

Ivan wiped up water on the floor with his handkerchief. He
mopped up as much as he could and tried to wring out the
handkerchief over the side of the cockpit. By the time he
brought the cloth back in, it was more wet than it had been
before.

Halifax tapped Ivan's leg and smiled. The smile hurt because
his jaw was trying to clamp shut. He needed to smile so Ivan
would not be afraid, and then if Ivan felt better, he would feel
better, too.

Ivan smiled back.

Halifax looked at the lopsided goggles on Ivan's face and the
soggy flight hat and started laughing. He couldn't help it.

Then they were both laughing. Rain ran down the sides of the
cockpit. Droplets snapped into their mouths.

Halifax gave up trying to wish the storm away. It was

exhausting him and he knew if he became exhausted, he would make mistakes and it would kill them both. That came to the same thing as this game of talismans. 'You are doing all you can do,' he said to himself, tasting the rain in his spit. 'There's no such thing as talismans.'

They dropped through a cloud and saw the ocean only fifty feet below. White caps scattered on the surface, sliding into the troughs of waves and riding back up to the crests. Halifax saw the water so close and felt the bread and caviar and chocolate ride up into his throat. Shock flashed through him. He put the Levasseur into a climb. He could smell the salt. They rose up slowly. Lightning blasted by.

Suddenly Ivan screamed and pointed past Halifax's shoulders. Halifax turned and saw the wing tips sparkle green. Ivan covered his face with his hands.

'Elmo's fire.' Halifax shouted. 'It's only Saint Elmo's fire.'

Ivan lowered his hands. 'Elmo?'

'Good luck.' Halifax nodded. 'Good talisman.'

Ivan mouthed the words "good luck" and covered his face again.

It took two hours to fly around the storm.

Shreds of blue showed through the clouds. The spider webs of frost melted off the windscreen. Now the Levasseur cut smoothly through the air. Halifax felt pressure dismantle itself slowly from around his bones and let him breathe again. He was freezing from the water that had soaked his clothes. His feet were wet but warm from the engine's heat. His socks clung to his toes like pockets of sponge.

Ivan tapped on Halifax's shoulder and pointed west. The brick-red Nova Scotia beaches were visible below. Beyond them, the land stretched out unbroken. Houses clustered near the sea.

Halifax banked left and headed south along the coast. He wanted to land the plane and walk home – he didn't care how long it took. The idea of bringing the plane in and just leaving it was something he had to fight back. He told himself he wouldn't die now. Whatever else happened, at least he wouldn't die. It was stupid. He knew he could still die very easily before the end of the flight, but the calm that washed through him, even as he knew he was tricking himself, was too pleasant to cut short. He allowed himself to think of his own life still intact and even to think of being home again. The Orteig Prize seemed small compared to that, and his name and Levasseur's and Ivan's resting like little pebbles in history.

Afternoon sun warmed the cockpit. Halifax felt sweat itch at his scalp so he pulled off his flight cap. The ocean glittered below. They made out the wake of a freighter heading north. Halifax's watch was set on French time. It said six-thirty in the evening. He couldn't remember if Eastern Standard Time was six hours behind or only five.

They passed the southern tip of Nova Scotia, seeing the white houses of Yarmouth like fragments of seashells thrown up into the green. Halifax looked at Ivan, ready for some word about the foolishness of heading out across the sea again or for a joke or a request that they turn back, but Ivan's eyes were closed. A block of sunlight rested on his face.

Five minutes later, the rumble of the engine suddenly died away. Halifax's eyes snapped up to the panel.

Ivan sniffed and opened his eyes, then his body jolted forward in panic, punching into the seat straps.

The rpm needle dropped back to zero. The Levasseur nosed forward. A blur in front of the engine casing turned into the solid paddles of the prop. There was no sound except wind and the echo of the motor in their ears.

Ivan's arm shot out to the three levers that controlled fuel flow. He switched from the centre tank to starboard. The engine groaned and started. The rpm needle bounced off zero and began to climb. Halifax cut back the throttle and opened it gradually, easing the engine's full strength up to full.

Ivan wrote on his note pad, CENTRE TANK STILL THIRD FULL.

'So why did it shut down?' Halifax shouted, feeling his muscles turn wooden.

Ivan wrote, AIR LOCK.

'What can we do about it?' Halifax's throat was already hoarse from shouting.

NOTHING.

Ivan switched back to the centre tank and they waited. Ivan's fingers stayed balanced on the levers, ready to switch again.

The engine continued to run. They settled back into their seats.

Ivan bent down, unscrewed the lid from the chart tube and

pulled out a map of the Eastern Seaboard. He drew a line from their position towards the coast of northern Maine. He cupped his hand over Halifax's ear. 'Head for land.'

Halifax shook his head. He cut the idea down with a sweep of his gloved hand. 'But we don't have the fuel to make another detour. We're only a couple of hours out of New York.'

Ivan reached slowly across. His hand closed around Halifax's collar. 'Listen to me,' he yelled. 'Head for land. If that air bubble in the centre tank moves into the main fuel line, there's no hope in hell we'll get started again. Do you understand?'

For a minute, they continued to fly straight. Then Halifax shifted his feet on the rudder pedals and eased the control stick over. The Levasseur rose on one wing and swung towards land. He wasn't angry to be heading in. If the engine held, they could still reach New York by following along the coast. He was angry that Ivan had to tell him to turn in. His own instincts should have told him first.

They felt it coming: a hammering shook through the plane and the engine died.

Ivan flipped to the centre tank. Nothing. He flipped to the starboard tank. Still nothing. Wind whistled through the flaps. Halifax felt the tugging at his veins as they began to fall. Ivan kept flipping from one switch to the other. He yelled at Halifax to throttle back.

Halifax cut the throttle, keeping the stick straight in case they nosed into a dive.

Ivan flipped all three levers at the same time and the engine spluttered. He leaned to his left and rested his hand on the throttle. Halifax pushed back his seat, giving Ivan space. The pressure of dropping gouged at their eyes.

Ivan moved the levers back and forth again and pulled out the throttle. The engine started. The prop became a foggy disc. Halifax felt power return to the controls.

They levelled out at three thousand feet and started to climb, heading towards land. Ivan took off his flight cap and used it to wipe the sweat on his face and matted hair. Then he dropped his cap on the floor and picked up the map. He checked the compass bearing and drew a large circle around an area of the Maine coast. He held the map up to Halifax and tapped at the circle. The map thrashed in gusts of wind that blew into the cockpit.

Halifax looked from the map to the rpm dial and back at the map again. He funnelled all his energy into feeling the pulse of the engine. He thought about nothing else, feeding off the smooth burning of fuel that kept them in the air.

Land showed in the distance. Halifax saw strips of rocky beach and then pine forest reaching back into the blurred horizon.

The engine squealed and oil sprayed back across the windscreen. They started dropping again. Nothing showed on the dials. Only the altimeter moved, falling backwards to the pin at the zero mark.

Ivan flipped the levers back and forth until the engine started. The Levasseur gained some altitude, crossing over land at five hundred feet. Their shadow cut across waves breaking on grey rocks. Then pine trees crowded below them. Ivan pointed to a scattering of lakes about five miles inland.

A smell of burning came from the engine. The windscreen was opaque with oil. Halifax had to loosen his seat straps. He raised himself and looked out over the top to see where they were going.

Even with its engine running, Halifax couldn't bring the Levasseur up to half power. The air lock must have caused a leak, he thought. Hardly any fuel is getting through.

Ivan had also loosened his straps and looked over the oil-splashed windscreen. The wind tugged at his hair and smoothed back his cheeks, showing the bones of his face.

They crossed a ridge of trees, clearing them by fifty feet. Lakes lay scattered among stretches of unbroken forest. There were no towns, no roads that they could see.

They circled a lake. Ivan looked out one side and Halifax looked out the other. Sun-light winked off the surface of the water, flashing silver and blinding them. Halifax banked sharply and the engine quit again. He levelled out and started to bring the plane in.

The prop stopped turning. Varnish gleamed on the wood. A breeze ruffled the surface of the lake. Trees huddled near the water. There were no signs of people.

Halifax began calling out instructions to himself. 'Flaps back. Too high! Flaps forward. Level. Flaps back.'

Ivan set his head against his knees and put his hands over his neck.

'Too high! Flaps back.' The trees swept out of focus. 'Zero rpm! Pedals back. Drop slowly. Slowly! Nose high.' The lake rose up to meet them. Halifax heard himself groan. The groan became louder and then his mouth was wide open and he cried out as a hiss of wind rushed past.

The Levasseur's tail struck water. The plane's belly slammed forward. An arc of water heaved over the nose and crashed down on top of them. It was freezing.

The plane sunk down and bobbed up. Waves slithered across the wings and spread out towards the shore.

Everything moved slower now. The water came up to their calves and he rocked back and forth in the cockpit.

Ivan stayed wrapped in a ball. Halifax was patting his own chest and legs, hunting for broken bones. The Levasseur drifted sideways and wallowed in the lake. Halifax heard water trickling in through a leak. Then he saw it, seeping in under the seats. He unbuckled his strap, and banged on Ivan's back as if it were a door. 'We're leaking. We have to get out.' Halifax smelled gasoline and pine. His knees ached and his feet were numb. He pulled down his seat straps and stood. Nerves in his back felt pinched from the shock of landing. The leak was slow but constant. The plane wasn't going down as quickly as he'd thought. 'We have a little bit of time. Not too much, though.' He still spat out the words, as if giving instructions to himself. It was all he could do. His legs were shaking with nervousness. He rapped on Ivan's back again. 'We're going to have to swim.'

Ivan stayed wrapped in a ball.

'Oh, Jesus!' Halifax sat down again and took hold of Ivan's shoulders. 'Are you all right? Are you hurt? Can you speak?'

Ivan made a snuffling sound.

'We have a first aid kit. Don't worry, Ivan.' Halifax grabbed for the little tin box fastened under the seat. His hands were shaking worse than his legs. 'What do you need, Ivan?' Halifax ripped the top off the box and bandages flew out around the cockpit. He pawed through the roll of morphine tablets and silk thread and needles and sticky tape for holding bandages down. 'What do you need, Ivan?' Halifax still shouted over the drumming echo of the engine in his head. He felt his eyes fill up with tears. 'For Christ's sake, what do you need?' He rested his hand on Ivan's shoulder.

Ivan snuffled some more. He was giggling.

'Oh.' Halifax slumped back in his seat. 'I thought you were dead, you stupid son of a bitch!' He ground the tears away with his knuckles. 'What's so funny?' Halifax listened to the rustle of water pouring into the fuselage. It was up to their knees now.

Ivan slowly lifted himself up. 'If I'd have known we were going to survive this, I might have enjoyed it a bit more.' His nose was bleeding. Red dripped off his chin and into the water.

Halifax held on to the greasy rim of the windscreen. His fingerprints smeared in the oil. 'I don't think it's anything to laugh about. We just lost the damn Orteig Prize.'

Ivan laughed even louder. 'Oh, who gives a shit? Nobody was expecting us even to survive. And there we were running up and down those stairs at the gym and sitting all night on those butt-freezing metal chairs at the café.'

Rainbows of gasoline drifted around the engine. Its ventilation slits were powdered black. Halifax cleared his throat. He just wanted to say the facts, thinking it would calm him down. He tried not to shake while he spoke. 'The Orteig Prize is for flying non-stop from New York to Paris or the other way around. They won't give us the prize for landing on some lake way the hell up in Maine.' Say the facts, he told himself. Be calm and say the facts. 'We just lost twenty-five thousand dollars!'

Ivan's laughter echoed across the lake. 'We didn't lose it. We never had it to lose.'

'We were close, Ivan. We were this close to winning.' He pinched the air.

'Oh, and what would you have done with the prize money, anyway? You'd give me half and then I'd borrow the other half and never pay it back. So there you are! Wait until Baturin hears about this.' Ivan slapped him on the arm. 'Wait until Serailler hears!'

'We came so damn close.'

'What's the matter with you?' Ivan wiped the blood off his face with the back of his hand. 'You just got in some bean tin of an aeroplane and flew it all the way across the Atlantic! Are you going to be ashamed of that? This is something you can tell your grandchildren about! This is something people you've never even met will tell their grandchildren about!'

Halifax scratched at the back of his head, squinting at the pine trees on the shore.

Ivan's whole face was bloody. He slapped Halifax again on the arm. 'You didn't do this for the money! If you wanted money, you'd have kept what you got off Serailler. All this is about, Charlie, is you coming home with something or coming home with nothing. And this is *Something!*'

Halifax looked at clouds shredding on the top of a mountain in the distance. Wind blew through the trees.

'Look around, Charlie.' Ivan waved his hand across the lake, at dark green saw-edge trees and water reflecting the sky.

Halifax reached down for the map and tried to pick it up. It fell apart in his hands. 'The whole world's waiting for us in New York harbour.'

Halifax thought of them, of the muttering crowds. He felt the chill of water on his legs. 'Did you see any towns on our way in?'

'I had my head between my legs. All I saw was my crotch.'

The water was up to their thighs. They were still two hundred feet from shore. They looked for a house or a path leading up through the trees but saw nothing. Ivan unstrapped himself and stood. 'I think we'll have to swim.' He tore a piece off the soggy map and dabbed it against his nose.

Halifax started to take off his jacket. The cold raked shivers up his back.

Ivan looked over the side of the cockpit. 'Do you think there are fish in this lake?' He held open his hands. 'I mean, very big fish with sharp teeth?'

Halifax stared at him. 'The plane is sinking, Ivan.'

Ivan pointed at the shore. 'And what about in there? Are there bears?'

Halifax climbed out onto the wing and saw the crack in the fuselage. He pulled off his boots and shirt. Goose bumps pebbled his back.

'What the hell am I supposed to do if I see a bear?' Ivan peeled off his clothes.

'Tell him you led the charge at Zovi Rog.' Halifax stepped to the end of the wing, ready to jump in.

'Hold it!' Ivan's voice bounced around the lake. 'You are forgetting something very important.' He held out one of the armbands that Mme. de Montclaire had given them and pulled it up over his bicep. He was naked except for the band. 'We don't want to disappoint Mme. de Montclaire.'

Halifax pulled on the other band and dropped into the water. Cold grabbed at his throat. He struggled to reach the surface, then broke through and breathed, his chest shuddering with the freeze. He started swimming for shore, dragging the heavy ball of his clothes. The Levasseur was going down nose first.

Ivan held his clothes against his chest and jumped in. A second later he popped back up, gasping.

Halifax's feet touched bottom. He felt sand. Holding his clothes against his chest, he walked toward the bank. The last few feet before the shore was thick with dead leaves gone black and crumbled apart. He sloshed through the reeds and threw his clothes on dry ground.

Ivan dog-paddled, chopping up spray. He finally found his footing on the sand and crawled through the reeds. The Levasseur's tail was a white fin rising from the water. The rest of the plane had sunk. Ivan hopped around naked under the canopy of trees, trying to get warm.

Halifax sat down in the reeds and jammed his feet into his boots. He took off the armband and threw it up into the trees and it didn't come down. Then he put on his shirt and jacket. He dug his hands into the soft ground and made fists. It would take a while, he knew, before he could believe where he was. Now he would have to take it in steps. Find a road. Find a town. Find people.

'I'm very hungry.' Ivan held up his trousers. Water dripped in streams from his legs. His armband was down by his wrist. 'Are there nuts and berries we can eat around here? You let me know if you see any nuts or berries, all right?'

Halifax started walking through the woods.

Ivan struggled into his clothes. 'Well, wait a minute at least!' Black flies flipped around his head.

Halifax turned and waited. Three dark birds with long beaks paddled toward him from the far shore, making a sad hooting noise.

Ivan hooted back at them and the birds disappeared below the surface. Then he ran to catch up with Halifax. His soaked boots squelched over the pine-needle floor of the forest. 'I suppose we'll just walk until we hit a road.'

Halifax didn't answer. He watched the Levasseur's tail dip

under the water. Waves spread out from the place where it went down. The lake was calm again. It reflected the pale blue early summer sky. Halifax turned and kept walking. The engine's thunder drifted slowly from his bones.

IN MEMORY OF

CHARLES NUNGESSER AND FRANÇOIS COLI


who attempted a nonstop crossing of the Atlantic from Paris to New York on May 8, 1927. They are said to have crashed in the woods near Machias, Maine. Their bodies and their plane have never been found.